Trading OHM

Book 1 of the Augurspell Mystery

Trading OHM

Book 1 of the Augurspell Mystery

By

Matthew Van Vlack

Strategic Book Publishing and Rights Co.

Strategic Book Publishing and Rights Co.
12620 FM 1960, Suite A4-507
Houston TX 77065
www.sbpra.com

ISBN: 978-1-62212-283-7

Dedication

For my muse, my wife,
The blessed love of my life,
Laura

Table of Contents

Author's Note

Although the following novel is a work of fiction and all characters, locations and incidents are fictitious and are not in any way meant to reflect actual persons (living or dead), actual locations or actual incidents, the novel does contain actual cultural, political and/or religious belief systems and some of their actual corresponding organizations that many (if not most) people believe to be factual (although other people believe they are fictitious). The author does not purport to deny, affirm or in any way suggest that these people are right. Neither does the author intend that this novel is in anyway a commentary on his personal belief in such systems. Also, the author unequivocally denies that he knows or purports to know any secrets or information concerning the systems and corresponding organizations described in this novel.

Having said all of that, all references to those belief systems, corresponding organizations and any singular individuals (factual or fictitious) connected to them, represented herein, have been painstakingly researched and verifiable from other sources (both factual and fictitious). In an effort to respect the Judeo-Christian elements contained within, the author has used traditional literary techniques when referencing said elements (i.e., capitalization of all personal or direct pronouns used in reference to any and all Judeo-Christian figures such as the Virgin Mary or Jesus Christ).

Finally, the author wishes to apologize profusely for any insult or effrontery he may cause through the writing of this purely fictional work (albeit satirical and somewhat cynical, if not mildly critical) by including belief systems, corresponding organizations and relevant individuals whether believed to be factual or fictitious. With that said, the author hopes you can enjoy the spirit in which this work was written. Don't worry about what you think it means or what you think the author means. Does any of it really matter, anyway? And if you do find yourself getting angry or stressed out during the course of reading this non-critical work of culture, religion and political systems, just fill a bowl with some sweet, sweet kush, light it up and inhale, baby, inhale.

Thank you for your attention in this matter.

Sincerely,
Matthew Van Vlack
(Not the author's real name, but close enough)
April 20, 2012
(Not the real date the author wrote this, but close enough)

Chapter 1

Deming, New Mexico

The United States/Mexico border town of Deming, New Mexico isn't Podunk. It isn't the corrupt, drug war battleground that most Americans, and certainly Fox News devotees, might think. Neither is Deming a metropolis that attracts the nosy, greedy, publicity-seeking bloodsuckers much larger cities like Chicago, Miami, New York and Los Angeles do. As a result, Deming proved to be the perfect place for the unemployed, formerly omnipotent, and all-seeing Nordic deity Odin to hide himself. It is a world divided between fundamentalist monotheism and fashionable atheism.

As far as Odin (aka Votan, aka Woden, aka "Mr. Grim") saw it, because of European man's conversion to a 5,000 year-old brand of Judeo-Christianity invented by an out-of-work Babylonian idol-maker, the whole world was engaged in a narcissistic massacre. What disgusted and consternated Odin and other out-of-work pantheistic deities about the religion of Abraham was its present-day fanatical, self-hating and incestuous incarnation that achieved nothing less than racial genocide and the slaughter of innocent billions.

As once-chief of the Nordic pantheon of gods, Odin (or "Grim Dog," which he chose back in 1973 when he worked as a truck driver and used the name as his CB handle) found that the only thing which kept him from wreaking vengeful havoc on Western Europe was drinking the pale imitation of the draught once drunk in the halls of his heavenly palace Valhalla, while watching barely-legal women who hung out at Deming's most popular karaoke country and western bar Wheels hit on aging bikers for free beer. It wasn't Valhalla to be sure and the women weren't his beautiful daughters the Valkyrie, but with no wars left to wage or warriors left to worship him, it provided Grim Dog enough of a distraction so that he wasn't constantly dwelling on his past as King of Asgard.

The one holdover that Grim Dog had from his glory days was the eye patch worn over his plucked-out right eye. It was a hell of a chick magnet with the less-reputable women at Wheels, especially since he had it bedazzled with the words: "Support Our Troops!" Attracting and exploiting women with daddy issues wasn't a problem for Grim Dog, because of how he and his Aesir brothers and sisters had been exploited by humans for centuries. After all, the most renowned interpretation of Grim Dog and his people was a hellishly long opera written by a famously bigoted Teuton whose operas were later used by another infamous mustachioed piece-of-shit to bring about the type of genocide previously described. It was enough to make any god a bitter old drunk.

But the exploitation of women flew right out of Grim Dog's head when he saw a certain dark-haired, dark-eyed babe, looking about nineteen years old, walk up to his table on that hot July evening.

He knew who She was and was surprised when She asked him, "Are you Odin All-Father?" Grim Dog spat his Michelob Genuine Draft on the table, barely missing the Young Woman. "Excuse me?" he asked, grabbing the nearest paper napkin and wiping the excess from his beard. The Beautiful Stranger pulled out a chair, sat down and leaned towards him. She repeated, "Are you Odin All-Father?"

"Yes, yes, yes, but keep Your fucking voice down. You don't know whose ears work for whom in this dive."

"Why? You think the collective intelligence in this bar could ever recollect a supposedly fictional Norse god—let alone that said god now looks like he lives in a truck stop?"

"The question is, how the fuck does a nineteen-year-old Jewish broad know who Odin is?"

The Babe smiled and rattled off, "Odin aka Woden aka Votan aka Wogun—"

"Okay! Okay!"

"In fact, I believe you're currently using a lesser-known variation of one of your many German monikers, am I right? 'Grim Dog,' isn't it?"

Grim Dog slapped his hand on the table, "Jesus Christ, shut the fuck up, Lady!" He looked from side to side, dropping his voice from a roar to barely audible.

The Babe giggled and swept back Her bangs. "It's ironic that you of all beings should use My Son's name in vain."

"Didn't mean any disrespect to You by it, honestly. I suppose foul language is a habit I picked up after spending too many centuries living amongst mortal losers. If that fuck-wad Hitler hadn't taken my sacred runes and used their power to propagate his Nazi bullshit, I wouldn't have had to leave my people's homeland to find the one place I thought no one like You could ever find me—so much for subterfuge. So, what is it You want, huh?"

The Holy Mother was about to answer when Grim Dog abruptly continued his stream of consciousness rant: "I mean—shit—look at You, barely old enough to be legal and Your so-called Lord-of-All-That-Is knocks You up. How old were You when that perv Archangel Gabriel planted the 'Seed of The Lord' inside you? Thirteen—fifteen, maybe—at most? Hell, He'd be up on statutory rape charges if He tried to pull that crap now! And He's the one those lunatics kill and slaughter in the name of—blowing up buildings and shit. You know I spent a few decades working on those skyscraper crews—talk about brave and all—barefoot some of those dudes were, especially the Native Americans. So please excuse my lack of respect for a deity to whom fringe-fundamentalist ass-wipes pray to when they kill thousands of innocent—"

"Shut up!" shouted the Blessed Virgin, desperate to get the old deity to stop rambling.

Inadvertently though, their conversation did attract some attention by confused humans around them. So, instead of saying anything else, for the moment Norse and Jew sat quietly until the people watching them returned to their own interests.

Finally the Virgin Mother said, "I'm looking for someone."

"And if You can't find them, what makes You think I can?"

"Listen, I don't have time to spill all the beans, okay? Not right now. A clock is ticking and there are several interested parties out there. If they could detect My power at work they would locate Me and then—" the Virgin surveyed one corner of Wheels to the other with a look of genuine fear that told Grim Dog this wasn't some fairy tale. This Being, this Mother of Christ was as terrified as any desperate single mother he had ever seen on the run.

Maybe it was Her kick-ass body, large brown eyes, or the fact that he hadn't been laid in a while and was hoping on some insane level he just might have a shot with Her that made Grim Dog decide to listen further. So, Grim Dog finished his beer and said, "Fair enough— but why me, huh? I'm far from the most powerful sky god in the proverbial phone book. How about Zeus, right—Indra even? Or what's the name of that hawk-headed Egyptian dude?"

"Atum-Ra," said the Virgin Mother.

"Yeah, that dude's older and maybe more powerful than any of us!"

The Virgin shook Her head and said, "No, there's no going there. He's still won't forgive my people for the whole Ramses/Red Sea debacle."

"Oh yeah, Moses and all that shit, right? Well, let's see—last I heard Zeus was shooting porn in Van Nuys. I think Indra is running one of those weird body exhibits in Cleveland, you know? The sort where you can see their insides and shit—blah! That stuff is seriously nasty!"

The Virgin leaned over the table and whispered in Grim Dog's ear, "I don't want them. I want you—because this whole thing's about something you're very intimate with."

Hearing the word 'intimate' come out of Her lips was enough to make any man (or fallen deity) feel shame. Fortunately for him, Grim Dog had absolutely no shame. He asked, "Me? What the?—"

"I'm stealing the Augur."

Grim Dog shot up out of his seat, standing to his full height of six foot-nine and shouted, "My Augur? You've found it!"

The Virgin fell back into Her seat and for a moment shook with fear at what no being had beheld in at least eleven hundred years, the countenance of the All-Father at the height of his anger. He was an all-together powerful figure and surely why the Christian monks decided to use the same familiar image for the One-God in order to scare pagans into converting.

The Virgin swallowed hard and said, "You heard Me. I won't repeat it."

Grim Dog placed his hands palm down on the table and fought as hard as he could to subvert his rage so as not to destroy Wheels and the surrounding eight blocks. The last person Grim Dog knew to have used his Augur was the previously mentioned mustachioed piece-of-shit bastard. As he had with everything good Grim Dog had ever made, the piece-of-shit twisted the power of the Augur to justify his evil "Reich." After the bunker incident, the Augur vanished like so many of the occult items stolen by the Nazis, and for some reason even Grim Dog could never locate it. Now She was here in front of him saying She had found it.

"Who has it?" Grim Dog asked in an even tone.

The Virgin looked down and said nothing.

"Who has my Augur?" Grim Dog asked in a slightly deeper but still even tone.

"I can't have you going off half-cocked and leveling the place. I'm not in this to kill or hurt anyone. I just need someone help me steal it."

"Steal? It belongs to me! If I take it back, it's not fucking stealing!"

The Virgin looked up at Grim Dog and said, "It's not you I want to steal it. Not even you could get into this place and back out again."

Then it hit Grim Dog. All at once, the All-Father knew who it was that the Virgin didn't want to say had his Augur. "Son-of-a-bitch," as he sat back down in his chair. "It's those bastard Catholics, isn't it? Those Opus Dei douchebags are keeping it in that wretched Inquisition-style basement they call 'the Vault,' right? And You don't want to tell me because they are 'Your' people and You'd rather me not run Gunghnir—(Gunghnir was the name of Odin's magical spear. It was common for the Norse gods and their worshippers to name everything used for just about any purpose. I kid you not when I tell you that Odin's eight-legged stallion Sleipnir had a different name for each horseshoe. They did this because as animists they believed that every physical object, organic and non-organic, carried a piece of the world's soul within it. Sorry, this parenthetical was too extensive. My wife is forever pointing out how verbose and long-winded I can be. So let's just start over again, shall we?)

Then it hit Grim Dog. All at once, the All-Father knew who it was that the Virgin didn't want to say had his Augur. "Son-of-a-bitch," as he sat back down in his chair. "It's those bastard Catholics, isn't it? Those Opus Dei douchebags are keeping it in that wretched Inquisition-style basement they call 'the Vault,' right? And You don't want to tell me because they are 'Your' people and You'd rather me not run Gunghnir through the hearts of every one of those slaughtering, pedophilic hypocrites!"

The Virgin looked down with Her face filled with hurt and disappointment and whispered, "They are not my people—not anymore."

"Bullshit!"

"No!" She shot back, pounding Her finger on the table—cracking the solid oak surface. "Maybe they were my people two thousand years ago, but the politicization, corruption and sadism committed in the name of My Beautiful Son and His Work disconnected them from Me long before the Inquisition! So don't you turn all self-righteous on Me or cast dispersions on My Son because of what those liars have said or done!" The Virgin Mother's tone changed. Anger passed and even temperament returned. She continued, "And just because you helped—helped being the operative word—make the Augur doesn't mean you have any more right to it than I do. So, My reasons for getting the Augur are none of your concern. All I need from you is help in finding Alberich Night-dwarf. And I know you know where he is!"

Odin spat on the floor. "That sack of shit? How dare You speak his name in my presence! If it weren't for his stealing the Rhinegold, my Aesir and I wouldn't have lost Europe to Your—those asshole monks! And what do You mean 'helped make the Augur?' It was my bloody right eye," he lifted his eye patch to show the Blessed Virgin the empty socket. "It gives the damn thing its power to see the future!"

The Virgin sighed and said, "I know. I know. But what's past is past and as much as you blame him for stealing your Ring of Power, you know it was the Holy Roman Empire and not the night-dwarf who converted your followers. And if you didn't have such a proclivity for putting your own power into objects—here, there, and everywhere—maybe you wouldn't have been spread so thin and—"

Grim Dog spat out, "Enough, enough of the psycho-bullshit! I know I was too materialistic! Now everyone's out there looking for my Ring, my Runes and now apparently, my Augur!"

The Virgin Mother leaned over the table and got as close to Grim Dog as She dared. After all, he was a giant to Her lesser five-five frame. "Don't you see, Odin? This is your chance to get back at them."

It was the chance at revenge combined with hearing his true name spoken by so beautiful a pair of lips that made him say, "Keep on yapping, Sweetheart."

"If the Catholic Church is not in My care, do you think My Son or His Father have any interest in saving it from the corruption devouring it from within? What do you say, G-Dog? Shall we party?"

"Okay, okay, You're saying that if I give You Alberich, and don't stop You from getting my Augur, I will be helping destroy the bastards who brought down Bi-Frost, Asgard and Valhalla?"

The Virgin Mary sighed. She was becoming exasperated with the back and forth restatement in question form. "I'm saying that if you help Me, you will finally be able to get back at the shitheads who cost you your job. What do you say, huh? Does that sound like an offer you can refuse?"

Grim Dog said, "For a virgin, You sure know how to please a man."

Chapter 2

Los Angeles, California

To say Charlie Hamor hated his life was like saying Rush Limbaugh was a moderately inclusionary egalitarian—an understatement as gross as the talk show host's fluctuating but generally morbidly obese proportions. The fact that Charlie was shagging one of the actresses listed on Maxim Magazine's online poll of "The CW's Primetime Hottest 100" wasn't enough to make him feel any better about his circumstances.

Charlie's actress/girlfriend's name was Deanne Ripper. Yes, Ripper. Which Charlie found all too ironic after he used one of those genealogical websites to discover Deanne did have a distant ancestor who lived in London, England in 1888 and was thought to be one of the most eligible suspects in the infamous Whitechapel murders. Coupled with Charlie having recently found out that Deanne's secretive activities made her a filthy whore, the karmic twist was not lost on him.

When you spend any appreciable time living in Los Angeles, you will discover that constitutional violations such as cruel and unusual punishment are most often carried out by gorgeous and intelligent blonde-haired, blue-eyed TV actresses with breasts that are naturally a "C" and need neither a tanning booth nor electrolysis to appear camera-ready. Unfortunately, this was not a truism Charlie knew when Deanne Ripper auditioned for the online video ad being shot for his organic medical dispensary OHM.

It was Deanne's first paying gig in the entertainment industry, and ever since that day he had a front-row seat to watch Deanne's stock rise in value along with the rise of her ego, her cup size, and her capacity for emotional cruelty. But as it so often is with the human heart, Charlie was stuck on the hook of addiction to Deanne, flopping and swinging about in the air while his intellect, sitting in a far corner of his mind, chilled with a mai-tai and repeated over and over again, "I told you so, I told you so—"

Unfortunately, it would take a stronger, sexier and lower maintenance drug to free this once-spirited man from that relationship and send him back into the tsunami of Los Angeles dating. But wherever that drug lived, she hadn't shown up in Charlie's life yet. So for now, he was still stuck with the mind-fucking Deanne.

So, as it was almost every Thursday night, Charlie stood drunk against the living room wall between the monstrous entertainment center and the kitchen entrance in Deanne's Westwood condominium. It was Guinness that got the best and fastest result for Charlie. There wasn't a party that Deanne threw at which Charlie had failed to bring a 12-pack of Guinness and by 9:30pm had drunk at least half the pack. Charlie had become a genuine alcoholic in the best tradition of his Belfast ancestors. Charlie took his 33rd drink of the dark, rich oblivion while he watched his "girlfriend" flirting with a commercial director named Tim Hamrod. The way Deanne's lips pursed, widened, swished from side to side and pulled back to reveal the orthodontic achievement called "caps" revolted Charlie because he had paid for them and now they were being used to seduce a man named "Hamrod."

Charlie thought, what the fuck kind of name is Hamrod? What ethnic origins could Hamrod have? Germanic, Scandinavian? Yeah, a brutal Viking raider who raped and pillaged—much the same way Charlie imagined this prick wanted to do to Deanne—could be named Hamrod. So, there Charlie had it. His girlfriend, who was no more emotionally committed to him than she was to white bread, was wanting to use her surgically-enhanced body parts to draw in some shitty commercial director for a couple of extra credits on her resume.

What was he going to do? Should he stay with her for the sex, however long that lasted, or should he break it off and walk away with whatever tattered dignity he had left?

It didn't matter. Whatever fleeting thoughts of rebellion he had were overtaken by the sudden, violent urge to vomit brought on by the thirty-third through thirty-eighth swigs of Guinness.

"Oh—shit—fuck," moaned Charlie as he slammed the Guinness down on the nearest counter and broke into a run across the living room, pushing aside shocked guests.

Banking the corner of the hallway that would take him to the bathroom, Charlie's shoulder bumped the shoulder of a woman he didn't know, Tracey Kipper. Fortunately, Tracey Kipper had an unusually gifted sense of kinesthetic motion. Although Tracey couldn't prevent her shoulder from being hit, she was able to maneuver and keep from slamming into the wall and grab Charlie by the shoulders to stop him cold.

"Are you okay?" Tracey asked.

Charlie shook his head furiously. He sputtered out, "No, no—gonna hurl, let me go—"

Tracey released Charlie immediately.

Charlie flew into the bathroom.

Tracey looked towards the living room and saw a few people watching. She looked at Deanne and saw her hand resting on Tim Hamrod's chest. Tracey scoffed and followed Charlie into the bathroom. She found Charlie on his knees, praying to the porcelain god. Although most people would find such a sight pathetic, if not altogether gross, Tracey felt genuine compassion and empathy for the turmoil that caused Charlie to bow before Lord Commode. Unknown to Charlie, Tracey was very aware of who he was and about his relationship with Deanne. Tracey was Deanne's first cousin.

Charlie vomited twice before the dry heaves hit.

Suddenly, someone appeared in the doorway behind Tracey. "Hey," said the man to catch Tracey's attention.

Tracey turned to him.

"I gotta shit."

"Can you not see it's being used?"

"Can you get him the fuck out of there?"

Tracey cocked her head and smirked, "Wow, you are as foul-mouthed as you are rude."

The man was taken aback. "The fuck is your problem?"

"Oh, I'm not the one with a problem, because you're going to go down the hallway into Deanne's bedroom and use the bathroom in there. If you should choose not to and remain here and continue to use that kind of pointless, idiotic and asinine vulgarity while speaking to me and trying to bother my friend while he's sick, then you will be the one having the problem. Are we clear?"

The man was so stunned he could only point down the hallway towards Deanne's bedroom.

Tracey smiled and patted the man on the shoulder. "Good choice," and handed him her empty Rolling Rock. The guest took it and left.

Tracey turned back to see Charlie sitting up, back against the bathtub, knees pulled to his chest, fighting to catch his breath. She walked up to him and kneeled down. She touched his arms and said, "Come on, Charlie, let's get you out of here."

Charlie looked up at Tracey and saw the hazy image of a girl he couldn't remember knowing, if he knew her at all. "Do I know you?"

"No, but I know you." She slipped her arms underneath his and lifted him up. It was effortless, which was belied by her petite size.

But Charlie would have none of it as a sudden burst of energy—the kind brought on by the panic of having just wretched a ton of alcohol and bacon-wrapped Spam hors d'oeuvres—overtook him and he shoved her off him. "Who are you?" he shouted.

Tracey was shocked and surprised. She realized that not only did Charlie not have a clue as to who Tracey was but he was so angry by what he had seen Deanne doing with Hamrod, being touched was the last thing he wanted. Fortunately, who and what Tracey was meant she didn't take it personally. Instead, she raised her hands in the international sign of "no harm" and said, "Sorry, sorry, I shouldn't have attacked your personal space. I'm just offering to get you out of here so, you know, you get home safely?"

Charlie was so surprised by Tracey's mature reaction to his immature actions, all he could say was, "Uh, yeah, out of here—thanks."

As the pair walked through the living room towards the front door, most of the guests ignored him. It was by choice, surely, because the egotism swirling in the room kept them from admitting that anyone of them could act just as pitifully.

When they reached the front door, Tracey grabbed the knob and turned it. Charlie looked through the bodies to see Deanne with her arms wrapped around Hamrod's shoulders, his arms around her waist, and decided that he would hate this woman for the rest of his life—or at least until he sobered up and realized it was his choice to have stayed in this situation for as long as he had.

In the parking garage below the condos, Tracey poured Charlie into her car and tried to put the seatbelt on him. Charlie fell forward, pushing Tracey back out of the car as he hit the glove compartment button. Tracey pushed Charlie back into the seat and the compartment door dropped open. Charlie was conscious enough to see the grip of a glock 9mm automatic pistol inside the compartment. He looked up at Tracey with a startled expression.

Tracey giggled and slammed the compartment door shut. She said, "LA, you know? My dad thought I needed the protection."

"Yeah, right," mumbled Charlie.

Tracey buckled the seatbelt around Charlie and shut the door.

Through the windshield, Charlie watched Tracey's body move gracefully around the front of the car. He was so smashed he was afraid he'd not remember either her or her rescuing him from the party. The fact that made him think he just might remember her and this night was how smitten he was with Tracey. Although he didn't know Tracey and Deanne were related, Charlie recognized Tracey's naturally blonde hair and blue eyes were similar to Deanne's, but her petite frame and naturally perfect proportions (he hoped) made her more attractive. But what he found the most striking about her was what he noticed when she climbed in behind the wheel of the car. The pale freckles on her creamy skin made Charlie's heart drop into his stomach. This woman had not pulverized her skin with artificial UV rays or altered what genetics had constructed for her looks. Because of it, she was the most singularly beautiful woman Charlie had seen in a decade. Her large eyes, tiny nose, well-formed lips—Tracey looked like a fairy tale.

Suddenly, Tracey noticed Charlie looking at her—really looking at her. A smile crossed her face as she said, "Hi." It wasn't spoken out of nervousness or embarrassment, but how naturally comfortable and happy it made her to have this drunken mess of a man giving her his full attention.

The drive to Charlie's house was fast, too fast, for Charlie to realize that Tracey needed no directions to find it. They drove from

Westwood to West Hollywood in traffic common for 11:30 on a Thursday night.

No one spoke, so Tracey had turned on the stereo so they could listen to some classic rock on the satellite radio. Charlie watched Tracey's lips mimic the lyrics of what started as a Genesis song and ended with a 1980's Yes song. Periodically, Tracey would glance at Charlie and smile—not at all embarrassed to lip-sync in front of him.

Since time never feels accurate to a wasted brain, for Charlie this car trip lasted hours—blissful hours—watching the face and sexy lips of his lady knight in shining armor. Abruptly though, bliss ended when Charlie felt Tracey park the car. He looked out the window and saw his house staring back at him.

"Oh wait," Charlie mumbled. "Reserved—placard parking only."

Tracey smiled and said, "I know, big guy." Tracey produced a green placard with an over-sized "W" in the center. "I got it from Deanne's before we left." She slipped it on her rearview mirror.

Although Charlie would never realize it, especially in his present state, Tracey was lying. She had not gotten the placard as they left that night. She had taken the placard from Deanne's car days earlier, because this was not the first time Tracey had been to Charlie's house.

Charlie tried to unbuckle himself, but wasn't able to manage it before Tracey had opened the passenger's door and gotten him out herself. Again, with little effort, Tracey put Charlie's arm around her shoulder, wrapped her arms around his barreled torso and helped him out of the car.

They made their way up the broken concrete walkway to Charlie's early 1940's house and stopped just short of the security screen. Charlie began searching his pockets, but stopped when Tracey dangled his keys in front of his face. "Wow, you're amazing."

"Am I?" asked Tracey. "Please tell my boss that—I mean, my employees that."

While Tracey unlocked the security screen followed by the double deadbolts, Charlie asked, "Employees? You got employees? What do you do?"

"I run a bookstore."

"Bookstore? You?"

"Why not me? Don't I look smart enough?"

"No, no!" shouted Charlie, who suddenly, desperately felt like he had insulted her without meaning to. "I didn't mean it like that! No, I mean—"

Tracey opened the front door with a laugh and said, "I'm just messing with you, Charlie. I know you weren't insulting me."

"Whew!"

After Tracey helped Charlie through the door, she shut it behind them. Instinctively, she locked the deadbolt and searched along the wall for the light switch. The house was as dark as ink. Almost no light bled in from outside. Given the small size of the windows in that style of house, it was common in areas like Hollywood and West Hollywood for them to be pitch-like during the day. So regardless of Charlie being sloshed, he was glad the room was dark because the sight of how he kept it would surely make Tracey run away, or so he thought.

Tracey found the light switch and flipped it.

"No!" screamed Charlie.

"What?" Tracey looked around, as if expecting someone to jump them.

But it wasn't an intruder that made Charlie cry out, it was the horror of his housekeeping, or lack thereof. The chaos, havoc and humanity of Charlie's living room re-defined casual bachelor living. Fortunately, Tracey could not care less. She brushed weeks-old (some months-old) copies of the LA Weekly, Los Angeles Times and the OC Observer off the sofa so that she could help him lie down.

Charlie groaned as consciousness slipped away. He fought to stay awake so he could engage this amazing woman who had done more in the last hour to help him than any girlfriend, most certainly Deanne, had ever done for him in the last twenty years.

Tracey found an afghan blanketing an old chair and grabbed it. She covered Charlie, who was already snoring. He would not remember this night again for a very long time. Tracey honestly did not care if Charlie would or would not remember. She looked at the coffee table and shoved aside the marijuana paraphernalia so she could sit on the edge. She interlocked her fingers and placed them on her lips. With intensity in her blue eyes, she watched Charlie. She studied his face and how youthful he looked. Suddenly, her breath caught in her throat and she felt a chill run up her spine. The scent of alcohol wafted from Charlie's pores. Tracey was afraid to leave him in case he vomited and choked on it.

Could Tracey live with herself having left him to die?

Chapter 3

Manchester, England

Lizzy Tate reflected on her life as a wrinkled old man, no taller than 4'9" or 4'11" at the most, sweated and grunted as he screwed her on the tattered and stained sheets covering the tattered and stained mattress. It was what Lizzy did, reflected on her life, while her tricks—men with absolutely no attractive qualities whatsoever—did what they did so she could earn her one hundred quid.

Lizzy was thirteen when her mum kicked her out. It was right after Lizzy had gathered the courage to tell her how her uncle, her mum's younger brother, had been raping her almost weekly since she was ten. That was four years ago. Now at seventeen, whatever soul was left in Lizzy was all but extinguished. Whatever pilot light burned to keep the spirit alive, even in a Manchester prostitute, was so close to extinguished in Lizzy that nothing short of a miracle would renew her soul.

No such complex or esoteric thoughts muddled the head of the wrinkled old man as he fought with all his strength to release the pressure building in his ancient groin.

Suddenly an explosion ripped through the room. The force of the blast picked up the bed and flipped it into the air. Lizzy and the john were sandwiched between the wall and the mattress. Fortunately, the mattress kept them from being crushed to death.

Lizzy screamed at the top of her lungs and used all her strength to push the mattress away from the wall and then knock the repulsive man off her once the mattress and bed frame landed back on floor.

As the cast-off john landed on the cold linoleum floor, he screamed, "Bitch, I lost my wood! You get nothing from me! Not a quid!"

Lizzy leapt off the bed and scrambled by hands and knees across the room, passing her own clothes, to escape through the entrance now unencumbered by a door. But she stopped dead in her tracks and screamed just shy of the doorway. Something, Someone was blocking her path and She made Lizzy literally shiver down to her bones.

The Virgin Mother stood where there had been a door. She looked even more radiant and awesome than She had looked in Wheels. Why the Virgin appeared so magnificent was a mystery. Maybe it was a difference between the atmospheres of Manchester and Deming. Maybe it was because Lizzy recognized Her.

Despite her mother's hideous qualities, she dragged Lizzy to mass twice every Sunday. As a result, Lizzy could still recite more than eighty percent of the liturgy by heart.

Whatever the reason, the Holy Mother's eyes, face and beatific countenance glowed with a halo; not the cheesy kind you see in Renaissance art, but the kind described in Scripture: a light that emanated from some unseen point behind and just above the crown of the Virgin's skull. She filled Lizzy's once-shrunken heart with both terror and total adoration. Her head dropped in supplication.

The Blessed Virgin reached out and placed Her gentle fingers beneath Lizzy's chin. She lifted Lizzy's face and said, "Go in peace, My Child, and know that you are beloved of the Mother, the Father, and of the Son, and that He grants His Grace upon you, always."

Tears ran from Lizzy's once-dim hazel eyes, now turned brightly green. The tears washed the years of shame and filth off Lizzy's skin and made it fresh, clean and full of life again. "Yes, Holy Mother. Thank You, Holy Mother."

Lizzy gathered up her clothes and ran naked from the flat. As she passed the Virgin and disappeared through doorway, Lizzy never noticed Grim Dog standing just beside the entrance.

Grim Dog walked past the Virgin and looked down at the pissed little man dusting his body clean of the stuff spread by the exploding door.

Before Grim Dog could say a word, the old man said, "Awch, I should have known you'd be behind this, Old Man!"

"Hello, Al. Looks like I caught you once again taking advantage of children."

His throat clenched with fear. "No fucking way," uttered the night-dwarf.

Grim Dog walked up to Al, grabbed him by the back of the neck and lifted him like a teddy bear. "Mary, Wife of Joseph, meet Alberich Night-dwarf. Pretty hideous, don't you think?"

"Fuck you," spat the dwarf. He swung his arms and legs violently. Of course he couldn't reach the Asgardian, but emotion doesn't always recognize physical impediment.

Grim Dog broke out laughing.

The laughter of his old enemy made Al even angrier, which unleashed a tsunami of curses and vulgarity in a dead tongue which sounded something like Norwegian. More likely though, it was some kind of language spoken several thousand years before there was a country called Norway.

Grim Dog said, "Okay, how's this: you either listen to this Lady or I kick the shit out of you with an iron boot?"

Al stopped his tirade and whirling body movements. He sighed and asked, "Have I got a fucking choice?"

"Nope."

Al shouted, "A beer! I need a goddamn beer!"

Grim Dog dropped Al to the floor and the night-dwarf scrambled for the refrigerator. "Al, focus! Do you know who this Lady is?"

Al looked at the Virgin Mary then opened the fridge. He took out a bottle of beer, bit off the glass neck, spat it out and took a big swig. He wiped the excess foam off his beard and answered, "I'm not a fucking retard! She's Mary, Mother of that Nazarene Rabbi!"

"Good, good, then how about you show the Lady some respect and stop fucking cussing. And put on some damn clothes!"

"It's alright," said the Virgin. "I don't mind."

Al smiled and said, "See, Dog? The ladies love the way my hammer swings."

Grim Dog looked at the Virgin. "You don't need him. I know a half-dozen other thieves who can do a better job than this little perv."

The Virgin Mother walked past the once-great All-Father to reach Alberich. She knocked the bottle of beer from his hand and said, "Alberich Night-dwarf, I have searched the worlds, upper, lower and in-between. I have been through lands once ruled by gods and heroes smote by the false worship of My Son and by the worship of His other brothers called by many names, but I have found no greater thief than you to do the task of which I now ask."

"Nuh-uh, not yet."

"Excuse me?"

"I've got to get my head clear." Al walked past both Immortals and stopped at the partially broken bureau next to the bed. Although overturned by the explosion, the drawers of the bureau were still intact. With a strength that belied his small stature, Al lifted the bureau back onto its legs. He opened the bottom drawer and started rummaging through it.

The Virgin looked at Grim Dog. "What's this?"

"I told you," Odin answered. "He's a loony. Ever since Ragnarok, he's been a pothead."

"Pothead?"

"Wacky weed?" Grim Dog put his thumb and forefinger together and pressed them against his pursed lips. He fake inhaled.

"Thank you, but I got it." Suddenly, the Virgin smiled as She realized She now had an "in" with the night-dwarf.

Al took out his stuff and sat down on the tattered bed. Within seconds he had packed the last of his kush in a beautiful pipe made of precious metal with a gem stone inlay. He lit the weed and took a long, very long, drag.

The Virgin Mother sat down next to Al and smiled a beatific smile. She waited for the night-dwarf to release the smoke.

Filled with a kind of bliss he could never remember feeling before, Al released the smoke and gasped a few times, fighting to keep as much of it in his lungs as possible. Then he let the final bit go and began to sway in satisfaction. "Oh, sweet Mother of G—" The dwarf realized who was sitting next to him and shot her a look. "Sorry."

"Don't worry, my clever friend. That's not what 'taking His name,' or Mine for that matter, 'in vain' actually means."

"Oh, wow, that's awesome—really awesome."

The Virgin looked at the now-empty baggie with only bitty bits of weed left in it. She asked, "Was that the last of your stash?"

"Stash?" the dwarf asked. "You know about the herb?"

"Please," The Virgin replied. "I raised two teen-age boys. I know about weed."

Grim Dog rolled his eyes.

The night-dwarf almost lost his pipe. "Say what? Who? You're shittin' me! Your Son—The Son? He toked?"

Mary patted Al on the knee and said, "All I'll say is that 'the Body and Blood of Christ' could be more aptly described as 'the Bud and Blood of Christ.'"

"Oh shit!" Al broke into a stoner's laugh.

Grim Dog smiled and sat down in a nearby chair. "And I thought I was the only one with an immortal son who smoked ganja."

Once Al stopped laughing he shook his head and said, "For that story alone I'll do just about anything You ask…"

"…but," the Virgin offered, "I know you are in need of some more herb."

"I'll tell You what, if You could get me some of that Last Supper kush I'd totally—"

"I can," the Virgin said.

"You can?"

"You can?" Grim Dog parroted.

The Virgin Mary looked at Grim Dog and nodded. She looked back at Al. "I will get you and the All-Father as much Last Supper kush as you want if you'll do just one little job for Me."

"Just give me the address and I'll Google-map it!"

Chapter 4

West Hollywood, California

Charlie woke the next morning without any conscious memory of Tracey Kipper or how he got home. His last memory was running across the living room to the bathroom after watching Deanne and Hamrod hitting on each other. Not knowing how he got home after a party wasn't anything new for Charlie, at least not since dating Deanne, but never had he found a way home and ended up under the afghan his "Gammy" made for him when he was in eighth grade.

"How'd I get here?" he asked himself.

A female voice answered from the kitchen, "Well, it wasn't you who put your pathetic, miserable body on that sofa."

It wasn't Tracey's voice or Deanne's for that matter. She was the other woman in Charlie's life and the one of the three whom he both knew well and trusted. She was Rita Ruano.

Rita walked out of the kitchen chomping down on a freshly made sandwich. She wiped excess mayo off her upper lip and plopped down in the chair once covered by the afghan.

Rita was in her late-twenties but looked no older than twenty. Her Italian-Latino heritage shone in her beautiful skin, hair and eyes.

Although she was short, Rita's high energy and spirit made her stand taller than anyone else in the room. Her tomboy nature kept her active (which kept her body in fantastic shape) while also keeping her from wearing nothing more than lipstick, mascara and occasionally eye shadow. And if anyone thought Rita was working to keep her feminine beauty hidden underneath ripped jeans, vintage t-shirts, and various caps and bandanas they might be right. But if they thought they knew the reasons, they'd be very, very wrong.

Seeing Rita brought Charlie some relief. He assumed that it was she who had put him on the sofa and under the afghan. "Rita, thank God. Thanks for putting me to—"

"Uh-uh," she muttered, mouth full, then swallowed and said, "I didn't do it, sailor. I got here ten minutes ago, came through the back door, found you like this. Figured I'd fix myself something 'cause whatever story you have to tell has got to be entertaining. I mean, hell, whoever put that afghan on you also cleaned this piece-of-shit-hole up."

"What?" Charlie looked at his living room and was stunned. It was clean. Someone had not only put him to bed but they had actually cleaned up his horrifically messy living room. "My living room—it's clean!"

"Very," said Rita. "Check out the rest of the place, too."

"What?" Charlie shot up on his feet and bolted towards the bedrooms. He disappeared down the hallway, while Rita finished up her sandwich. She could hear Charlie's gasps and exclamations of disbelief.

He reappeared in the living room and said, "Clean, orderly, every room. How did all of this happen? Did you do this? Because you've done this before—"

"I'm not in love with you anymore, Charles! I mean, I love you—you know, but the last time I cleaned this joint up was when we were more than friends, more than boss and employee. You don't think you might have been so drunk you actually cleaned this place?"

"No way! Or at least I don't think so. I can't figure any of this out."

Rita shrugged her shoulders and said, "Then I haven't got a clue, Boss. But what I do know is that we are late."

"We are?" Charlie asked, looking desperately for a clock and found the cable box reading 10:43 a.m. "Oh shit!"

"Why do you think I'm here?" Rita asked.

Charlie scrambled for his wallet, keys and jacket, all of which he found nicely placed on the side table next to the sofa. He picked them up and looked at them. "Do I have a fairy godmother or something?"

"I'm pretty sure only teenage girls and virgins get those, neither of which you are."

They headed for the front door. Charlie opened it but dropped his arm across the doorway to stop Rita from leaving first. He asked her, "Pony! He knows what he has to do today?"

Rita said, "Take it easy, Boss. I talked to him last night. I'm gonna drop you off and then run by his place with the cash."

Charlie shuddered. "Pony with cash—God, why do we trust him to get the hydro from Buddha?"

"Because the only thing in the world he cares about more than his own life is weed. Weed's his religion."

"Right, it's his religion."

They went out the front door, and Charlie locked it behind them. They headed down the walkway towards Rita's car, which was parked in the same spot Tracey's had been the night before. They reached the sidewalk but Charlie froze.

Rita asked, "What's wrong?"

Charlie looked back at his house and then at Rita's car. He looked for a second time followed by a third.

Rita said, "Charles, we'll have a line at the dispensary! We have to go! Can we play Columbo another time, please?"

"Yeah, right, okay, sorry. It's just—it's just—"

Rita scoffed and pushed Charlie with all her strength to her car. She unlocked it and opened the passenger's door. Charlie was mumbling about how couldn't for the life of himself remember last night but really wanted to. Ironically, as if repeating last night, Rita buckled Charlie into the seatbelt and did the same for herself before driving them to work.

Fortunately, it was only a ten minute drive from Charlie's house to Charlie's marijuana dispensary OHM. Below the decorative three-letter script on the sign were the words: "Organic & Homeopathic Medicinals" (in the kind of ethnically-insulting pseudo-Irish style font made popular by the live shows of pop-Celtic music aired in unending loops during PBS pledge drives) underneath the much larger letters O H M (in the equally ethnically-insulting pseudo-Viking font made popular by the Renaissance-faire explosion of the early 1990s). The bad grammar of "Medicinals" notwithstanding, the competitive environment of legalized medicinal marijuana dispensaries in the city of West Hollywood meant that how you named your dispensary could make all the difference. Charlie hired Rita after she came up with the name OHM. It was easy, non-offensive and ironic in a Hindu and Buddhist way.

As Rita pulled up to the curb in front of OHM, Charlie saw the line measured eleven patrons long. "Son-of-a-bitch, how will I get this place opened and everyone serviced if you have to go over to Pony's first? I'm no good at appeasing potheads! I'm too high-strung!"

Rita put the car in park and grabbed Charlie's knee. She said, "You're right about that. Okay, so listen: I'll go inside with you, call Henry, and then—"

"Yes, Henry!" Charlie shouted. "Call him and then you can—"

Rita was out of the car and shouting at the line of patrons before Charlie was finished talking about Henry. She used her charm, her hips and her humor to turn all of their spirits up. It was a hot morning in the City of Angels, but by the time Charlie was out of the car, keys in hand and unlocking the front door, Rita had made the sweating, uncomfortable customers eager and willing to wait. Once they had entered and gone through the security foyer and were inside the front room/lobby of the dispensary, Rita and Charlie were able to switch on the lights, turn on the satellite stereo system, get the air conditioning blowing, and bring the lobby computer and sales room registers to life. It was far from their first time opening the dispensary late, and with the number of times they had run this drill, OHM was ready for business within fifteen minutes of their arrival.

Five minutes before Charlie and Rita were ready to receive the patrons, the last component to operating the dispensary walked through the back door: Ian Olczwicki. Technically, Ian was a bouncer by trade but since he was a fan of Star Trek: The Next Generation and always wanted to be "Security Chief Worf." As a favor, Charlie gave him the same title—not the name Worf. He became Security Chief Ian (Yeah, not as menacing, I know).

"What's up, my lue-zers?" was how Ian greeted whoever was inside OHM on whatever day it was.

"Fuck you, Ian!" was how Rita always returned his greeting.

"Did you munch sweet rug last night, Rita?" was one of several common comebacks for Ian, as he double-checked the equipment on his belt before heading to the front door where he would sit and check the credentials of their customers to make sure they had the legal card required to buy medical marijuana or related edibles and equipment.

Before Rita could come back with another retort, this is the point at which Charlie would get very bossy and shout, "Both of you, shut it! You love each other, we all love each other, this is a place of love, now shut the fuck up, get along and Ian, open that goddamn door so we can make some motherfucking scratch!"

Like Charlie, Ian was in his mid-thirties. Unlike Charlie, Ian was a former NFL line backer. He played for three seasons with the San Francisco 49ers, but blew out his knee in a pre-season game against the San Diego Chargers before his fourth season began. It was a contract year for Ian and he was sure to make a load of dough. He had been picked to the Pro Bowl the year before and was on schedule to have another devastating year full of sacks due to his all-pro pass rush. But Ian was so bitter at the loss of his fame and football career, he spent the next three years squandering his accrued wealth. It left him working odd jobs and nothing stuck until he ran into an old friend, former USC alum Charlie Hamor.

Although not as athletic or well-defined as during his pro-days, Ian was still tall and powerfully built. He continued to lift weights and do light cardio, but his continued bitterness at God and San Diego for what happened all those years ago prevented Ian from getting anywhere close to the development he once had. He had a bit of a belly but it wasn't anything anyone would criticize for fear that Ian's giant paws would become a fist in their face. He shaved his head and sported a full beard and kept them both well-groomed.

Charlie hired Ian as his security for the dispensary when he first opened it two years ago. Over that time they renewed their deep and highly dysfunctional friendship which began in their sophomore year as Trojans. The third member of that four-man entourage (Pony Macreedy was the fourth) was Henry Leturnoe (pronounced exactly like LeTourneau of the famous Christian university but because Henry didn't want to be confused with this more "fanatical" institution, he legally changed the spelling), who Rita rang up that morning to come in and cover her while she went to find Pony for his hydro run. Henry and Charlie were co-owners of OHM together. His genius was in growing the medicinal magic sold at OHM. The only product they sold that Henry didn't personally develop was the hydro Pony was to buy from the supplier Buddha Jesus.

While Ian spent the better part of his twenties as a 49er, Charlie and Henry wrote and published a series of five novels that were relatively successful. Only the first book in the series was a New York Times bestseller, while the following four were only modestly successful. After the fifth book, something happened to Charlie that changed the direction of his and Henry's life. Charlie's kid brother Daniel was diagnosed with a devastating form of cancer that took his life when he was only twenty-six. It tore Charlie up emotionally. He was devastated seeing his only sibling wracked with pain.

During this time, Charlie and Henry discovered the natural wonder of marijuana. Fortunately, Daniel was able to use Henry's first personal strain to find great comfort towards the end of his life. Once he was gone, Charlie and Henry took the money they had made as authors, developed their own weeds and opened OHM. It wasn't just a lark or a desire by stoners to have as much weed as they could ever want, whenever they wanted. For Charlie and Henry, medical marijuana and OHM was a calling, the fulfillment of a promise to Danny to give the kind of comfort and relief from pain that they wanted to make for him.

Over the years though, that calling had become like any other business: stressful, competitive, life-consuming and financially risky. It was only a photo of Daniel, Charlie, Henry and Ian that hung on the wall in the front room of OHM that served as Charlie's ballast under the weight of what had been a crushing six months. OHM wasn't in any real threat of financial collapse, but the arrival of a network of ten dispensaries which had popped up all over Los Angeles County owned by the same shadowy figure was choking the life of independent dispensaries like theirs. In the last year, twelve other indie-dispensaries had gone out of business. Charlie, Henry and their most trusted employee Rita would be damned if they were next. This was why the Buddha Jesus hydroponic weed was so important. Charlie had an exclusive deal for "Buddha Blend," which made it their best line of defense.

Twenty minutes after they had opened the dispensary, Henry arrived to relieve Rita. She took off in her car and the three ex-Trojans were left to keep the flow of clients moving in and out. Those clients who had come in just for Buddha Blend were able to purchase only an eighth each on that day since they were low. But if they came back on Monday, there'd be a fresh shipment and no limit on how much they could buy.

That's why Charlie was so tense on the way to OHM about Pony having cash. And that concern—the reasonable, rational, all-too-often-proven-valid concern of Charlie's—rolled through Rita's brain as she drove from West Hollywood by way of Santa Monica Blvd. to Wilshire to Ocean Blvd to Venice Beach. As if it could make a difference to Charlie back at the dispensary, she kept one hand tapping the money bag containing the cash while the other steered the car. Rita reached an alley between two beach-front stores and parked in a spot where she knew she was risking a ticket. But under the circumstances she decided it was better to pay the fine than wasting time finding a legal place to park. She grabbed the money bag and got out of the car. She ran out onto the promenade and saw the store she wanted. It was a t-shirt shop, amongst other things.

Dodging skaters, skateboarders and the occasional bicyclist, Rita reached the store and found an almost invisible little staircase behind a slender glass door that ran up to the floor above the t-shirt store. She entered and raced up the stairs to the weathered door at the top. No number, no name—the door could be to a janitor's closet. She knocked and waited. Nothing. She knocked, again. Still nothing.

Rita sighed and shouted, "Pony! Wake the fuck up, you slacker! You have one job! Just one job! I need you to do it now!"

There was the sound of someone groaning from inside.

Rita tapped her forehead against the door and moaned. "Pony Macreedy, get your sorry-ass excuse for a body to this door and open it up or I'm gonna tell every loser on the promenade outside where you keep your spare—"

The door flew open and a smiling Pony Macreedy greeted Rita. "Hi, Rita! No worries, babe! I'm here and I'm one hundred percent ready to go! Wanna come in?"

Rita quickly examined Pony: his clean but bushy red hair and hippie-like beard showed that he had showered that morning. His psychedelic-style t-shirt with a rendering of the late Richard Manuel, a member of the legendary The Band and Pony's personal idol, and faded cut-off jean shorts were also clean. But none of this was any guarantee that his apartment was in any way likewise or not a HAZMAT zone.

"In your apartment?" exclaimed Rita. "Please! I do not want scabies!"

"I don't have—what the hell are scabies?"

Rita shoved the money bag into Pony's chest. He grabbed it with both hands. "This! This is your life, right here! You got that?"

"Oh, is today the Buddha run?"

Rita scoffed. "Yes, dummy, today is the Buddha run. Charlie is counting on this, Pony, you cannot let him down! He is all but out of the Buddha Blend, got it?"

"I got it! I got it! But Charlie knows that—what are scabies?"

"Forget the scabies, okay? I'll tell you some other time. Focus! Focus! Now, Charlie knows how long the trip will take you—that you won't be back until tomorrow. But if you don't get going now it'll be next Thursday before you get back! So move it!"

"Gotcha, Cap'n! Hey, Rita, did you see the news this morning? You won't believe what's going on at the Vatican. The Pope is—"

"I've got to get back, okay? OHM is swamped." And with that, Rita was down the stairs and out through the filthy glass door before Pony could say or ask anything else.

Chapter 5

Manchester, England

Breaking into the Vatican's legendary Vault, located below the Basilica of Saint Peter, at first seemed to be an impossible task. In fact, the night-dwarf argued with Grim Dog over the absurdity of the Virgin Mary's objective, regardless of how big a stain he'd turn into if Grim Dog stomped on him for refusing to do the job.

After several minutes of trying to get the Asgardian and the night-dwarf to stop bickering, the Virgin shouted a single word to stop their fight. "Faith!"

"The fuck?" Alberich asked as he turned to Her. "What the hell are You on about?"

"I'd think that someone as worldly as you, Alberich, would understand exactly what I mean. Are you not a creature of magic? Is faith not an important component to having magic work?"

"Oh, I get it!" It was as if a light went off in Alberich's brain that revealed the why of the Blessed Mother's choosing him to pull off this theft. "You mean 'faith' as in 'belief,' right? You're saying that because no Christian in the modern world is allowed to believe in the existence of night-dwarves, they won't have any defenses against my magical powers. There is no gate, no alarm, no gun, no video surveillance whether known to the general public or kept secret by even the most powerful military which can capture, see or affect a night-dwarf. So, I can walk in and out of the Vatican without even using my night-invisibility! Why didn't I think of this before? I could be stinking rich by now!"

Before the Virgin Mary could respond, Grim Dog piped up, "Don't be stupid, Al!"

"What? How am I stupid?"

"Do you think we're the only three 'supernatural beings' that even know about, let alone want the Augur? Even the Mother of Christ isn't omniscient! We haven't got a clue whether anyone else might be trying to get at it. And regardless of whether the devout in that palace of hypocrisy accept your kind as real, it doesn't mean all of them won't be able to see you. You can avoid the technology, no doubt—but even the lowliest security guard might have bought into Grandmama's childhood stories. Remember, outside the Romanians, the Italians are the most superstitious Westerners of all."

"The All-Father's right," the Virgin said. "You can't take for granted what any given human might believe or not. So you have to use whatever supernatural talent you have to keep yourself hidden from the human eye. On top of that, who knows what other artifacts are kept in that vault? There could be all sorts of devices to countermand your powers."

"Shit," Alberich mumbled, clearly sobering up fast. "I'm gonna need to take a few tokes before I hit that pit."

"No!" the Virgin shouted. She stood up and knocked aside his pipe, shaking both the night-dwarf and the former Asgardian deity.

"Hey! Whoa! That was the last of my kush, bitch!"

The Virgin grabbed Alberich by the chin and shook his head. "Hear this, Alberich Night-dwarf, I will give you the most precious kush ever grown on this earth, but you will not—you cannot—go into that fortress with anything other than the purest mind and heart. The Augur will not respond to anyone who isn't both! Do you understand me? You cannot hold the Augur if you are not pure!"

Grim Dog laughed.

The Virgin looked at Grim Dog.

He saw Her glare and said, "The truth is that little bastard right there hasn't been pure since he stole my ring to rape the Rhinemaidens."

Suddenly, Alberich broke down weeping. He fell to the floor wailing. "He's right," he cried out. "I am not worthy to serve You, Fairest of All Mothers, let alone hold the most precious item in the world! I am a pathetic, bent, corrupt little spirit! I am a thief, a rapist, a fornicator, a murderer, a really shitty dad to a couple of kids I stole!—"

"Oh shit, I had forgotten about the kidnapping of Siegmund and Sieglinde," Grim Dog whispered. "I liked that opera Wagner composed about it, although it was a bit long. Too bad that mustached lunatic and his bastard Nazis got our stories caught up in their bullshit racism."

Al said. "I've done some bad shit, but never genocide—never that!"

The Virgin Mary smiled and kneeled on the floor in front of Alberich. She placed Her hands on his face and lifted it so that their eyes met. "But you are repentant, are you not? Is not your heart full of sorrow, regret, shame and grief for all that you have done before this very point in time?"

"Aye, yes, yes I am," muttered the night-dwarf.

"Then I forgive you. He forgives you. All of life forgives you and you are pure."

Then as if from above, a light shone down through the ceiling from some greater, higher love on the face of the night-dwarf.

Grim Dog saw the light, too. He rolled his eyes and scoffed. To himself he mumbled, "Show-off."

Papal Household, Vatican City

Every hall, every room in the Papal private chambers was quiet. No one dared speak as they waited for word regarding The Holy Father. Just outside the private chambers of The Holy Father stood Cardinal Patrizio Tindiglia, Cardinal Vittorio Giordano and Cardinal Aleksy Walczak, who appeared to be the only persons in the Papal Palace in verbal discussion. With quiet intensity, the three highest-ranking members of the College of Cardinals discussed between them what was happening inside The Holy Father's private rooms.

The chambers' door opened and a physician walked out.

All three Cardinals looked at the physician. The physician approached them with his attention focused on Tindiglia. He said, "The Holy Father is asking for you, Cardinal."

Tindiglia nodded. He looked at his colleagues, both of whom gave him a nod. Tindiglia followed the physician as he returned to the Pope's private chambers. Tindiglia entered the bedchamber of the Pope and found another physician and two nurses monitoring the extensive machines being used to keep the Pope from slipping into the abyss.

Without a word, Tindiglia walked to the side of the bed closest to the Holy Father, hands together, and muttered prayers in Latin. Were it not for the machines with their trademark beeps, pings and bells, Tindiglia might think the Pope already dead. After a few more prayers, Tindiglia spoke. "Holy Father, I have received your summons. What may I do to serve you?"

The Pope took in as deep a breath as he could and spoke something that more closely resembled a broken hiss with a hiccup or two inside. Tindiglia bent over and placed his ear as close to the pontiff's mouth as he could without his flesh touching the Holy Father's.

"I beg your pardon, Holy Father, but could you please repeat your request?"

The Pope uttered the sounds—words—into Tindiglia's ear.

The shock which crossed Tindiglia's face suggested he was surprised but understood the pontiff's request. The fact that Tindiglia's expression was one of awe suggested the Cardinal found his superior's request hard to believe.

"You are certain, Holy Father? This is your request?"

The Pope muttered some more and nodded to affirm what he has said.

The Cardinal bowed and said, "As you wish, Holy Father. I will move with all speed to see that he is brought here." Tindiglia remained bowed but moved so that he could kiss the ring of the Pope without touching or lifting his superior's hand.

Tindiglia stood up straight and walked over to the same physician who had escorted him inside. He grabbed him by the arm and led him back towards the doors.

"Yes?" the physician asked.

"Drugs?—has the Holy Father been given psychotropics of any kind?"

"Psychotropics?" the physician repeated, clearly taken aback by the accusatory tone in Tindiglia's question. "If you're asking have we given the Holy Father anything other than what's required for his comfort—no, of course not. However, due to the incredibly high level of pain caused by the final stage of his cancer, we are administering morphine, but no more than the required amount."

"Forgive my tone, doctor. I do not mean to sound—it's just that—please forget I asked. You are doing a fine, fine job. Would you please notify me of any other changes in his condition?"

"Of course, Cardinal, immediately."

Tindiglia slipped out of the room and met his colleagues in the hall outside.

Walczak asked, "How is the Holy Father?"

Tindiglia took a deep breath and said, "As well as one can expect, but it will not be long before he is with Our Heavenly Father."

Walczak sighed and looked at Giordano. Giordano asked, "What did he want with you, Tindiglia? What news did the Holy Father give you?"

Tindiglia put space between himself and his colleagues. Clearly he was trying to find the words to explain what the Pope had told him. Finally he said, "It is almost not to be believed. He asked for us to summon his mentor for the last rites."

Walczak stepped towards Tindiglia. "What? You mean Father Agosto!"

"Not I!" Tindiglia fired back. "It is the Holy Father that would see him!"

Walczak shook his head, much, much too upset to think rationally. "No! No! We cannot allow his return to the Holy See!"

Tindiglia shouted back at Walczak, "We? There is no 'we'! There is only he who is in that bed, Walczak! He's the Holy Father! If he wishes a visit from his mentor than we shall bring him, regardless of what you, I or the entire College of Cardinals thinks about the Holy Father's request or Father Agosto!"

Tindiglia turned to the quiet Giordano and asked, "Do we know Father Agosto's location?"

Giordano nodded and said, "South America."

"South America?"

"The Amazonian Rainforest, to be exact."

"Exact?" shouted Tindiglia. "Do you know how big that Rainforest is? We'll never find him in time!"

Giordano said, "We have a way to find him, and bring him here in time."

Walczak shot a look at Giordano. "We do?"

Giordano looked between both his peers and said, "Oh yes."

Tindiglia threw his hands out to Giordano. "Well, don't make us play a game, Giordano. Where is it and why wasn't I told about our having any such means to do such an impossible task?"

Giordano said, "I don't know why you weren't told. All I know is that it's in the Vault."

"The Vault?—" whispered Walczak, his face turned a pale yellow color.

Tindiglia only nodded and took a few seconds to absorb what Giordano had just revealed. "I see," he said. "Then since you have the clearance, Walczak, I need you to get down there and help me find this means to get Agosto here as fast as possible."

"What is it?" Walczak asked. "I mean, what is it the Holy Father asked you to get besides Agosto?"

Tindiglia answered, "The Augur. He said the thing I need to get Agosto here as fast as possible is the Augur."

Walczak and Giordano looked at each other at that exact moment and repeated, "The Augur?"

Tindiglia sighed and rolled his eyes. Exasperated he said, "Please, Cardinals, this isn't the Dark Ages. We aren't at war with the Saracen; we aren't confronting the Great Schism or Martin Luther. All we have to do is take the elevator down to the Vault, open the door, get it out, use it to find Agosto and bring him back here.

"What about that could possibly go wrong?"

Chapter 6

The Basilica of Saint Peter, Vatican City

As impressive as the Basilica's security system appeared to be to Alberich (Al had completed six months of a security analyst degree at the Tucson campus of the DeVry Institute of profit-based learning back in 1981), everything the Virgin and Grim Dog had told him about belief seemed to be validated as he cruised through laser defenses, passed within a few feet of several Swiss Guards and went un-photographed by video surveillance.

How did the night-dwarf pass through solid doors and locks? Good question. After all, doors and simple locks—or in this case, retinal-scan locks—can be an impediment to any living or organic creature, supernatural or not, as they are themselves solid and contain some kind of organic material. Al was able to bypass these by employing his magical powers to warp the laws of physics. As a night-dwarf, he could de-materialize his physical self and operate through whatever shadows or darkness was present. His entire body transformed into a kind of "dark energy" and easily passed through even the smallest of openings, visible or otherwise. Unfortunately for the Vatican, no matter how advanced their technology, they were still dealing with good old fashioned air-conditioning. When Stuart Cramer invented the first modern-day application of air-conditioning in 1906 North Carolina, it was Al's second cousin Mimlier who discovered he could use the vents and pipes as an ad-hoc tunnel system to get in and out of any given building. Unfortunately, Mimlier was not prepared for what Freon would do to his digestive system when he decided, on a dare, to chug it with a beer chaser.

Once Al was inside the central air matrix, it took him less than five minutes to reach the vent that fed the hallway directly in front of the Vault door. The one thing about the Vatican's Vault which captured Al's curiosity was how deep below the earth's surface he had to descend to reach it. Throughout the whole complex, Al found indicators that a technology not historically associated with the Catholic Church had been employed to construct the Vault. In fact, Al wondered if certain cousins of his night-dwarf species had been employed to help build it. Whatever the case, Al's mind was locked into doing his thievery and getting out before any special surprises stopped him.

Once transformed, Al passed through the vent slots and became a solid humanoid shape in front of the Vault's door. He looked down both sides of the hall and saw what might or might not be guardsmen posted at the far ends. Whether they were or weren't, they didn't appear to detect Al's presence. So Al gave the door his full attention, and after a quick review of the retinal lock and sizing up the door itself, Al suddenly gasped and stepped back. He couldn't believe what he was sensing about the door.

Iron! Fucking iron, he thought to himself. With all the types of steel in the world, what are the goddamn odds these ass-backwards bureaucrats would build the fucking vault door out of iron? Well, that does it! Clearly whatever else Grim Dog and the Virgin said, these bozos definitely believe in creatures like me!

"Shit, shit, shit," Alberich mumbled over and over again.

But he wouldn't let this sudden complication beat him. Hell no! The light of redemption that shone on him back in his rat cage of an apartment (not an absolute conversion, mind you; in fact, it was more convenience than conversion) had imbued Al with an unwavering conviction to fulfill the wish of the Virgin Mary. Well, that and the payment of Last Supper kush.

Suddenly, Al heard a pair of metal doors open. Due to the acoustics of the hallway, Al was not sure exactly where the doors were. With nothing but instinct, Al transformed himself further until he was part of the shadows already present in the hallway.

Into view appeared the three Cardinals led by Tindiglia, accompanied by a trio of armed guardsmen behind Giordano and Walczak. As the clerics neared the iron door, it began to open. The Cardinals didn't even need to use the complex lock system, since someone on the inside of the door had seen them approach and didn't want to make his superiors wait.

When the Vault door swung open, a sudden burst of unearthly light shone forth from within the ancient chamber. Instinctively terrified of the light, Al scampered as far along the wall as he had to in order that shadow kept him cloaked. Fortunately, the Cardinals and their Swiss Guards were so distracted by the clerics babbling to each other no one either heard or noticed Al's movements. The Cardinals and Swiss Guards entered the Vault and the door began to swing shut behind them.

Al gasped in desperation. He suddenly realized that his fear of the light made him scamper away from the place he needed to enter, and the door was freakin' open! He knew that entering under the guise of dark energy was taking a chance, but so was going in solid. Either way, he had only seconds to decide.

"Fuck it," he mumbled to himself.

Quick as lightning, Al dashed through the closing space and immediately sought out the closest space with darkness in it. It didn't take conscious effort. Again, this was all done by instinct being a night-dwarf who had lived for more than a thousand years.

Once inside, Al realized the light was more like a curtain, obscuring the vast size of the room and the number of items, crates and artifacts held within. There was no way to estimate the size of the Vault with the naked eye. Al could not see any other wall. Above his head the night-dwarf could see no ceiling. The room went up and up until it disappeared into darkness.

"Bollocks," Al mumbled. "This will take for bloody ever! I definitely think this deserves another five—no double the original ten bricks." Realizing he was actually making noise and that the Cardinals and the Swiss Guards were no more than ten yards away, Al clamped his hand on his mouth.

Tindiglia swung his head around in the direction of Al's voice. "Did you hear that?" he asked the others.

A guardsman asked, "What, Sir?"

"A voice—thought I heard—" but Tindiglia could see nothing and no one.

"Down here," said Walczak, "there are only ghosts."

But it didn't matter who was looking in Al's direction, he was completely obscured. Soon the clerics and guards continued along their way forgetting altogether the voice Tindiglia thought he heard.

Al sighed, having dodged a bullet. All he had to do now was actually find "the Augur" and get it the hell out of the Vault, the Vatican, the Holy See and back to Los Angeles, where he had agreed to meet the Holy Mother and Grim Dog.

Reassessing the situation, Al decided that no matter how exhausting it was for him to maintain his shadow-form, it was his only fail-safe protection. So he slipped from one shadow to the next, passing bookshelf after bookshelf, guard after guard without anyone noticing him. Once he was invisible, the only thing Al needed in order to find the Augur in so huge a chamber was his olfactory sense—aka his big, red, bulbous nose.

Their nose was the most gifted sensory apparatus born to the once-vast population of night-dwarfs. Having spent the majority of their great years dwelling inside mountain ranges all over the world, it was the ability to sniff out precious metals and stones in the darkness of the earth which allowed them to find and then craft the kind of beautiful objects appreciated by deities and mankind alike. That was until the goddamn Industrial Revolution came along and fucked up the whole economic and social balance between mortal and immortals— but that's a diatribe for another time.

Additionally, the amazing noses of the night-dwarves allowed them to sniff out items of great power and magic because these objects, believe it or not, actually put off a smell—a "stink"—as the night-dwarfs would call it. This is how back in his heyday Alberich found and stole the Great Ring he once forged for Grim Dog. The ring had a stink that told any night-dwarf that Alberich had made it.

So, Al set his nose to sniffing. At first he was overwhelmed by the powerful stink of many, many arcane objects. He almost vomited from the overwhelming sensations, but as quickly as he could, he ferreted out in his mind the odors that were distinct to the kind of objects that would contain something of Grim Dog. Although he, like every other supernatural person or occult junkie, had heard of the Augur, Al had never set eyes upon it. Being that its form is somewhat malleable and non-descript before one's eyes first set upon it, there wasn't much with its physical description that either the Virgin or Grim Dog could help with, even though Grim Dog's right eye was undeniably a part of its construction. Since a part of Grim Dog's physical body was in the Augur, Al used his powerful olfactory sense to trace the scent he knew all too well.

Unfortunately, although Al's nose unerringly led him through the labyrinth of shelves, cases and smaller vaults (containing many millennia of magical objects, some Christian, some pagan), when he found the specific vault containing the Augur he saw it was protected by Swiss Guards. More challenging still, the Cardinals Giordano and Walczak and their personal Swiss Guards were standing right there in front of the vault's open door.

"Shit," mumbled the night-dwarf.

Only Tindiglia wasn't present, but that soon changed as he appeared from inside the Vault holding something in—well—a bowling bag. Yes, it was a large blue-green bowling bag from approximately the late 1950s or early 1960s. On one side was sewn an insignia of a hammer with the words "The Hammers" below it. Tindiglia wasn't holding it by the handles, though; he was carrying it by the bottom with both hands.

Walczak asked, "A bowling bag? It's kept in a bowling bag?"

Tindiglia said, "This is exactly how it was found when it was recovered on the twenty-sixth of November, 1963. The fact that it was—is in a bowling bag is inconsequential. Probably just the kind of unlikely place the previous holder would think to put it so it wouldn't be found easily when looked for."

Walczak asked, "Where?"

"Dallas, Texas," answered Tindiglia.

"Why there?" was Walczak's next question.

Before Tindiglia could continue the history lesson, Giordano shouted, "Inconsequential, Walczak! It's our job to use it, not discuss it! Now let's find Agosto so the Holy Father can be at peace!"

But if that was meant to end the discussion, it failed. Instead an argument broke out between the three Cardinals over how to use the device, if using it was possible at all. No one, including Tindiglia, was willing to unzip the bowling bag to look at the Augur, let alone remove it or use it.

Al was salivating. He was so close to the bag, the Augur reeked to him. But to grab it when it was actually in the hands of his enemies and their weapons close enough to slice and dice the night-dwarf (they were immortal from aging, but not weaponry) would be folly.

How fast could these apes run, though?, thought Al. If I grabbed it, kept the dark energy going and really ran, I might be able to—shit! The sudden recollection of the iron door stopped Al's mind before it finished the thought.

Tindiglia, Giordano and Walczak ended their bickering by agreeing to take the bag and its contents to the Holy Father and determine at that point what to do next with the device. Were it not for the mortal state of the princely pontiff, the Vault managers would not have even allowed the Augur to leave the chamber. Fortunately for Al, the managers agreed.

Al was almost giddy as his enemies bore the bag through the iron door and into the hallway outside. He was barely able to contain his giggling. The only material in the whole of the tiny nation which proved impossible for Al to beat was now moot. But while Al was praising his good luck, he saw the iron door closing after the Cardinals and the bag. He made an odd little screech in desperation and then broke into a full run. Still in dark energy form, Al escaped through the closing gap of the door just before it slammed shut and locked.

Al sighed in relief. He caught his breath just in time to see the Cardinals, guards and the Augur disappearing down the hallway. Al had no idea where they'd end up going, or if he'd be able to intercept them through the intricate ventilation system before they were someplace where the Augur would be even better defended. His gut told him it was now or never.

If necessity is the mother of invention, then desperate greed is the molesting uncle of dumb courage. So it was for Alberich Night-dwarf as he broke into a faster-than-human run, maintaining his concentration on his dark energy form, and crashed into the legs of Giordano, one guard and Tindiglia himself. The three men dropped like bowling pins.

The other men left standing were caught by such surprise they instinctively scattered towards the closest wall. After all, it wasn't a person or even a dwarf they saw smash into them and seize the bowling bag. All they saw was a two-dimensional shadow or, more accurately, a patch of darkness swoop back around after knocking them to the ground and sweep up the Augur.

"What in the name of Christ?" shouted Walczak. He looked to the Swiss Guard still standing and ordered him, "After that, erm—bag!"

But the Swiss Guard couldn't see anything. Al and the bag were well out of sight. "But, Cardinal, I do not see it! I don't see a thing!"

Walczak screamed at the top of his lungs as his fellows rose to their feet with the help of the other Swiss Guards.

"What was that thief?" asked Tindiglia.

"Nothing human, I'll warrant!" shouted Giordano. "It must have been an evil spirit! I felt it hit me but I saw no solid form!"

"Evil spirit? Evil spirits is what the Holy Father will call us when we tell him we've lost the Augur!" added Walczak.

Through all the chaos, Tindiglia remained composed. He looked down the hallway where Al had disappeared and said, "Now we have another reason to summon Father Agosto to the See."

Chapter 7

West Hollywood, California

Charlie walked up to the door of his house completely wiped out. Anyone who thinks running a pot shop is "totally bitchin'" or "awesome, dude" would be terribly, terribly wrong. The majority of your customers are not laid-back hippies or Cheech and Chong; they are genuinely chronically ill people who can find no relief from "legal" pharmaceuticals and must resort to means society deems "wrong" in order to be comfortable—not cured, just comfortable enough to tolerate their suffering. This means they will be cranky, impatient, and sometimes assholes. Having watched his baby brother suffer endlessly, Charlie accepted these peoples' right to be assholes, but that didn't mean he was any less frustrated and physically drained at the end of the day.

Each night when Charlie sat down on his sofa with beer in hand to decompress, he spent at least five, sometimes fifteen minutes chatting—well, not chatting so much as complaining—to the spirit of his brother about shitty customers in order to renew his calling. Eventually, he'd fall asleep watching Craig Ferguson, wake up the next morning and go back to work. Most days this ritual served its purpose. But on that night (the night after Tracey had brought him home) something different happened.

As Charlie sat down with beer in hand and clicked on the local news, ready to chat with his brother, his land-line rang. He decided to let the machine pick it up. As the greeting droned on, Charlie took a swig of his beer but stopped when he heard the click of the machine and Deanne's nasally pitch:

"Hi, Charlie, it's me. Um, I tried you at OHM, but—um—Rita told me you'd left—like a while ago? Guess you're walking, but," she coughed, "maybe you stopped at Fatburger's on the way home? If you did, you deserve a treat, you really do. Rita told me what a shitty day it was there. Anyway, um—call me? I need to make up last night to you? You'll never guess how I found out about you leaving. It was crazy. But I was upset, I was. That Hamrod prick I talked to for an hour was like—well, listen, call me, okay? We can talk about it then. Kiss kiss!"

Deanne hung up.

Charlie groaned. This is why he didn't have a mobile phone. In the age of wireless communication, Charlie felt privacy was sacred and so was not being reachable when your bitch of a girlfriend was trying to make up for whatever emotional scam she pulled the night before. How the fuck did I get home last night? Charlie thought to himself. I have no fucking memory! Jesus, have I become that much of an alkie that I can't even remember? Shit, it isn't the weed. I haven't smoked any since last weekend.

Wondering how he got home and how Deanne found out about it was reason enough for Charlie to call her no matter what the cost. So, after drinking the rest of his newly-opened beer in just two long swigs, Charlie reached for the phone and picked it up. He was about to dial Deanne's number when it rang in his hand and made him jump.

"Shit—fuck!" he shouted. He shook himself calm and answered it on the third ring. "'Ell-o?"

It was Henry.

"Hey, Henry, what's up?"

Charlie listened to what Henry was saying. What Henry actually said wasn't as relevant as how it made Charlie's gut tighten up, which led to a huge belch that spat out of his mouth because of the beer sloshing in his belly.

"Oh God, Henry, man, dude, I'm so sorry. I just drank a beer and my gut—"

Henry cut off Charlie and said more that made Charlie's gut tighten again. Thankfully no more gas was left to blow out either end.

"You and Rita? Yeah, sure, okay."

Then Henry asked if Charlie needed a ride to where they were waiting for him.

"No, no, I'm not far. I could use the walk—you know, and make sure all the gas is out before I sit in public. Even a Fatburger deserves respect, right?"

Charlie hung up without another word. Henry and Charlie were so close that they almost never said, "Good-bye," or "See you soon," or "Later," or even that really annoying colloquial "Late!" It's what they did—or didn't do—that they picked up from Charlie's brother.

What did Henry tell Charlie on the phone? Whatever it was, Charlie struggled to absorb it. It made him tell his brother's spirit, "Danny? I'm sorry, man. Guess our talk has to wait until later. I've got a date with an A-bomb."

Charlie stood up and walked out of the house. He locked the door and headed towards the street, turning in the direction of Santa Monica Blvd.

Fatburger Restaurant (Yum Freakin' Yum!)

When Charlie reached the doors to Fatburger, he stopped short of opening them because he saw Henry, Rita and Ian seated at a booth not eating but drinking fountain drinks and chatting. They had a code, these friends, not to order any food until everyone had arrived, no matter how hungry they were. It just wasn't what they did. It could have come from the weed-smoking custom of smoking only with friends and not alone. Whatever the reasons, Charlie knew that he had no appetite and hoped that for once his friends would break with tradition.

Charlie opened the door and entered. He made a bee-line for the booth where his friends sat.

Ian was the first to spot Charlie. He was seated on the outside with Henry on the inside. Rita was on the opposite side next to the window. Ian smiled big and said, "Finally! Shit! I'm starving! Anyone else want anything?" To Charlie specifically he asked, "How about you, big guy? King Burger?"

"Nada," said Charlie as he slid into the open spot next to Rita.

Ian shot out of the booth and headed for the order line.

Before anyone said anything else, Rita wrapped her arm around Charlie's and squeezed it tightly. She kissed him on the cheek and asked, "Who has the sexiest boss in the whole wide world?" Which was an awesome thing to say from someone as hot as Rita, but to Charlie hearing those words kind of told him that something really shitty was about to be said.

"It's the gut, right?" Charlie asked. "It's this wobbly gut that makes me so sexy."

Rita gently poked his soft belly and said, "Absolutely, yes. I hate tight abs, you know? I like to have some skin I can sink my teeth into and—" she made silly noises with her teeth and lips.

Charlie smiled and laughed.

That's when Henry decided the flirting should end, because although it wasn't real for Charlie it was likely real for Rita. No one in their little group was ready to admit or deal with that kind of a complication, most of all Henry. So Henry said, "Uh-uh, stop! No more talkie-talkie re: nibbly-nibbly—no more talk of soft guts or any other sexual fetishes, 'kay?"

Rita and Charlie looked at Henry with expressions that suggested they had no idea what he meant.

"Good," said Henry.

Suddenly, Ian plopped back down in the booth next to Henry and slammed his open palm on the table top. It made a loud snapping sound that made the other three all but leap out of their seats. "Charlie, guess what?"

Henry knew exactly what Ian was going to say and knew it was not the right time. He grabbed Ian's shoulder and squeezed it, shouting, "Shut up, Ian! No!"

Wincing in pain, Ian yelled, "Ow, motherfucker! What? Shit!" Ian knocked Henry's hand off his shoulder.

Rita reached across the table and popped Ian on the forehead with the palm of her hand, "Listen to Henry, stupid! No speakie! No speakie!" Clearly Rita knew what Ian was about to say and was joining Henry in shutting him up.

"Ow, fuck!" Ian repeated as he swiped at the empty air where Rita's hand had hit his forehead. "What am I, a fucking monkey? Jesus Christ, people! You think I'm so insensitive that I'd just spit out, 'Hey Charlie, guess what? I heard your girlfriend is fucking a hairdresser!' I mean, c'mon!"

Henry sighed and sank down in his seat, lightly banging his forehead on the table top.

Rita also sank down in the booth and said under her breath, "I hate him—hate him—why? Why is he our friend?"

Ian appeared to genuinely be surprised by Henry and Rita's reactions. He looked at them and then at Charlie, who spoke not a word—simply ran his fingers along the table top.

Oblivious to what he had done, Ian said, "See, people, our man's not made of glass, right? He's no pussy! This dude's tougher than Ronnie Lott! So, Charlie, you want I should tear this motherfucking hair-jockey in half? I can, you know. I'd love to—"

Henry was still tapping his head on the table top.

Rita stood up and reached over the table. She grabbed the much-bigger Ian by both shoulders and shook him with all her strength. "You are a son-of-a-bitch, and I will make you pay for spitting this out! I swear to God!"

Ian laughed as Rita's shaking had no effect on him whatsoever. "What, Rita? Does this mean I can't watch you give head to the trannies across from The Seventh Veil?"

Charlie grabbed the closest part of Rita's arm and coaxed her back away from Ian. He kept a hold of her hand. "It's okay, Rita. Henry, I'm cool, man. I am all cool."

Although he remained sunk down in his seat, Henry stopped hitting his head and sat up.

Just then the cashier shouted out Ian's order number, and without another word, he was up and over to pick it up.

Charlie said, "I appreciate you guys being sensitive, but I'm not angry at Ian. Ian didn't rip my heart out and piss on it."

Rita placed her hand on Charlie's face and turned it so she could look him straight in the eyes. "Then I second Ian's motion to kill the hairdresser, then the cunt. Yeah, I said it!" Then she switched tones, speaking in the softest, sexiest voice she could (which is hard-on sexy, man). "In fact, let me cut her fucking tits off and carve the name of that hairdresser into her deceptive fucking heart." And she meant it, too. Rita would do it for Charlie, no questions asked.

Charlie smiled at Rita's heart-felt offer and said, "Thanks, babe. I know you and Ian mean well, but this is my problem and I'll handle her. Plus, I can't lose OHM's best employee." He took her hand and kissed it.

Henry said, "Sorry, brother. I know how big and bad your heart can break. And something tells me you aren't completely surprised?"

Rita asked, "You aren't? Did you know?"

Charlie shook his head. "No, not for sure—I thought it was this other guy I saw her flirting with last night."

Rita said, "Knowing that whore, she's doing both guys—plus half the executives at the W-fucking-B!"

Henry said, "It's called the CW now. See, the old UPN network and the WB decided to merge under the control of Warner Bros. and—"

Rita slapped her hand over Henry's mouth. "Who cares what that Mickey Mouse network is called!"

Through Rita's hand, Henry managed to say, "No, no, not Disney—not Disney Channel."

"Hey, hey, guys," Charlie said. "Let's not forget it was the CW that bought Danny's pilot before he died. So we can't go shitting on them too hard."

"Good point," conceded Rita.

Ian sat back down with his tray of food and began separating it out and digging in. Without a word or any permission, Rita began eating Ian's onion rings.

"Bitch! My fucking rings?"

"Yeah, your fucking rings—bitch!"

All four laughed.

Henry asked Charlie, "Something tells me your mind is actually focused on something else? Is it still how you got home last night?"

"Yeah," said Charlie. "I really can't get it out of my mind."

Ian said, food half-chewed in his mouth, "You gotz a guardian angel, dude! It's Danny! Danny's fucking protecting your ass from wrapping around a tree."

Rita said, "Ian, stupid-boy, no car? The man had no car? Apartment all cleaned up, organized? Danny never would have done that."

"You got that right," Ian conceded.

Charlie said, "Just before you guys called me to meet you, Deanne left a message. Said she was sorry for her behavior at the party. She definitely doesn't know what you guys told me, but she knows how I got home."

Rita asked, "So, how're you gonna handle it, Boss?"

"Believe it or not, it's our anniversary tomorrow night."

Ian groaned, "Man oh man, it's always on an anniversary that shit goes down."

Henry said, "You have plans?"

Charlie said, "Not officially, but I think I've got an idea how to corner her and make her admit the truth."

Rita snuggled close to Charlie and asked, "Can you take me with you, please? I gotta see you rip that bee-atch a whole new one, please? I won't be a bother, honestly. You won't even see me. I'll creep in behind you, take cover in the kitchen and watch through the pass-through."

Charlie said, "Rita, you can't know how much I'd love for you to be there with me, but like the condemned man, I must face the gallows and hangman, thereon, by my lonesome."

"Well, one thing's for sure," Ian said, "that means when we get together to smoke on Saturday night, we're gonna have some good story to go with it. Pony's gonna get us the shit, right? I mean, I don't want that guy—"

Rita cut off Ian and said, "Don't worry about Pony, okay? I gave him the money, and the one thing this boy never fucks up is getting weed."

Same Fatburger

In the back of the restaurant, unseen in the L-shaped section behind the fountain drinks near the bathrooms, were Grim Dog and the Blessed Virgin. Invisible to Charlie, Henry, Rita and Ian, it was those four the pair of immortals had come to see—that and the fact that Odin absolutely loved the Triple King Burger. In fact it was a Triple

King Burger, along with onion rings, fat fries (both Texas-sized large), bowl of chili, and a large chocolate shake that Grim Dog was happily chowing down on while the Blessed Virgin drank a Coke Classic and nothing else (That's right—no diet anything for the Mother of Christ).

Between large bites of burger, Grim Dog said, "You know he might just vanish. He might get so damn scared he won't show his ugly face."

The Virgin smirked at Grim Dog. "You think he'd miss ten bricks of 'Last Supper' because he's afraid? But he's not the only reason why I picked Los Angeles."

"Ah, I thought it wouldn't end with the dwarf."

"Nope, and they're sitting right over there," The Virgin Mary turned in Her seat and pointed back at the four friends.

"Them? What the hell do they?—"

"Quiet, Grim Dog, and look at the sad one."

"They're mortal! They all look the same to me!"

The Virgin Mary sighed. "Not the two men with African-American heritage or the Latina." She was dismissing everyone except Charlie.

Grim Dog squinted at Charlie.

"He has your blood, Grim Dog. He has the blood of—"

"By Gungnir's blade, You're right. He is almost one-hundred percent—but how? I thought all of them were wiped out by those bastard Templars before they could carry on their lineage."

"First of all," said the Holy Mother, "I don't claim all Templars. Not all of them are as bad as those stupid movies and books say they are. Second, yes, intra-breeding has all but eradicated your Vikings and Celts, but a handful of them remain. But this one isn't just any descendant, Grim Dog—he's—"

Then it hit Grim Dog, as he saw Charlie stand up and make his way towards the counter to order food. Rita had followed Charlie up to the register but it was only the blonde-haired, grey-eyed Charlie that Grim Dog watched. Grim Dog's expression seemed to all-at-once change, becoming softer somehow, as if he were watching a grandchild for the first time—a grandchild he never knew he had before now.

"This one—he is—Vanaesir?"

"Yes," confirmed the Virgin.

Grim Dog looked at the Virgin with a glint in his eye that told Her he understood the how and why of Her choices. "You didn't just find me because the Augur has part of me in it, or because You needed that son-of-a-bitch Al, but because this boy, this descendant—my descendant—"

"Charles Arthur Hamor. His friends call him Charlie."

"Charlie? Yes, Charlie. Sure, why not? And I suppose You know the secret I've been keeping from You?"

The Virgin Mary took a drink and nodded.

"And You're not offended?"

The Virgin shrugged. "Why should I be? I come from desert people. Yours were of the sea. You are Sky-god. I am Earth-goddess. Everything in your bones means We should not only distrust Each Other but actually fight Each Other. Fortunately you have evolved, as have I, well past the pathetic constraints of the hypocritical distortions of modern-day Christianity and paganism."

The Virgin went on to say, "No, I wasn't offended because I had already learned that the secret of the Augur was…"

"…the Augurspell," finished Grim Dog under his breath. As if for the first time in a millennium, he was allowing himself the memory of something so glorious and so ancient it seemed to be only a dream, the word Augurspell as it left his mouth became an electric charge in the air.

"Yes, the Augurspell," repeated the Virgin. "It was necessary for both you and Me to act cooperatively towards retrieving the Augur without full disclosure. So…"

"…by working to help You find Al, and You trusting me not to hijack the operation—You knew You could trust me with the rest of Your plan."

The Virgin nodded and said, "Something like that. You are so much more than any story that has ever been recorded about you."

Grim Dog raised the eyebrow over his eye-patch and said, "Don't let that get around, Sweetheart. I learned a long time ago that no matter how hard you try to change human perception, they will only see in their gods what they want to see in themselves—and unfortunately, a compassionate All-Father isn't something that my human children ever wanted. Consequently, we beings took on the rather cruel and ambitious façades our human worshippers demanded of us."

"And I know that you helped create both the Augur and the Augurspell to try and change that reality. You wanted to show human beings they could create a better future, a better world, from the most beautiful part of their souls."

"You really did Your research, didn't You?"

The Virgin smiled.

Grim Dog nodded and said, "Maybe now by helping You I can see that better world come to pass—I hope."

The Virgin knew that Grim Dog was referencing what might be the darkest event in his personal history, when those Aesir gods (over whom he was king) decided to stab and burn to death the fertility goddess Gullveig of the Vanir (a rival race of gods who were the basis for the legends of faeries and elves) because Gullveig had taught magic to mankind, threatening the Aesir's dominion over Midgard (the Aesir word for Earth).

Fortunately, Gullveig was almost immediately resurrected from her ashes each time she was burned (as an Earth goddess, Gullveig was able to reassemble her original form from the genetic material of the earth in which she was buried). Although Grim Dog was ashamed of how his fellow Aesir behaved, he aided them in fighting the Vanir who declared war on those who had tried to kill their immortal cousin.

It is likely that no matter how misogynistic Grim Dog spoke or behaved towards women in his present persona as a biker/trucker type, his shame and guilt for this terrible crime was what kept him trapped in a world that had decided many centuries ago to abandon him.

As a form of penance, and to help ensure such a vile chapter never repeated itself, Grim Dog formed an alliance with other kingly immortal beings (whose names won't be listed here, because it would take too long and isn't important to this book—maybe look for it in one of the future ones?) to locate a force—a power that could create a universe of peace and plenty. Of course, it doesn't always follow that good intentions create positive results.

Once the Augur was built and its Augurspell power became accessible to anyone with the right combination, even evil could be manifested through it. But Odin and his allies had not thought all of that through before imbuing certain DNA with a trigger that could fire off the Augurspell. Now, for the first time in a thousand years, he was looking at someone with that trigger in his DNA.

As much delight as it brought him to reminisce about those naive days when the Vanaesir were first born, he was now looking at the other side—someone with the power to destroy the whole world.

"Our being here is not just about him or his blood holding the key to activate the Augur," the Holy Mother said. "But I can see by your expression you are thinking about how much he reminds you of—"

"Don't say the name, please!" begged the All-Father, tears welling up in his eye. "It's too painful."

"Then it will also pain you to know that We are in Los Angeles to find the other half of that particular child."

"Other half?" asked Grim Dog. "You found the other half?"

The Virgin smiled. "Neither side can unlock the Augur on their own."

Grim Dog shoved six onion rings in his mouth at once and laughed. Through a mouthful of food he asked, "You really are fucking with this world, aren't You?"

The Virgin said, "And I'm about to release the biggest storm against them all."

Chapter 8

Amazon Basin, Brasil

For Father Aitor Moreno, the vast and dark unknowns which hid behind the thick tree lines along either shore of the great Amazon River terrified him. What terrified him more was that he was coursing the waters in a hollowed-out tree trunk boat with a pilot who was only fifteen years old. The priest's mouth recited the hundreds of prayers he had learned since childhood to ward off the superstitious forces that no modern-day Catholic would admit to believing but no doubt still did. If this assignment had not been given to him personally by Cardinal Tindiglia of the Holy See, he would have done whatever was necessary to avoid it.

The thirty-one-year-old Moreno dobbed the rivulets of sweat running down his face with the semi-clean towel he kept firmly grasped in his left hand. He peered into the dark waters and saw what he was certain to be schools of deadly piranhas, just waiting for the boat to capsize and eat him for lunch. Or maybe what he saw was a twenty-five-foot anaconda snaking its way underneath the bottom of the boat, of which he was sure was a poor barrier against such a deadly creature.

Neither of these scenarios was true, but it wouldn't have mattered if Moreno had been told that by a PhD in marine biology. Piranha and anaconda are present in the Amazon, but it wasn't those particular monsters plaguing the waters beneath Aitor's boat. Whatever it was, Aitor's imagination would make it the worst of the worst, even Nessie herself!

As another two hours passed, Moreno's mind was soon stolen from the river itself as the pilot took them down a narrow tributary that led them deeper into the darkness of the last great rainforest on Earth. Moreno's mind raced back to his days at university when he read Conrad's Heart of Darkness.

Moreno thought to himself, Am I Marlow sent forth into the wilds of Africa and is the long-lost priest I'm searching for the legendary Kurtz?

He might as well be, since to the tribal natives and foreign exploiters along the river banks, the priest whom Moreno was dispatched to retrieve was believed to be a hundred-year-old missionary called "Espada de Deus" ("the Sword of God" for those of you, like me, who might have taken French or even German as opposed to Spanish in high school). His appearance varies with as many sightings told over the last three generations. Most commonly, Espada de Deus is described as having eyes of blue flame and hair braided with the tongues of the devils and liars who refused to convert to the Word of God. Although Moreno was pretty confident the priest he knew only as "Agosto" was unlikely to be so colorful or ordained with body parts, Moreno couldn't help but wonder if he might not find a more Brando-like Colonel Kurtz sequestered deep within the heart of the forest living like the crazed creature folklore made him out to be. Fortunately for Moreno and his overactive imagination, he wouldn't have to wait much longer to confirm Agosto's existence.

The pilot docked the small boat to an anchor post on the bank after only an hour since they entered the tributary. Out of the boat and onto solid earth made Moreno feel just a little less nervous. At least nothing in the water could get him, but now he had to worry about the rainforest. Although Moreno spoke beautiful Portuguese and his pilot understood every word, the guide gave no verbal response to any question Moreno asked. Instead, he would only smile at the priest or motion to him with his hand in the direction they were heading.

"Faith in God is one thing. Faith in humans is entirely different. It's our job to have faith in God. Faith in humans is the downfall of the priesthood."

It was what Moreno's mentor, Monsignor Ernesto Garcia, was forever telling him whenever Aitor would ask him, "But how can we know that the other person, not ourselves, is living in order with God? How can we trust them not to betray us or God?"

So it was that truism which played with Moreno's head as the guide led the nervous agent of the Vatican, hacking away at the brush in front of him. Moreno was obsessed with knowing if he was being led to his target or death at the hand of some terrible superstition. But nothing so dramatic lay at the end of their trek from the bank to a clearing in the forest, wherein the guide revealed with the sweep of his hand a small church providing the only light they had seen in the last two hours.

Candlelight flickered in the two windows, one on each side of the door, inviting a relieved Moreno to rush past the guide and up to the door of the church. Very gently, he rapped his knuckles on the door and then looked back at his guide. Although it was dark and the candlelight didn't provide a great amount of light, it would appear that the guide had disappeared. Now, did that mean he had simply moved and was somewhere in the dark or had he for whatever reason suddenly fled? It was a question Moreno would never have answered, because he would never see the guide again.

The door to the church opened and Moreno hopped back a few inches, but who he saw was not a bone-haired, fiery-eyed monster. The man standing in the doorway of the church appeared to be a modestly sized and modestly good-looking Tuscan priest whose hair was shoulder-length (a bit unkempt but acceptable under the present conditions), with eyes bright blue, and who stood at least six feet, if not an inch or two taller. He wore the kind of black vestment that hung like a single tunic, reaching the tips of the priest's boots and belted at the waist.

In his hand this priest held a Bible and nothing else. Behind him Moreno could see that the tiny pews were empty. It appeared as if this priest was delivering mass to no one.

"Excuse me, Father?" spoke Moreno in Portuguese.

"Yes?" responded the priest.

"Are you Father Agosto?"

The priest did not respond. Instead, he turned on his heel and walked back down the single aisle in the single room of the church until he reached the modestly adorned altar at the rear of the building and kneeled before it. He continued the mass in Latin where he was first interrupted by Moreno's rapping.

Moreno was surprised and felt a bit insulted by this priest's abrupt turning away from him, not answering and continuing with a mass to no one. So Moreno stepped through the door and closed it behind him. He double-checked to see that all the pews were empty and, seeing that they were, he walked down the aisle and stopped just short of entering the gap between the altar and the front pews.

"Excuse me, Father," said Moreno. "I need to know if you are Father Agosto. Please? I have been sent here by the College of Cardinals to retrieve him to the Holy See."

The priest stopped speaking Latin. Instead, he spoke in fluent Portuguese and not from the mass. "Cardinals, did you say? The Vatican calls for my return?"

"Then you are Father Agosto? I found you?"

The priest stood up and turned to face Moreno. "You have not found me or Father Agosto. Only Christ, the Holy Mother or the Holy Father can find Agosto. What you have found is a man serving God in the only part of the world not completely bereft of God's Grace. In the eyes of Agosto as in the eyes of God the Father, you are as a child, Aitor Moreno."

That made Moreno aghast! He choked on his own spit and started coughing. He was so shocked that this stranger knew his name! Who was—what was this priest?

After Moreno caught his breath he asked, "How—how do you know me?"

The priest turned slightly towards the altar and placed his Bible there. Then he walked up to Moreno and said, "I am the Father Agosto for whom you were sent. And I know more about you, Aitor, than you will ever know about yourself. Do not question how, just accept that I do."

Suddenly, the very modest looking man he had first seen at the doorway of this building was no longer the man into whose eyes he now gazed. Instead, he was seeing someone—no, something—more powerful, more charismatic, more ancient in the eyes of this priest than he had ever seen before—ever—including the day he kneeled before the Pontiff himself and kissed the Papal Ring.

As if caught in a trance, Moreno spoke in monotone, "I was sent here by the order of Secretary of State Cardinal Tindiglia to tell you these words, 'Find Agosto in the darkness of the Amazon, and tell him that the Pope is dying and a thief is on the loose.'"

Agosto turned away from Moreno and walked up to the altar. A tiny smile broke through his stony face as he said, "So, Tindiglia is second-in-command? I always knew that boy's ambition would take him far."

"I'm sorry, Father, did you say 'boy'?"

Agosto turned back to Moreno and asked, "You said the Holy Father is dying?"

Moreno answered, "Yes, Father, but—and this sounds unusual—he apparently asked for his mentor to administer the last rights, and that mentor was—you? Considering you don't look a day over forty, it couldn't possibly be the—"

Agosto raised a hand which all but struck Moreno dumb as the words caught in his throat, as had his breath, and he was silent. "I will administer them."

"Then you are returning with me?"

"Yes, I will return to the Holy See." And with those words all the candles lit in the small church suddenly extinguished.

It was like magic to Aitor but he already knew better not to question everything about this enigmatic cleric. Instead he asked, "Uh, Father, excuse me? I came with a guide but he seems to have—"

Agosto said, "Fear nothing, child. When you are with me, you are in the presence of the Father, and as He protects you so do I."

"Um, excuse me, Father? I'm not sure I understand what you're saying?"

Agosto sighed and shouted, "I'm telling you to stop pissing in your pants, boy! I will get us out of here and back to Rome! How could they have sent such a child after me?"

Shocked by Agosto's outburst, Moreno thought better of saying another word. He simply waited for Agosto to motion for him to leave the church with him. Once they were outside, Agosto stepped several yards away from the building and knelt facing the church. Moreno felt compelled to do the same. As Agosto began to recite a prayer in Latin, the kind of which Moreno could never remember having learned in seminary, the younger priest saw the entire look of the church begin to wither, as if in just a few moments it aged a hundred years.

Moreno stopped reciting and asked, "How?"

Agosto finished his prayer, which left the church as a dilapidated building hardly recognizable, and said, "The power of faith and prayer, belief and beatitude is the key to power and the key to time. Remember this, Aitor, and you will find those childish fears you carry will vanish come the first light of morning."

Moreno nodded to the elder and said, "Yes, Father."

Agosto stood up and said, "Now, rise. It's time we get our transportation out of here."

Before Moreno could ask Agosto exactly what transportation he meant, he was aghast to see Agosto rip off his body in one sweeping motion the black vestment and reveal an entirely different outfit underneath: a pair of black jeans, military boots, and a modern black priest's shirt with white collar under a leather motorcycle jacket. Agosto reached into his coat pockets and took out black gloves which he proceeded to slip on.

Moreno was once again speechless at the morphing Agosto.

"Something to say, Father Moreno?"

"I, uh—I—what? How did you—is that a leather jacket?"

Agosto smiled and said, "Wait here, Father." And into the dark brush behind the ruined church disappeared Agosto, leaving Moreno to shake his head and look around anxiously, terrified of the dark. Suddenly, there was the explosive roar of an engine followed by a blinding light that came right at Moreno.

Moreno squealed in terror and dropped to his knees, shivering. He covered his head and began to pray. Then he felt the brushing air of something passing by and stopping right in front of him. Slowly, he dropped his arms and looked up to see Father Agosto astride a fire-red chopper with silver flames painted along the body and outfitted with ATV tires that would surely allow it to manage the unforgiving terrain of the rainforest.

Agosto held out a helmet to Moreno and said, "Climb on, Father."

The younger cleric thought again about being told not to ask this priest too many questions, but such wonder and strangeness compelled Moreno to ask, "By the Grace of God, who are you?"

"Put your trust in the Lord God Our Father, and you will see more and learn more than any man twice your age."

Father Aitor Moreno stood up and took the helmet. He placed it on his head, secured the chin strap, climbed on behind Agosto and wrapped his arms tightly around the strange priest's waist. He closed his eyes and, with lips quivering, prayed silently.

Agosto revved the engine and opened it full throttle. He, Moreno and the bike vanished into the jungle, leaving deep tire grooves as the only evidence that anyone had ever been where the centuries-old church now stood in ruins.

Chapter 9

Calabasas, California

Calabasas lies north of Los Angeles in the San Fernando Valley. Considered an affluent city, Calabasas (like any city in the Valley) hides a darker underbelly. Within several of the magnificent houses and complexes dotting the mountainous landscape, reside citizens of less reputable note. Many of them would appear to be perfectly average and join in the annual neighborhood block parties and barbeques with their neighbors who were none the wiser.

Of course, this generalization didn't apply to the estate house and combination paramilitary compound of one Buddha Jesus (Hey-suess, not Gee-sus), who resided in that same Calabasas community. The acreage and placement of the house ensured a distance far enough from his neighbors that none of them knew any specifics of what happened in Buddha Jesus' house. And even if they have any kind of inkling, it's very likely they'd act as ignorant as possible about it all, because Buddha Jesus (born Jesus Alejandro Angelia Delgado on his Los Angeles County birth certificate) was suspected (but never convicted) of being the second-most powerful drug lord on the West Coast. Only a mysterious figure called Mickey Murrow who resided somewhere in the Seattle area was rumored to be more powerful than Buddha Jesus. But that wasn't the most interesting, and certainly not the most unique part of the man Buddha Jesus. What made Buddha Jesus more interesting than anyone else in Calabasas was the fact that he genuinely believed he was the reincarnation of a Tibetan Lama, but not just any Lama. He believed he was the reincarnation of the Great Fifth Dalai Lama Ngawang Losang Gyatso, who lived between the years 1617 and 1682.

Now, as absurd as it might seem to anyone raised as a Catholic (as was the man formerly called Jesus Alejandro Angelia—wait, we did that already) to believe that a Calabasas drug lord could be a reincarnation of not just any Dalai Lama but the Dalai Lama to be termed "The Great," think how absurd it would be to anyone raised Buddhist or to those monks to whom Buddha Jesus visited over the course of ten years to prove he was this reincarnation. Of course, not a single monk would believe Buddha's claim, but it was this very rejection that proved to be the final great passage in Buddha's mind that he was in fact just such a reincarnation – and it was the words of His Holiness the Fourteenth Dalai Lama himself that sealed the deal!

During his studies, Buddha Jesus came upon the controversial sect of Buddhism called Dolgyal (a kind of sectarian school of Buddhism that relies on the appeasement of spirit guardians to bring good luck or desired results as opposed to full faith in development of the compassionate Buddha within as a source of good life). To a boy raised with a Catholic heritage that included prayers to and the incorporation of Saints who were prayed to more than Jesus, let alone God, such a pseudo-pagan style of Buddhism was very appealing. If one could attain any kind of immediate gratification from Buddhism, Dolgyal was as good as it got.

Moreover, the revelation of the Gyalpo in Dolgyal by Buddha Jesus was the absolute turning point for the whole of his life and spiritual existence—and was the rationalization for how a drug lord could both commit and participate in such illegal and cruel activities while still believing with the whole of his heart (if not with his borderline-psychotic mind) that he was the reincarnation of any, let alone the Fifth, Dalai Lama.

Simply put, Gyalpo are troublesome buggers who make things all together difficult for humans. Like poltergeists who have unfinished or nasty business to perform on the living, Gyalpo spirits can be anything from the cause of a stubbed toe to the force behind the levies breaking in New Orleans after Hurricane Katrina. Gyalpo are progenitors of karma and, in some cases, outright evil. And it was the Fifth Dalai Lama who was known by some Buddhists to have brought the most to bear against the power of these Gyalpo in an effort to stop their worship and therefore, diminish their power. Conversely, there were some Buddhists, not many but they do still exist, who actually believed that the Fifth Dalai Lama encouraged the practice of Dolgyal and used Gyalpo to further the development of inner power and wisdom. Buddha Jesus was one of the latter.

In a final desperate effort to find recognition for his belief of being the reincarnation of such a Dalai Lama/Gyalpo, Buddha Jesus used a great deal of his criminal fortune in an effort to achieve a private face-to-face with His Holiness the Fourteenth Dalai Lama, only to get nothing more than a phone call from the great humanitarian. The conversation one might imagine was – well, unimaginable? Suffice it to say that after Buddha Jesus verbosely explained his peculiar theory of Gyalpo/Dalai Lama reincarnation/drug lord karma/dharma to improve the lives of mankind through cruelty/mischievousness, the reply of His Holiness was something like: Well, I guess if anyone would be such a Gyalpo reincarnate, you'd be a fair candidate. Just please, Brother, leave the Great Fifth Dalai Lama out of it, okay?

Whatever His Holiness' exact words, Buddha Jesus was overwhelmingly pleased by the non-confirmation of his whacked-out theory. Sadly, the drug lord would continue to blacken the name of the Great Fifth Dalai Lama, Ngawang Losang Gyatso. Following the phone call, Buddha sent more than $500,000.00 in donations to the charitable work of the Fourteenth Dalai Lama, who promptly returned the check. Having proven not to be easily dissuaded, Buddha Jesus continued to make an effort to achieve his face-to-face with His Holiness.

Those who actually had the courage to ask Buddha Jesus how and when he first got the notion he was this reincarnated Dalai Lama, were told that Jesus had an epiphany while dropping acid at Burning Man. And for anyone who's been to Burning Man, the fact that he dropped acid and had some kind of hallucination/epiphany was the only part of the story that sounded plausible. Of course no smart person would say to Buddha Jesus that everything else seemed to be bullshit—not if they wanted to walk away from him alive. Whether real or not, the epiphany also ensured Buddha Jesus would never again touch his own illegal merchandise.

The epiphany also inspired the cultivation of the drug lord's popular hydroponic marijuana blend dubbed "Buddha Blend." Buddha Jesus believed his formula for this unique indiga strain was inspired by a recovered memory from his life as the Fifth Dalai Lama. Of course there is absolutely no evidence that any such weed (or any type of weed for that matter) was ever grown by the Fifth Dalai Lama. This question of fact versus fiction was academic, though. What mattered was that purchasing Buddha Blend was the whole reason for Pony Macreedy to arrive at the gates of Buddha's sprawling compound; a definite fact which would forever change the present lives of both the hippie stoner and the second-most powerful drug lord on the west coast.

The cab carrying Pony stopped just outside the gates to Buddha's estate. Pony took a bill out of the money bag to cover the rate plus tip, and climbed out with the money bag in one hand and a raggedy knapsack hanging from his shoulder.

As the cab pulled back onto the street, Pony walked up to the intercom button and pressed it. He waited for the voice on the other end to say, "Yeah, what do you want?"

"Hey, it's Venice Pony. I'm here for OHM?" which was followed by a buzzing and the lock on the side door next to the gates clicking so that Pony could open it and enter.

Pony made his way along the curving driveway up to the sprawling mansion that was filled with no fewer than nine Cadillac Escalades (black, of course) and one pristine vintage 1962 Bentley S34. It was the one thing that always made Pony stop dead in his tracks and wolf-whistle. He was also tempted to run his fingers along the two-tone hood, but always remembered that being alive was better than touching a car.

Pony reached the front door and saw it open. Standing before him was one of the most beautiful—well, likely the most beautiful woman Pony had ever seen. Her name was Claudia (just Claudia—like you-know-who and that other you-know-who—at least for now) and she was well-known to Pony, because they used to be friends. She was long and sleek, with a vintage beauty that rivaled the '62 Bentley. Her Peruvian blood gave her the kind of skin that Parisian models would die for, and hair as black as midnight. She wore a blue/black skin-tight leather jumpsuit that showed off her perfectly toned musculature, with waist-length jacket and dual automatic pistols holstered to each hip.

Claudia had been in the employ of Buddha Jesus for the last two years and was always the first to greet Pony with the same question each time, "Macreedy, how's Charles?"

"You always ask me that, Claudia, and I always tell you to call him! You think he can't accept you working for the Buddha? He's not judgmental like that! Plus, you guys were hot together—H-O-T, hot, hot, hot! Not to mention that Deanne bitch he's seeing right now. Man, she's the worst—"

"I don't care," interrupted Claudia.

"Then why do you ask me every time I come here?"

"Because your ceaseless blathering amuses me?"

Pony shook his head and said, "Nope, don't buy it. But I'll tell him you asked, again."

"Whatever suits you," she said. Then she turned on her heel and walked back inside. "Come on, he's waiting."

Pony entered the house and closed the door behind him. He followed the cat-like Claudia through the ironically minimalistic yet ostentatiously built mansion until they exited the French doors on the other end of the kitchen leading out to the magnificently landscaped garden with an Olympic-sized swimming pool. Five half-naked women were swimming, while ten gunmen armed with military-grade weapons patrolled the garden grounds.

Claudia walked up to Buddha Jesus, who was reclining in a modest lawn chair wearing nothing more than the kind of groin-wrapping made famous by the Mahatma Gandhi. As a devout Buddhist, his head was shaved. Conversely, a pair of sixty-five-thousand-dollar, Style 23 turtle-shell sunglasses sat on the drug lord's nose.

"Macreedy's here, Buddha," was how Claudia announced the Venetian stoner. She stopped and stood on the other side of Buddha's lawn chair.

Without budging, Buddha Jesus said, "Brother Venice Pony, you have come again in the name of the business called OHM?"

"Like always, Buddha!" He held out the money bag. "And I got the scratch for your back!"

Claudia rolled her eyes.

"Your gift for gab is astounding, Brother Pony, but not what amuses me." He put his hand out for the money bag. Pony inched closer with the bag out until it met Buddha's hand. Buddha's hand closed on it and he took it and placed it on the lawn chair beside him. "Claudia will retrieve your bricks. Would you care for a mojito or daiquiri while you wait?"

Claudia headed back inside the house.

Pony answered, "No, no, I'm good. I'm gonna be skating home and the alcohol dehydrates me."

"Very wise," acknowledged the drug lord.

Pony's eyes found their way over to the beauties swimming in the pool. A few of them waved at Pony and blew him kisses, which made him instantly blush. That's when Pony's mind remembered something interesting he'd heard on NPR and might be a good point of conversation with Buddha Jesus. "Hey, Buddha, did you hear about the Pope?"

"Excuse me?"

"You know, the Pope? I mean, I know you're Buddhist and all, but I wondered if you heard about the Pope being sick."

"No," muttered Buddha, "I guess I missed that on last night's TMZ."

"No, no, it wasn't TMZ! It was on NPR! Anyway, apparently the College of Cardinals—"

Then Claudia returned, carrying a backpack with ten bricks of Buddha Blend inside and interrupted Pony's story with, "Here it is, Macreedy!" She forcefully tossed the pack at Pony.

Pony almost missed catching the backpack and fell onto his butt, gripping it in both hands. "Uh, thanks, Claudia."

"Take care, Venice Pony, may the Gyalpo be with you."

Pony stood up and said, "Yeah, may Goo-poo be with you too." He slung the backpack over the shoulder opposite the one holding his own ratty pack and followed Claudia back through the house and to the front doors.

Claudia opened one of the doors for Pony and said, "Be careful getting back to the city with those bricks."

"I always am, Claudia. I always am. And I'll tell Charlie you said, 'Hey?'"

"Tell him what you want. I don't care."

"Yeah, okay, sure."

Pony walked out through the door, but Claudia reached out and grabbed one of his arms pulling him back inside. She asked him, "There really is trouble between him and this Deanne bitch?"

"I'm telling you, Claudia, she is cheating on him big time, putting Charlie through the emotional wringer."

Claudia nodded and released Pony's arm. She pushed him back out through the door, saying, "Well, as the Buddha says, karma equals out all dharma."

"I hear that! Especially if that karma is called Claudia," but Claudia closed the door on Pony before he had actually finished his sentence. Pony wasn't insulted though, he smiled and nodded. "Yeah, she's still got it bad for the boy—can't wait to tell Charlie!"

Chapter 10

Los Angeles, California

Tracey Kipper locked the doors to Bird's Books at 11:00 p.m. As owner and manager of Bird's (named after the late great Charlie Parker, her favorite jazz musician), she wanted to show her younger employees she knew what Saturday nights were for. After all, it wasn't like Tracey couldn't remember her twenties. She was only thirty-two (but genetic good luck gave her an appearance of no more than twenty-five) and kept herself incredibly fit. So unless other duties called her away, Tracey was always the person to open and close the shop Friday through Sunday morning. Being the owner of your own business had its advantages and being nice to your employees was one of them.

Once Tracey got into her car, parked in a narrow parking lot behind the row of buildings in which her bookstore was housed, it was a straight shot home from West Hollywood along Santa Monica Blvd. into Westwood. The only turn she took was into the parking garage below the condos where she lived down the hall from her cousin Deanne Ripper.

Although only two days and nights had passed since she had taken her cousin's boyfriend Charlie home following his collapse at Deanne's party, the urge to call Charlie and find out how he was doing had fluctuated between strong and weak and everywhere in between. Although it was only an assumption on her part, she assumed Charlie did not remember Tracey taking him home.

She had heard nothing more from Deanne after Tracey had told her Charlie had made it home safely. But when Tracey began to discuss with Deanne what had brought on Charlie's collapse, Deanne told her cousin to stay out of her business and to stay away from Charlie. Tracey tried to assure her cousin that there was no ulterior motive in her wanting to help her keep her boyfriend, but Deanne didn't believe it and told Tracey she should find her own cock to suck and keep her lips off hers.

That was all Tracey needed to have thrown in her face to tell her that Deanne was playing some kind of dangerous game and she'd be smart to stay the hell out of it. But Tracey wasn't sure she could stay away from Charlie. She genuinely wanted to help this—well, pathetic guy. Maybe a therapist would analyze Tracey as having a Nightingale Complex, and was becoming obsessed with Charlie because he needed to be rescued. That is may be, as the British would say, but for Tracey it was simply because she knew something about Charlie that even he did not know about himself. This meant Deanne couldn't let him get too far away or Tracey would lose more than she could tell anyone.

As Tracey rode up the elevator from the garage to her floor, she decided that she couldn't wait any longer to contact Charlie and get confirmation that he was okay. She knew about his dispensary and she decided that before she'd approach him face-to-face, "accidently" of course, Tracey would reconnoiter OHM and see if he was back to work and functioning well. That meant she'd have to get to sleep at a decent hour and rise early enough to—

Wait, wait, wait, Tracey told herself. How stupid am I? It's Sunday tomorrow, and that's the one day no dispensary in West Hollywood is open. Shit, she thought, if I'm going to confirm he's okay before Monday, I'm gonna have to set up something and run into him, which should be do-able. He was so wasted after Deanne's party; he probably doesn't remember a thing about that night. Maybe I can work up something fresh, organic, like we're meeting for the first time and—

The doors to the elevator opened at Tracey's floor and she walked down the hallway towards her front door. As she searched through her purse for the keys she knew she should have kept out after locking the car downstairs but had without thinking dumped back into her black hole of a purse, Tracey continued to self-analyze her behavior regarding Charlie Hamor. Damn, girl! What's going on with you? You haven't had your head on straight about him since—well—day two of first learning Deanne was sleeping with him. Not that that isn't coincidence enough, but you made all sorts of slip-ups: the gun in the glove compartment—

That's when Tracey reached her front door and found her keys in her purse. She took them out but froze when she heard two familiar voices shouting at each other through the walls of the hallway.

Tracey turned to look at her cousin's door she had just passed, and knew that what she was hearing was Charlie and Deanne having it out but good.

"What the hell?" she mumbled to herself. "I don't believe it."

Tracey couldn't make out the words being said, just the tenor of the argument: heated, very heated and bad going on worse. She couldn't resist slinking down the hallway and putting her ear next to the crack between door and frame hoping to hear something, anything discernable.

Deanne's voice was the first Tracey could make out. "Who the hell do you think you are? What gives you the right to tell me how to live my life or judge what I do?"

Charlie's voice was clearer because his was louder. "I don't have to judge, Deanne! It's a fact! I have witnesses! You have been sleeping with that son-of-a-bitch hairdresser Bruce! What am I supposed to think, Deanne? You're fucking cheating on me!"

Tracey felt a kick in the gut. She knew that name Bruce. She knew that hairdresser. He was her hairdresser, and it was Tracey who had first suggested that Deanne go see him. Oh shit, was all of this her fault?

"Think whatever you like, Charlie! Who I see, who I want to see, is my business—not fucking yours!"

"Seeing does not mean fucking, Deanne! Last I heard we were monogamous! If that changed somewhere 'long the way I didn't get the text!"

"Text? I wish I could text you! You don't even have a fucking cell phone, Charlie! Christ, when are you going to join the twenty-first century, huh? Maybe if you did I'd let you know a little more of what goes on in my life!"

"Oh shit! Oh shit!" laughed Charlie. "So this is my fault now is it? If I had a fucking cell phone, if I were as brain-dead and talked with my fucking digits like everyone else in this pathetic city, I might have known a little earlier that my girlfriend was banging a clipper jockey? How sad are you, Deanne? How the fuck did I ever think there was a soul inside your cold dead heart?"

Those last words made Tracey cringe. The "cold dead heart" was a fact she knew about her cousin, but she was blood and you have to accept that kind of fact when a person's kin.

"Well," said Deanne, her voice calming down, and taking a moment to let the next comment really simmer, "at least Bruce knows how to fuck."

"Oh my God," mumbled Tracey. She did not think even Deanne capable of hitting someone like Charlie so far below the belt.

There were a few moments of silence. The air was crackling with tension both inside and outside the condo. Although the couple (or what used to be a couple) inside had no idea the third person listening through the door was as wrapped up in the emotional electricity as they were.

Charlie said, "I can't even believe you'd say that. Are you so morally bankrupt you have to attack my physical attributes to justify your constant need to fill that emotional void in your chest with the one thing you can give a partner, your pussy?"

That was followed by a slap, then another, and both sounds made Tracey jump a bit and suddenly she wanted to run back to her door and inside her condo. But well, curiosity and the cat and all that stuff prevailed.

After that last comment from Charlie, Deanne's voice and approach changed completely and it surprised even her cousin. She said, "Are you finished now? Had your little rant? Ready to be an adult and sit down and eat this anniversary dinner I made for you?"

"No fucking way," Tracey whispered. "This is their anniversary?"

Charlie shouted back, "Adult? Me act adult? Fuck you, Deanne—fuck you!"

Suddenly, Tracey heard Charlie storming down the entry way towards the front door. She gasped in fear of being discovered crouching against it and scampered as fast as she could back to her own condo door.

As the front door to Deanne's apartment flew open and Charlie stepped out, Tracey had just enough time to get her key into the lock, turn it and open it just as Charlie appeared and stepped out into the hallway. But he was so focused on Deanne who stayed inside the doorway that he never saw Tracey disappear into her apartment.

Tracey crouched down behind her door leaving it open just enough so that it appeared closed while still able to hear the drama in the hallway.

Deanne said, "Don't walk away, Charlie! Not tonight, not like this! I made you linguini!"

Charlie crossed his arms and said, "Fuck your linguini!"

Deanne huffed and disappeared back inside the apartment.

Although Tracey could only see Charlie and not what was happening with Deanne inside, she saw Charlie throw out his hands and say, "What the fuck are you doing with that, Deanne? Don't you even try! Don't you even—"

But before the word "dare" could pass his lips, a bowl full of linguini flew out through the door and struck Charlie square in the face.

Tracey cringed and said, "Uh-oh."

Charlie was on the floor, groggy, without a doubt concussed. Clam sauce, linguini and the cracked bowl covered his face, shoulders and chest.

Deanne walked out into the hallway and stood over Charlie. She crossed her arms and smiled at her defeated opponent.

Tracey decided there was no point in hiding any longer and that she could just as easily convince Deanne she had come out after hearing the commotion. She walked halfway towards Deanne and her target before her cousin acknowledged her.

"Hi, Tracey."

"Um, hi, Deanne. I just got home and heard—you know, something out here and—is he alive?"

"Oh yeah, I can see his chest going up and down. Plus he's making those pathetic little noises, grunts, shit like that. He just needed to know who the dominant one is in the relationship. Now that he does—" she let her words trail off. Then she changed the subject and said, "Oh, thanks for recommending that hairdresser Bruce."

"Bruce? Yeah, did you like his work?"

"Did I like his work?" Deanne grabbed some of her hair and pulled it around so she could sniff the ends. "I didn't just like it, I loved it. He gave me more than I could have ever hoped for."

"That's good, I guess."

Deanne looked back down at Charlie. "Don't worry about him, really. I'll call maintenance to come around and carry him out with the rest of the garbage."

Deanne went back inside her apartment and closed the door. Tracey could hear the door lock.

Tracey walked up to Charlie and kneeled down. Gingerly she lifted the bowl off Charlie's face and the most of the linguini so that he could see her and she could see his eyes. "You okay in there? I mean, are you hurt badly—anything broken?'

Charlie groaned and moved his head from side-to-side. It could have meant no, but it could also have just been him trying to see if his neck was broken. Either way he said, "I hate clam sauce."

Tracey released all the tension caught in her chest with a big sigh and said, "Here we go again. Come on, you. I can't let you ferment out here alone." Using all the strength in her smaller frame, Tracey lifted and placed one of his arms around her neck and shoulders. Then slowly, steadily Tracey stood him up. She walked him down the hallway and into her condo. Once inside, she closed and locked the door.

Tracey walked Charlie, now a bit more steady but reeking of clam sauce, into the living room and plopped him down on the sofa. Charlie sank back without falling over or lying down. Tracey stepped back and saw that now she had the stuff on her. She scoffed and said, "Damn, Deanne, still cleaning up your leftovers."

"Okay, Charlie, you just hang right there, okay? I'm going to go to the bathroom, get some stuff and then—I'll be right back to clean you up, okay?"

Charlie's response was to groan—groans and what Tracey could swear was the occasional "bitch—hate her—hate myself—should have—should have—" which might or not actually be what Charlie said. Either way, it was Tracey's hope that those were things Charlie was thinking, because it would mean Deanne was out of the way.

As quickly as she could, Tracey ran into the walk-in closet and changed out of her clothes. She dumped them in the basket on the floor and slipped on a t-shirt and sweat pants. Then she went to a section of the walk-in, tucked away in the back and pulled out a man's tee. It was an old University of Texas Longhorn tee. She checked the size—XL—and took it out of the closet. Finally, Tracey entered the bathroom where she grabbed a box of baby wipes on the top of the commode cistern as well as the towel hanging on the rack behind the door.

"This should do for now."

When she came back into the living room she found Charlie slumped forward as if—well, as if he had suddenly died in an up position. Only his groaning reassured Tracey he was alive if not well.

She carried the gear to the coffee table and sat down next to Charlie. With the kind of concern that only comes from someone who really cares about another, Tracey dug into cleaning up her cousin's now ex-boyfriend. She appeared unfazed and unconcerned about the nasty food, sauce and general trouble while cleaning Charlie with the baby wipes.

Charlie gave no resistance. He was like a baby in the hands of a caretaker who went to town on every crack and crevice. She removed his shirt and found herself into his armpits—it was all quite personal. But however he was bonked from the bowl, there were no cuts or blood, only his completely dazed mind.

Finally, Tracey had done as good a job as possible. "There," she said to him. "It's not great, and I think you should take a shower when—you know, your head is clearer. But for now—" She slipped the tee over his head and helped thread his arms through the sleeves. Gently, she guided him down onto the sofa, lifting his legs, so that he was laying face up, flat on his back. Lastly, she removed his shoes and set them down under the coffee table.

"You should rest now. I can't see any sign of a break or blood. You might have a mild concussion, but I don't think you can't sleep. I'll keep an eye on you, though. I've had some medical training so…"

"Who are you?" managed Charlie.

"Oh, you really don't remember me?"

"I know you? I hope I know you. You cleaned me. You cleaned me everywhere."

Tracey suddenly felt flushed and nervous. Spit caught in her throat and she began to cough from the reflexive closing of her throat. She regained her breath and said, "Not everywhere, okay? Just—well, like I said you'll need to shower when you—"

But Charlie had begun snoring—lightly, but it was snoring.

Tracey sighed and wiped the sweat off her forehead with a fresh baby wipe. She couldn't believe she had so suddenly become self-conscious and actually lost her composure. Come morning, she'd make sure that wouldn't happen again. She stood up and walked out of the living room and into the bedroom. She went back to the walk-in closet, checked the shelves behind the door and found a pair of blankets. She took them out and grabbed a pair of pillows off her bed.

When she returned, Tracey put a pillow under Charlie's head and covered him with one of the blankets. She took the other pillow and blanket and fixed herself up with them after sitting in the cushy chair next to the sofa. Tracey grabbed the remote, turned it onto a news channel and settled in to watch it, while she watched Charlie.

Chapter 11

The Apostolic Palace, Vatican City

The Pope had died in the night, but not before Father Agosto had arrived and performed Last Rites and heard the Holy Father's final confession followed by the granting of absolution. The Holy Father was genuinely happy to see Agosto as he knelt beside the Pontiff's bedside and kissed the Papal Ring. He and Agosto spent several minutes in private conversation before Agosto began the full order of rites.

Afterwards, Tindiglia (named Cardinal Camerlengo by The Holy Father just before his death) immediately declared Conclave. Because of his unique status to the previous Pontiff, Father Agosto remained within the hallowed and now sealed-off Apostolic Palace. While the whole of the College was summoned, Tindiglia (joined by Walczak, Giordano and the third member of the Capita Ordinum, Cardinal Boris Alexikov) summoned Agosto to a private audience within the Sistine Chapel.

Agosto was escorted by the Marshall of the Conclave into the chapel to a chair placed directly in front of the four Cardinals. He took his seat and waited for them to address him first.

Tindiglia said, "Thank you for coming so quickly at The Holy Father's request, Father Agosto."

"Eminence," was all Agosto said, followed by a nod of his head.

"But it is not the only reason for your being summoned. Are you aware of this?"

Agosto nodded and said, "Yes, Your Eminence. Father Moreno told me a thief was on the loose. I can assume the Vault was broken into?"

"Yes," said Tindiglia. "How this occurred is, of course, an absolute mystery."

Not to three of the four Cardinals present. After all, it was they who were knocked off their feet and in their very physical presence had the bowling bag containing the object called "the Augur" stolen. But that was something that Tindiglia, Walczak and Giordano were keeping to themselves for the time being.

Agosto said, "If I may, Your Eminence, the 'how' is of less importance than the 'what' which was stolen."

"The Augur," said Tindiglia.

Agosto raised both eyebrows and shifted in his seat. He crossed one leg over the other and swept his hand over the knee on top. "I see."

"So, as you can see, we must find the Augur if we are to…"

"…locate the new Pontiff?" offered Agosto.

"Yes," confirmed Tindiglia. "Of course, we are also well aware of the other catastrophic implications should that relic end up in the hands of souls with lesser spiritual fortitude and validity?"

Agosto said, "I am quite familiar, Your Eminence, with the voracity and capabilities of the Augur."

Walczak piped up with, "Yes, wasn't it the Templars who first brought the Augur to Vatican City?"

Agosto answered, "Yes, Cardinal Walczak, almost a millennium ago. In fact, it was the Augur that earned the Templars confirmation by Pope Honorius II."

Walczak offered, "I think it was on those grounds that the Antipope Celestine II opposed him, was it not?"

Agosto looked down at the floor and said, "If I recollect my studies correctly, yes it was."

Tindiglia shouted, "Enough of the history lesson! What matters is getting that relic back here and done as soon as possible! Without that relic we cannot be assured we will choose the right Holy Father to continue leading Holy Mother Church intact!"

Everyone but Agosto seemed shocked by Tindiglia's outburst but said nothing as he was now Camerlengo.

Agosto broke the tension by asking, "Camerlengo, does intelligence know where the thief has taken the relic? Is the college aware of how to locate the Augur?"

Tindiglia answered in a much calmer voice, "The Holy Father shared with me which of the other relics could be used to locate the Augur and its thief. I know that we are not allowed to verbally speak of the relic used to locate the Augur, so suffice it to say that we have confirmed its location as Los Angeles, California."

Agosto showed the tiniest of smiles. "I am familiar with the city."

In a disapproving tone, Tindiglia said, "Yes, the Holy Father told me about that, as well."

Walczak added, "We have all heard the story of your prior mission to Los Angeles."

Agosto shrugged.

"I haven't," said Alexikov.

"Shut up, Boris," spat Giordano.

Tindiglia stood to his feet and shouted, "Shut up! Enough! We all know that only Agosto can carry out this retrieval and it was the dying wish of the Pontiff that he does so! As Camerlengo it is my duty to be the voice of the Holy Father until the new Holy Father is crowned!"

Again there is silence and tension, except for Agosto. Nothing and certainly no hierarchical position seemed to shake him.

Still on his feet, Tindiglia clapped his hands three times. Everyone but Agosto looked at the doors to the chapel. They opened, by the hand of the Marshal, and inside walked Father Aitor Moreno. In both his hands, Moreno bore an ash wood and cedar box. On the box's lid, engraved in gold filigree, shone the image of two knights riding the same mule, bearing a flag upon which was the red Crusader's Cross; this was the symbol of the Holy Order of the Knights of the Temple of Solomon (aka The Knights Templar). Moreno carried the box past Agosto, never looking at the priest, and stopped just short of Tindiglia and the Capita Ordinum. He bowed his head and held the box out to Tindiglia.

Tindiglia took the box from Moreno and said, "Thank you, Father Moreno."

Moreno bowed at the waist and said, "Thank you, Your Eminence." He turned and walked back towards the doors. As he passed Agosto he stole a glance at the priest.

Agosto gave Moreno a small smile and nodded his head.

Once Moreno was out of the room and the Marshal had closed the doors, Tindiglia said, "Rise, Father Agosto, and approach us."

Agosto did as ordered.

Tindiglia handed the box to Agosto, who took it and opened it. Inside he saw something he thought he'd never again see in his long life: a pair of uniquely designed 9mm automatic pistols with the Knights Templar symbol and cross inlay in pearl handles. On top of these there was a leather case for an identification card.

Agosto looked up at Tindiglia who said, "Go ahead, you can look at it."

Agosto walked back to his seat and placed the box down on the chair. He took out the wallet and opened it. Inside was a card that read: "License to Kill in the Name of the Lord God Our Savior as ordained by the Vatican." Below that was Agosto's name, physical description, Templar identification number 003 (you thought I was gonna say 007, didn't you?) and finally the phrase "Diplomatic Immunity Applies" with the general information number for the Sacristy of the Vatican (+39.06.698.83712—seriously).

Agosto looked at Tindiglia and asked, "Thank you, Your Grace."

"Yes." Tindiglia stepped down from his chair and walked up to Agosto. He placed his hand upon Agosto's shoulder and squeezed it. He said, "Your status as a member of the Holy, but secret, Order of the Knights Templar has been reinstated."

Agosto bowed his head. "Thank you, Your Eminence. It is humbling to once again be in the trust and faith of Mother Church." Agosto slipped the wallet inside his jacket and took out the two pistols.

As he checked to see if each cartridge was full of bullets, then slid them back into the grip of the gun, Tindiglia said, "The fate of Holy Mother Church and God's Will on Earth rests on your shoulders, Agosto. Whatever heretics, blasphemers, pagans or assholes try to get in your way, do whatever it takes to get that relic back here before eight days are over."

Agosto spun the guns, one in each hand, and slid them effortlessly into shoulder holsters hidden under his jacket. "Of course, Your Eminence, I can be in Los Angeles by tomorrow. But I will need the other relic to locate the Augur."

"Right, right," grumbled Tindiglia. He looked back at the other Cardinals, all of whom looked disappointed to give up whatever it was.

"Well, give it to him," spat Giordano. "It's not like he doesn't need the damn things."

Tindiglia reached underneath his vestments and took out a glasses case. With a heavy sigh, he handed them over to Agosto. "Now look, Agosto, losing the Augur is one thing—but if you lose these glasses…"

Agosto took the case and popped it open. Inside was a pair of purple-tinted sunglasses, the style of which was made famous by one John Lennon. "Camerlengo, who do you think brought this relic back and presented it to the Holy Father? You shouldn't worry about these lenses. When I brought them here they were just a pair of amethyst crystals. They hadn't even been polished, let alone put into this form."

Agosto slipped them on his face and put the case inside his jacket pocket. With a smirk and a nod, Agosto walked out of the chapel.

Once the door was closed and the Cardinals were alone, Giordano stood and said, "I know who he was to the Holy Father, and that bringing him in was necessary. But, Tindiglia, I don't like him not only having the Lenses but also getting his hands on the Augur."

Tindiglia whipped around on his heel and shouted at Giordano, "I appreciate your suspicions of this…of Agosto! But we have no choice but to trust him! With the Holy Father dead, we are the only four that know who and what that…"

"…man? Is that what you were going to call him?" finished Alexikov. "Do you know that bastard's reputation in my country? He's called М'ясник Христоса!"

"Butcher of Christ?" asked Giordano.

"What does that even mean?" asked Walczak. "Does that mean he's like Christ's butcher and gives him good cuts? Or does it mean he literally cuts up the bread to be the body of Christ, you know, butchers him—"

"It means," shouted Alexikov, "That in the Ukraine he's considered a demon—a demon, man!"

Tindiglia shouted, "Shut it! All of you just shut up!"

Alexikov said, "Camerlengo, you understand what I'm saying, don't you? He's a—demon! There! There, I've said it! No one can live as long as he has and not have a pact with—"

Giordano slapped Alexikov in the back of the head (ala Moe to Curly) to shut him up. Alexikov whimpered and sat back down.

"Look," began Tindiglia, "I appreciate that none of you trust Agosto. I'm not sure he should be trusted, at least not when it comes to any living man. The one thing I do know is that the only reason he lost his License to Crusade is because of the extent he will go to in order to carry out the mission of Holy Mother Church. So, as long as we are all on this side of the fence, none of us have anything to fear from his—conviction."

Walczak sunk down in his chair and nodded his head. "Good point, Camerlengo. I guess the only ones who have to worry are the bastards who took the thing."

Tindiglia said, "Let's just hope our lockdown of the See was fast enough and secure enough to ensure that absolutely no one could get any word out about the theft. I dread to think about what other groups would do if they thought they could get their hands on the relic."

"Yeah, especially those apocalyptic cults," said Giordano. "Talk about butchers of Christ, those lunatics could cause real havoc with the Augur."

Giordano raised his hand and said, "There is one other wild card in all of this—"

The other Cardinals all looked at Giordano.

Giordano continued, "—which none of us has yet to speak?"

Tindiglia said, "Then speak it, Giordano. Go on. Speaking the name alone won't make it appear before us."

"Opacus," was all Giordano said. It was a single word that visibly shook everyone except Tindiglia.

"Is that what you think, Tindiglia?" asked Walczak.

Tindiglia said nothing. He took several seconds to ponder his answer before he said, "All I can say is that every possibility is on the table."

"I pray it's not them," said Alexikov. "Everyone thinks Opus Dei holds the dark secrets of Mother Church; were anyone outside of our college to know what Opacus holds—"

"Enough prattling!" ordered Tindiglia. "We focus on what we know. And what we know is that with the Augur outside of the See, the whole world teeters on the edge! We must get it back at any cost, no matter who or what has stolen it."

Chapter 12

Silver Spring, Maryland

For a Christian denomination obsessed with the gory "End-times," the Seventh-day Adventists ("SDA") had their world headquarters located on an absolutely beautiful twenty-six acres of land a mere twelve miles north of the capitol city of the very nation which they believe is the seat of absolute evil. As a consequence, Washington, DC will be ground zero for Armageddon. Probably the reason they want to be so close—you know, so they can claim dibs.

After the world is wiped clean, Jesus will return on Trigger (maybe Silver?) his white horse, along with the Adventists into what's left of DC. Jesus and his Adventist groupies will be armed to the teeth with top-of-the-line firearms (as well as the appropriate concealed gun permits). The Big Guy and those Adventists will rebuild the nation's capital as their own capital called New Jerusalem. Of course, Jesus won't arrive until after the general slaughter of those not-so-lucky bastards who didn't convert to Him before the shit hit the fan. But just in case any unlucky heathens are still hanging about, JC will have his trusty Smith & Wesson to blow away their hell-bound asses.

It's a fortunate irony then, that apocalyptic groups like the SDA have the ability to locate the most visually stunning real estate for their multiple centers of operation. After all, according to their take on the Good Book, the whole world will be wiped clean (literally) including the very properties on which their expensive modern facilities stand. To waste that kind of money and effort in building such large complexes while believing that at any moment the Lord Jesus Christ will come-a-callin' and squash all that hard work and proof of their utter devotion like so many cockroaches shows just how blissfully ignorant they really are.

Although they will never admit it in either the media or at your front door, Adventists believe that it is their destiny to be the best chosen people of God with the duty to bring about the very End-times that will kill all unbelievers and take the Adventists up to Heaven where they will party like it's 1899. After all that is over, the Adventists will be sent back down in a huge galactic elevator with a clean slate to re-create Eden. With that as their core reason for existence, the SDA have put their considerable resources towards discovering each and every possible pathway to usher in the End-times. Among all the hundreds, certainly thousands, of methods is the Augur, and the Adventists know about the Augur. In fact, they not only know about the relic, they know that their rivals the Catholics have had it in their possession for—well, since long before the Adventists rolled onto the scene.

Not recognizing the Catholics as Christians (even though they actually built the first beast, so to speak), the SDA declared—not publicly of course—that Catholic Church is satanic. No kidding, for real! They see them as blasphemers who helped Satan warp the Bible. As a result, the SDA began infiltrating the Catholic Church (CIA-style) several decades ago, even to Vatican City itself. With the help of modern wireless communication, they can instantly relay information, say—oh, like the Augur's been stolen—within hours of its becoming rumor in the Basilica cafeteria.

Unfortunately, the news (or rumors) of the theft was left on the general information voice mail of the Biblical Research Institute. Apparently, the SDA's spy in the Vatican had dialed the wrong branch. It was the Adventist Mission organization who was assigned the job of monitoring all activities within the Vatican. As result, it took almost twelve hours after the rumor was heard by the spy to reach the desk of the Vice-President of Adventist Mission, Mr. Carl H. M. Eiderbrook.

Eiderbrook's assistant physically handed him the short two-sentenced communiqué: "Augur stolen. Advise what to do?"

Eiderbrook looked up at his assistant and asked, "This is it? Are you kidding me?"

"No, Sir, that's all the Biblical Research Institute had on their voice mail."

Eiderbrook scoffed and leaned back in his ergonomic chair. He shook his head and muttered, "What kind of idiot do we have working over there? I mean, is this asshole a retard or brain damaged?"

"Um—sorry, Sir, I can't comment on his mental development or intelligence level."

Eiderbrook sat back up and grabbed a notepad on the desk. He took a pen out of the holder and began scribbling a note. "I can't work with this little information. I need to know what this shithead's talking about, okay?" He handed the note to his assistant. "Can you do that for me? Can you figure out how to get me more information?"

The assistant took the note and nodded. "Yes, Sir. I will get you all the information you need." He turned to leave the office, but stopped when his boss called him back.

"Yo, wait! Look, if this is the Augur and it really has been stolen, I want to know about it ASAP, right? I don't want that rat-fucking Governing Body of the Jehovah's Witnesses to move on this before we do. Hey, that Elder something-or-other?—what's that prick's name?"

"I'm sorry, Sir, which Elder prick exactly?"

"Come on, come on, do I have to spell everything out for you? I mean, if I knew which prick it was I wouldn't be asking you for his name! He's the Los Angeles JW Elder in charge of this—look, I had to talk to him at last year's Apoca-Con."

Then the assistant realized who his boss was talking about. "Yes, Sir, I remember him now. His name is Brother Laurel—Nathaniel Laurel. He is the Los Angeles Elder in charge of relic retrieval. I also remember meeting his assistant Brother Williams. He was—"

"Quiet, Barker!" It was the first time he had used his assistant's name in the conversation. Eiderbrook hated using the names of his underlings because it gave them a sense of equality to him; the one thing Eiderbrook got off on more than thoughts of the Apocalypse was having dominion over others (but that's more than we need to know about his personal fetishes).

"Yes, Sir," said Barker, whose own mind was starting to drift to memories of last year's Apoca-Con in Denver. It wasn't that when Barker met Brother Williams either of them had an expectation of anything. I mean, they weren't total strangers. Previously, they had spoken twice on the phone because their respective bosses had to communicate over some reliquary issue between the SDA and the Jehovah's Witnesses.

There was no clue when the two assistants spoke on the phone that there was any kind of spark. Certainly Barker liked the tenor of William's voice as Williams told Barker that he liked the alto of his. All either expected upon meeting in person in the lounge of the Hilton Garden Inn in downtown Denver was a friendship that both hoped could breach their rival apocalyptic viewpoints. What they ended up experiencing however, was something so much deeper than just friendship and a shared hope for the destruction of the planet.

For Barker and Williams, their physical meeting was the kind of revelatory connection that both men later confessed to feeling was for them absolute confirmation that the Lord God had given unto each of them a great gift (each other). In fact, it would have been an affront to Lord God Himself if they didn't fully immerse themselves in those gifts. This was the description of their first meeting, shared between the two attractive men as they shared champagne and chocolate-covered strawberries, naked under the sheets in Williams' room after a long and lovely afternoon of coitus.

"Barker!" shouted Eiderbrook. "Wake the fuck up in there, you idiot!"

Barker snapped out of his beautiful memory to the present face of his angry, bitter, foul-mouthed, servant-of-God boss.

"Yes, Sir—sorry, Sir—I was trying to remember the contacts we have in LA and who I should call to make sure Brother Laurel is monitored to assure he doesn't move on this before you can." The assistant left Eiderbrook's office and shut the door behind him.

Eiderbrook rapped his fingers on the desk for a few more seconds then he picked up the phone. He dialed a number and waited. When it was answered he said, "This is Eiderbrook. I need to speak with Iverson." He waited a few more moments before he said, "Iverson, listen—we have a situation and I need you to be ready to mobilize the minute I give the word—" Another lengthy pause was followed by, "Excellent. You're the man, Iverson." Eiderbrook hung up.

Brooklyn, New York

Unfortunately for Eiderbrook and the entire SDA, the Jehovah's Witnesses were amongst apocalyptic cults the crème de la crème. Through their supreme global operation called the "Watchtower," there wasn't a single point on the planet Earth that the JWs couldn't monitor and therefore couldn't reach. Why? The Watchtower had its own satellites! And I'm not talking about your average catalogue-order communication satellites. The JWs' satellites, of which there were twenty-one, gave them near-omniscience (well, they like to think of it as omniscience—how quaint is that?) which put them so far ahead of every other fundamentalist or new age group that even the Scientologists had to acquiesce to the JWs' technological superiority—and if you know anything about that old dianetics crowd, they don't like kissing anyone's ass. (Lord Xenu's and Tom Cruise's notwithstanding—which I absolutely and genuinely respect as their right to do. I mean it! I'm no fool!)

The underground complex where the satellite intelligence is gathered, processed and reviewed is a vast bunker below the world headquarters of the Jehovah's Witnesses at 25 Columbia Heights, Brooklyn, New York. The offices above are occupied by the Governing Body who assembles weekly in a secret conference room to study the satellite intelligence. And on the same day Eiderbrook at the SDA was alerted as to the theft of the Augur, the entire Governing Body (all eight non-elected white men) was seated around the conference table reviewing a twenty-page report recounting what their secret agent inside Vatican City had obtained.

All eight men might as well have been cloned, with the only differences being some used Grecian Formula, others did not, and some were Hair Club for Men clients while others were not. Regardless, they all wore the same slate grey suits with dove grey pinstripes and ties with the Watchtower logo nicely embroidered on them. Wanting to play up the whole "Oooo, we're-the Governing-

Body-tremble-before-us" kind of effect, the table around which they sat was much too large for practical purposes, having a gap of space so far between each elder they had to have blue-tooths to actually hear each other. The final touch was the spotlights shining down on their heads so as to obscure their features, completing the "spooky-badass-mothers-for-God" package.

The last effect to the conference room that ensured anyone who entered it that they weren't dealing with just another goofy cult of End-timers was the twenty-one separate HD TVs built into the wall so that while in conference, the Governing Body could observe whatever Watchtower Central was seeing from their command room several hundred feet below them.

So with reports laid out in front of them, the Eight were ready to speak with the chief Los Angeles elder-in-charge of relic retrieval Brother Nathaniel Laurel, who walked into the room accompanied by his assistant Brother Williams (who had made such an impact on Barker of the SDA).

One of the Governing Body motioned for Laurel to take a seat at the table nearest the door so that all the Eight could see him. Brother Williams was left to stand behind Laurel as any good supplicant would.

There was a few moments of tense silence before Elder Northcutt of the Governing Body asked, "You have read the report from the Vatican?"

Laurel looked at Brother Williams who handed him a copy of the report. Laurel put it on the table in front of him and said, "I did, on the flight here from Burbank."

"And what's your opinion?" asked Northcutt.

"Well, without absolute proof of the theft, all I can say is it's tantalizing to say the least—to imagine the Augur is out there in the world, unguarded, unprotected and retrievable? Whoever got their hands on this power would be, well, invincible."

Another of the Eight named Carriage asked, "Then you don't believe it's happened? You think the rumor is a lie?"

Laurel shrugged his shoulders and said, "I understand that I am here because I am in charge of sector Los Angeles, and if this report is true and the relic has been in that city for only twenty-four, maybe thirty-six hours—I'm not sure as anyone could verify it."

"What are you saying, Laurel?" shouted Carriage. "Are you saying if this," he threw the report across the table at Laurel, "is either true or a lie, you still cannot confirm it?" He shot up to his feet and slammed a fist on the table. "Then what the fuck are you doing for us in LA? What's your point in existing?"

Laurel was afraid of the elder's rage but wouldn't show it. Instead he took a deep swallow and said, "I understand your frustration, Elder Carriage. All I can do without breaking the commandment of bearing false witness is to say I will mobilize each and every resource at my disposal to ascertain the validity of this report. Is that acceptable to the Governing Body?"

The Eight looked at one another, and after several head-nods, Northcutt said, "That is acceptable, Laurel, but you will report to us every eighteen hours as to your progress. Understood? The last thing we will tolerate is one of our enemies getting their hands on this providence of God before we do."

"Especially those Adventist bastards," added Carriage.

Laurel stood from his seat and, in unison with Brother Williams, bowed to show their acquiescence. Without another word, Laurel left the conference room. Williams scooped up their copy of the report and sheepishly bowed twice more to the Governing Body as he left the room.

Watchtower Private Jet

After they travelled back to Burbank from LaGuardia, Brother Laurel finally let his frustration fly. He kicked one of the chairs on board the plane no fewer than ten times, until the bolts keeping it secured to the floor of the compartment loosened and the chair fell. Then Laurel plopped himself down on the long sofa, hands entwined, elbows on knees, and lips pressed against hands.

Brother Williams seemed unfazed by the outburst. It was something he had seen more times than he could count. "Brother Laurel, can I get you a beverage? Kool-Aid?"

"Fuck your Kool-Aid!"

"Water perhaps?"

Laurel stood up and shouted, "Stop with the commandment bullshit, Williams! Get me some fucking bourbon!"

Williams nodded and disappeared behind the curtain separating the galley from the passenger compartment.

Laurel sat back down and saw that Williams had tossed the report onto the sofa next to him. Laurel picked it up and flipped through the pages. Although he had worked hard to sound rational and skeptical to the Governing Body, Laurel knew that what had happened in the Vatican was an actual theft. Who and how it had been carried out was what was making him so angry. He didn't like to be on the short end of the stick, because unlike many of the other elders with whom he associated, Laurel had resources of a very different, dare to say blasphemous nature. These would be what Laurel would have to use to find out who had the Augur.

Chapter 13

Los Angeles, California

Tracey woke in the chair with the blanket still covering her and immediately looked at the sofa to see Charlie, eyes closed and breathing shallow, alive if not well after last night's food melee. Having twice put this man to sleep on living room furniture after some kind of excessive night's activities, she marveled at how much like a little boy he looked while sleeping. It made her stomach drop a bit when she saw that look because it made her feel emotions she wasn't exactly comfortable with—not yet anyway.

Having dropped him off once at his house and seeing his private environment was personal enough, but now Tracey had brought Charlie into her house, her private environment. She had definitely crossed a line whether she had consciously meant to or not. For some time this man had been an author whose books she had read many years ago and admired greatly. After that, he was the boyfriend of a cousin about whom she heard nothing but negativity. These two "Charlies," the author and boyfriend—contradictory at best—were now one person whom she had let into her life. What Tracey was feeling for Charlie was more than she expected, and she was entirely unprepared to confront it.

Trying to make as little noise as possible, Tracey got out of the chair and entered the kitchen where she began fixing coffee. After filling the carafe with water and pouring it into the reservoir, she opened a cabinet and took down some ground espresso. She also reached up to the top shelf and took down a bottle of whiskey.

From behind Tracey she heard, "You dressed me?"

Surprisingly, Tracey didn't jump. She turned around with a smirk and said, "Your clothes had to be burned. Deanne left no part un-sauced."

"I can believe it. So, I guess I should say thank you for rescuing me?"

Tracey proceeded to start the coffeemaker and then poured two shots of whiskey, one of which she held out to Charlie. He took it without question while Tracey downed the shot she kept.

Charlie took his shot and shook his head. "And how is this supposed to help?"

"Is your head still hurting?"

"No."

"It's working."

"Ah, clever."

"Another?"

Charlie handed out his shot glass, which Tracey quickly filled. Charlie drank the shot and placed the empty glass on the counter closest to him. "Wow, I don't know how smart it is to have two shots first thing in the morning, but—who are you? And how do I thank you for rescuing me?"

Tracey put her shot glass in the sink and said, "My name is Tracey, Tracey Kipper. I'll tell you what, why don't you take a shower, okay? You really do stink from the whole thing last night, and I'll get coffee made and answer all your questions, fair enough?"

"Yeah, you're right, I reek." Charlie turned to leave but stopped. He turned back to face Tracey. "Um—can I keep wearing?—" as he pulled on the neck of the tee.

"Of course, Charlie, it's yours."

Charlie turned again to leave but once again turned back to ask, "Bathroom?"

Tracey smiled and giggled. "Follow me." She walked past Charlie, who then spun around to follow her into the back of the apartment and through her bedroom.

To Charlie's surprise he saw that Tracey's bedroom was, well, not immaculate. It wasn't a sty, either. It was the kind of bedroom someone might have who spent more time away from home—at work, perhaps—so that the chaos of the room was not a reflection of bad habits as much as a reflection of how busy someone's life was.

Tracey reached the bathroom and quickly put together a small pile of stuff for Charlie, including a towel and a face cloth, which she then handed to Charlie and switched places with him without his really noticing.

Tracey closed the bathroom door saying, "Have a good shower. We can talk when you get out."

Charlie put the stuff down by the sink and worked with the shower faucet until it was the right temperature. When it was just right, Charlie quickly stripped down and got inside, closing the curtain and doing as hasty but thorough a job as possible.

Returning to the kitchen, Tracey found the coffee brewed and ready to be poured. She fixed herself a cup and drank it pretty quickly. Her face was flushed and she was feeling nervous as hell. It wasn't exactly what she expected. Yet it wasn't exactly going badly either. She had imagined Charlie—and her—many times before, but it never began with him thinking her some stranger who just happened to take him in after ending his relationship with a she-demon.

"Stay cool, babe," she told herself as she poured a second cup of coffee, this one with cream and sugar. After taking a more modest sip of the second cup, Tracey began putting together a tray (well, a baking sheet to be precise) to carry out the coffee carafe, a mug for Charlie and whatever else he might like to add to it.

She entered the living room and placed the tray on the coffee table and waited. As if waiting for the big interview to start, Tracey kept telling herself—Stop it, Tracey! Why are you acting like this is prom night? Why are you getting all hot and bothered? I admit he's cute and all but—Tracey, get a grip!

Her cell phone rang. It was a somewhat muted tone as it was deep inside her purse.

Tracey jumped and looked in the direction of her purse, not sure if she did hear it.

It rang again. This time it was definitely a ring.

Tracey looked at the clock. It read 10:15 a.m. on Sunday. She scrambled for her purse, dug out the phone and said, "Hello?"

On the other end was the voice of a middle-aged man that said, "Hi, niece, it's your Uncle Leo."

"Uncle Leo! It's so great to hear from you. How are you?"

"I'm great. You?"

"Just fine, but I have company."

"On a Sunday morning?"

"It's the young man I mentioned to you?"

"Oh yes—yes," said Uncle Leo. "Charles Hamor? The one who owns that dispensary? Isn't he dating your cousin Deanne?"

"Um—yes, but—um—I'm sorry, Leo, but I think I hear him coming back into the living room."

"Well, I'd best let you get back to your date. Have fun."

"Thanks, Uncle Leo. I'll call you later with all the gory details."

"I love you, niece."

"I love you, too," and Tracey hung up.

She was putting the phone back in her purse when Charlie entered. He was dressed in the Longhorn tee and his pants. He was still drying his hair with a towel. He saw Tracey putting her cell back in her purse. "Were you talking with someone on the phone?"

Tracey spun around and saw Charlie. She was surprised that she hadn't noticed him entering. "Um—yeah—I guess. I mean, yes, sure."

"I hope you didn't cut it short because of me. I mean, I can book and let you—"

"No, no, no!" insisted Tracey. "It wasn't you, really. It was just my Uncle Leo. He lives in New Hampshire and totally forgets about time difference, you know? He calls at really weird hours."

Charlie nodded. "Yeah, relatives, I hear that. I have one, an aunt who lives in Georgia, forever calling me a week before my birthday to ask when my birthday is. I got so tired of it that for the last couple of years I've told her it was two months later than it is—you know, just to fuck with her."

Tracey nodded. "Yeah, my Uncle Leo's kind of absent-minded too. Maybe I should try something like that. I'd love nothing more than to just be left alone sometimes—sometimes—by him."

There were a few moments of tense silence as Charlie finished up with his hair. Tracey watched him, studied him really as if she needed to for some reason she wasn't entirely comfortable with. Then finally she realized what was on the coffee table and spat out, "Coffee! I made coffee!"

"Excellent!" said Charlie. "I've got to have that caffeine fix."

"Great!" So Tracey raced to the sofa and poured him a mug. "Cream only?" She handed it to him.

"Yeah, that's right." Charlie took the mug. "How did you know I hate sugar in my coffee?"

"Lucky guess," giggled Tracey.

Charlie nodded and took a drink. "Espresso too, my fave." He put the mug down on the table. He looked around the room and said, "Listen, Tracey, I don't mean to sound weird or not appreciative, but—I get the feeling you know me and I sort of don't know you, okay? I mean, I'm sorry to come off sounding weird or even paranoid, but I'm not even sure—you're familiar to me and all but—"

Tracey sighed and stood up. She said, "It's okay, Charlie. I'm sorry. I should have just come out and told you everything. I just wasn't sure if you remembered me or not, 'cause we've definitely met before and yes, I know a lot about you."

"Really?" Charlie sounded even more uneasy.

"Oh shit," Tracey mumbled. "I'm not a stalker, okay? I'm Deanne's cousin, and we actually met at her party the other night."

That put Charlie immediately at ease. "Oh, okay, that's great. Right, Deanne's cousin—Tracey—yeah, I remember Deanne mentioning you a couple of times."

"Please sit down, okay?"

Charlie sat down in the chair Tracey had slept in and picked up his coffee.

Tracey sat down on the sofa. "Deanne and I are cousins, yes. But we are far from close and have never been good friends."

"But you know about our drama—from her end?"

"I've heard some of it, yes, but if you want to know if I'm on her side? Hell no. Truth is, Deanne's always been—well—I love her 'cause she's family—but she is cold. She's not the most empathetic person on the planet."

Charlie took a sip of coffee and said, "Most? I'm sorry, but your cousin's not empathetic at all."

"Fair enough."

"Look, forget what I said. Like I have a right to say anything, you know? I was dating her, right?"

"No, no, you have a right, but you really don't remember the other night?—"

"Why? Did we?—" Charlie waved his hand between him and Tracey.

"No, no, sorry, I don't mean that kind of thing. No, I meant—I was the one who drove you home."

"It was you—you," said Charlie in great relief. "I mean I didn't remember details or, um, being conscious, but sure, when I woke up and when I was in the shower, I knew there was something familiar—you cleaned up my apartment?"

Tracey sighed and grimaced, "Too much, huh?—too weird? It's just that your place was kind of wrecked beyond—well, I felt it was the least you were owed after someone in my family treated you the way you were treated."

Charlie laughed and said, "You in the habit of making up for your cousin's bullshit?"

Tracey smiled and answered, "No, of course not, I just—honestly—"

"Don't get me wrong, I appreciate it, but making up for family shit can lead to some real trouble. I mean, look what happened to the Kennedy kids when they tried to make up for what Papa Joe did to get rich?"

Tracey laughed a bit and said, "No, you're right. I get it. It's just that I was worried if I left you that night without making sure you hadn't alcohol-poisoned yourself—well, I couldn't have lived with myself. So, I cleaned your place to stay awake."

Charlie nodded. "Well, I can say this: you did a fantastic job and a big favor for me. However you did it, I was able to find everything you moved and organized. I don't know if I could ever do it again, without asking you to do it for me."

Tracey smiled a genuine smile of pleasure and her cheeks turned pink. "I'm glad, really glad."

After a few more moments of silence, not tense silence, pregnant silence—but chemistry starting to bubble, Charlie asked, "What do I owe you, then?"

"Owe me? Money?"

"No, not money—I mean, unless—uh, of course I don't mean money. No, I mean what can I do to say?—you know, thank you? How can I say thank you for rescuing me from your cousin two nights in one week?"

Tracey was quiet. She wasn't sure if she should answer. If she were honest with Charlie, she would tell him exactly how he could show his appreciation. The problem was that even the most modern of women wouldn't say to a man, "Fuck me!" without it being frowned upon. Damn, Tracey was horny. It had been a long time, a helluva long time. But now Tracey was finding herself so rapidly and so powerfully attracted to Charlie it overwhelmed her. And she was alone with him—in her apartment.

"Tracey?" Charlie asked. He could see she was daydreaming. "Tracey, you there?"

Suddenly, Tracey was back in the present and realized Charlie was waiting for her to respond. "Oh, yes, sorry! I was just kind of—lost in a thought. Hey look—um—" Tracey stood up from her seat and walked over to her purse. She reached inside, hunted around and took out a business card holder. She walked back to Charlie and popped the lid. She took out a card and handed it to him. "Here's my card. I'd love, you know, dinner—sometime—anytime that works for you? Just call me and let me know?"

Charlie took the card and said, "Um, yeah sure." Charlie saw the name "Bird's Books," and Tracey's title was "Proprietor." He said, "Great word—proprietor—don't hear it a lot. You own a bookstore?"

"Guilty. I've always been a book-geek."

"Me too! I own—uh, I have my own business, too."

Tracey smiled and sat down on the arm of the chair, as her arm gently touched Charlie's shoulder. "I know you own a dispensary. I think it's cool, really."

"Oh, great—yeah, so I guess we're a couple of entrepreneurs, huh?"

"Guess so."

Charlie slipped the card in his pocket and said, "So, I'll call you and we can set a date when we both kind of have a better idea of our weeks?"

"Sounds great," agreed Tracey.

Suddenly, Charlie shot out of his seat. His face showed he just realized something he had forgotten—something important. "Oh shit."

Tracey stood up too, and asked, "What's wrong? What—"

Charlie put his mug down on the coffee table and gently took Tracey's hands in his. It was something Tracey wasn't expecting and she almost shuddered from his touch.

"What is it, Charlie?"

"Shit. I just remembered: my dispensary isn't open today, but I am getting a shipment in from someone, and my friend's bringing it in—God, Tracey, I'm so sorry. I really hate to do this but I've got to go. I've got to take care of this today or my customers will be pissed off."

Tracey smiled and said, "I totally get it, Charlie. It's the same with books. If I don't have my intakes ready to go out the day I promise to, I get some very angry bookworms."

Then Charlie pressed his hands against the tee and hissed through his teeth. "Shit, my clothes!"

Tracey put her hands on Charlie's shoulders and said, "It's cool, okay? It's all cool. Keep the tee. It's my brother's and way too big for me, anyway. I'll just, you know, I'll take care of your dirty clothes. That way you have to follow through with your promise for dinner—otherwise—"

"You'll hold them hostage?" finished Charlie.

"You bet," and spontaneously Tracey kissed Charlie on the cheek.

They were both surprised and now, very nervous.

"Okay," Tracey said, breaking the nervousness. "You have your car down in the garage, right?"

"Right, right, downstairs, so—"

Then without another word, Charlie double-checked his pants for his wallet and keys and sort of fumbled, stumbled and with many nervous smiles and laughs got to the front door and opened it after wrestling with the lock.

Tracey found herself smiling nervously too, and giggling even. She made her way to the door as soon as Charlie was out in the hallway. Holding it open as Charlie made his way down the hallway, she flashed him her hand in good-bye. Charlie did the same.

Charlie passed by Deanne's apartment on his way to the elevators but never even took a glance. His eyes were firmly locked on Tracey. Once Charlie had disappeared into the elevator, Tracey closed the door and locked it. She stood motionless for about ten seconds, then slumped down to the floor and started laughing.

"Oh God, Tracey, you are such a dork! Don't let this guy get to you! But he's so damn cute." She shot up to her feet and stomped them. "No! Don't say it! Don't say he's cute! Oh shit! You just said it! Damn it! And he's sexy!"

Tracey covered her face and screamed. "Leo's going to kill me! He's going to kill me!"

Meanwhile, as Charlie rode down the elevator, he was reprimanding himself via forehead bumping on the elevator wall. "Shit, shit, shit. She's Deanne's cousin. Shit, she's hot—damn, so hot—freckles! Why does she have freckles? God, I love freckles! Plus she took care of me! Twice she fucking took care of me! She's got to be into me—twice—has to be into me!"

Reaching the parking garage, the doors opened and Charlie stormed out with a mixture of giddiness and anxiety battling in his stomach. "I've got to ask Rita—Rita! She'll know if she likes me! God, she is so incredibly cute! Tracey Kipper—kipper's a fish, right? A flat, salty fish the British have for breakfast—"

On went the self-babbling between the two, as Charlie got into his car and drove off to meet Pony at OHM with the Buddha Blend; and Tracey got herself ready to go open Bird's Books—late, but she'd get it open and hope for the rest of the day that Charlie would call her later to set up their date.

Unfortunately, something very cosmic and very mythic was about to drop into both their lives, and that dinner date would never happen—or at least not in a way they could have ever planned.

Chapter 14

Bourbon Street, New Orleans, Louisiana

The Cat's Meow is the kind of karaoke bar that features the finest in youthful indiscretion and lack of genetic musical talent. The only way to survive the karaoke experience is to be drunk, and the only way to really cut loose and sing karaoke is to be drunk. It's a winning formula. When you add a near-immortal night-dwarf to the mix who has just stolen what might well be the most powerful relic on the planet Earth—well, you know that means it's just gonna be one helluva great par-tay!

Unfortunately for Al, the near-immortal night-dwarf who successfully swiped the Augur from right under the nose of Cardinals in the Vatican, his choice to hit The Cat's Meow in order to celebrate his success sent the wrong message to the very immortals who had hired him to steal the Augur. In fact, when Grim Dog walked through the doors of the bar (on his own with no Holy Mother Virgin in tow, looking for Al and the Augur) and found the night-dwarf up on stage butchering the lyrics of "Don't Stop Believin'" by Journey, Al had no idea how unfortunate it was that he had chosen to stop off in New Orleans on his way to Los Angeles to celebrate his victory.

When the bouncer at the door asked Grim Dog to show him identification, Grim Dog just looked at the bouncer with his one smoldering eye. Immediately the bouncer (who was almost the size of Grim Dog) said nothing other than, "Have a good time, Sir. If you'd like any extra fun," he produced a card and put it out for Grim Dog to take, "text me and I'll…"

Grim Dog walked off towards the stage completely blowing off the bouncer's offer. The former All-Father made his way through chairs and tables and a large crowd who were whooping and hollering in encouragement of Al's butchery and stopped just at the edge of the stage.

Up until this point, Al had his eyes closed in an effort to really, really feel the energy of Journey's power ballad. He also wanted to make sure he had a firm grip on the microphone in one hand while clutching that bowling bag with the other, inside of which held the most powerful relic on the planet. But when Al heard the thunderous—and I mean thunderous, not just a metaphoric use of the word—sound of Grim Dog cracking his gloved knuckles he opened his eyes and saw the rather perturbed deity within arm's length (well, Grim Dog's arm) of him and his prize.

Al stopped singing and the crowd moaned their disapproval. He said, "Hi, Grimmy."

"You son of a dragon-whore," mumbled the Asgardian. "Give it to me!"

Instinctively, Al pulled the bag to his chest with both arms and smiled. "Where are my bricks?"

"Bricks? They're where they would've been if you had arrived where you agreed to meet us."

"Oh, so, 'cause I wasn't there—you're going to—" Al broke into a run. It wasn't a human run or even the run that a desperate human makes when certain doom and ass-kicking is definite. No, this was the kind of running that only supernatural persons do when they have other supernatural persons (or beings—it really doesn't matter which term, both are politically correct) about to kick their ass for services not rendered.

From the second Al ran and Grim Dog pursued him, the crowd went from seeing an elderly giant chatting with an elderly little person to seeing whoever it was on stage butchering a Cher song. None of them would remember the immortals, only the caterwauling—that's how magic worked. At a later date, a few who were really smashed would say they had the weirdest feeling something really extraordinary had happened, but for the life of them they couldn't remember any details. The details, if they could recollect them, might best be described as a "wind storm" contained within the building, which rattled the chairs, tables, bottles behind the bar and the bodies of patrons, but soon blew through the front doors and spilled out into Bourbon Street. And like those in The Cat's Meow, the people on Bourbon Street would not be able to recollect details of this whirlwind pursuit either, although being out in the open they were more likely to remember having encountered something which knocked them physically to the ground. In actuality, Al had taken to ground—which is to say—he burrowed into the earth via a manhole cover in Bourbon Street and was tunneling through the sewage system, creating his own tributary with the vast magical powers born to his ancient people to escape above-Earth enemies like Asgardians.

Conversely, Grim Dog was above Earth using his vast reserves of supernatural power to follow the night-dwarf's movements through this planet that he had, when called Odin All-Father, ruled over. In those years he knew every rock, every river, every natural or man-made feature as it was all connected to the roots of the Tree of Life, whose branches reached up to his once-heavenly kingdom of Asgard and Valhalla and would tell him anything he needed to know about Earth and her goings-on. Now it was no different.

Grim Dog used his own powerful form to run in pursuit of the dwarf who was really doing a very bad job of keeping his promise to the Holy Mother. Unfortunately, supernatural or not, deity or not, neither of these venerable beings had infinite resources of power, and it wasn't long (in supernatural terms) before they began to slow down and peter-out. That happened somewhere outside El Paso, Texas, actually not that far from Deming, New Mexico!

"That's ironic," said Al as he fought to catch his breath while Grim Dog held him by his shirt collar, well off his feet.

"Not ironic, stupid—coincidental. Now—" Without another word Grim Dog unleashed on Al, pounding the dwarf in the face and gut. The pounding wasn't as personal as Al might have thought. It was more of a beat-down that said, "You promised to do something for me and you broke your word. That means you will be punished." Grim Dog would have done the same to anyone who broke their word to him. Of course, the fact that it was Al did make Grim Dog smile.

By the end of the spanking, Al was sprawled on the shoulder of the I-10, under the "Welcome to El Paso" sign.

Grim Dog glared down at Al. He held the bowling bag in his now-bloody grip. Grim Dog decided to peek inside the bag and say, "Yep, it's there. You weren't stupid enough to take it out." Grim Dog looked back at Al and said, "I really wish we could have buried the hatchet with this one, old man."

"Me, too—" said Al, meekly.

"And if it were me, I'd make sure you never saw your bricks. But the Virgin wanted me to tell you when I found you, that when you get back to your pad in Manchester you'll find your bricks there."

"Thanks?" Al went unconscious.

Grim Dog smiled and stuffed the bowling bag in the pit of his massive arm. He began to walk into El Paso, whistling Journey's 'Don't Stop Believin' while brushing his white beard.

Once inside El Paso, Grim Dog hooked up with an old biker brother of his from the Reagan years. Although this friend had aged considerably, wheelchair-bound due to crippling arthritis, the friend could swear Grim Dog wasn't a day older. Grim Dog owned it up to good genes and asked if he could borrow his Harley Davidson to get back to Los Angeles. Considering his current condition, the friend saw no problem with it and gladly gave Grim Dog the keys.

As Grim Dog took the keys, he patted his friend's knees and rolled out of El Paso on I-10 West with the bowling bag secured to the back of the Harley.

The next morning, Grim Dog's friend woke to find he was able to use his legs for the first time in more than ten years.

Muscle Beach, Venice Beach, California

Being a supernatural force of awesome power, Grim Dog was able to roll onto Muscle Beach in Venice a mere six hours after he left El Paso. "Now, it isn't exactly Superman speed or nothing," as Grim Dog might say to himself. "But shit, dude, the chopper can only handle so much enhanced power without falling to pieces!"

In any case, when Grim Dog arrived he saw a sight that made him at once want to laugh at the irony while also hurl from the pathetic display of basest human nature. He saw the petite but stunningly beautiful Virgin Mary sitting on a bench near one of the muscle cages, flirting with six muscle-bound men. Each one was doing what they could to display their physical qualities in an effort to influence This Two-Thousand-Year-Old-Plus Hottie's favor. Of course, none of them knew they were hitting on the Mother of their personal Lord and Savior.

"You've got to be shittin' me, dude," Grim Dog mumbled. He parked his bike, stepped off it and carried the bag to the bench where the Blessed Virgin was seated, ogling the men.

"Please," Grim Dog mumbled to his counterpart.

"What? I might be the Virgin but I'm no prude."

"Wow, how many centuries have You been waiting to use that one?"

The Virgin was about to respond when one of the muscle-bound boys shouted at Grim Dog, "Hey, Grandpa! Howz about youz leave the Lady with us."

Grim Dog walked up to the wire fence that stood between him and the face of the would-be instigator. Grim Dog was at least six inches taller than the younger, even without his boots. With inhuman reflexes, he reached through the fence with his fingers and grabbed the collar of the boy's muscle shirt. He pulled the boy to the fence and kept pulling until the corpuscles in his face burst and his skin turned purple.

The boy screamed and his fellows began to yell and beg for Grim Dog to let him go.

Grim Dog smiled and said, "Boy, your muscles are like your grasp of the English language—chemically enhanced. So, how about you and your girlfriends here just leave me and My Granddaughter alone? Gotz it?"

The frightened boy nodded his head up and down repeatedly.

Grim Dog let the boy go and he and his muscle-bound entourage began to quickly leave the cage with their stuff.

Grim Dog turned back to the Virgin who was glaring at him. "What? I didn't hurt him—too bad."

"I gather you found Al?"

Grim Dog sat down with the bag and put it on the bench between them. "Yep."

"Did you leave him alive?"

"Only because You asked me to, but I warned You. I knew he'd never trade something so powerful for simple weed."

The Virgin said, "I suppose you were right, but fortunately the guardian I've chosen to entrust the Augur with will trade it for weed—or more likely trade weed for the Augur."

"Wait, wait, wait! Are You shittin' me? You're going to give it to some mortal after all the bullshit We went through?"

"The point is to find the mortals We can trust it with, All-Father. I have already revealed Charles Hamor to you. Now it's time to reveal to you the other descendant."

"Finally! Let's go!"

A Not-So-Clean Apartment in Venice, California

Pony Macreedy was asleep on his couch face down; drool from the corner of his mouth soaking into his pillow. He was wearing the same clothes as he had worn two days earlier when he went to Buddha Jesus' compound to purchase the bricks of Buddha Blend. He also still had the skates on which he used to make his way from Calabasas to Venice: an odd way to travel, perhaps, but a system that Pony and Charlie devised some time ago to keep Pony from ever being caught on the radar of any authorities. It also gave Pony the adrenaline rush he so badly craved in between weed sessions. The paraphernalia on the weathered coffee table in front of the sofa-bed showed that Pony enjoyed his private weed session with the Buddha Blend.

The only sound that filled the apartment was the clicking of the stylus on the turntable of the stereo system located under the window. It was caught in the lock groove of Pony's favorite album "Music From Big Pink" by the seminal rock group The Band. It was his first choice whenever he settled in to enjoy whatever herb he had chosen to smoke on a given afternoon. His love of The Band had already been confirmed by the t-shirt he wore to Buddha Jesus' compound, which he was still wearing even though it had been two days.

Watching Pony sleep, Grim Dog and the Virgin Mary stood behind the sofa. Grim Dog's expression was perplexed, while the Virgin's was unmitigated admiration and love for what was to Her a blessed child dreaming of a better world.

Grim Dog asked, "You're telling me that this?—I mean he is also a descendant of my Vanaesir?"

"He and Charles Hamor could be no more brothers than if they been born twins in this life."

"Wow—uh," Grim Dog rubbed his face and then scratched his beard, hard. "I just—I mean—You need them to unlock the secret of the Augur?"

"I am disappointed that you cannot see it in him."

"See what? Do you hear that noise?"

The Virgin moved around the sofa so She could push aside the pipe, the bong, and the remaining brick of weed, all of the things cluttering the top of the coffee table and sat so She could reach out and very gently caress the side of Pony's cheek.

She said, "Can you not see it in his blood? He is as much Vanaesir as Charles."

Before Grim Dog could respond, he cringed as Pony made a terrible snoring-coughing-gagging sound that only a deviated septum could create.

"Aw shit," Grim Dog mumbled. "Apnea? There's never been apnea in my family. Never, never, never had any troubles like that. Please, tell me he's not Vanaesir. I mean, other than the hair coloring, the skin, the height—I can't tell what color his eyes are—" so Grim Dog leaned down over the couch and opened one of his eyes to see it bright blue. "Yeah, yeah, okay, those are—I mean, he's genetically one but, please, do I really have to?—what is that fucking clicking noise?"

The Virgin shot up to Her feet and for the first time looked as hurt and pissed as he had ever seen Her. Her dark eyes were alight with the glow of a Mother whose dearest Son had been scorned by others who cannot see the beauty that shines from within Him. There was no word—no sound to accompany the fury that burned within the Holy Mother's eyes. It was the kind of fury not seen since the days when Grim Dog's ex-wife Frigga would berate him for coming home covered in gore after a great battle and not wiped his shoes off on the welcome mat before treading all over the newly-cleaned bear rug.

Suddenly, the Norse god realized what it was that was making the incessant noise filling the apartment. He walked over to the stereo and took the record off the turntable. He smiled as he read the label. "Hey, if The Band is his choice in music then I can buy what You're saying about this kid. Second best decision I ever made was suggesting to Bobby Dylan that he hook up with those guys."

Grim Dog put the album back down on the turntable. "I'm sorry," muttered Grim Dog. "I can see that he and Charles have the DNA to unlock the Augur—absolutely! No doubt! Would bet a million dollars on it! How could I have not seen it before? I guess being stuck on Midgard—uh—Earth this long has made me kind of dumb."

The Virgin Mary's eyes softened and She went back to sitting on the coffee table and stroking the hair of the snoring Pony.

"But do We have to give it to him first? Can't We give it to the Hamor guy—"

Again, the Virgin shot a look of scorn that shook the old deity in his boots. He threw his hands up in the air and finally, he handed Her the bowling bag over the couch. She took it and smiled at Grim Dog.

"I guess I should go now?" Grim Dog asked.

"We are almost finished with Our part, yes. There is one last task that must be done by ritual to try and protect all those whom We cannot protect in the coming battle."

Grim Dog shook his head and said, "I really hope You know what You're doing here, Mary." It was the first time Grim Dog had used Her proper name, and it did not go unnoticed by Her. "Are You sure, really sure, the boys will not just get wiped away by their enemies? Because the minute You pass it on to him, We release it from Our care, and just about every wingnut on this planet—"

The Virgin said, "Do not fear for Our children, All-Father. Although You and I cannot fight this battle for them, nor can We let them know who We are right now, We will not be too far from them. And not all those coming for the Augur will be the Enemy."

Chapter 15

Venice Beach, California

Pony woke to the sound of knocking on his door. He lifted his face off the sofa and felt the dry spit in the corner of his mouth and saw the stain on the cushion that served as pillow.

The knocking continued.

Pony didn't want to verbally answer, at least not yet, because who knew who the hell it was? He knew it could be Charlie coming to get the Buddha Blend. It might have been Rita, because he had not talked to her since getting the money, and if Charlie for whatever reason couldn't make it, he would have sent Rita.

Regardless, Pony was no dummy and was not going to answer until he looked through the peephole. But if he did not get moving in time, whoever it was might book. If it was Charlie (or worse, Rita) then they would be pissed he didn't answer. So, Pony moaned and shifted, genuinely struggled to get conscious enough to rise and reach the door.

Pony managed to make his way across his apartment knocking over as few things as possible. He stumbled twice when his size-thirteen-feet hit both the ratty backpack and the duffle containing the bricks of Buddha Blend. Fortunately, Pony's apartment wasn't so long that he had a lot of room left to fall over and hit the floor after meeting the backpacks. Instead, he fell into the front door and used his long arms to catch him while he peeked through the peephole.

The woman who stood outside the door was holding the bowling bag—the same one once held by Holy Mother Mary and Grim Dog. She was attractive, of that Pony had no doubt. Her hair was dark, as were her eyes, but she wore very little make-up, if any at all. She was dressed like a hippie, so to Pony she appeared very much the kind of girl you'd see up and down the Venice boardwalk.

"Hmm," Pony muttered to himself. "Don't know her, never seen her. Course she could have been here before; could have gotten high here before. Don't see a baby with her—that's good—condom worked."

"Pony!" shouted the voice of the woman through the door after a fifth knock on the door. "Pony Macreedy, I know you're in there. I need to talk about something very important with you."

"Listen," said Pony, "I don't know you, but you know me. Until we ascertain who you are and why you're here I really don't think I should—"

Suddenly, a photograph appeared at the peephole. It was such a shock to Pony he fell back onto the floor absolutely stunned by what he saw in the photograph.

Before Pony could say anything else, the woman at the door said, "I'm sliding it through the door, Bug. Does that help make you understand it, Bug? Should I keep calling you Bug?"

Pony started shaking. He pulled his knees to his chest and began to rock. In one powerful moment of clarity, he realized who it was on the other side of the door.

The photograph came through the space between door and floor and slid right up to Pony's legs. He looked down at the photograph with tears in his eyes.

"Bug?" said the woman. "Bug, believe me. I'm not trying to shock you. I just—I have something I need to give you."

Pony (aka Bug) picked the photo off the floor. It was the kind of curve-edged, perfectly symmetrical, faded colored photo taken by the 1970's popular style of camera called the Instamatic. In the picture he could see a ten-year-old boy with fire-red hair and jean cut-offs with a polka-dot button-up shirt. Pony knew it was him. The other person in the picture, that's the person who scared Pony, because it was his best friend in elementary school, his only girl cousin—who died not long after this picture was taken. She was dressed in the same outfit the adult woman was wearing on the other side of the door.

"Bug?" asked the woman. "I know you're scared. I get it. But I also know that if you didn't believe it was me, you wouldn't be scared. Could you please open the door and let me in?"

Pony stood up and walked to the sofa. He sat down holding the picture firmly in his hand. He still didn't know what to say or what to do.

"Bug, I swear to you, I'm not a vampire! I'm not a scary Romero-zombie that'll eat your brain. I mean it, Bug, I'm not!"

"Bug, bug, bug," reverberated inside Pony's head. It was his first nickname. His cousin Claire gave it to him because he once ate a bug just to impress her.

"Bug, do you remember how we were going to get married one day? Remember? We didn't care that we were cousins. We knew that we were connected, special to each other in a way we would never be to anyone else ever. I know I've been dead a very long time, but I know you never got married. I know you always compared every girl you were with to how you and I felt together. Come on, Bug! It's me, Claire! I love you, Bug!"

Then it was quiet, for as much as ten minutes. Part of Pony hoped she'd—it'd gone away, but as he looked at the picture—really looked at Claire and him as children with arms around each other's shoulders, something in his head clicked. Pony stood up, walked over to the front door, unlocked it and opened the door.

The adult Claire was still there, standing with both hands holding the handles of the bowling bag. "Believe me now?"

Pony shrugged his shoulders and walked back to his sofa.

Claire entered and looked at the messy pad. "Wow, this is cool, Bug."

"I'm not Bug anymore. I go by Pony."

"Okay, Pony it is. But I like this place. It's very free, you know? It's where I thought you'd live when we were kids."

Pony wasn't looking at Claire so much as he was looking at the opened brick of Buddha Blend.

Claire saw the brick, saw Pony's eyes and said, "Ah, you think this is because of the grass, right? You think—"

"I was stupid," Pony said. "I should never have smoked that shit after hours and hours of skating. I never have good reactions when I do weed after being pumped up with adrenaline."

"Well," said Claire as she plopped the bag onto the coffee table by the brick, "I'd tell you it was the brick if it'd make this easier for you. Does it make it easier for you?"

"Yeah."

"Okay, then it's the grass. And I'll tell you what; I'll take that weed off your hands in exchange for this bag."

"What?" That offer made Pony sit up and stare at Claire as if she were anyone else. "I can't do that. It's not mine to begin with. I bought it for Charlie—for OHM."

"Right," said Claire. She stood up and started pacing the floor. "Charlie's your friend, right?"

"Yeah, more than friends, he's like…"

"…family?" Claire finished.

"Yeah, family."

"And you think he'd want to sell grass that makes everyone go psycho and see dead relatives?"

"No, of course not."

"Wouldn't that be bad for business?"

"Yeah, I guess so."

Claire walked over to the sofa and sat down next to Pony. She put her hand on his knee and said, "Of course not. Of course it would be bad for business. But if you help me by taking this bag off my hands," she pointed at the bowling bag, "I'll take these bricks off you and you'll never see them again. Sound like a deal?"

"But what's in the bag?" Pony asked Claire.

Claire smiled and said, "Just the most fabulous object in the entire world."

"Wait, wait, wait," said Pony. "Is this like that scene in the movie 'Time Bandits' when The Evil Genius tries to seduce Kevin in the guise of his parents to steal the Most-Fabulous-Object-In-the-World? But the Object really isn't Most Fabulous, 'cause the Most-Fabulous-Object-In-the-World really doesn't exist. So if Kevin takes it, he'll fall into the pit of despair just like the Time Bandits do?"

Claire's face went blank. She looked Pony in the eye and said, "I have no idea what you're talking about."

"That's right," thought Pony out loud. "You died before that came out."

Claire stood up and went to the sliding glass door that opened onto the tiny balcony overlooking the beach. She slid back the door and took in a deep breath of ocean air. "You're right, Bug—sorry, Pony. You shouldn't trust me. In church they taught us the Enemy will often times use those we love most to make us lose our way. I cannot really prove to you one way or the other that I really am the spirit of Claire come to offer you something so magnificent in exchange for some hydro, or that I'm not the Enemy."

"So what do I do?"

"I'll tell you what, Pony. Why don't you open the bag, look inside, and check out the gift before you decide."

"Really?"

"Sure."

"It won't burn out my eyes, like 'Raiders of the Lost Ark'?"

Claire shrugged her shoulders and shook her head—same clueless look in her eyes as when Pony referenced "Time Bandits."

"Damn, that hadn't come out yet either— "

Pony reached out and picked up the bowling bag. He unzipped it and looked inside. What he saw was definitely nothing he expected to see, but then again what would anyone expect to see if they were told that they were looking at arguably the most powerful object in the world?

"A radio?" Pony asked Claire.

"Yes. What were you expecting?"

Pony reached inside the bag and took out a vintage transistor radio circa 1964. For a piece of electronics almost half-a-century old it appeared pristine. It had a bright red plastic shell with its antenna retracted and snapped behind the handle. The plate that showed the brand name read Armageddon 420 (in that fancy kind of Dark Ages script), which Pony thought had to be the oddest if not the kind of the coolest brand name ever.

"Armageddon 420," whispered Pony. "Whoa, that must have been some kind of limited edition model or something, man. And how cool is that, huh? 420? That's like stoner code for—well, you know what for—so how cool is that?"

Claire asked, "You like it then? You like this radio?"

"Yeah, man, totally cool and shiii—" Pony cut himself off when he noticed the large plastic dial. It showed markings for both AM and FM dials, and in the middle—the center was not round but almond shaped with a slit in the center, as if it opened up. It was a stand-out feature that absolutely fascinated Pony, but exactly why he could not say, at least not then. "What's with this dial, huh? Does it look weird to you?"

"Weird to me?" asked Claire. "I'm kind of dead, Bug. And seeing as I died in 1981, everything I've seen since I got here looks weird to me. But none of that matters. What matters is that you seem to really like this radio, is that right?"

Pony smiled and nodded and kept inspecting every inch of the funky device.

Claire sighed and said, "Bug, nodding is not enough, okay? You have to like say it, you know? You have to say you love it—out loud, I mean!"

"Okay, okay, I love it!"

"And you would say it's worth the Buddha Blend? You'd trade it for the Buddha Blend?"

Pony didn't answer—still too wrapped up in checking out the radio for anything else that made this a one-of-a-kind device.

Claire rolled her eyes and shouted, "Pony!"

Pony looked at her. "Sorry, sorry, what?"

"You can check it out all you want, very soon. I just need you to say it out loud, that you'll trade me the Buddha Blend for that Armageddon 420 transistor radio."

"Shit, yeah!" but then Pony stopped and realized he had to say it in the way his cousin asked him. He wasn't sure why it had to be said in this particular way, but he also did not feel that it was so weird he wanted to question it or dig for answers. "Right, let me see—uh—I am willing—I mean I want to trade the Buddha Blend for this kick-ass Armageddon 420 radio. Cool?"

"And you aren't worried about the consequences?"

Pony stood up and proclaimed, "Hell no! This thing's got to be worth serious bank! Not that I want to sell it, I don't. But it's an antique, man! It's totally 'Road Show,' baby! And when Charlie sees it, he'll see what bank this is too. I can see it all now! We'll make it a totally righteous centerpiece for the dispensary—that'll bring in even more clients, which will mean more and more dough."

"Great then!" Claire walked over to the remaining brick on the coffee table and collected it in both hands. She walked it over and dropped in into the open duffle full of the untouched bricks of Buddha Blend. Quickly she zipped it up and lifted the bag with absolutely no effort whatsoever.

Pony looked at his "cousin" and said, "That's it? You're leaving, now?"

"I can't stay here, Bug, and I've given you what I came to give you."

"Okay, yeah, but—I mean—what—"

"Why?" asked Claire. "Why now? Why at all?"

"Well, yeah! I mean, there have been a lot of times in my life when I've thought about you—wished you were with me—could've used your—"

Claire walked up to her living cousin and put a hand on his cheek. "I'm sorry, Bug. It never works like that. The Universe never works on our timetable, just its own. Be good, Bug." Claire kissed Pony on the lips. "I love you, and be strong, okay? Everyone will attack you for the choice you've made today. Just remember, you know why you did this and that's enough."

"Why did I do this?"

Claire put her hand back on Pony's cheek and said, "Because you love and trust me, and because you want to make lots of bank!"

Pony sat amazed as his cousin—his dead cousin, who carried the duffle full of Buddha Blend to the front door, opened it and walked outside onto the landing. He had no words as she took one last look over her shoulder at him, smiled and descended the stairs. A few seconds later Pony put the radio on the sofa next to him, jumped up and ran to the landing. He stepped out and looked down the long narrow stairs to the glass door that opened onto the boardwalk. He ran down and went out through the door. He saw many, many people walking by but no sign of Claire. She and the hydro were gone.

Chapter 16

West Hollywood, California

Charlie drove directly from the condos where Tracey and Deanne lived to OHM. As it was Sunday, it wasn't an issue if he got there in time to open the doors for customers. All that mattered was that he arrived in time for Pony to get there and to intake the Buddha Blend which Charlie thought Pony still had.

As one might think, on the drive over to OHM Charlie's mind could hardly think of anything or anyone other than Tracey. It was more what she did to help him, the now ex-boyfriend of her cousin, than who she was that was an enigma to Charlie. His somewhat pessimistic tendency would lead him to think, what's her agenda? But the fact that she had previously rescued him, taken him home and even cleaned his pad without calling him or in any way harassing him after that first night contradicted an agenda theory. And after the second rescue, Charlie could not think of anything else she would get out of it, either. He had offered to take her out to dinner, but she genuinely seemed pleased, if not more surprised. What was this woman all about?

Again, Charlie's mind, as rational as he was, as thoughtful as he was, didn't last long in the area of her motives. His mind went back to thinking how incredibly hot and attractive she was. Physically she was dynamite! But her capacity and level of concern for him, basically a stranger—a loser who had been the victim of his own poor judgment, staying with Deanne, whom Tracey had acknowledged to him wasn't the best of people—turned him on for reasons way beyond the fitness of her body.

Thank God I have a business, if not a life, to keep my mind off her, he thought to himself. Otherwise, I could drown in her! I'd still be there acting all stupid—no, not possible to be more stupid than covered with linguini and clam sauce—and making the kind of mistakes that would get him kicked out of her place. Fortunately, Tracey also had a life, if only a business, to show Charlie she was grounded enough to be in charge of something, someone who has an objective, a goal—a bookstore, too. That meant she was smart, always a fantastic quality in a woman as physically beautiful as Tracey. And no matter what else he did, Charlie kept thinking about her over and over and over again.

Now, he decided, all he had to do was figure out exactly how long he wanted to wait to call her for their date—and—ugghh, he thought, how long to wait to call Deanne, officially end it, and if she should know about Tracey.

His mind reeling from Tracey, Deanne and all things chemical, Charlie found himself passing his own dispensary before he realized he missed his turn.

"Shit!" he screamed out loud.

Charlie took the nearest side street off Santa Monica, drove down to another cross street, turned right, went back two blocks, turned right again, and pulled into the narrow parking lot behind the row of buildings in which his dispensary was housed. He parked in one of the faded parking spots next to the back door to OHM.

As he climbed out of the car he spotted another car in the same area behind OHM. It was Rita's car. That was a good sign, as he went to the back door, took out his key and unlocked the door. That meant that Pony was likely here or had been here already and Rita was divvying up the hydro to put in bottles and bags.

Unfortunately for Charlie, as he entered through the back door and heard the sounds of an early Hawkwind album playing over the stereo system, he was in for a big disappointment. Instead of shouting he was there, Charlie stayed quiet and walked through the back of the dispensary, where Henry would spend almost all his time prepping the weed and tending the plants, to the sales room. There he found Rita, Henry and Ian all looking confused and perturbed.

"What's up, guys?"

They all looked at Charlie.

"Pony not here yet?"

Rita stood up and walked over to Charlie. "Nope, haven't heard a word yet."

Ian shouted, "And that little fucker should have been here two hours ago. Where the fuck have you been? We've been trying to call you for the last hour!"

Henry stood up and put a hand on Ian's chest. He said, "Calm down, Ian. Don't yell at Charlie. He's your fucking boss. Show some respect."

Ian said, "You're right, Henry. Listen, Charlie, Henry's right, I'm sorry, man. I didn't mean to shout at you. We were just worried."

Rita said, "Yeah, we thought maybe Deanne took you out or something."

"Close," said Charlie as he walked over to a phone behind the sales counter. "We had it out big time, and she hurled a bowl of linguini and clam sauce at my head that cold-cocked me but good."

Ian and Henry started laughing.

"No fucking way," said Ian.

Rita looked at Ian and Henry with a scowl. "It's not funny! He could have been hurt!" Rita walked over to Charlie, who was dialing Pony's number and asked, "Are you okay? Are you hurt anywhere?"

"No, I had a knight in shining armor—" then he heard Pony pick up the phone. "Pony, where are you?"

Rita looked confused. She repeated, "Knight in shining armor?"

Charlie said, "Dude, what does that mean?—delayed?"

Henry and Ian walked towards the counter, very interested in whatever it was Pony was telling Charlie. The only thing they could discern from Charlie's expression was confusion.

Charlie said, "Pony, look—Pony, listen! Man, you are not making a lot sense. You said your cousin came by—some kind of present? Pony, Pony, Pony, shut up! Yeah, just a second, okay? I'm going to send Rita and Henry over there to get you and the hydro, okay? Then you'll come back here and we can find out what all this cousin business is, okay? Can you do that?"

There was another pause as the other three saw Charlie look even more confused by whatever Pony was telling him.

Charlie said, "Pony, you obviously just woke up. I don't know why you are warning us about Buddha Blend—no, we've never had anything—Pony!" Charlie shouted to shut Pony up. "Hang up the phone, get everything together and they'll be there in twenty, okay? No, twenty!"

Charlie hung up.

Henry asked, "What the hell's wrong with him?"

Charlie shook his head. "That stoner's in a bad way this morning. He's babbling on about seeing his dead cousin, Buddha Blend being bad for you, something about a radio and—zombies? I don't know."

Henry patted Rita on the back and said, "We'd better get over there, sister, before our boy explodes."

Rita nodded distractedly, and said, "Yeah, okay. But Charlie, I want to know more details about last night, okay? What's with this knight business?"

"Okay," said Charlie. "Just go get Pony and bring that weed back here!"

Rita and Henry left the way Charlie came in, leaving Charlie and Ian alone.

Ian leaned against the counter and said, "You want a beer?"

"Kind of early, isn't it?"

"Yeah, but I can tell you need it. That bump on your head is nasty."

Charlie touched the knot just underneath his hairline and winced in pain. "Yeah, I'm lucky that fucking bowl didn't gash my forehead."

Ian went back behind the sales counter and opened the refrigerator in which they kept perishable edible hash treats, reached way into the back of the lowest shelf and took out two Dos Equis. He twisted off the caps with his hands and handed one to Charlie.

They both took a long swig and released satisfied sighs, after which Ian asked, "Okay, give me the whole skinny, bitch. I want to know exactly what that ho Deanne did."

A Few Miles West in West Hollywood, California

Bird's Books opened on time—well, it actually took Tracey an extra fifteen minutes to unlock the front door, but it might as well have been on time as no one was queued outside. The luxury of not opening until noon and the routine of putting on makeup, getting dressed and driving to West Hollywood in order to open the store helped Tracey not think too consciously about Charlie—or Deanne.

On the drive over to the store it was more Deanne in her thoughts than Charlie because being the kind of stand-up, low-drama gal that Tracey was, she wanted to tell Deanne that Charlie had been at her place last night as soon as possible. But was that the brightest decision? Being Deanne's cousin might actually make that news worse.

Tracey and Deanne's mothers were sisters—and about as different as the two cousins. Tracey's mother was a much more practical person, while Deanne's was a failed supermodel who had poured all of her passive-aggression into a daughter who was on the verge (if CW primetime is considered a verge) of stardom. Were it to fall out that Tracey had gotten something Deanne already had or wanted to have, Deanne's mother would certainly take it as a front against her and let her sister know about Tracey's failure as a good cousin. But that whole drama was only a momentary concern of Tracey's. The bottom line for Tracey was that she wanted Charlie to know that her feelings for him—whatever was happening inside her towards him—was as real and right as rain and that no matter what secrets about her he might eventually discover (and how those secrets directly concerned him) had no effect upon her attraction for him. She had been down that road once with another man and it totally scared her—and it kept Tracey single and mostly celibate for more than three years.

Ironically, it was Charlie who had in a way helped Tracey survive that very destructive relationship. After Tracey had learned about her ex's betrayal and chosen to swear off men, it was reading Charlie and Henry's books that kept her moving forward. It gave her hope that one bad relationship and how a partner treats you in it does not mean both partners are terrible people or that all sexual/romantic relationships are doomed to failure. Now, Tracey was finding herself face-to-face and emotionally awake by the author who had given her strength to move on. In any case, Tracey's efforts to tell Deanne that morning failed. She had stopped by her cousin's apartment, knocked on

116

the door, even entered with her spare key—but found no sign of Deanne. She wondered where Deanne would have gone, considering the break-up had happened at a very late hour. Of course, Deanne might have planned it that way and had a location already chosen for after the break-up?

To answer that question, Tracey did a masterful job of checking Deanne's computer—even broke through her password protection— as well as desk drawers and other hardcopy books for just such an address. It wasn't like Deanne had all together vanished, and nothing was conspicuously gone from bathroom, bedroom or walk-in closet, plus her kitchen was still a mess from making the linguini and clam sauce dinner.

Tracey decided not to make a bigger case of it and left a simple hand-written note taped to the back of Deanne's cordless phone that read: "Call me at Bird's or as soon as you can. We need to talk– xoxo."

Although Sunday wasn't a customer-heavy day, it was the day for Tracey to catch up on the mundane aspects of her job as owner-manager, and she welcomed the busy work. Her best friend and employee Jenny Sway was scheduled to come in and work the register from one until six (when Bird's closed on Sunday). Until then Tracey stayed up front checking inventory and making sure books that had been thumbed through by customers, then left out or not put back in their right place, were shelved properly.

For the next forty-five minutes, Tracey used this mundane work to help her not think about when Charlie might call her. She also tried not to think too much about how sexy she thought Charlie was. It might seem odd that someone as incredibly smart and grounded as Tracey would find a man so completely caught up in a depressive spiral as Charlie was either sexy or attractive, but she knew so much more about him than anyone could.

Damn it, she thought. This is going to get me fired! But I don't give a shit! I want to tell him! I want to tell him so bad!

So caught up in her thoughts, Tracey didn't hear the front door open and Jenny Sway, a dark-eyed, dark-haired beauty in her late twenties, come in announcing at the top of her voice, "Tracey, honey, I'm here!"

Jenny's voice definitely snapped Tracey back to the present and she responded, "Hey, honey! I'm back here in mysteries!"

117

Jenny bounded down the main aisle and located Tracey in the mysteries, stocking copies of Charlaine Harris' most recent Sookie Stackhouse novel. "Hey girl, what's up?"

Jenny and Tracey hugged each other.

"Not a lot," answered Tracey, who didn't want to get into it with Jenny.

"Why don't I believe you?" Jenny asked her.

Tracey shrugged her shoulders and looked back to her books.

Jenny waited a few seconds and studied Tracey's face. "Uh-huh, right."

Tracey looked at Jenny and blushed. Tracey had a terrible time hiding when something emotional was really eating at her. Her skin and freckles betrayed her every time. "What?" asked Tracey with an "I have no idea what you're talking about" tone in her voice.

"Nope! Uh-uh! Bullshit!" Jenny insisted. "I see it in your pink cheeks, sweetie! You are in it bad and I bet its name is Charlie Hamor!"

"Shut up!" insisted Tracey with a smile, and she pushed Jenny back.

Jenny shook her head and said, "I'm putting my things up and then you're going to tell me everything that you don't want to tell me, okay? Because I can see you're bursting to say something!"

Back at OHM Dispensary

Ian and Charlie were now seated in the front lobby of the dispensary where customers would first enter and wait, while Ian checked their identification before allowing them through the door to the salesroom. Not that the door or wall separating the lobby from the salesroom was much to worry about. It was rather flimsy and seemed to act as more of a reminder that people who came to get their marijuana here were supposed to be getting it for legit reasons and not because they were losers who couldn't face the ordinary boredom of their ordinary life.

The serious reminder that this was a very dangerous, very monitored business was the heavy bars covering the front windows of the dispensary and the "cage" in which the customers would first enter after coming off the street and then wait while another kick-ass electronic security door would open only after the door to the street was closed and locked. Of course, when you're there to get your pot, you didn't think of these bars, cages and double-locked, double doors as anything other than part of the ambience that comes from getting the best pot money can buy.

Charlie and Ian were seated on the leather sofa, drinking their beers and smoking a joint. The Hawkwind CD "In Search of Space" Charlie had heard playing on the stereo system when he first came in was still playing loud, cool and smooth.

Ian asked, "So she was the one who drove you home from Deanne's the night of the party?"

"Totally was—totally was."

"And she saved you, again!"

"Dude, she didn't just save me, man. She fucking clothed me, man. She cleaned me up, gave me shelter. Shit, she was my Florence Nightingale!"

Ian laughed and shook his head. "I don't get it, man. I don't get it. You say she's Deanne's cousin, right? That you never met her until the night of that party? But you don't remember her that well from that night. And so you really didn't talk to her until last night—no, no, no, this morning—because you were fucked up from being beaned in the head, man! I don't get it! How does she know you to rescue you? And did you fuck her? Did you fuck her?"

"No, I didn't fuck her, man! I wouldn't do that to her! She was too nice—too nice…"

"…to fuck?" Ian finished. "Is that what you were going to say? You only fuck chicks that are mean fucking bitches to you, like Deanne? Like Marina! Like that killer-bitch Claudia! Whoa! Remember her? Remember how mean she was? Oh, shit."

Charlie laughed, "You're right, man. You're right! Claudia was mean! But, no! It's not that I didn't want to fuck Tracey—I mean, wait, no, wait! I mean, I wanted to hold her—make love to her—"

"Oh God, you're in love with her!" shouted Ian. He laughed as loud as he could and with Ian's size that rocked the whole sofa.

"Yeah, so—so what if I'm in love with her? Can't I have love at first sight?"

Ian grabbed Charlie and shook him. "Dude, you cannot be in love with the cousin of that bitch Deanne, because when Deanne finds out she will cut your balls off and shove them down your throat and with her other hand pull them out your ass!"

"Fuck Deanne!" the drunk and high Charlie shouted. "I'm not scared of that bitch! She was nothin' when I first met her! If it weren't for me, she wouldn't have that fuckin' role on that fuckin'-piece-of-shit-CW, piece-of shit-teeny-bopper, fuck-me-I've-got-some-STD-soap-opera she's on now!"

"Whoa!" shouted Ian. "I don't believe I've ever seen this side of Charles Hamor! You sound liberated!"

"I am! I am liberated from Deanne! I am liberated from all bitch girlfriends! And I am going to make Tracey mine! Mine!"

Back at Bird's Books

In Bird's Books, Jenny listened intently to Tracey's whole account of last night and the night of Deanne's party. Basically, Tracey poured her heart out about Charlie, which is what Jenny asked Tracey to do but it was the amount of stuff Tracey had to share that stunned Jenny.

The women were behind the counter, near the register. Jenny was resting her arms on the top of the counter, her face showing her processing the information. Tracey looked nervous, worried that now she had said it all out loud to someone, especially her best friend Jenny, that for the first time everything having to do with Charlie made Tracey sound way too desperate.

There were a few moments of tense silence. Then Tracey asked Jenny, "Well, come on? What do you think? Am I desperate? Am I crazy?"

"Yes, to both."

"I am?"

"Yes, but it's because Deanne's a bitch."

"I know! She's going to kill me!"

"No, I wouldn't worry about her, really. She obviously wants to get rid of him. I mean, she almost killed him with pasta! No, I think she's the kind of person who just holds onto people to use them, because she hates to be alone."

Tracey nodded. "I hate to say it, but you're right. I think that's it, too."

"But here's the real question," said Jenny. "If he's cute and all, that's great, and I know it's been like a while for you, Trey, but is this really the kind of guy you want to be with?"

"What?"

"If he lets this kind of person walk all over him, basically use him, treat him like crap—I don't know, hon, sounds like he's kind of a loser?"

That surprised Tracey. She wasn't expecting that to come out of Jenny's mouth. "You think he's a loser? Because of what I?—"

Jenny shook her head and said, "Listen, Trace, you're a hot chick, you know? You live in one of the hottest cities in the world. I just don't think you should settle for someone who doesn't have the guts to shirk off a bad relationship, you know? And I know—I know you're a fan of those books he wrote and all, but how many times does the real thing fail to live up to the fantasy?"

"You think I'm attracted to Charlie just because I liked his books?"

"Well, look at your job, hon! I mean, he was a bestselling author!— kind of, maybe—"

"Jenny, yes, I was a big fan of his books, but he hasn't written anything in a long time. And I don't think he's the person in his books, okay? I mean, look at him now. He runs his own business."

"A head shop!" snapped Jenny.

"No, it's a medical marijuana dispensary."

"Because he's a stoner, and I bet his friends are all stoners! Come on, Trace, who're you trying to convince here?—me or you?"

Damn it! thought Tracey. This wasn't going to work at all! If she could tell Jenny everything she knew about Charlie, she knew she could change her friend's mind. Tracey knew why Charlie had started OHM. She knew about Danny's cancer and what it did to Charlie. But she wasn't supposed to know—Charlie or Deanne had never told Tracey about that tragedy, and it wasn't something revealed in his books or articles about him after he quit writing. So, if Tracey was to tell Jenny about Danny, she'd have to tell Jenny how Tracey knew and that wasn't going to happen. There would be too many lives blown apart; Jenny's life would be in danger if Tracey told her everything she knew about Charlie—and how. For now, Tracey would just have to play dumb and desperate in front of Jenny. At least for other reasons, that would play well for Tracey.

Tracey put her elbows on the counter and rested her chin on her fists. She sighed.

"So do you have any idea when he's gonna call you for this dinner?" Jenny asked.

"Nope."

"Then can we still go out tonight?"

Tracey perked up and looked at Jenny. She waved a finger in her friend's face and asked, "Is that what you're worried about? Is that it?"

"What? What?"

"You don't want to lose your wingman?"

"Well, I mean, of course I don't! But, I mean—"

Tracey took her friend's hands in her hands and said, "You aren't going to lose your wingman, okay? And yes, I'll go out with you tonight. Okay?"

Jenny smiled, looking relieved. "Good. Because there's this totally kick-ass band that we're going to go see!"

Chapter 17

Airspace Somewhere Above the Atlantic Ocean

Having a private Lockheed SR-71 Blackbird at his disposal (compliments of Vatican City) was not going to stop Father Agosto from following his gut due to long years of experience of hunting down rare objects and even rarer living targets, which the Holy Mother Church ordered him to locate and either return or destroy. It wasn't as if Agosto had become a certain "double-O" who drank a certain kind of cocktail. But with his License to Crusade reinstated, Agosto had carte blanche to do whatever was necessary to retrieve the enigmatic Augur. With the Revelator Glasses atop his nose, allowing his eyes to partake of their omnipotent capacity to identify the truth, good or ill, of anything or anyone seen through the Glasses—Agosto was going to go wherever the Holy Spirit guided him.

Without spending too much time on the Templar phenomenon of the Holy Spirit, because it would just keep us away from this particular story for too long, let it suffice to say that for Knights Templars—for those who have been made true members of the Holy Secret Order of the Knights of the Temple of Solomon (I'm not talking about those Masonic posers or those weenie dudes in the other Mr. Brown's books)—the Holy Spirit could best be equated with clairvoyance, clairaudience and clairsentience all rolled into one. But whereas those three are gifts attributed to some kind of psychic power, born of some kind of human capability not normally accessible to the average person, the Holy Spirit is the power of God or Lord Jesus Christ itself operating through the Templar to give them special vision, special auditory or special knowledge not normally available to humans. For Templars and the Faithful, the Holy Spirit is not a Power that is in anyway interpretable as pagan, witchcraft or sorcery. The Holy Spirit is a Power given directly by the Will of God—or at least that's how it's been for two thousand years (give or take a century).

Agosto is not a fanatic, by any means; it would be wrong to think of this priest as anything similar to a Pat Robertson or an Osama Bin Laden. In fact, this is a man (and believes he is just that) who would rather spend his life in isolated prayer—a monastery, and who did for a while live as a monk. However, because he is a devout man of God, he cannot refuse the call to service. To do so would be to practice pride and reject humility. Agosto understands that his faith is not the only faith—that Christ is not the only power, the only Word of God. It is just that for Agosto, his existence is to serve the Christian God. As a result, Agosto will employ (when necessary) the Holy Spirit when confronting other Ways that get in the way of Holy Mother Church.

Back to the immediate moment of Agosto and using the Holy Spirit in order to hunt down the Augur and its thief: when Agosto was told that the Augur was located in Los Angeles, he knew that guaranteed nothing. In fact, the Holy Spirit told Agosto that Los Angeles was not the place to start. The place to start was to inspect the Vault itself and, with a little Holy CSI work, determine that arcane powers—ancient, pagan forces—were employed to get in and out of the Vault. Agosto had encountered enough "fae" powers in his time to know what is magic and what isn't. He could tell that something magical had gotten in and out. That immediately eliminated several possibilities and narrowed Agosto's focus. He was looking for someone or something whose power came from the Elder Gods.

Once aboard the Blackbird and in flight to the United States, Agosto placed the Revelator Glasses on his nose and began a prayer. With this prayer he summoned the Holy Spirit to activate the ancient lenses so that he could scry the location of the thief. Unfortunately, the platitude "The Lord works in mysterious ways," is a platitude for a reason; the Holy Spirit manifests Its Power as It sees fit. In other words, even someone of Father Agosto's experience can never know exactly how the scrying will manifest. In this case, locating the thief meant hearing the awful karaoke singing of one Alberich Night-dwarf.

The shrill and tone-deaf rattling tore through Agosto's ears, not with the singing of Journey's 'Don't Stop Believin',' but from another 1970s rock super-group REO Speedwagon and their hit 'I Can't Fight This Feelin' Anymore.' It was like liquid metal being poured into his ears and it made Agosto shout out loud and yank the Revelator Glasses off his nose.

"By all that's holy!" he shouted, as the Glasses plopped onto the cushion of the sofa next to his chair. "Why must those horrid creatures of the dark earth insist on singing?"

After recovering from the blast of unholy sound, Agosto put back on the Revelator Glasses and once again prayed—this time including a request to Lord Jesus Christ not to let him hear any sounds—to learn exactly where this night-dwarf was located. Perhaps the Holy Spirit was taking pity on Agosto, for this time It showed him the name of a karaoke bar in El Paso, Texas named Rock Ur House Down.

After taking off the Revelator Glasses, Agosto dialed up the pilot on the phone-intercom to tell him where they were to stop before heading for Los Angeles. Once they changed direction, Agosto went to the hold over his seat and took out a duffle bag, which he laid on the sofa and unzipped. Inside was an arsenal—things in which a proper Catholic priest would never employ for any reason whatsoever, at least not one who didn't fight in the Mediaeval Crusades.

Agosto's duffle was full of guns—not the pearl-handled beauties presently holstered under his jacket—but ordinary military-grade guns such as a pump-action shotgun (aka riot gun), an M240 machine gun, a high-powered sniper rifle, a pair of Uzis, a Swiss long-range machine gun and assorted automatic pistols. Along with these more common modern weapons was an assortment of hand-held weapons that included a beautiful broadsword in scabbard, all of which looked as if they were brand-new. The only weapon in the duffle that seemed ancient, as if it has been taken from the display case of a museum, was a long dagger in scabbard that Agosto took out to more closely inspect. He slowly drew the dagger from the weathered scabbard to reveal an iron blade, which neither shone like steel nor appeared in anyway modern. This was the weapon he slipped into the inside pocket of his jacket and then zipped up the duffle.

Biggs Army Airfield, El Paso, Texas

The Vatican's private jet landed at 11:30 p.m. A ramp lowered from the cargo bay near the tail of the plane. Out of it drove Father Agosto, wearing no helmet but with the Revelator Glasses on. He was driving the same fire-red chopper that had taken him and Father Moreno out of the rainforest.

It was an altogether peculiar sight for the very small ground crew who came out to service the private jet. But none of them said a word as the priest revved the engine and tore out of the airfield south on Wright Street. The route took less than twenty minutes, and Agosto was parking in the lot already filled to capacity.

Agosto entered the Rock Ur House Down karaoke bar and saw it packed with locals who had come for a night of fun and relief from the week's everyday stresses. It was something that Agosto could not empathize with but certainly sympathized with, and it was his genuine hope that none of them would get caught up in his reasons for coming or scarred by his appearance there.

It was critical that no matter how much latitude the Camerlengo had given Agosto, he not draw too much attention. This wasn't like a Robert Rodriquez/Quentin Tarantino "Grindhouse" film where explosions, piles of bodies and scores of raped women went either unnoticed by the mass media and the authorities or was accepted by both as "There's nothing to see here."

Agosto's first test of subtlety was upon him the minute he entered the bar, because just inside the door sat a tall, rotund bouncer. Due to the poor lighting, it wasn't immediately evident to the bouncer that a Catholic priest had entered, considering this man was wearing a leather jacket, John Lennon-style sunglasses and black jeans.

The bouncer said, "ID, man."

Agosto looked at the bouncer without saying a word.

Again the bouncer said, "ID, man. I gotta see your ID."

Agosto pointed to the priest's collar, as well as the rosary hanging just below it, now visible since he was facing the bouncer.

The bouncer actually jumped a bit on his stool and gripped his own rosary hanging around his neck under his black t-shirt. "Sorry, Father. Of course you can go in."

Agosto crossed the air in front of the bouncer and said, "May the Lord bless you and keep you, My Son."

The bouncer crossed himself and said, "Thank you, Father. Thank you."

On stage he saw some co-ed singing a Justin Bieber hit that had just recently made it to the karaoke world. So he began to casually patrol the bar looking for any sign of the night-dwarf or anyone who carried the scent, as it were, of the creature upon them. This is where the Revelator Glasses came in useful. Other than its scrying powers, the Glasses could also function to reveal the truthfulness of peoples' appearances right down to their souls. This also included the lint, one might say, left behind by magical or inter-dimensional creatures.

As inconspicuously as possible, Agosto walked the floor of the bar and between the tables looking for any sign of the thief. Suddenly, the Templar Priest spotted him: the night-dwarf was closest to the karaoke machine. He would be invisible to almost everyone else, but everyone else wasn't wearing…

Al was enjoying watching the breasts of the co-ed rise and fall as she gyrated to the Bieber tune, until he saw a deadly iron-bladed dagger that he immediately recognized as twenty-seven hundred years old and capable of slicing his throat open in mere seconds. Once the iron met his blood, he'd burst into flames and be reduced to ash. The question now in his mind was, who the fuck would not only have this fossil, but also would know to use it against a night-dwarf?

"My friend," spoke the soft voice of the Templar Priest, "I think it would be wise for us to talk outside where these ignorant folk won't be confronted with a reality none of them can handle."

"Is that your best pick-up line?"

Agosto actually touched the blade to Al's throat and it stung him like a snake bite.

"Grrrgggh," growled the night-dwarf. Not wanting to draw the attention of the people near them, he bit down on his tongue and held back from screaming as loud as the pain demanded. Without another sound, offering no resistance, Al shifted so that Agosto walked behind him out the back door of the club.

Once he was outside in the night air, Al made his move. He summoned all of his magic and began to metamorphose into dark energy, becoming a shadow so he could disappear from his unknown attacker. But Al could never have comprehended the skills of this opponent, or the fact that with the Revelator Glasses, Agosto could see Al's natural body even when transformed. None of that mattered though, because in one swift swipe of the iron dagger, Agosto severed Al's right hamstring. The night-dwarf fell to the ground and cried in agony.

"My hammy, you son-of-a-bitch—you've fucking crippled me!"

Agosto picked up the whining night-dwarf and carried him off to some nearby bushes where he dumped him out of sight of anyone coming or going from the bar. "Stop your complaining, foul creature. I know this iron is painful to you but you are hardly disabled by it. You'll heal slower but soon enough."

Al rolled on his back, side-to-side, whimpering and crying.

Agosto kneeled down and grabbed him the collar of his shirt. He pulled Al close to him and placed the blade of the knife as close to Al's throat as he dared. "Now, I do know that if I swipe this through your neck and sever your head from your body you will perish—no healey, healey. Got that?"

Al stopped crying and just moaned in pain. "You bastard Templars, I could never decide who was worse—you or those motherfucking Inquisitors."

Agosto said, "If I was an Inquisitor, I'd not be talking to you, now would I?"

"Okay, okay, you son-of-a-bitch, but not for nothing," Al began to snicker, "if you had any idea who it really was—really was who hired me to—" Al broke into a full-throated laugh.

"What?" asked Agosto. "Who are you talking about?"

Al began to laugh harder and harder, so hard he was fighting for air.

"Who hired you to take the Augur?"

But Al was laughing so hard he couldn't make words that sounded intelligible to Agosto. Frustrated, the priest stood and kicked the dirt close to the night-dwarf's head. He was a lot of things, Agosto was, but he wasn't going to harm the creature any more than he already had—not without a good reason. Laughing and irritating the Templar Priest didn't count as a good reason. So, Agosto waited for Al to stop laughing, but it took Al another good five minutes to calm down. While he waited, Agosto took off the Glasses and rubbed his eyes. He didn't like this weird twist or the night-dwarf laughing. Then he put the Glasses back on and saw something shimmering on the cuff of Al's shirt. Agosto grabbed Al's arm and gripped the cuff with his fingers.

"What? What are you looking at?" asked Al. No longer laughing, his brain and mind clear from the healing pain of his cut hamstring; Al recognized what it was on Agosto's face. "Holy shit, the Revelator Glasses."

"Who touched you here?" Agosto asked the night-dwarf. "Someone, something more powerful, more holy, someone very—"

"She did," said Al. "She did."

Agosto released Al's arm and shoved the little man back several feet. The priest rose to his full height and drew out both his pistols. He aimed them at Al. "It's not possible. She would have nothing to do with you."

Al was definitely frightened by the guns. He had no way of knowing what kind of munitions were inside the magazine. But he also knew he was close as he could ever be to having the Knight Templar's balls in a vice. Being a naturally clever creature, he decided to play it up for all it was worth.

"Yeah, well, I'm sure you and your oh-so-powerful Holy Mother-child-fucking-Church would like to think that, wouldn't you? Truth is, asshole, that The Holy Virgin Mother of Your Boy Jesus Christ did come to me and ask me to steal the Augur out of your piece-of-shit vault. And if those are the Revelator Glasses, you know everything I'm saying is true, just like you can tell it's Her aura still showing on my cuff."

Agosto could see it. Through the Glasses and through the Holy Spirit Power within him, the Templar Priest had absolutely no doubt that what Alberich Night-dwarf was telling him was the truth. It utterly turned his stomach, made him physically nauseous, but what the pagan creature was saying was true and he couldn't deny it.

Without showing a single crack in his steely façade the priest said, "But I can also tell that she is done with you. You are no longer under her providence."

That was true too, Al thought. But uh—oh shit—"Yeah, so?" spat Al. "You need me to tell you the details, 'cause if you're working for the Vatican then you're working for the Enemy of the Virgin, shithead!"

As abhorrent a thought as it was to someone as dutiful to the Church as Agosto, both the Glasses and the Holy Spirit Power flowing through the Templar Priest told him this dwarf wasn't lying. "Los Angeles," Agosto said to Al. "The Augur is in Los Angeles, is it not?"

"Yes, but it is pointless going after it, because the bastard who took it from me is in cahoots with your Virgin. Plus, I think he and the Virgin are doing the high hard one, and if you try to cross their path, he's going to—"

"Who?" asked Agosto.

"Fuck you," said Al.

Agosto fired one bullet from each gun, capping Al in each knee.

Al screamed in bloody terror and fell to the ground rolling and rolling and rolling—

"Who the fuck are you saying is with the Holy Mother?"

"Grim Dog, you fucking fucker fuckface! It's Grim Dog!"

Agosto lowered his guns. He was stunned. He hadn't heard that name in a very, very long time but he knew it was just one of many names used by someone, something that was for the Knight Templars as sworn an enemy as Satan itself.

"The One-eyed Wanderer?" Agosto asked.

"I don't mean the one-eyed trouser snake, stupid! Yes, I mean motherfucking Odin All-Father, you stupid child-fucking priest! And when he finds out you're trying to take back the Augur, he'll take Gunghnir and—"

Before Alberich Night-dwarf could finish his sentence, Father Agosto raised his guns and unloaded both magazines into the screaming creature which had, until that moment, lived for almost two-thousand-five-hundred years. When he had emptied both guns, as Al's body convulsed against the blessed silver bullets in an effort to have his own magical genes attempt to survive the assault, Agosto holstered the guns, took the iron knife and cleanly decapitated Alberich Night-dwarf.

Seconds later Alberich Night-dwarf's body sizzled and popped several times until the whole of his body became ash. Only the head remained intact, gripped in Agosto's fist. The eyes were open and the mouth gaping.

Agosto said, "Truth or not, vile creature, I'll not allow you to say that such a beast as Grim Dog would sully the Holy Mother. Plus, your head will serve to keep the Vatican occupied while I find out what the Cardinals true intentions were in summoning me. No one deceives Agosto, no one."

Chapter 18

Washington, District of Columbia

As much as certain religious groups were mobilized in an effort to recover the Augur, earlier that same evening, while Agosto was still in transit in the Vatican jet over the Atlantic Ocean, political wheels were also spinning as word of the theft from the Vatican's Vault hit the wires of the United States government and specifically, the Office of Homeland Security.

But as it was also Sunday, the offices of both supervisory agents and their management bosses were vacant. Only the most junior agents were monitoring any and all intelligence coming in from sources all over the globe. And whereas more than a single chapter of this book could be dedicated to how having only junior officers and agents monitoring said data could lead to—well, let's just say certain repeat performances—the point of stating who was there and who wasn't there when word of the theft arrived has to do with who was the first to get the information at Homeland Security and to whom that information was next taken.

Special Agent Dale Curb was seated at his desk in his cubicle, working on his computer translating some kind of pointless rambling from recordings of an "al-Qaeda in the Arabian Peninsula" operative yakking away to his cousin about how he was going to be part of some operation involving bombs, a new hotel being built in the UAE, etc., etc. There was no way to verify at that point how legitimate this claim by the AQY operative was until Curb had finished the translation and gotten it into the hands of one of his superior officers, SA Michael Lombard. But that wasn't going to happen anytime soon because a fellow junior officer appeared at his desk with a printout in his hand.

"Dale?" asked the officer.

"Yeah," said Dale as he looked away from his translating to see the worried expression on his colleague's face. "What is it, Harris?"

"Dale, I know you're in the middle of another assignment, but this just came down directly from the Director's desk."

"My uncle?" asked Dale.

"Is he your uncle? I literally had no idea."

"Not a lot of people do," said Dale. "And I'd like to keep it that way, if you don't mind? Because if everyone here knew then they'd think I got where I am so quickly because of…"

"Nepotism?" finished Harris. "Believe me; I'm sure you passed the test all on your own."

"I did, as a matter of fact," insisted Dale. "The first time—I mean, I studied my ass off. I bet you passed it the first time, didn't you?"

Harris smiled and changed the subject, "Anyway, here's the memo from the Director's desk. He wanted you to personally handle this."

"But what about—?" Curb turned halfway to his computer and was about to point out what he was working on.

Harris insisted, "Dale, dude, he made this sound really, really important. Don't worry, man, I'll cover what you're working on." Harris peeked around Dale's taller frame to see what was on the monitor. "Oh, it's a translation? No biggie! I do those all the time!"

Dale took the printout and said, "Okay, if you're sure?—but I'm not on this alone, am I?"

Harris patted Dale on the shoulder and said, "Dale, it's all good. It's all on the printout. Just get going and read it on your way to the elevator."

Dale smiled and nodded. "Yeah, okay. I guess so. Thanks so much, Harris! It's great to have a friend like you!" Dale patted Harris on the shoulder as he headed away from his cubicle towards the elevators.

Harris watched Dale disappear down the aisle. Suddenly, his face became a scowl. Under his breath he said, "Son-of-a-bitch—passed the test first time, ass-kissing, nephew of the Director. God, I hate fuckers like you, Dale." He looked at Dale's computer and sat down at the desk. He smiled an evil smile and in one quick moment deleted the complex translation Dale had spent all day working on. "Let's see how your nepotistic uncle likes that."

But the repercussions of Harris' nasty attack on Dale Curb would go unnoticed and unrecognized for quite some time. At the present, Dale was definitely focused on the paper in his hand and reading it while he rode the elevator down to the garage level. In a nutshell, it told Dale that his uncle, the Director of Homeland Security, wanted him to find Supervisory Special Agent Ephraim Syde and inform him "The Shell has broken! The Shell has broken!" Shell had a capital "S" in the memo, too.

What this meant was unclear to Dale Curb. Why his uncle would ask specifically for him to deliver it was also unclear—other than it was a rare instance where Curb's uncle actually did think that maybe he could trust family more than department to carry out the mission— maybe it was so damn important that only blood could do the task.

This rationale was viable from a certain point of view. If the Director recognized this was a volatile situation, that things could go sideways easily, his best bet would be to put it in the hands of a family member rather than another agent. If something did go wrong, a family member was less likely to spill what they knew to the media. A regular agent might go public and really screw the department. But Dale never wanted to think ill of his uncle—never. So he would never see that his uncle was sending him to an agent whom Homeland Security was stuck with after its formation, because every other intelligence agency had gone through the ringer working with Ephraim Syde, a burned-out relic of the Cold War.

Sunday nights (or more precisely late Sunday afternoon into late Sunday night) found Ephraim Syde at Madam's Organ Restaurant and Bar, located not far from where Agent Syde lived in his one-bedroom apartment on 18th Street NW in downtown DC. As hip a jazz, blues and alternative crowd scene as one could find anywhere in the nation's capitol, Madam's Organ also functioned as the kind of place where someone of Syde's age with roots firmly planted in Southside Chicago could reconnect. Many similar joints might claim to be timeless and ageless, but Madam's Organ was exactly that, which was why every Sunday Ephraim Syde would sidle up to Big Daddy's Love Lounge &

Pick-Up Joint (on the second floor of Madam Organ's) and order his one true love: a Manhattan in a frosted martini glass—the last true Manhattan in all of DC.

The other love of Ephraim Syde's life (which he was likely to find in Madam's Organ as well) was red-haired women. Oh yes, fond memories of a former KGB agent whose beautiful red hair and brown eyes had almost been the downfall of Syde twice while working in Europe during the early 1980s. However, her demise, shortly before the Berlin Wall's demise, left him with daydreams of finding her one day there in his favorite joint, or at least his flirting with the DC beauties that frequented there.

Although the memo in Dale's hands told him nothing about Madam's Organ, other than its location on 18th Street, or that Ephraim Syde's passions were extinct cocktails and KGB agents, it did tell him that this is where he should go to find Ephraim Syde.

Once he was in his car and out on the streets of Washington DC, Dale drove to the bar on 18th Street and parked in a no-parking zone. Having those "special plates" made him think it was the best choice—not wasting time trying to find a parking spot. To a more experienced agent, it almost made it clear that Curb was doing something so important he'd be reckless enough to park in a spot that made him stand out.

Once inside the bar, Dale quickly moved through the first floor and then up to the second where he found Ephraim Syde seated at a table drinking his Manhattan. However, Syde was not alone. There were three younger women (much younger) seated in the booth with him. Although Syde was 55, he also looked a lot like Josh Brolin, save being bald and having a Van Dyke beard. He dressed nicely, indeed, and was by no means a depressive personality. Like a certain Nordic deity who was introduced earlier in this tale, Syde had no problem being the surrogate for any young woman with daddy issues.

Curb, who himself resembled a Hollywood actor, namely Keanu Reeves (with less character and even less charisma), wasn't sure how exactly to attract Ephraim. Then an idea popped into his head that made him very proud of himself. He took out his mobile phone and went to another empty table. He sat down and dialed the main switchboard of Homeland Security. Once an operator answered, Dale identified himself (name, rank, serial number) and asked to be connected with SSA Ephraim Syde. A few moments later he saw Syde stop chatting with the women and motion to them that he had to answer his—

"This is Syde," came through Dale's phone, and he watched Syde's lips move.

"Agent Syde, I'm Agent Dale Curb. I've been asked by the Director himself to contact you about…"

"Curb? Who the fuck?—listen, kid, I'm off the clock, okay?" Syde disconnected the call.

Dale was shocked and insulted. He had identified himself in the proper manner taught to him by his previous supervisors and his uncle. He dialed the number again.

Again, Syde answered. "This is Syde."

"Agent Syde, the Director himself has asked me to—"

Again, Syde ended the call and went back to chatting up the women. He motioned for the waitress to bring them all another round.

Oh, now Dale was getting really steamed. He knew that he couldn't be too conspicuous and just bust into the conversation. Who knew who these women were? Although they only appeared to be co-eds from American University, they could be spies. Nothing was impossible in Dale's mind. It was a challenge. Like the test that got him into his position in Homeland Security, which most folks assume Dale didn't pass the first time, Dale wouldn't let everyone else's underestimation of him get in his way of fulfilling orders given to him by his uncle.

Dale quickly reviewed the memo and saw nothing specific that told him to tell SSA Syde immediately, so he waited to see how the situation with the women developed. Over the next ninety minutes of observing SSA Syde and the women, Dale ordered four diet sodas, an order of potato skins, mozzarella sticks and bean and cheese nachos (deluxe). Dale had a big appetite.

Eventually, two of the three women left the table, presumably giving up and allowing their friend dibs at Syde. Dale figured his window would open soon, as their numbers dwindled. But when the waitress came to Dale's table for the tenth time to see if he wanted anything else, he said he'd like a hot fudge sundae with lots and lots of nuts on it. The waitress was polite but anyone with any real common sense could see that she was getting really, really tired of Dale taking up so much time at one of her better tables.

As the waitress walked off to fill the fourth food order, Dale looked over to SSA Syde's table and saw that he was gone! The red-haired co-ed was still there but Syde was nowhere to be found. Dale began to panic a bit. He didn't want to draw too much attention but he was unable to keep his face from tightening and his eyes getting wider.

Just then, SSA Syde slid into the seat opposite Dale with his gun drawn and pointed at Dale under the table. "All right, bucko, here's the score. I've got my 9mm under this table and ready to blow your fucking nuts off. Now, to avoid this you're going to tell me why you've been watching me and the women for the last two fucking hours."

"I'm a—I'm an—agent. My card—my badge—in my jacket? Please?" Sweat beaded on Dale's upper lip. He audibly swallowed and his mouth turned instantly dry.

"You look like the kind of crispy cut assholes they hire these days, so I'll let you get it out—if you've got it. Go ahead."

Slowly, Dale reached into his pocket and took out his identification wallet, which he put on the table. He slid it over to Syde, who flipped it open and saw the proper credentials inside. "Well, SA Dale Curb, why the fuck are you bothering me on my one day off in my favorite fucking place left in this pathetic world?"

Without a word, Dale took out the memo folded up in his other pocket and handed it to Syde. Syde holstered his gun and opened it. As soon as his eyes scanned it, the look on his face changed. A light twinkled in his eye, although his face turned to stone. His posture straightened up and he looked directly into Dale's eyes. "Who gave this to you? I mean, who actually physically handed this to you?"

"SA Harris? He works directly under—"

"Yeah, the Director. I fucking know. I also know that you're the fucking nephew of the Director."

Dale sighed and said, "Yes I am, but I passed the test on my own, the first time…"

"Shut the fuck up, Dale."

Dale shut up.

SSA Syde looked around and saw the hot fudge sundae making its way to the table. He looked at Dale as the waitress put it down in front of the agent and asked, "Will there be anything else after this, Sir?"

"No," spoke up Syde. "It's okay, Hillary. I know this kid. Put it on my tab and we'll be out of your hair here in no time."

"Yeah—okay, Ephraim."

"Oh, one other thing, kid," he said to the waitress Hillary. "Will you tell that cute doll at my table that I had to jet for work but if she'd leave her number with you I'll call her when I get back in town?"

"Yeah, okay." The waitress headed over to Syde's table.

Syde looked at Dale and said, "Do you have any idea what this is about? I mean, do you even have an inkling?"

"No."

"Jesus, I've got to babysit on this assignment? What the fuck is your uncle thinking? Goddamn it."

Dale was really feeling insulted and really getting pissed. He took a big spoonful of the sundae and said with his lips and tongue already turning numb, "I will have you know, SSA Syde, I am as accomplished and trained an agent as any—"

"Okay, look, Curb? I got nothing personal against you. I will tell you that you and I have been given the biggest assignment to come down the pike since the fucking Bay of Pigs, and I guess you learned how that turned out in history class? So, take your fucking sundae and pick up your fucking credentials and let's get the fuck out of here, because according to this memo, not only has "The Shell broken," but we have the fucking NSA already one step ahead of us on this fucking case."

Dale took another bite of his sundae and said, "No, I don't need to take it with me. I'm fine."

Syde stood up and headed out of the lounge with Dale Curb fast on his tail.

Chapter 19

Venice Beach, California

Although the movement of organized religions and political forces in response to the theft of the most powerful object in the world appeared awesome, the ultimate fate of this object lay in the hands of ordinary people (at least they considered themselves ordinary). People like Henry and Rita, who had earlier that same day driven over to Pony Macreedy's apartment to find out why he hadn't arrived at OHM with the Buddha Blend indiga.

Henry was more baked of the two, so he allowed Rita to take the lead. He knew how important it was for her sense of self that she drive, walk ahead of everyone, open that door or this one, and he was happy to oblige. Plus, he knew she was a lot more pissed at Pony than he was, and didn't want to get caught in the crossfire when the shit started flying.

As they arrived at the glass door that led up to Pony's apartment, Rita threw it open with all her strength. She was through the door and up the first few steps before Henry had a chance to catch the heavy door from snapping back and hitting his shoulder.

Suddenly, Henry became concerned by Rita's level of anger and said, "Rita, honey, don't lose it, okay? Don't!"

But Rita was already on the landing and ready to knock on the door when she said, "Henry, I'm not going to kill Pony. I'm just gonna let him know that his incessant need to test Buddha's shit and sleep it off all day is no longer an option." Rita knocked loudly on the door.

There was no immediate response from inside the apartment. Rita knocked again and shouted, "Pony? Pony, it's us! Are you in there? Come on, man!"

Henry reached the landing but took two steps down because both he and Rita couldn't fit comfortably on it. He looked back down on the steps and noticed how odd the whole stairwell looked in the shadows made by the sunlight coming through the dirty glass door. There were light fixtures at both the top and bottom of the well but they had not worked for years. As a result, it was an altogether pretty filthy set of steps. That's when something halfway down caught Henry's attention.

Rita knocked a third time and began going through her own keys to find the spare to Pony's lock. Meanwhile, Henry stepped down to where he saw the something that he knew was a plastic wrapping, unique as it was used to hold bricks of weed. When he reached the step, he knelt down and picked it up. He smelled what was an indiga leaf stuck to the plastic and muttered, "What the fuck is this?"

Rita had found the spare and put it into the deadbolt lock. As she was about to turn it, it unlocked from the inside and the door opened. Rita stepped back as she saw an ashen-faced Pony, still holding the bowling bag, staring her right in the face.

"Where the fuck have you been?" asked Rita.

Pony gave her no answer. He turned and walked back to his sofa. He sat down, wrapped both arms around the bowling bag and squeezed it.

Henry came up from where he found the wrapping and walked past Rita into the apartment. "Pony, what happened here?"

Rita entered behind Henry with a look of curiosity on her face. She asked Henry, "How do you know something happened here?"

140

Henry walked over and sat down next to Pony on the sofa. He lifted the wrapping with the traces of weed inside and asked, "I found this outside, Pony. Why was this outside?"

Rita walked around to the other side of Pony and sat next to him on the sofa. She looked at the wrapping and asked, "What is that?"

Henry said, "It's the wrapping for the bricks of Buddha Blend. It shouldn't be outside on the steps."

It appeared that Pony was ignoring them. He kept staring straight ahead out the sliding glass door to the balcony that overlooked the beach.

Henry put a hand on Pony's shoulder and gently nudged him. "Come on, Pony. I don't like what I'm feeling here. You've got to talk to us. If something happened—"

Rita put her hand on Pony's knee. She said in a voice much softer than any she had used since arriving, "Pony, we're your friends. You're starting to scare us a little, okay? If something bad happened—"

Without looking at either friend, Pony said, "She came in. I saw her actually walk inside and—"

"Who?" asked Rita. "Who's she?"

"Claire."

Rita looked at Henry with an expression that asked, who?

Henry looked at Rita and shook his head.

Rita asked, "Pony, who's Claire?"

"My cousin—my dead cousin."

Rita continued to ask, "Okay, and you say she was in here?"

Pony gave no answer. He only squeezed the bag tighter.

Henry asked, "How can a dead person have been here, Pony? And what does it have to do with the?—"

"She took it," said Pony. "She took the weed with her."

"I'm sorry, what?" asked Henry.

Rita said, "Pony, you're not making any sense."

Henry said, "I'm going to look around for the weed, okay? I'm sure it's here somewhere. Pony, when I finish looking you're going to talk to us and make sense, okay?" Henry stood up and began to search the small but incredibly cluttered one-bedroom apartment for any sign of the indiga.

Rita tried to take Pony's hands in hers, but as she tried to pry Pony's hands away from the bowling bag they would not relent. "Pony, come on. You're really starting to scare us, okay? I don't understand what you mean about your dead cousin and—let go of the bag, okay? Okay?"

But Pony, who offered nothing else to say, would not release the bag. Finally, Rita gave it one massive pull and fell back on the sofa as Pony's hands suddenly opened and the bowling bag came crashing into Rita's chest.

"Ow," she muttered as she sat back up and looked at the bag.

Pony stood up and walked towards the sliding door. He opened it and stepped out onto the balcony.

Rita looked at the bag and then unzipped it. She pulled it open and saw the radio inside. "The hell?—" she muttered.

Henry walked back into the living room and pronounced, "Okay, I'm really kind of getting pissed now! Pony, where is our fucking weed?"

On the balcony, without turning around, Pony said, "I told you. My cousin Claire came to the door and swapped the weed for the radio."

Henry shouted, "You have finally lost your fucking mind, Shaggy!"

"No," said Rita. "I mean, I don't know about Claire—but, Henry—" she pulled the radio out of the bowling bag, "—this is the radio he's talking about."

Henry walked over to Rita and took the radio from her hands. He quickly looked it over and said, "This is like a vintage 1964 Sears or maybe Philips transistor radio? Holy shit, this thing is like mint— never looks used. I mean, to a collector it must be worth—" Henry's eyes grew wide. His jaw dropped open and he looked at Pony, or Pony's back, with a really freaked-out expression.

Rita looked up at Henry and said, "Henry, you look freaked out. What's—"

Henry handed the radio back to Rita and walked up to the sliding door. "Pony, I need you to turn around and I need you to get really serious with me. I can't find the weed. You have a mint-condition piece of electronics almost fifty years old, and I'm thinking that—"

While Henry talked to Pony, Rita inspected the radio closely. She saw no cord, no compartment to hold a cord and especially strange, no compartment for batteries. But that wasn't the strangest feature; that was in the center of the dial. The center was an eye, a human eye.

While Henry was talking to Pony trying to get him to make sense, Pony turned around and said, "I don't know what else to tell you guys, but—my dead cousin Claire walked into the apartment, took the Buddha's weed and left that radio in exchange. That is the fucking truth!"

Henry was speechless. Something in Pony's voice, something in his eyes was something that Henry had never seen in Pony before—grounded conviction. He should have been angry, Henry knew that, because Pony had lost the weed, the bricks of weed that were worth thousands of dollars. But something else—something in what he said about a dead cousin made Henry not angry—just worried.

Then Rita said, "Henry, I'm not sure but, uh, could you come over here and look at this—radio, please?"

Still looking at Pony, who was still looking at him, Henry said, "Rita, I'm trying to talk with Pony here and—"

Rita said, "I know that, Henry, but I don't think you noticed that not only does this thing have no cord or place for batteries but the center of the dial is a human eye."

"What?" Henry snapped his head around and looked at Rita. "What the fuck?"

"I know! I know!" shouted Rita. "But there it is!" Rita turned the radio towards Henry and held it out so that he could see the peculiar feature on the dial.

"Okay, okay," muttered Henry. "That's some weird and wacky shit, right there."

Pony said, "Now do you believe me about my dead cousin Claire? She gave that to me. She gave me the human-eye radio for the weed!"

"What the hell is going on, Henry?" asked Rita.

Henry put both hands on his head and said, "I haven't got a fucking clue. All I know is that Charlie is going to really freak out when he realizes that the weed is gone and for nothing—for some weird fucking radio."

The radio turned on. The dial lit up, the eye blinked and the sound of it tuning itself to a station crackled through the air.

All of them screamed.

Rita dropped the radio on the sofa and leaped up to her feet. She ran over to Henry and Pony. "It blinked! Did you see the eye blink?"

"Holy shit!" shouted Pony. "It blinked, dudes! I saw that creepy fucking thing blink, man!"

"What the holy motherfucking shit ass-wiping shit?" screamed Henry.

All three friends wrapped their arms around one another in sheer terror. They watched the eye on the dial blink a few more times, then the dial turned as the speaker crackled until it hit a station that played the rock and roll classic "Bad Moon Rising" by Creedence Clearwater Revival. The three friends were speechless. All they could do was grip each other tightly and listen to John Fogerty shout about flooding rivers and terrible things coming out of the night. He begged us all to stay indoors.

Then it shut itself off. As quickly as the eye had blinked, the dial had turned, and the speakers crackled one last time before the radio stopped working.

None of the three spoke a word for several seconds. Then Rita said, "I peed myself—a little. I'm glad I'm wearing a pad."

Pony said, "I don't have a pad and I peed a little."

Henry muttered, "This is 'Twilight Zone,' dudes—fucking Rod Serling-time!"

Still no one moved.

Rita looked at Henry.

Pony looked at Henry.

Henry looked at Rita and then he looked at Pony. "Me? I'm gonna have to—"

Rita said, "You're the smart one."

Pony said, "You're a best-selling author."

Henry said, "What does that have to do with this? How does that?—"

Pony asked, "Have you ever seen your dead cousin?"

"No, no I haven't," answered Henry, who peeled himself free of Rita and Pony and slowly, very carefully walked towards the radio. Acting as if the radio were some kind of feral rodent that might at any moment jump on his face and gouge out his eyes, Henry grabbed the bowling bag, turned it upside down and leapt onto the radio, covering it with the bag and zipping it back up. He fell onto the sofa and hurled the bag across the room where it landed next to the door.

All three sighed in relief.

Rita and Pony clung to each other as they scooted across the room and plopped down on the sofa next to Henry.

Rita kissed Henry on the cheek and said, "You're my hero."

Pony did the same thing and said, "You're my hero, too."

Henry stuck a finger in Pony's face and said, "Don't you ever do that to me again—ever."

Pony put up his hands and said, "Right, sorry. And I am sorry about the weed, I really, really am. I just—I just—"

"I know, I know," repeated Henry, "your dead cousin—how could you resist your dead cousin? The question now is…"

"…how do we tell Charlie?" finished Rita.

Henry nodded.

Suddenly, from inside the bag, they heard muffled crackling and the muted sounds of the 1980s' mega-hit "In the Air Tonight."

Henry, Rita and Pony all screamed.

The radio went silent again.

"I don't know how," said Henry. "I don't know how we're going to tell Charlie. But if that fucking thing does that in front of Charlie and Ian, the weed will be the last thing we'll have to explain."

Chapter 20

West Hollywood, California

Charlie and Ian were seated quite comfortably on the sofa in the lobby of OHM and watching the forty-two inch HD TV with satellite hookup. They were watching a game between the Dallas Cowboys and Washington Redskins and deriding both sides equally. Neither was a fan of the teams and with Ian having at one time been a professional player with the San Francisco 49ers, knew just what trash to say about the players whether in person or hundreds of miles away.

Being high made the kind of foul-mouthed insults Ian was hurling not only bearable, but actually humorous to Charlie. At that moment, he just wanted to forget about Tracey and Deanne and his upside-down life and that's what Ian afforded Charlie—low-brow distractions. It seemed a truism that the more intelligent or more naturally philosophic a person, the more likely they were to find a genuine value in the kind of antics or vulgarity presented by the Three Stooges or Cheech & Chong as they would the musings of Alan Ginsburg or the histories of Howard Zinn. This was absolutely Charlie Hamor. The deeper he found himself slipping into emotional aesthetics or intellectual curiosity, the great equator between the two vast hemispheres of Charlie's head and heart was weed.

It is important to note, however, that not all weed is equal. Ask a hundred cannabists (Yes, it's a real word. Go ahead and look it up on urbandictionary.com) and you'll get a hundred different answers as to what is the best cannabis and for what purposes. Suffice it to say that to be a purveyor of cannabis is to be like a purveyor of fine wines or beer. You will inevitably find that different brewing and fermentation techniques will result in absolutely different products. In general though, you have two general types of weed: indiga and sativa. Because sativas take longer to grow and involve more cultivation, the result is a stronger, more energetic high. Indiga is just the opposite—having a more relaxing, not stimulating effect. And now one can imagine that when the term hybrid is used in referring to weed, it is a cross between these two strains—and hybrids have over the last ten years of medical marijuana use become more and more popular.

"What kind of person are you? And what is the malady for which you require medical cannabis?" is the kind of question Charlie, Henry or Rita would ask when helping a new client evaluate whether indiga, sativa or a hybrid is required.

The more scientific and intellectually serious Americans become about cannabis, the more derivatives and applications are discovered that help to destroy the silly stereotype of potheads, surfer-boys and weed as something other than a legitimate form of medicine. Prior to Danny's cancer, Charlie had never taken a toke, let alone smoked a quarter-ounce of indiga a week. He was by no means a grass prude; in fact, Charlie was great friends with Pony from the seventh grade, who began smoking pot in the tenth grade. Henry, who didn't discover his talent for cultivating it until Danny's death, had smoked sativas since they were both freshman in college. Charlie had just never thought it would help him—he was wrong. Charlie was now an advocate for the emotional and psychological benefits of cannabis as much as the physical. Whenever either his heart or head was careening towards the proverbial Dead Man's Curve, a nice 70/30 indiga/sativa hybrid helped Charlie apply the brakes before impact.

Where did someone like Ian sit on this controversial fence? Simple: the man had blown out a knee and lived with chronic arthritic pain from years of football—the stronger the sativa, the better for cutting off the pain receptors in his fiery brain. For his part, Ian had become something of a controversial figure in both the professional sports world and the world of cannabis because of his outspoken stance on the legalization of marijuana and use of it in the NFL, NBA, NHL and MLB.

A particular rant of Ian's that had been a YouTube sensation from a couple of years back gave birth to an organization called Athletes for Legalization of Medical Marijuana (ALMM). Ian didn't take the legendary rant that began during an appearance made at media day before "The Big Game" too seriously. He was simply answering a reporter's question about how he had recovered from the pain and suffering of multiple ligament tears and degenerative cartilage. When Ian owned his recovery and full relief from pot—oh, the shit hit the fan! Ian was never asked back to another media appearance. His agent dropped him and it seemed the whole world turned against the former Niner.

Then one day Ian received a call from an old college football friend who asked him to stand as ALMM's first president. Not believing himself to be in anyway articulate or even remotely intelligent enough to represent such a serious movement, Ian only accepted after Charlie, Henry and Pony explained to him what it would also mean to OHM's reputation. But when certain African-American organizations, led by highly visible black social leaders came out against a black man fronting an organization that "encouraged" the use of marijuana, the firestorm became more than Ian was willing to handle. After only one year, Ian stepped down as president. Defending his individual rights as a black man against black organizations became an irony that he just wasn't willing to deal with.

Regardless of the former pro football player and his former bestselling author friend having to defend their reputations, Ian and Charlie remained clear on what cannabis, weed, grass and Mary Jane really meant to them—relief and relaxation. Unfortunately for Charlie and Ian, relief and relaxation were about to hit the wall when Henry, Rita and Pony arrived at OHM with a vintage 1964 transistor radio in an old bowling bag and the most "fucked-up story" either of them had ever heard.

In order to be clear on the story that Pony recited to Henry and Rita, as well as how Henry and Rita reacted to it (along with the "activation" of the radio with the eye in the dial) it was decided that the most rational member of their group, Henry, would tell all the stories. However, it seemed that Henry's calm and cool demeanor, as well as his effort to make the whole sequence of events sound in anyway rational, still left Charlie without any clue what to say—although his wide eyes, slack jaw and ashen skin expressed his feelings perfectly.

On the other hand, Ian had words which he directed at Pony, "A radio—a bowling bag and a radio—you traded all the bricks of Buddha Blend for some lousy, piece-of-shit radio?"

"But it was my cousin, Ian! She came back from the dead—and I'm not talking George A. Romero—I'm talking Patrick Swayze 'Ghost'!"

Ian nodded his head furiously, bobbing it up and down and muttered, "Swayze 'Ghost,' right, right, right—cousin—right." Then Ian launched himself at Pony, hollering at the top of his lungs, huge hands grasping for the slighter, shorter man's neck. "I'll fucking kill you, you piece of fucking shit!"

Pony screamed and scrambled behind the greeting desk.

Henry and Rita intercepted Ian and used all the strength they could muster to keep the huge man from reaching Pony.

"Whoa, hold it there, big guy!" shouted Henry.

Rita added, "No, no, Ian! Kill him and we'll never figure out what's really going on!"

But Ian wasn't giving in. Fortunately, his being under the cloud of weed was keeping his body from reaching its full power and couldn't break through the sober wall of Henry and Rita.

Henry looked at Charlie, who had moved to the floor with his ashen face now completely vacant of any and all color. "Charlie, dude! You got to help us! Are you okay?"

Rita said, "Henry, he doesn't look good at all."

Finally, Ian stopped fighting against Henry and Rita. "Okay, fine! I won't kill the little shit! Now let me go!"

Cautiously, Henry and Rita let Ian go, but stayed between him and Pony just to make sure. Ian sat down on the sofa and rubbed his face with his hands. "What the fuck? That was a lot of fucking money, and we are going to have some really, really pissed-off clients."

Henry sat down next to Ian and said, "I know, Ian. I'm already thinking about that, okay? We'll figure out something."

Rita moved over to Charlie and sat down on her knees in front of Charlie. She could see he looked petrified. "Charlie—honey—you okay?"

Charlie gave no response. He lifted his head and looked at something on the other side of the room. It was like he was staring right through Rita.

Rita turned her head around to see what Charlie was looking at but saw nothing out of the ordinary, nothing that would have his attention. "What is it, Charlie? Say something!"

Pony stood up from behind the desk and put the bowling bag with the radio inside down on the counter. He said, "I know it won't make any difference to either of you, but I'm really, really sorry. I know rationally no one in this room should believe me when I say my dead cousin Claire was in my place talking to me or that because she asked me for the weed I couldn't help but give it to her and take this bag. I know that all of that is bullshit and you think I'm just full of bullshit and that I'm just fucking crazy, fucked up, stoner-head Pony—but…"

"I believe you…" muttered Charlie, his voice high-pitched and distant sounding, but everyone heard it—even Ian.

"You what?" shouted Ian. He shot up to his feet and clenched his fists.

Henry stood up with Ian, ready to block his friend from his friends.

Rita asked Charlie, "You believe Pony? Why?"

Charlie asked Rita, "Help me—stand? Too much of the stuff—too relaxed—"

Rita said, "Of course, honey—of course." Rita put Charlie's arm around her shoulders and stood him up.

"Okay, okay, I'm good. Thanks, Rita. Thanks."

Rita gave Charlie enough space so that he could stand on his own. The color returned to his cheeks and he licked his dry lips wet. He rubbed his own face and stretched the skin a bit to make feeling return to it.

Henry looked at Ian and asked him, "You good, man? You good?"

Ian scoffed and said, "I won't kill him. I mean, it wasn't my money that bastard lost, but if it hurts my paycheck this month I will kill the shaggy-looking motherfucker. Yeah? Okay?"

Henry nodded, "Sounds fair."

Pony looked at Ian with a weak grin and said, "So, I'm good to live as long as you get your regular paycheck? I mean, as long as—"

Ian said, "Let me put it like this, Pony. If this place takes any kind of a financial hit—loss of revenue, closure, drop-off in clientele—as a result of you losing all that Buddha Blend, then you will die, right after you fill out the reams of paperwork for my unemployment insurance."

Pony nodded. "But wait, didn't you tell me you actually don't need this job? Yeah, I mean, last week we were talking about how you very smartly invested almost all your NFL earnings in…"

Ian shouted, "Pony, I will kill you just to kill you if you don't shut the fuck up!"

Henry shouted, "And I'll let him this time!"

Pony put his hands up in mock surrender. "Yeah, right, okay, okay, it's all good guys—all good."

Rita was still focused very intently on Charlie and why he was reacting the way he was to Pony's fuck-up. "Charlie? You said you believe Pony? So, what do you want to do about this?"

Charlie said, "Yes, I believe Pony, because I've seen the dead, too. I see Danny all the time."

Ian scoffed, "Come on, Charlie! You can't compare Danny to this whatever cousin of his! I mean, we all love and miss Danny! We all see him in the work we do here and stuff—"

Charlie looked at Ian and said, "Ian, please. I'm not going to waste time explaining what I mean, okay? And it's pretty shitty to say that Pony's cousin Claire isn't as important to him as Danny is to all of us. Danny was friends with Pony, too! Whatever is going on here is way beyond any of us to understand—right now. The bottom line is we have two problems: a practical one—buying more bricks; and an esoteric one—what is the ghost of Pony's cousin doing giving him a weird radio? We can solve the practical problem. As for the other—I have no idea, right now. What I do know is I have enough cash in the 9-11 safe to cover buying another set of bricks. After I grab it from my place, we'll go to the compound and get the Buddha Blend—that'll be the end of it, okay?"

Pony asked Charlie, "Really, Charlie? You don't hate me? You accept my apology?"

Charlie said, "Pony, it's cool, honestly. Look, whatever happened to you—maybe it'll make sense later. All that matters is that you're okay, we're all okay, and—hey, after we get back with the new bricks maybe we can figure out what all that stuff you guys were talking about with the radio, huh? Now that sounds like a real mystery."

Ian looked at Henry and said, "Charlie sounds kind of weird, don't you think?"

Henry said, "He's baked, dude. Plus, he's right. That radio is the real mystery. I'm definitely looking forward to figuring out what's what with that thing."

Charlie put his hands together as if begging and asked Rita, "Would you please drive? I'm too fucked up!—oh, we need to hit my place first and get what money we need out of the 9-11 safe!"

Rita smiled and shook her head. It was a habit of Charlie's to repeat things when high as well as get loud sometimes when excited. She said, "I'll be happy to drive."

"Great!" shouted Charlie. "Pony will come with us! Henry and Ian will stay here and figure out this radio! It looks like the real mystery! Sound good, guys?"

Henry shrugged his shoulders and said, "No problem for me."

Ian said, "Well, I could hang for a little while, but then I have to split. I have an old teammate who's got this band he's managing. He wanted me to come and see them, give him my opinion. How about maybe after you guys get back you can meet me there? You know, have a few? And listen, Pony, we good?"

Pony ran over to Ian and vigorously shook his hand. "Yeah, man, definitely! Please man! I'd love to buy a round, you know? You forgive me too, man, really?"

Ian struggled to get his hand free of Pony's after the fiftieth shake. "Well, I'm not totally sure about forgive—but we are like family, man."

"Okay, okay," said Pony, "I can live with that, man. That's a lot more than I deserve, I know. I don't know, man, seriously. I just don't know why I did it and I wish I could explain—"

Rita walked over to Pony and grabbed him by the arm. She pulled him away from Ian and towards the salesroom door. "Come on, Pony. Let's quit while we're ahead, shall we?"

Pony nodded in agreement and disappeared through the door with the rushing Rita. That left Charlie with Henry and Ian. Charlie walked up to Henry and hugged him.

"What's that for?" Henry asked.

"For being there when Pony needed you—and for being here, in my life, as a partner." Charlie patted Henry on the cheek. "You're my brother now."

152

Henry smiled and said, "You're my brother, too."

Charlie walked over to Ian, who stepped back and raised his hands in mock fear. "Whoa, dude!—uh—how about we take the affection as given?"

Charlie said, "Ian, don't be afraid of love, man! Arms aren't just meant for tackling and waging war, bro!" Charlie spreads his arms wide. "Now, come on! Give me some love, you cool cat!"

Ian looked at Henry, who looked back and shrugged his shoulders. Ian sighed and hugged Charlie. Charlie really bear-hugged Ian as much as he could, being considerably smaller, and made all the sweet noises a guy who is baked makes when expressing his platonic man-love for another guy. Finally, the hug ended and Charlie walked into the back to join Rita and Pony.

Ian looked at Henry and said, "That is one seriously funky white boy."

Henry said, "Tell me about it. If all white guys were like Charlie, you can bet Reverend Jesse and Reverend Al would be out of a job."

"I hear that," said Ian. "Now, what's this shit about this radio having a fucking eye or something? And no batteries or power cord?"

Henry walked over to the bag. "Yeah, come check this shit out. For the life of me, I can't figure out how the fucker came on and started playing CCR and Phil Collins."

While Henry unzipped the bag and took the radio out, Ian said, "Shit—CCR—fucking Phil Collins? Why couldn't it play some good shit, you know? Like Marvin Gaye or Wilson Pickett?"

Chapter 21

Hollywood Hills, Los Angeles, California

If your impression of Los Angeles and the surrounding areas (including the San Fernando Valley and the Hollywood Hills) is based upon images shown through contrived TV shows titled after zip codes, famous Los Angeles streets or generic geographical features, than you will likely labor under the misapprehension that Hollywood proper and its surrounding areas are geographically flat or swallowed by concrete a la New York, Chicago, Miami or even Dallas, Texas. Nothing could be further from the truth.

Greater Los Angeles is tightly woven around and through the Santa Monica Mountains. The famous Hollywood Hills are part of its foothills. When you live in the Hollywood Hills you live in another world. Far enough above the rabble of Sunset and Ventura Boulevards, you believe you are safe and protected from the scum of humanity. At the same time, the land is vulnerable to rain, mudslides and wildfires, not to mention those howling little bastards called coyotes. Also, at any moment you could lose that two-million-dollar house to force

majeure or a literal Act of God. Since this is the absolute truth
facing anyone who chooses to live in the Hollywood Hills, it's only
rational then to believe that anyone who chooses to live in such a risky
environment is either addicted to edginess, has absolute faith in some
kind of god, or is just fucking nuts; conversely, a person could be all
of these. This latter definition applies to Brother Nathaniel Laurel,
a very successful real estate attorney and faithful Jehovah's Witness
elder of the Hollywood Kingdom Hall.

Once Laurel's jet had landed at the Bob Hope Airport (near
Burbank) following his meeting in Brooklyn with the Governing
Body, he immediately dispatched his assistant Brother Williams to
locate, in person, seven particularly faithful Witnesses whom Laurel
called his Zealots; and have them congregate at Laurel's home in
the Hollywood Hills at ten o'clock that night. No use of electronics
or communication devices were allowed for fear of the Devil
eavesdropping. Laurel handed the keys to his Porsche to Williams so
that he could find all the Zealots, wherever they worked, and get back
to him as quickly as possible. Williams recognized how important his
mission was because he was given this particular car, but he had one
more meeting in mind.

Meanwhile, Laurel took a limousine from the airport to his house
in the Hills. Once he arrived, he went through the house screaming
for his wife Mary and his daughters Rebecca and Esther to meet
with him in his library. Laurel's tone was abrasive and dogmatic. But
his wife and daughters were devotees of Watchtower and dared not
speak a word against their "leader" for fear of reprisal. Instead, they
immediately stopped whatever they were doing to meet with Laurel
in the library to be present before the elder had even sat down in his
recliner.

Without letting his family know in any detail the specifics of
what he spoke to the Governing Body about, Laurel said, "I have
been granted by the Governing Body a most sacred and solemn task.
Nothing I have been asked of at any point in my life, nor in any of
your lives, is as important as what I have now been asked to do."

There was no response, no questions made by the women; in
fact, there was never a sound made by any of these women through
their entire role regarding the mission to retrieve the Augur. After all,
according to whatever teachings the Jehovah's Witnesses used (and
believe you me, they used no teachings of Jesus of Nazareth found

in either the Bible nor any subsequent or previous material), women are just another tool to be used by all-powerful men to carry out the Governing Body's self-serving power games.

As servants to the man, these women were ordered by Laurel to prepare for him a special bath with special ingredients: holy water, oils and flower petals that will purify his mind and body, which they will also wash by hand. Both wife and daughters wore (supposedly) sacred garments and waded into the bath with Laurel and physically washed his body while he recited some kind of arcane sounding prayers. Presumably the prayers were spoken in Aramaic, the language most often credited with being the language spoken during the living days of Christ. But who in Hell knew in what tongue Laurel was speaking? It could have been Klingon for all that his wife and daughters knew. It didn't really matter, anyway. Whatever this self-styled servant of Jehovah (aka megalomaniac) thought was happening to him in the bath, at best it was preparing his ego to withstand the oncoming battle for the Augur, at worst it was practicing incest. Either way, Brother Laurel thought he was getting ready to commune with the Host to locate the powerful relic and destroy those who presently held it.

As make-believe as this all sounds, it is what groups like the Jehovah's Witnesses believe is not only their right, but their duty to fulfill the will of their deity. All apocalyptic sects and/or cults rooted in Judeo-Christianity have their origins in the Western European tradition of Christian Mysticism. Although Mysticism is a world-wide phenomenon and appears in all major belief systems, Christian mystics believe that they can achieve a state of ecstasy wherein they directly connect with the God-head or his servants (aka The Host, Angels, etc.) and become, as it were, the medium or channel for God's Will. Imagine if the Holy Spirit could be ordered up through your cable's On-Demand system. The irony is that these modern-day apocalyptic mystics will espouse the most humble of messages and, in many cases, actually put themselves down in order to create the falsehood that they are nothing until that Holy Spirit takes them over and makes them a bad-ass. The truth is that nothing is more arrogant than to think that any genetically unstable creature like a human could even for a moment carry inside their form a portion of all-creation without physically blowing to pieces. But these idiots think they can and they think they do, and moreover, people give them money to carry on the sideshow. Men like Laurel not only carry on this kind of scam, but actually believes he is that medium for the Holy Spirit.

By the time the incestuous bath is finished, Brother Nathaniel Laurel's brain was well into its fugue state of being "Jehovah's Instrument." His wife and daughters, once out of the tub, bowed to the human tool and then dressed Laurel in some kind of vestments that looked like a 1980s New Romantic take on the robes worn by the same Cardinals who had dispatched Father Agosto after the same Augur.

Once dressed, Laurel looked to his wife and motioned with his fingers for her to give him something. She took off from around her neck a golden chain on which hung a key. She placed the key and chain in Laurel's hand. Laurel dismissed his family and walked alone to a door next to his private study. He used the key to unlock the door. After removing the key, he put the chain around his neck and hid the key inside his shirt. He opened the door to reveal a staircase that led down to a room beneath the surface of the mountain.

When Laurel reached the end of the staircase, he faced a door made out of iron and stone covered with many ancient sigils and symbols specific to some long dead Mystery Religion. Laurel raised his hands with palms facing the door, lowered his head and prayed. Once done, he placed his hands on the door and with little effort, pushed the door open to reveal a pitch-black chamber.

As Laurel entered the chamber, six oil sconces set into the walls of the chamber suddenly burst to light. The walls, like the door, were covered with etchings and artwork reflecting all sorts of symbols that harkens of a more primitive pagan time. Naked women and animal-headed men entwined in all sorts of peculiar sexual positions enhance the forests, mountains and unusual ancient structures. The only "thing" in the room appears to be a stand or pillar that rises to a height of five feet and stops. A bowl, or more precisely a grail, sits atop the pillar. There is nothing inside the grail.

Laurel continued to recite prayers as he walked up to the pillar and touched the rim of the grail with his index fingers. Suddenly, the bottom of the bowl separated and out from the pillar rose a wooden box that looked really old and really important. Laurel lifted the lid of the box and took out a mirror with four lines of cocaine and a razor blade on it. He also took a rolled-up fifty dollar bill out of the box. Closing the lid, Laurel put the mirror down and used the fifty to quickly sniff two of the lines of coke.

"Thank fucking God!" shouted Laurel. Then he sniffed the other two lines of coke. He picked up the stray powder on the mirror with his finger and ran it along the top of his gums, sucking whatever he could off his finger.

Once he was done, Laurel put everything including the bill back into the box. He put the box back into the center of the bowl and touched the sides of the bowl so that it once again opened. The box fell back into the opening and something different rose up from where the box first had appeared. It was a small control panel of some kind, like a mounted remote control.

Laurel pushed the top two buttons on the panel and the sounds of whirring accompanied several panels opening in the erotic walls of the chamber to reveal large monitors—seven in total. All of which receive their feeds directly from the same satellites as those used by Watchtower Command Center in Brooklyn. But unlike the feeds monitored by Watchtower, Laurel's are only linked to Los Angeles and about eighty-eight percent of the rest of Southern California.

Laurel grabbed the command panel and dislodged it from the pillar so that he held it like a giant remote. He stood next to the pillar, which was an equal distance from all the monitors and began to switch between the multiple feeds, as if getting an overall feel for the technology and how he will use it.

Elsewhere in Burbank

Out on the streets, since leaving the Burbank Airport in Laurel's Porsche, it's a whole other experience for Brother Williams. There was no bathing, no vestments, no cocaine and no daughters to touch your naked body. Of course Williams had no desire for any woman to bathe him, but he could think of at least one very significant person with whom he would like to bathe. Unfortunately, there was no time for Williams to think about the man called Barker, assistant to Laurel's rival and sworn enemy the SDA. Brother Williams had to find those seven Zealots and he had to find them now.

Oh, and now that it's been revealed that Brother Laurel and all his "mystical" antics and deeply-held Christian beliefs are a crock of shit (other than being a great beard for his drug habit and lust for power and money), it can be revealed that Laurel named his seven Zealots not for the generic definition of fanatically faithful but after the original Jewish Zealots who, during the time of the Roman occupation of the Holy Land, were forever attempting to revolt and oftentimes committed murder or crimes that irritated the Roman Governors.

"Having such warriors at one's command is helpful for trying to keep your real intentions obscured," was what Laurel once told another Jehovah's Witness elder whom he trusted to know his real reason for faith. Now the Zealots were themselves the most genuinely brainwashed—uh—faithful followers in the Jehovah's Witness sect. If they were to ever think their leader(s) were not as faithful, it would be like learning that Jesus was really the Serpent who had been yanking the world's testicles since day one.

Not being able to use the "communication devices" for the reasons that any such signal could be intercepted by pretty much any bush-league technology, it took Williams a total of four hours to round up all the Zealots and get them heading over to Laurel's house in the Hills. And let me tell you something, it wasn't like Lauren, Adrina, Stephanie, Brody, Spencer and Heidi gathering for a party in the Hills when these seven lunatics showed up at the door wearing nothing but black suits, ties and carrying one briefcase each. They were polite though, to Laurel's wife and daughters. Each of them entered and stood by the door next to the study, not speaking a word, until all seven Zealots and Brother Williams were present.

When Williams showed up with the last of the Zealots, the door opened as if by magic (just monitoring by Laurel below and then opened electronically). The eight men descended the staircase and saw the creepy iron and stone door. It also opened on its own to reveal the even creepier chamber, which to the seven Zealots was like walking onto the bridge of the Starship Enterprise set for a Trekkie (or Trekker, as they prefer to be called).

Williams was less impressed but never let anyone else detect it. He simply smiled in awe and joined his boss who watched in gleeful mania at how orgasmic the Zealots appeared to be reacting, without completely losing their cool, of course. I mean, let's not forget they are the best of the best and no warrior of Jehovah could ever totally lose their cool. Williams watched his borderline boss observe the devotion of the Zealots for a few more minutes before he nudged Laurel and pointed to the door still open. Laurel nodded to Williams and he hit the remote control that had been opening and closing every damn thing in the house since taking it off the pillar.

When the door closed the Zealots all looked to the Elder Laurel, and from wherever they were standing in the room went down on one knee and bowed their heads to Laurel.

"Hail, Elder Laurel! Hail, the voice of Jehovah's Will!"

Laurel tried not to let his smile get too damn big, and Williams tried not to vomit in his mouth.

Laurel reached out with his hands just above his head and said, "Zealots, you are Jehovah's Swords, chosen by the Lord Jesus Christ Himself, through me, to deliver unto my hands and then to the hands of our sacred and solemn Governing Body, the single most wicked and destructive instrument ever built by the Antichrist Beast in the fires of hellish Babylon!"

The Zealots shouted at the top of their lungs!

It made Williams jump, because he wasn't expecting it, at least not at the ungodly volume reached by the seven voices.

Laurel continued, "This object is of one name as are all those things of and cast out of Heaven. It is called Augur! A word that reveals the truth of our world's future—a gift given only by from God—stolen by the Devil—of the Apocalypse! Yes, my Brothers! The Augur can foresee—foretell of the future! In the wrong hands—in the hands of the Antichrist Beast—it can change the world! It could destroy all mankind and the whole of the Earth before the appointed time!"

Again, the Zealots shouted at the top of their lungs!

This time Williams didn't jump, but he crept a bit back into some heavy shadows so he could cover his aching ears. But his boss and the Zealots weren't finished. Laurel continued to rant some more about needing to get the Augur before their enemies got it and how they had to eviscerate whoever it was that presently had the damn thing. But when Laurel mentioned who those enemies might be specifically, and brought up the arch-rival of the Jehovah's Witness—Seventh-day Adventists—all it made Williams think about was how wonderful it would be to see Barker again, to be inside Barker again, and to have Barker inside him again.

That's when Williams knew what he had to do—what he was being called to do—in his heart by God—his God, whatever that kind of God would turn out to be.

160

Laurel said, "As you can see, my Zealots, we have technology here given to us directly by God—so, yeah, this is clean technology, okay? This is not bad technology! Good technology!"

The Zealots repeated, "Good technology."

"That's right! Good technology, which is tied to the very powerful systems of the Governing Body from Watchtower itself. Watchtower is currently monitoring the whole of this city, Los Angeles, wherein we know the Augur and its evil possessors are located. Once they have located it, they will notify us and I will dispatch you to recover it!

"Are you ready? Are you ready to fight the Devil's forces?"

The Zealots shouted their agreement!

Williams motioned for Laurel to speak to him off to the side. Laurel went up to Williams and asked, "What is it?"

"Elder Laurel, perhaps it would be prudent to put me back out on the streets and let me observe our hated enemy the SDA, so that if they make motions towards the Augur or have any way to trace it like Watchtower—"

Laurel interrupted Williams with, "Yes, yes, I understand what you're suggesting and I agree that it would be prudent. Good thinking, Williams. Take my Porsche, and keep your mobile on and clear, understand?"

Williams said, "Yes, elder," and was out the big iron and stone door before any of the Zealots noticed he was gone.

Completely ignorant to Williams' ulterior motives, Laurel turned his attention back to his Zealots, whom he continued to pump up by having them take their Bibles out of their briefcases and take turns reading scripture out loud. While they did this, Laurel looked to the monitors and the feeds from Watchtower Command Central hoping and praying that at any moment the signal would be sent that the Augur had been located. He salivated with the thought that he was going to be able to get his hands on the Augur first, that his own personal squad of fanatics would slaughter anyone in their way, and even protect him should he decide to use the Augur to broker his own opportunity with the Governing Body.

Chapter 22

Washington, District of Columbia

The private jet chartered by the SDA church sat idle on the tarmac of Ronald Reagan Washington International Airport waiting for its most important passengers: the self-esteemed SDA V.P. Carl Eiderbrook and his quietly sexually-conflicted assistant Kyle Barker. They had been held up at the world headquarters when the president of the SDA himself called to discuss the matter of locating and obtaining the Augur before anyone else could.

"You understand, Carl, that we are at a disadvantage," noted the president on the video conference with Eiderbrook.

"Begging your pardon, Sir, but I'm not entirely sure what you mean by disadvantage?" asked Eiderbrook.

The president answered, "Your faith in the SDA is commendable, Carl, but the facts are these: we are not the Vatican and we do not have the material resources to the extent of our primary opponent Watchtower."

"I appreciate your point, Mr. President, and I think I could agree if I didn't genuinely have faith that it is the SDA's destiny to possess the Augur."

"Really?" asked the president with a tone of genuine curiosity.

"Absolutely, Mr. President, if you wouldn't mind?—" Eiderbrook put up a finger so that the president could see it.

"Please," said the president, using his own fingers to signal Eiderbrook to do whatever he needed to with a wave.

Eiderbrook stood up and went to the bookshelf next to his desk. He quickly scanned the books and pulled out the one he needed. Taking the book back to his desk, he sat and opened it so that he could read to the president what he found inside. "Inside this text written by Forefathers Crosier and Hahn, a magnificent study and interpretation of Ezekiel, I believe they directly reference the Augur—"

The president interrupted Eiderbrook with a shocking, "How? How could they have known about this relic when no Protestant groups mentioned even knowing of its existence until 1910?"

"That's what they explain, Sir, by saying they didn't physically know. They had a vision—a shared vision—in the days immediately following the Great Disappointment—

(Sorry, just have to interject at this point: yes, this was literally a really big disappointment by the entire SDA community of that time, because they had reached the date predicted by their then-leaders for Armageddon—but, of course—well, we're all still here, right? So see, they were disappointed because none of them croaked—no Armageddon means no-second-coming of Christ which means no salvation and they all burn in Hell.)

Eiderbrook continued: "So many were left despairing, but Father Crosier received a vision from the angel Uriel—who was the same angel that spoke to the Prophet Ezekiel—who spoke of a device that would determine the true date for Christ's second coming. He spoke of it specifically as a device born of both Holy and unholy blood and bone to make it greater than all others, and that is held within the very Holy Spirit born of Christ as God worked through him—"

The president stopped Eiderbrook again and said, "Whoa! Whoa! Are you saying that the text you have reveals Arianism as the truth?— delivered by Archangel Uriel himself?"

"That is what Crosier and Hahn contend, Mr. President."

"And how—erm—how is that we do not know of this already?— that you alone have brought this text to my attention?"

Eiderbrook said, "I believe there are two main reasons, Sir. First, it does not stand well for the SDA to be accepted as a legitimate Trinitarian denomination if it is discovered that the first Forefathers had scriptural truth of the Trinity being false. Second, if this text were brought to general knowledge within the SDA, it could cause a schism from which the church might never recover."

"Good reasons, Carl, but how is it you know this?"

"Mr. President, you put me in charge of relic recovery for a reason—I am good. I had my assistant Barker go through texts we discovered over the last few years to find out what, if any, indication they give to the Augur. This text was only discovered last April in a barn in Illinois."

The president rubbed his chin and looked like he was fighting to contain his excitement. "And according to this, we have a claim that both through a vision from Uriel and the fact that we know the nature of the construction of the Augur—both Christian and pagan—but still containing the Holy Spirit—that proves that Christ was not greater than God—that the Trinity is a lie! The Adventists of old were right! We were right and everyone else is wrong!"

Eiderbrook smiled. "Yes, Sir, that is why I believe we have nothing to worry about from the greater resources of our enemies."

"Yes," said the president, "Indeed, Carl. You have shown me that we have both providence and prophecy on our side."

Eiderbrook added, "Crosier and Hahn could not both have been wrong, because Uriel itself chose our Adventists to know of the Augur."

The president nodded. He said, "You have proven that you alone have the right, the power and the grace to do this job, Eiderbrook. Whatever you need from me, from the church, it is yours."

Eiderbrook said, "Sir, I need a jet to take me to Los Angeles. I have no doubt that it is where I will find the Augur. But I will need to have our best technological minds compile the list of materials and resources I will need to carry out my mission. With these items I can trace the frequency with which the Augur receives its divine word."

"We can do that? We can trace it?"

Eiderbrook said, "This is how Watchtower and the Vatican will be tracing it, no doubt. I will also need to enlist the Light Warriors."

The president's eyes went wide and his jaw dropped. "The Light Warriors—are you sure?"

"Absolutely, Mr. President."

"Won't that result in bloodshed—lots and lots of—I mean, buckets of—these guys can create absolute tubs full—are you absolutely sure you'll meet with that kind of violent resistance?"

164

Eiderbrook nodded his head and spoke in a very deep, very confident voice. "I hate to say it, Sir, but I do. I have no doubt that the lust and avarice others have over the power of this relic will lead them to the heights of sin and wanton destruction. We need our Light Warriors to ensure minimal damage and casualties, as well as the clean recovery of the relic. I promise you, Sir, I will not unleash them in an offensive way—only in defense."

The president said, "I shall authorize them to be sent to Los Angeles and under your personal directive." The SDA president signed off.

Eiderbrook sat back and exhaled loudly. He smiled and clapped his hands. As if activated via the Clapper, the door to his office opened and Barker entered.

"Yes, Sir?" asked Barker.

"We're going to LA, Barker, and we are going to be getting everything we need to recover the Augur. I am going to send you—"

Barker interrupted Eiderbrook and asked, "LA? Did you say LA?"

"Yes, you idiot, that's what I said!"

"I see. I see." Barker was excited for another reason all together but had already made one mistake by interrupting his boss. So he diligently kept his mouth shut while Eiderbrook began listing the steps he needed Barker to follow in preparation for their mission. Barker knew he had to follow the instructions perfectly for fear of Eiderbrook's wrath. But something was bugging Barker too much to ignore, so he asked Eiderbrook, "Um—Sir, I don't mean to tell you I was eavesdropping on the call to the president or anything, but did I hear you right?—um—did you mention the Light Warriors?"

"I did, Barker, but I already put a call into Iverson about them in Los Angeles. They'll be waiting for us when we land. Now, get on with those preparations I gave you, right now!"

"Yes, Sir! Yes, Sir!" and Barker was gone.

By the time Eiderbrook and Barker arrived at Ronald Reagan Washington International Airport and boarded their private jet, Barker had spent the last few hours getting all the resources into motion so that when they arrived in Los Angeles, they would have the technology Eiderbrook required to track down the Augur.

Bob Hope Airport, Burbank, California

Eiderbrook and Barker's private jet landed no less than forty-five minutes after the Jehovah's Witness' private jet carrying Brother Laurel and Brother Williams had landed. In fact, the two jets had come in on the same runway and after Eiderbrook and Barker disembarked, would both be parked in the same private hanger. It would seem coincidence had a sense of humor.

What was different for Eiderbrook and Barker when they disembarked their jet was being welcomed by a tall man in a solid black camouflage uniform with a military-style buzz cut and wearing sunglasses (at night—Cory Hart style). He walked across the tarmac to meet them after climbing out of an unmarked, government-plated, black Jeep SUV. Because the windows were blacked out in the SUV, the number of people, if any, who had accompanied him was uncertain—other than a driver, which could be assumed because this man exited from the front passenger's door.

He stood and waited for Eiderbrook with a cold steely expression. He shook his hand when Eiderbrook reached him.

Eiderbrook said, "Iverson, good to see you."

"And you, Mr. Vice-president. Your ride is this way," and motioned towards the SUV.

Eiderbrook raised a finger to Iverson and turned to Barker. "Rent a car and ascertain what the JWs are doing, understand? Then meet us back at Iverson's compound no later than eleven p.m. Do you have the address?"

"Yes, Sir, it's in my cell."

"Good."

Barker headed off towards the closest terminal, while Eiderbrook followed Iverson to his SUV.

Eiderbrook asked Iverson, "Have you already gathered them?"

"I had them at my place and ready for debriefing an hour after you called. Five came with me. The rest are back at the compound practicing and running maneuvers."

Eiderbrook nodded. "Good. Good. And you have arranged for the full ordinance we discussed?"

They reached the SUV and Iverson opened the front passenger door for Eiderbrook. "I have everything you asked for. It will be ready for your review when we get there."

While Eiderbrook climbed into the SUV, a near-clone of Iverson exited through the driver's door and climbed into the back of the SUV. Iverson closed Eiderbrook's door and walked around the front to take the driver's seat.

Inside the SUV, Eiderbrook could see that there were three men in the seat directly behind them and two more men in seats added to the rear of the SUV. All of them looked like clones of Iverson, save for minor hair color differences and some differences in the bone structure of their faces. But seeing as they were all wearing sunglasses there was no difference detected in their eyes.

Iverson punched the ignition button and drove off the tarmac at high speed.

Eiderbrook pointed to his eyes and said, "Sunglasses—your sunglasses?—how?"

Iverson touched the frames of his glasses and said, "Chromographic lenses, Sir. We can see the entire color spectrum, which also includes digital transmission and information feed on everything we see. The monitors back at the compound see what we see."

Eiderbrook nodded and said, "That's cool. That's cool. Do—um—they?—"

"No, Sir—the heretical JWs don't have these. Custom designed these myself, Sir."

"Excellent, most excellent. Do you?—um—think you could?—"

Iverson reached past Eiderbrook and punched the glove compartment button. It dropped open and an extra pair of chromo-glasses dropped out and into Iverson's hand. He held them out for Eiderbrook. "Yours, Sir."

Eiderbrook smiled and nodded his head, "All right." He put them on and flipped down the cover of the lighted mirror in his visor and checked himself out. "Yeah, these are fucking sweet!"

"Yes, Sir, they are."

Through the glasses Eiderbrook could not only make out the detail of everything either cloaked in darkness or fully lit, but he could see information being scrolled digitally along the edges of his vision that provided him full information on whatever he was looking at.

It took another hour to reach Iverson's compound, which lay west of Calabasas between the Malibu Mar Vista and Monte Nido regions of the Santa Monica Mountains. It was well buried from ordinary view, helped by the ridiculous cost of development in that region of

Los Angeles County. It was unlikely that anyone would come across, let alone be bothered by any activity in the compound, even though it was no more than a forty-minute drive to the hustle and bustle of the Santa Monica Pier.

As the SUV drove through the gates and up the steep roadway to the front of the main house, Eiderbrook was awed by the spectacular combination of Spartan efficiency and modern-day technology to create what might well be the paradigm for Adventists' vision of how to prepare for the Rapture.

"It's fantastic, Iverson—absolutely fantastic."

"Thank you, Sir."

As the SUV stopped in front of the main doors, two fully-armed and body-armored sentries emerged from seemingly nowhere to open both the driver and passenger doors, allowing Eiderbrook and Iverson to step out without lifting a finger.

Eiderbrook asked Iverson, "Is the gate below the only barrier between them and us?"

Iverson answered, "Oh no, Sir, you wouldn't have seen it coming in. There is an invisible electronic wall halfway between the main gate and the house. It's something similar to what the Republicans proposed for the border, but our gate is much better and actually exists."

Eiderbrook said, "Those retards and their Tea Party lackeys are fools not to listen to our advice and take our assistance."

Iverson replied, "Soon enough they will be begging for our leadership."

"You are always looking towards the future without sacrificing the present, Iverson, and I admire that."

"Thank you, Sir."

"Now, take me to see the Light Warriors?"

"You see seven of them here, Sir—the five who accompanied us and the two out here. Follow me and I'll show you the others."

Iverson took the lead as they entered the main house. Eiderbrook followed with the five men from the SUV. The two men outside remained as sentries.

Eiderbrook continued to inspect the house as they walked through its expansive hallways and spacious rooms, marveling at the minimal furniture, décor and distractions. Whatever décor was present reflected the apocalyptic visions of the Rapture, Tribulation, evil Babylon and forthcoming New Jerusalem as interpreted by SDA interpretation of Revelations and Old Testament prophecy. Some of the artwork appeared truly graphic and nightmarish, with a particular emphasis on sexual deviancy and physical torture—in particular of women and even children—at the hands of absurdly muscular creatures with animal and demon heads. Why this was the case might only be answered by the artist, although it could also be a peculiar fixation of Iverson, as it was his property.

Whatever Iverson's proclivities represented in the distribution of object d'art, mural and statuary, Eiderbrook didn't care. He was certain he had a man here who would follow any instruction, without question, that was necessary to retrieve the Augur.

As Iverson reached the other end of the main house he opened a set of French doors that revealed a huge balcony that overlooked several courts and arenas in which were assembled no fewer than ten men each, for a total of forty to fifty men, practicing a variety of hand-to-hand combat and weapons training.

Eiderbrook walked to the railing and looked down onto the Light Warriors in training. He smiled the smile of a power-hungry megalomaniac who was seeing for the very first time his goal of kicking the other guy's ass all over the playground coming to fruition.

Iverson asked, "I gather from your expression this is what you were hoping to see, Mr. Vice-president?"

Eiderbrook answered, "Oh yes, Iverson. I don't think seeing Angelina Jolie naked, covered in baby oil in my bed could give me more wood than I have right now."

Iverson looked back at the five men who had followed them in and saw them look at him. None of them showed an expression of either approval or distaste at Eiderbrook's metaphor.

Eiderbrook looked back at Iverson and said, "Loosen up, idiots! We might be believers but it doesn't mean we don't get horny!"

Iverson said, "We have no problem with that, Sir. It's just that Light Warriors don't have the luxury of such sexual distractions."

"Of course not," said Eiderbrook. "So tell me, Iverson, is there anything the JWs have that can in anyway match what you have shown me today?"

"Our intel on what both the JWs and the Vatican have dispatched is limited, but from what I have heard the JW forces are no match for our Light Warriors, and the Vatican disbanded their greatest fighting force almost a thousand years ago. I sincerely believe we have nothing at all to be concerned with."

Eiderbrook laughed out loud, "I can't wait! I can't wait to get that Augur in our hands! Ours!"

"The streets of the city will run red with blood, Mr. Vice-president."

"Do you promise, Iverson? Do you promise?"

"Oh yes, Sir. Whoever has that Augur and is foolish enough to get in our way will meet the dark lord Satan himself when we send them to Hell."

Eiderbrook laughed the laugh of madmen and really, really bad guys. It echoed across the mountains surrounding the compound.

The Other Side of the Hill, Los Angeles

Unbeknownst to the SDA Vice-president and his army of Adventist soldiers, his assistant Barker had left Burbank and was combing the streets of Los Angeles and the surrounding area to do as he was asked: find the Jehovah's Witness' operation and get what information he could about them. However, Barker was more interested in finding just one Witness in particular. While driving a rental car through Glendale, he dialed the number of that Witness and got an answer on his mobile.

"Hello," spoke Brother Williams in a soft voice.

"It's me," answered Barker in an even softer voice.

"Oh God, it's so great to hear your voice. I've missed you so much, but I can't talk long. My boss has called for no communication devices to be used, so—"

"Then meet me—right now. I can't wait."

"Okay, do you know Pink's on La Brea in Hollywood?"

"Pink's? Is that some kind of joke about us being?—"

Barker laughed and said, "No, no!—just a coincidence, I promise. I grew up not far from LA, and during the summers it was my favorite guilty pleasure—best hot chili-dog in the world! You really haven't heard of it?"

"Now you're joking, right? What's Watchtower's view on us watching too much TV, reading too much news, knowing too much about—"

"Right, right—fair enough. I'm going to get off the line so I can find some place to pull over and send you the directions from where you are."

"I'm texting my location—can't wait to see you!"

"Me too! See you soon." Barker hung up immediately. He found an empty parking lot in a business complex and pulled into it. He parked the car but didn't turn off the engine. Looking at his cell he saw the text from Williams giving him his location. Barker quickly sent instructions to Williams' phone via a map-app so that he'd know exactly how to reach Pink's. Before he could receive confirmation of Williams getting directions, he took the SIM card out of the back of his mobile and tossed it out the window. He then reached into his pants pocket and took out a fresh one which he placed in the phone. He slipped the mobile in his jacket pocket and headed towards Brand Boulevard which he could take to connect with a series of other city streets until he hit La Brea in Hollywood.

After Williams studied the information sent by Barker, he did the same with the SIM card in his phone. He had just left his boss with the Zealots in the Hollywood Hills house and was able to reach Pink's much sooner than Barker. And while he waited for his lover to arrive, Williams began to think about how he and Barker could work together to get their hands on the Augur and use it as a bargaining tool against their bosses and the terrifying sects to which they both belonged, to ensure that they could be together forever.

Chapter 23

Calabasas, California

By the time Rita, Pony and Charlie arrived at the front gates to Buddha Jesus' compound, Charlie's buzz from his early afternoon with Ian was gone. He went quiet about halfway through the trip, and being seated in the front passenger's seat, Rita and Pony noticed that the buzz-happy Charlie was gone and that pensive Charlie had returned. His expression told them that Charlie was working out what options were available for dealing with Buddha, but neither of them could imagine for even a moment what they were.

Fortunately, as Rita looked to the back seat at Pony who met her gaze, they knew they could trust that whatever decision he would make would be a much more grounded, practical and intelligent choice than either of them thought they could choose. That's why they were both very, very surprised when Charlie asked, "Pony, do you have a fatty?"

"Excuse me?"

Charlie turned around to look at Pony with a look as serious as Pony could ever remember. Then Charlie insisted, "A fatty—big fucking spliff?"

"Um—yeah, right—uh—" Pony searched his fanny pack for a joint.

Rita asked Charlie, "You sure you should do this before?—"

Charlie looked at Rita and cut her off with a firm hand on her knee, "Rita, trust me. I need this before we go in there."

Pony produced a tightly wound joint, which he lit and took a drag from to get it nice and going, then he handed it to Charlie. Charlie took a good long drag and held it in for quite a few seconds. He offered it to Rita, who knew she did not want to be the only one of the three not high when they went inside.

Being intelligent smokers, even Pony, the three did not take too much. None of them wanted to be in-orbit. Instead, they had a measure amount from which years of using had become instinctive, so that when each had the right amount in their systems they killed the roach. Pony placed it back inside his fanny pack where it would be safe and sound. Now they were calm, focused and anxiety-free, which is a good state to be in when you're about to face the most dangerous drug dealer west of the Mississippi.

"Do it," Charlie told Rita.

Rita reached out of the car window and pressed the call button on the intercom post.

"Yes?" It was Claudia's voice.

Charlie cringed a bit when he heard it—one word was all he needed. And believe me, we've all had that relationship that left such scars that no matter how long it's been since we've seen that someone or heard their voice, our balls (and I mean literally) shrink into the safety of our body.

"Claudia, it's Rita, Pony and—um—Charlie to see the Buddha?"

"Charlie? Charlie's with you?"

Rita sighed and shook her head. Under her breath she mumbled, "Jesus above, why the fuck do I have to?—" and Rita looked over at Charlie and motioned for him to speak directly into the intercom.

Charlie dropped his head and swung it from side to side a few times, then unbuckled his seatbelt, leaned over Rita and said through the window, "Hey Claudia, it's me. Is the Buddha around to talk with?"

There was no immediate response.

Charlie looked at Rita whose face was only inches from his, their lips so close they could feel each other's breath, and his shoulder was brushing her breasts. Charlie looked very uncomfortable but that could have been simply because of his weird position. Rita, on the other hand, was clearly nervous because she was having a very hard time not being affected by her attraction for Charlie and his being so fucking close to her.

Pony noticed nothing between them and was simply looking out the windows at the surrounding landscape.

"Sorry," Charlie whispered to Rita.

"No, no, no—it's all good, really." Rita swallowed and it was quite audible.

Claudia spoke again saying, "Okay, come on in. He'll see you."

The gates electronically unlocked and then rolled open.

Charlie sat back in his seat, smiling at Rita. Rita finally relaxed and wiped her forehead and neck of sweat. She drove through the open gates and up the long driveway to the front of the compound's main house. Rita parked the car directly in front of the long steps that lead up to the porch and turned off the engine. She looked at Charlie, who looked at her and smiled.

Rita grabbed his arm and squeezed it gently, "Charlie, you can't reason with this guy. You know that, right? The whole reincarnated Lama, Buddhism thing is just bullshit. He's a psycho."

Charlie patted Rita's hand and said, "I'm not stupid, Rita. I know Jesus isn't what he thinks he is. But he thinks he is, so he is."

Rita shook her head. "What?"

Charlie said, "I'm not afraid of dying, either."

Pony crossed his arms and said, "Yeah, I'm not afraid of dying too, but I am afraid of your psycho-ex. I mean she's got to be the hottest creature, easily on par with Adriana Lima. But dude, she's the one who could cause real damage."

Charlie looked back at Pony and said, "That makes more sense than being afraid of Buddha."

Pony looked out the window and saw Claudia walk out of the front doors. "Speak of the she-devil."

Claudia stopped at the top of the steps and looked out across the distance at the group of stoners she was once a part of.

Charlie looked out the window and for a moment swore that Claudia, even at that distance, met his eyes with hers.

Rita lowered her head and leaned over Charlie's lap to look out and see Claudia. "God I hate that fucking bitch."

174

Charlie asked, "Why? Why waste your time with hating her, Rita? You've got a better heart than that."

"Because you weren't the only one she betrayed when she broke up with you and went to work for that psycho. She was my friend and I introduced you two. She broke your heart because of me."

Pony said, "That's her bullshit, Rita. No one blames you for that."

"Pony's right," agreed Charlie. "I don't blame you."

"I know that, but she thinks because she's Peruvian and I'm Mexican she's like, superior or something—hag. And I hate that she and I used to room at that convent school. God, she makes me sick!"

Charlie said, "Let it go, Rita. Your grudge against Claudia—that was all a million years ago. We need to get in there and get back with the blend before Claudia gets suspicious as to why we're sitting in here doing nothing."

Rita opened her door first. "Fine, let's get in there and get out."

Charlie and Pony followed Rita and they all walked up the steps to meet Claudia, who kept her eyes locked on one person and one person only—

"Charles," spoke Claudia in a long, sexy tone.

"Hello, Claudia."

Rita sighed loudly and rolled her head around.

"You look good," said Claudia while looking up and down his torso slowly and purposefully. "Have you dropped weight? Looks like at least twenty pounds."

Before Charlie could respond, Rita piped up with, "Yeah, he dropped the emotional bullshit you left him with, Claudia."

Claudia looked past Charlie to Rita.

Pony slapped his hands on his face and grunted.

Claudia said, "Couldn't use it to get into his pants, Rita?"

Rita grimaced and clenched her teeth. She balled her hands into fists and started to move past Charlie.

Charlie stopped Rita and said, "Claudia, Rita, no games! We're here on business!"

Through the main doors and onto the porch stepped Buddha Jesus in his full lama vestments. The bright yellow and red colors shone lavishly and wholly contradictory to the reality of this man being a drug dealer and killer.

"Claudia!" shouted Buddha Jesus.

Everyone looked at Buddha Jesus.

"Charlie's right. This is business. Please, put your passions in check."

Claudia said nothing else. She stepped aside and let Charlie, Rita and Pony walk past her and through the door following Buddha Jesus.

However, Rita could not resist throwing a quick glance at Claudia as she walked past her, to silently tell her she had not forgiven her for her part in their friendship ending. Claudia quickly returned the look, but then gave her full attention to her ex-boyfriend.

Once everyone was inside the large foyer, Buddha Jesus turned around to face the group and stopped them walking with a raised hand. Clearly he didn't want them coming any farther into his massive house. "Why are you here again so soon? I know you couldn't have smoked all of it yourselves? And I can't remember the last time I saw you here, Charles Hamor."

Charlie looked at Pony, who knew that Charlie was silently reminding him it was entirely his fault that Charlie was there in front of Buddha. Pony was embarrassed and decided to avoid Charlie's eyes. So for the first time, Pony took a really good look around Buddha's foyer. It was lovely.

Charlie knew he had gotten through to Pony and so turned his eyes back to business and Buddha Jesus. He said, "Well, Buddha, you might be seeing a lot more of me. I'm here to get more Buddha Blend. I need eight bricks, and I have the money—" Charlie reached into his jean jacket and took a money bag out of an inside pocket.

Buddha raised a hand and said, "I'm more than happy to provide you with another eight bricks, and I know you have the money for it, but—well, my spirit feels there is something unusual taking place with you. It's something I can't help but be curious about. We've always had a system, a routine, and in the last two years you've never deviated from that routine until now. Why?"

Charlie handed the money bag out to Buddha and said, "It's nothing you need to concern yourself with, Buddha, I promise. Believe me when I say that nothing like this will happen again."

But Buddha didn't take the money bag. In fact, he motioned for Claudia to come around and stand next to him. She did. Then Buddha motioned with both arms, which made Charlie, Rita and Pony look around them with their faces showing shock and worry. Their bodies tensed up and the three instinctively drew closer to each other.

Eight armed gunmen entered the foyer. They surrounded Charlie, Rita and Pony with Buddha and Claudia completing their circle.

"What the fuck is this, Buddha?" shouted Rita.

Before Buddha could answer, Charlie grabbed Rita's hand and said, "It's okay, Rita. Let's not lose our cool. It's all we've got."

"Ah, but that's not what I understand," said Buddha.

"What do you mean?" asked Charlie.

It was dead quiet as Claudia stepped forward and walked up to Charlie. She got so close to his face everyone thought she might be kissing him, but she didn't. Instead, she studied his face, his eyes, his lips, his nostrils, even his ears. It was like she was inspecting a newly made piece of equipment for quality clearance.

"What the fuck are you doing?" Rita asked her.

Claudia ignored the question. Her eyes and mind were focused entirely on delving as deeply as she could into the darkness of Charlie's pupils, the windows to his soul, which she did at one time know more intimately than any human being ever could. But whatever that intimacy was could not tell her what Charlie might be hiding from her boss.

Pony's expression turned to real fear and he began to jitter.

Claudia ended it by giving Charlie the tiniest of smiles followed by a wink.

Charlie crinkled his nose and furrowed his brow. Clearly he had no idea what the hell was going on.

Claudia walked back to Buddha Jesus and said, "Sorry to say, Buddha, but he doesn't have any idea what you're talking about."

Buddha suddenly grabbed Claudia's chin by the hand and tightly squeezed it. He flipped her head around so that he was staring straight into her cringing eyes. Her whole body squirmed and she tried not to scream in pain from the painful pressure applied by his fingers on her chin. "You wouldn't be trying to protect this former love of yours, would you?"

"No," Claudia whimpered. "I don't—him—not lying for him—"

Rita snickered.

In a voice both loud and authoritative Charlie said, "Chill Buddha! Shamatha!" Its power shocked everyone in the foyer—but none as much as Buddha Jesus.

Buddha Jesus looked at Charlie, still holding and squeezing Claudia's chin even harder. "What did you say to me?"

Charlie looked Buddha in the eye and with a calm, even voice said, "Shamatha, my brother—abiding calm—and Vipashyana—see it clearly, man."

Buddha smiled and released Claudia's face.

Instantly she shrank back and put a good distance between her and her boss. She rubbed her chin, clearly in pain.

Buddha said, "Good man, Charles Hamor. Even an untouchable can instruct the greatest teacher how to center and retain his sati." He bowed to Charlie. "Thank you, my brother."

Charlie returned the bow and said, "Think nothing of it. I would not know how to share with you had you not taught my spirit as the great lama you have been when I was just a meager servant."

Buddha laughed and wagged a finger at Charlie. "Oh that's good ass-kissing, Hamor—very good. Now, if I am to believe that Claudia is not trying to protect you because you used to fuck, then you don't know what I know, but am I willing to take that chance."

"Buddha, if I had any clue what you were talking about then maybe I could, you know—um—if I knew that something you knew could get me killed, bring out these guns, would I have come here? Do you think I'm that stupid?"

Buddha nodded and said, "You've got a point. However, I know what I know. And I know that you are not just here because you need more weed. I know you are here because of something else—something bigger than you, bigger than me—bigger than weed."

The entire time Buddha and Charlie had been talking, since Charlie had evoked the language of Buddhist meditation to get Buddha to back off Claudia, Pony had grown more nervous and fidgety. His eyes darted from the exchange between the two charismatic and intelligent men to the gunmen who clearly were there to kill them the moment Buddha gave the word. Once the conversation switched to discussions about Buddha knowing more about them being there than just to buy extra weed, Pony realized that his only hope to get his friends out of the compound alive was to come clean about what happened to the weed, accept full blame and see if at least Charlie and Rita could walk out alive. Pony recognized it was his choice to let that hybrid go in exchange for the weird radio, and that it was that action alone that brought Charlie and Rita to the house of this psycho.

That's when Pony exploded with, "It's my fault, okay? It's my fucking fault!"

Rita, "Pony, don't! Just shut up!"

Charlie and Buddha looked at Pony.

"No, Rita, it's my fault! I won't have anyone here get hurt because I fucked up and traded the weed away!"

Buddha asked, "Traded? The weed?"

Charlie said, "Buddha, don't listen to Pony. He's scared and—"

Pony stole Charlie's attention by grabbing his arm and stepping in front of his more rational friend so that he was almost right in Buddha's face. "Thanks for trying to take the heat, Charlie, but we know the truth and if Buddha believes all the shit he says he does, this shouldn't freak him out too much."

Buddha repeated, "Umm—'believes all the shit he says he does'?— what exactly are you talking about, Macreedy?"

Pony said, "What I mean is that if you're really a Buddhist, then what happened to the weed won't freak you out and you'll see that something bigger and badder is going on here, and you'll let us go."

Rita whispered in Charlie's ear, "We can't let him tell Buddha. He'll think he's crazy and kick the shit out of us anyway!"

Charlie whispered back, "Actually, I think Pony's got something here. If Buddha really wants people to believe he is what he says he is, he'll want to hear this story. Buddhists believe very much in the power of the spirit reaching out to the living from the land of death, especially when challenging us to grow and change ourselves for the better."

"I'm sorry," Rita said, "but I don't get half that shit. I was raised Catholic."

"Trust him, okay?" and Charlie put an arm around Rita's waist to hold her close, to make her feel better and safer.

Buddha said to Pony, "Go ahead, Macreedy! Tell me your story! And I'll have no interruptions!" Buddha swept everyone with his eyes, including his own gunmen. Pony told his tale of how he tried some of the Buddha Blend, as he normally did after picking up a shipment, fell asleep, woke to the sound of knocking at the door and was visited by his dead cousin Claire.

During the telling, of Buddha's gunmen, six of the eight were Latino and instilled with the very strict and much paganized Catholicism rampant throughout Mexico and Latin America. The details Pony described regarding his cousin's visit actually resembled tenants characteristic of myths and legends told by Latino elders of visitations by family spirits and even saintly figures such as St. Michael, St. Gabriel or even the Holy Mother. It made these six men look at each other and struggle to hide their concern.

The other two gunmen were ex-military Anglo-Americans, born and raised in the Midwest and possessed of a practicality that meant they could care less about stupid ghost stories.

Even Claudia showed more attention to the story than anyone might expect. As Rita had said earlier, she and Claudia did attend the same convent-run school as girls, so their religious background should be approximately the same depth; however, where Rita claimed a Catholic upbringing, hers was more steeped in the true Roman Catholicism of her Italian family. Unlike Claudia, whose upbringing more resembled the kind of paganized Christianity of Latin origin. Finally, Pony finished his tale of ghosts, radios and bowling bags. He looked back at Charlie and Rita and then at Buddha. "That's it," Pony said, "the whole freaky story."

Buddha was silent. He looked at his men, Claudia and then his would-be captives. Finally, the drug-dealing reincarnationist said, "Yes, I can appreciate that this story is at the very least fantastic. But—um—do you have this bowling bag or the radio given to you for the weed?"

"No," Pony said. "We—um—we kinda left it back at the shop, you know? Didn't even think to bring it, you know? We should have brought it, really should have. I bet someone as smart as you are, you could have told us a lot about it," Pony looked at Charlie and Rita. "Don't you think so, guys? Don't you think the Buddha could've helped us figure it out?"

Charlie and Rita looked at each other and nodded. Charlie said, "Sure."

Pony looked at Buddha and said, "Yeah, too bad we didn't bring it."

Buddha nodded and said, "Well, clearly you were visited by a spirit."

"You think?" Pony asked.

Buddha nodded, again, and said, "Absolutely, Macreedy. I can't say why, it's not my dharma to know. But certainly, it means something significant and I would not dare stand in the way of Spirit. Therefore we will take the payment and give you an equal replacement of our blend." Buddha snapped his fingers and the gunmen, along with Claudia, disappeared.

Pony grabbed Buddha's hand and shook it vigorously. A huge smile crossed his face and he looked very, very relieved. "Thanks, Buddha! Thanks for understanding! Man, you really are a spiritual dude, dude! You are the best—the absolute best! You totally live up to your name, dude, you know, like a wise Buddha?"

Buddha fought to get his hand back from Pony. He said, "Okay, okay, Macreedy! Enough!"

Charlie and Rita both grabbed Pony and pulled him away from Buddha Jesus. Charlie said, "Thanks for understanding, Buddha." He handed the money bag to Buddha.

Buddha took the money bag and smiled. He said, "When you do figure out this radio, do please share it with me. I'm definitely curious."

Charlie said, "Absolutely. Absolutely."

Buddha pointed a finger at Pony and asked, "Wait, Macreedy, did you notice if the brand of the radio said Armageddon 420?"

Pony was totally flabbergasted that Buddha knew the brand name. "Totally, man! Totally! How did you know the label, man?"

Buddha did not answer. Instead he shook and waved his pointing hand at Pony in a good-bye motion.

Claudia returned with only one of the eight gunmen, carrying the same kind of duffle that Pony had previously taken the first set of bricks. Buddha motioned for her to hand the bag to Charlie. Pony moved to grab the bag, but Rita grabbed his arm and pulled him back with all her strength. She said, "Nope, never again are you touching it."

Pony looked dejected.

Charlie took the bag from Claudia. "Thanks, Claudia. Are you okay?"

Claudia said nothing. She walked back to Buddha and stood just behind him.

Everyone looked at each other in a moment of awkward silence. No one knew what to say but sort of waited for the other person to say something.

"Take care," Charlie said to Buddha.

"Let me know," Buddha said. "I really am interested."

Rita walked through the doors alongside Pony. Charlie followed them with the bag of weed.

The gunman followed Charlie and closed the doors as soon as they were gone.

Claudia asked, "Why didn't you tell Charlie you knew he was being watched by the DEA? I don't get it!"

Buddha Jesus said, "That's right, Claudia, you don't get it. You have no idea what's just been dropped in our lap. It's something bigger than any amount of drugs, weed or cash. It's bigger than the fucking DEA watching OHM and trying to use him to shut down my business. In fact, if I can get my hands on that radio, I will never have to fear any man or government ever again!"

Claudia looked totally confused. "Buddha, I let you grab me and almost break my fucking jaw, and I might work for you but you also know I could kill every one of these motherfucking gun-toting eunuchs you have peppering this compound, so I don't need your bullshit riddles! What the fuck are you talking about?"

"I am talking, Claudia my dear, about that fucking radio they've got."

"The one Pony claims some fucking ghost gave him? What the fuck?"

"Listen to me, woman, you are the best bodyguard and hit-person I have working for me, but I will fire your ass if you keep talking to me like that. Now, do you want to keep working for me?"

Claudia said nothing.

"Good. I want you to follow them back to their dispensary, and I want you to find out everything you can about that radio. When you have a visual, call me and tell me what you see. Then, and only then, will I tell you what I want you to do with it next."

Claudia said, "Fine, I can do that. But what about what your contact in the DEA said? Do you know how many people are watching Charlie and OHM?"

"No, so keep hidden. I don't want them to know what we know. If you spot anyone that even remotely looks like a spook, let me know. Got it?"

"You're the boss." Claudia walked out of the foyer in the direction of her private quarters.

Buddha smiled and left the foyer in the direction of his meditation chamber.

Outside Buddha's Compound

Rita drove the car through the gates and onto the road that would take them out of Calabasas and back to the 101 Freeway. This time though, Pony was riding shotgun and Charlie was in the back with the duffle sitting on his lap.

Pony looked at Charlie and said, "Can't I try just a little bud—just a little—"

Rita and Charlie both shouted, "Hell no!"

Pony threw up his hands and said, "Okay, okay, but I'm telling you—if clients start seeing dead relatives, you'll wish you'd let me try it out."

Rita looked at Charlie in the rearview mirror and saw that he looked deep in thought, staring out to the setting sun. "Hey, Boss, I know what that look means."

Charlie sighed and said, "Sorry, I just—"

Rita said, "Yeah, I don't trust him either."

Pony shouted, "Me three, guys! Seriously, I don't like the way the whole vibe felt. It's like the only thing that he took away from the story was the radio, you know?"

"I know," said Charlie. "That's why I'm thinking the Buddha's got an idea what that radio is."

"And the gunmen?" asked Rita. "What were they for? It's like he was going to blow our asses away, until Pony's story and then— shazam—we're like his best customers again."

Charlie nodded and said, "Yeah, there's definitely something going on. When we get back to OHM, we need to find out what's up with that radio. My Spidey-sense tells me it's a Pandora's Box that could let loose all kinds of unholy hell."

Chapter 24

West Hollywood, California

The streets of Los Angeles proper and those of the interconnected metropolis were no mystery to SSA Ephraim Syde of the Department of Homeland Security. During the 1970s and 1980s, Syde was stationed in Burbank, working to root out the communist and related sympathetic element in the motion picture industry. He also targeted the rising technological arena, later dubbed Silicon Valley. This experience made him the best candidate in the eyes of the Director to accompany his young nephew to recover the Augur.

Of course, the fact that SSA Syde never once made a formal arrest of any would-be target during his two decades in Southern California, because there weren't any, was of no consequence to whether Syde was actually qualified to carry out the mission. During his time in that city over those two decades, Syde became very well acquainted with another lesser-known area of investigation for his then-department of employment, the Federal Bureau of Investigation. That area was the rising phenomenon known to the public as the New Age movement.

While tracking the activities of many suspects in his pursuit of communist sympathizers (and also shadowing several women), SSA

Syde became attracted to living the Southern California lifestyle and became familiar with many New Age/occult practices. Occult is not a term comfortable to those who practice alternative or pagan religions, but it is the term used most often by the less-educated members of the government. This was the case with Ephraim Syde, so for the sake of telling Syde's story, the term occult is more apropos.

Syde never became a convert to the occult, even after visiting a very convincing psychic/medium that channeled a rather impressive spiritual entity called Rulphé, who predicted Syde would have a bout with testicular cancer over which he would triumph. Although that prediction came true, Syde did not believe in the authenticity of such entities or that the practitioners of mediumship were anything other than charlatans.

However, the one phenomenon of the New Age he did come to believe was authentic was Relic Magic. A lesser known phenomenon of the New Age, Relic Magic was the belief in the imbuing of physical objects by higher intelligences (extra-terrestrials, angels or even the Creator itself) for the use of obtaining great power by humans or other forces. Now, it might seem odd to believe that anyone would believe such a reality was possible, but that was the case with Ephraim Syde. He didn't believe in mediumistic or channeling power, but he did believe in higher intelligences (in particular extra-terrestrial) who were trying to mess with the human race—in particular, these great and mighty United States of America.

Completely drawn into the world of relics, the subsequent folklore and controversial magic cast by them, SSA Ephraim Syde discovered he was not the only member of the FBI or other government services who believed in the existence of such phenomenon, or its ability to influence the course of United States history. As a result, he became a member of an unsanctioned operation involving multiple intelligence and justice agencies to monitor such relics appearing, their use, theft and/or sale. The operation attempted to recover such relics to warehouse them or even use them for the benefit of this great nation.

This was the primary reason for Syde being sent by the Director of Homeland Security, because the Director also believed in such supernatural forces and knew what the Augur could potentially mean in the wrong hands. It wasn't something that the Director's nephew SA Dale Curb necessarily believed just yet, but that's why the Director wanted him with SSA Syde. So he could see for himself not only what was really at play in their battle to control such objects, but also because he knew Curb wouldn't give away any information to anyone since he didn't know shit about it. SSA Syde liked working with agents who didn't know shit. Like when he went to Madam's Organ on Sundays to hit on younger women with daddy issues, it made Syde feel superior.

Regardless of the fact that SSA Syde was a misogynist, a philistine to inferior officers, and a general misanthrope to everyone else; he was a thorough agent and knew that before he and Curb landed in Los Angeles they had to find evidence of the Augur's activation.

Although Syde had never set eyes on the Augur, he was well aware of its reputation. He had encountered (or believed he had) other scrying and divination relics while on previous missions, and knew that they all caused ripples in the quantum field surrounding—well, everything. And for the purposes of what Syde bothered to learn about how they actually operated, he knew only that it affected quarks, those wonderful little bastards that make up—well, everything.

While on the jet from DC to Los Angeles, he made a call to a colleague in San Diego who had "the means" of scanning all of Southern California for any evidence of the quark-quakes created by divination devices. There was no guarantee that the Augur worked along these same quantum principles, but it was worth a shot. Fortunately for Syde and Curb, the shot worked.

When the Augur had first crackled to life in Venice at Pony Macreedy's apartment and played both CCR's and Phil Collins' classics, it rippled through the quantum field monitored by one particular satellite owned by the University of California–San Diego that was leased out to the Office of Homeland Security. The reason why Cal–San Diego owned such an unusual piece of machinery when the majority of the world considered these kind of magical relics and quantum science a load of horseshit was because the United States government is nothing if not clever in its distrust of its population. It has had since its birth in Philadelphia in 1781 a belief that the public at large is incredibly naïve and stupid. This meant that the government was "big daddy" and knew what was best for everyone, even though it was comprised of the same naïve and stupid members of the public.

After Homeland Security was established and the President at that time resurrected the Crusades (oh sorry, that's right: "the war on terror is not a religious war." The government believes Islam has just as much a right to exist as Christianity—blah, blah, blah), the government adopted the unofficial position that any religion (including Judaism and Catholicism) outside of good old-fashioned, homegrown, Protestant, apocalyptic Christianity, is absolute horseshit.

Between the Roosevelt and Clinton administrations, the government was totally open to any and all possibilities (even during Reagan) when it came to who and what God was. But there's no point in rehashing the whole Roswell/Area 51 controversy or the recognition by the Allies during World War II of the Nazis using all sorts of crazy occult shit. Those days of fun and free exploration of the truth for the sake of all mankind, not just good ol' America, are ninety-eight percent dead.

Suffice it to say, as far as the United States government is concerned there is only one God—theirs. Make no mistake, they will go to any lengths (already invaded Afghanistan and Iraq, didn't they?) to put money, innovation and technology towards acquiring whatever will prove that American Christianity is the one true religion. This is one of the primary directives of Homeland Security.

In order not to be obvious in their pursuit to strengthen the one true American God, Homeland Security turned to state universities and, in exchange for extra bucks and funding for this and that, put their religious war operations on their lesser-known campuses. This quark-quake sensing satellite monitored from the Cal-San Diego campus was a prime example of this insidious plan.

(An interesting coincidence, though—the same technology developed for this Homeland Security satellite ended up in the satellites used by Watchtower and Seventh-day Adventists, but that story can wait for another time.)

Once the Homeland Operatives at Cal-San Diego registered the Augur's activity, they were able to follow its movements to the very medical marijuana dispensary where the unwitting souls whose lives had been chosen earlier by two deities to hold the relic remained, ignorant as to the forces rallying against them. But all these operatives could tell SSA Ephraim Syde was the address of OHM and that the Augur was likely in that location as the quark-quake had become stationary there over the last few hours.

SSA Syde didn't give all this information to SA Curb, though. Keeping the younger agent ignorant gave Syde a sense of greater importance and control over the operation. It also kept Curb from having any ideas of his own or contradicting anything Syde told him to do. Fortunately, Dale Curb wasn't the kind of agent who wanted to break the rules. He liked following orders and preserving the system. This meant he'd do pretty much whatever Syde asked him to do, like rent the car when they landed at Bob Hope Airport.

Although it had been some years since Syde was in Los Angeles or West Hollywood, he knew that the address of OHM placed it near the intersection of Fairfax and Santa Monica Blvd. When they arrived there, they found that a Sunvalley Organic Market was almost directly across the street from OHM. Being Sunday night, the agents expected the dispensary to be closed, and they were correct.

"It's as dark as the grave," said Syde in the self-important tone he liked to use when stating the obvious.

Syde parked their car in the parking lot of the Sunvalley Organic Market behind a wall that separated the lot from the sidewalk. He took out a pistol scope and used it like a telescope, focusing it on the front of the store.

Curb took out his mobile phone and began scrolling through apps at a near-inhuman speed. "Sir, may I ask you a question?"

"You can ask."

"Do we know who the other agent is that you were told was here before us, or what agency they are with?"

Syde said, "I know the agency—NSA. As for the agent's name— no, my contact didn't have that."

Curb asked, "Why would NSA be interested in whatever it is we're here to deal with?"

Syde turned away from the scope and looked Dale in the eye. He said, "They are interested because we are interested, Curb. Don't you get that?"

"I'm sorry, Sir, I'm not so sure I do."

"Wow, you really don't know how things work, do you?"

Curb shrugged his shoulders.

"No one in government trusts anyone else in government. If we did, then we wouldn't need different agencies, bureaus, departments or whatever doing the exact same jobs. The only impetus to actually get anything done is to prove that a rival agency isn't as good as you are, and if you are shown up by a rival agency then you just have to work harder the next time."

Curb said, "But that's so cynical."

"Of course it's cynical, stupid! That's the whole point! If we weren't cynical and actually trusted the citizenry to do what they have a constitutional right to do, we'd be out of a job. Worse than that— what if people all over the world actually started fucking cooperating with each other—could you imagine? We'd really be up shit-creek. So, don't give me none of that positivity bullshit, okay—not a syllable of it!"

Curb continued to rush through apps, never taking his eyes off the screen the whole time Syde rambled on.

Syde suddenly became bothered by Curb's paying more attention to his phone than him and asked, "What the hell are you doing?"

"I'm using the internet to find out what I can about this place and the people who run it. According to this—"

Syde swiped the mobile phone out of Curb's hands and dangled it out his side window. "Fuck this! I've been with the FBI twenty-five years without needing some fruity piece of techno-shit to give me help capturing bad guys."

Looking like a hurt child, Dale Curb reached across Syde and tried to grab back his phone. "Hey, that was a gift from my old girlfriend! It's all I have left of her! Please, don't—"

Syde grabbed Curb's collar with his other hand and shook the younger agent until he shut up and stopped reaching for the phone. "Calm down! Calm the fuck down! I won't break your precious little lovey-dovey phone, all right? But we do this my way, got it?"

Dale didn't respond.

Syde repeated, only louder, "Got it?"

"Yes," agreed Curb in a very meek and nasally voice.

Rhetorically Syde asked, "What did I do to deserve the Director's nephew? What?"

"I told you already. I passed that test fair and square."

"Sure you did."

Curb asked, "May I have my fruity piece of techno-shit back, Sir?"

"Here," and Syde handed the phone back to Curb.

Curb took it and double-checked to make sure it wasn't in any way damaged.

Syde returned to watching OHM through the gun-scope.

Curb said, "So, do you not want to know what I found out before you took my phone or what?"

Before Syde could respond his own mobile phone rang. He reached into his coat pocket and took it out. He answered with, "Syde."

Curb watched his superior officer as he mostly listened with a few "Uh-huh's" and "Got it. Got it." Finally, he hung up and put the phone back in his coat pocket.

"Who was that?" Curb asked.

"It was my old-fashioned way of finding out shit—getting other people to find things out for me. It was my contact at the NSA. I know who it is they have working for them. They are definitely closer than us."

Curb asked, "So, what do we do?"

Syde started up the car and pulled out of the parking lot, taking Fairfax south. As he did he explained, "Their contact has something we don't and it's an advantage we can't openly challenge. So we're going to find the contact before they do and make it clear they aren't going to fuck up our operation."

"Wait!" Curb shouted, "You're going to face off against the NSA agent?"

"No, stupid—we're going to break into the agent's house! They aren't there. We're going to find out what they know so we can use it get the relic first. Now do you get it?"

Curb nodded and said, "Yes, Sir, I do—but why don't we just break into the dispensary and see?—"

"Have you not heard a goddamn thing I've said? If our job was just to break into that shitbox and nab the relic, we'd do it. But that's not the job! We aren't just here to steal a relic! We are here to find out who took the relic, why they took it, for what reason they took it, why the NSA wants it, and why they picked the particular agent whose place we're going to ransack, as well as find out who else these bastards might be in contact with."

Curb looked very curious and asked Syde, "But wait—isn't 'why they took it' and 'for what reason they took it' the exact same thing?"

Syde shouted out loud and slapped Curb squarely across the face. "Are you fucking retarded, deaf or both? Who the fuck cares what means what? I run this op so you do what the fuck I say and how I fucking say it!"

Curb made a strange noise when Syde hit him followed by a series of hisses and "ows." Gently, he rubbed the spot where Syde hit him.

After listening to Syde ramble for a bit, Curb finally shouted, "I get it, okay! I fucking get it!"

Syde nodded and said, "You know what, kid? I think I'm going to make an agent out of you yet. And if I seem to be harsh on you, it's only because I want to make your uncle really proud of you."

"Really?" asked Dale, his eyes lighting up, a stupid grin crossing his face and his whole demeanor becoming that of a five-year-old. "You think you can make my uncle proud of me?"

Syde winked and clicked his tongue. "You betcha, kid. Just listen close and keep your trap shut."

Curb smiled and said, "Yes, Sir!"

Chapter 25

West Hollywood, California

The Troubadour nightclub, located on Santa Monica Boulevard in the heart of West Hollywood, is a legendary venue that has been credited with unofficially launching the West Coast Hard Rock and Hair Band movements of the late 1970s throughout the 1980s. Van Halen, Motley Crüe and Poison are just a few of the acts who got started on the Troubadour's bi-level bar/full-stage set-up. But the year the Troubadour began was 1957, and it continues well into this twenty-first century to be arguably the hottest venue for any genre of music. So to say it has only contributed to a small era of rock is limiting its ongoing influence—not only on the West Coast but all across America's fields of popular music.

Ian's friend Ricardo Lujan, who managed the band Happy Jack's Back, knew what it meant for the fledgling band to get booked at the Troubadour and wasn't about to blow the opportunity. He invited as many friends as he could scare up off of Facebook and even MySpace, as well as calling up several A&R people to appear from six different music labels. He also arranged for reviewers from newspapers, the internet and TMZ to cover the happening scene. All in all, it was going to be a huge event. Unfortunately for Happy Jack's Back and Ricardo and all those assembled for a good time, it would be quite a while before any of them would hit a club to enjoy good music, good booze and good friends for a very long time.

It didn't take Ian very long after leaving OHM to get to the Troubadour. It was just a straight shot west on Santa Monica, and seeing as Ian rode a motorcycle, it usually wasn't difficult for him to find a place to park. But that night, when he pulled his bike into the back of the club where the parking lot met the alley street, he saw a red chopper with flames painted on the tank and fenders, parked in his unofficial spot.

"Son-of-a-bitch better hope I don't see his ass inside—take my fucking spot."

OHM was Ian's first oasis, the Troubadour his second. He was friends with the manager André and often hit it on the weekend to find a hook-up for the night. Plus, he had picked up more than a few nightshifts as bouncer since OHM was only a daytime gig.

After Ian parked his bike opposite the invading chopper, he walked over and inspected it. It was a gorgeous machine, no doubt, and for that Ian had to respect the driver—until he spotted a crucifix etched into the headlamp of the bike.

"The fuck?" he muttered to himself.

It was a very peculiar decoration and one he never expected to see, even in the large Latino biker gangs Ian knew.

"Fucking religious fucking freak," and with that wonderful sentiment, Ian walked to the back door and greeted the bouncer there with the customary combination handshake and hugs used by the hip and cool cats who were bouncers in Los Angeles. And yes, this bouncer was also a friend of Ian's. Ian had a lot of friends.

"Who owns that fucking bike?" Ian asked the bouncer.

"Can't say, dude—was here when I got here."

"Seriously? When did you come on?"

"Just before seven."

"No shit? That's a long night for you, man." Ian slapped him on the shoulder and grasped it with a friendly show of machismo friendship. "Cool, bro, cool."

The bouncer opened the door for Ian, who went on inside. By the time Ian hit the main floor (standing room only) and saw Happy Jack's Back up on stage, he had gotten himself a brew and found both

Ricardo and André. He joined in their conversation about the band's set and soon the chopper out back disappeared from his mind. Over the next hour, he had nothing but fun as the problems of his other friends Charlie, Henry, Pony and Rita escalated.

Yes, Ian had left Henry alone at OHM before Charlie, Rita and Pony returned from Buddha Jesus' compound. He couldn't have had any idea that they were in danger or that the very strange radio—which Henry was still working on cracking—was making them a target of at least five extremely powerful forces on the planet Earth. All Ian cared about was getting laid.

Jenny Sway and Tracey Kipper entered through the front doors.

Jenny was able to get herself and Tracey through the security line, because of her own connection to Happy Jack's Back. Whereas Ian knew Ricardo, Jenny knew Meister, the band's drummer and lyricist. Before becoming good friends, Jenny and Meister had been quite the item for about three weeks. Regardless, fate (or certain deities?) had conspired to bring these two people to this same place at the same time. Because it wasn't long after Jenny and Tracey first arrived that Ian's eyes fell on Jenny Sway's beautiful face and buxom body. The rest, as they say, was all chemical.

Tracey had to scream just about every word she spoke because the din of the music was loud as hell. "I'm gonna get us drinks," was the first thing she shouted, and if someone didn't know better they'd have thought Tracey was pissed.

Jenny nodded vigorously and shouted back, "Mike's Hard Lemonade!"

Tracey shouted back, "You don't want a LIT?" (That's a Long Island Iced Tea for you self-righteous teetotalers.) "I'm driving!"

Jenny thought about that and said, "Yeah, okay, get me a LIT! Thanks, babe, I love you!"

Tracey smiled back at Jenny and headed for the closest of the three bars set up on the wall opposite the stage.

Meanwhile, Ian saw Tracey move away from his prey, leaving the gorgeous Jenny all alone and ripe for the picking. Brushing his hand across his shaved head, as if he had hair or anything that needed grooming, followed by a quick check of his beer-saturated breath and finally checking out his black t-shirt and jeans (none of which would make any difference to Jenny), Ian made his way over to her.

Tracey was almost at the bar when she collided with someone who she swore must have materialized out of thin air. It was a hard collision too, not the casual brush or even typical shoulder-bump one encounters in that kind of crowded place.

"Excuse me!" Tracey shouted, hoping that the person heard her or would respond in kind.

But the person who collided into her did no such thing. All this tall man in a leather jacket did was look at Tracey with his John Lennon-style sunglasses and an expression that was impossible to read. It was the Vatican's Father Agosto and in one of his hands he held a small duffle bag. He was there in the Troubadour, and bumping into the woman who was falling for the man who was in possession of the very relic Agosto would do anything to get his hands on.

From Agosto's perspective, in other words through the Revelator Glasses, he could see that Tracey was not just an ordinary woman. Agosto couldn't quite understand why it was that the clothes she was wearing kept morphing from one look to another. All he could assume from what the Revelator Glasses were showing him was that this woman was not who or what she appeared to be. It made him stop and look hard at her after she asked for his excuse.

Tracey had no such advantage of the Revelator Glasses and could only assume that Agosto was a big asshole who didn't apologize to anyone else, even when he was clearly in the wrong. But now to have him just standing there, staring at her, wearing those stupid sunglasses in a dark bar and blocking her from getting drinks really made her mad.

"Hey, could you move, please? I need to get to the bar! Okay?"

Still Agosto didn't move.

"I said move! Please!" and then for reasons Tracey would later regret, something instinctive clicked inside her head. In a trained aikido move, Tracey grabbed the priest's larger hand and twisted his wrist in such a way that he instantly dropped to one knee in pain.

Agosto was too shocked to take any evasive move and found himself at Tracey's mercy. But he made no sound, no noise of any kind. The pain should be crippling, but it clearly was nothing more than a total surprise to the much bigger man.

"Next time act polite," Tracey said, as she let his hand go and walked around him and continued on her way to the bar.

Agosto stood up and shook his wrist. He looked at the strange woman who had just sent him to a knee, and then walked to the mezzanine level of the club. There he could stand and keep an eye on this woman whom he suddenly had a great interest in.

By the time Tracey had gotten Jenny her Long Island Iced Tea, and herself a gin & tonic, she saw no sign of Agosto and was happy to be rid of him. Unfortunately, she was not. He was high above her, watching her every move, trying as hard as he could to use the scrying powers of the Glasses to discern what it was about this constantly-shifting woman that this powerful relic was unable to clearly ascertain.

Tracey carried the drinks back to where she left Jenny but saw no sign of her friend. "Oh shit," she said to herself. Again, employing deft skills of movement and speed indicated from her move on Agosto, Tracey wove her way through the dancing and swaying patrons without ever once hitting, knocking or straight-on bumping into anyone else. She held the drinks firm without spilling a drop.

All of this Agosto watched from above and marveled at, the duffle bag still gripped in one hand. Finally, Tracey spotted Jenny seated at one of the tables lining the walls all around the interior of the first floor and sighed with relief. Of course, Jenny wasn't alone. Ian was seated next to her and chatting her up like a real pro. As Tracey approached the table, she could see Jenny was totally digging on Ian and his banter and knew there was nothing she could do but to sit down opposite them, slip Jenny's drink across the table to her and relax. She took a sip of her own drink and began to scan the crowd.

Of course the crowd was not what Tracey was thinking about. She wasn't thinking about the strange man she had just bumped into and put down on the floor. She wasn't even thinking about Jenny and the man Jenny had just picked up, and they were acting like Tracey wasn't there either. The person Tracey was thinking about was Charlie Hamor, and how incredibly sweet and sexy he looked as he lay sleeping on her sofa the night before. In light of her thoughts about Charlie, Tracey's mind lost interest in everything else. All she really wanted to know was when she would see him.

Tracey reached into her pocket and took out her mobile phone. She checked it for missed calls or messages, hoping that maybe, just maybe—with it being on vibrate and all the confusion since coming into the place, he might have—she could have missed—shit, she thought to herself. Shit, shit, shit—he's not going to call me. It's because I'm

Deanne's cousin and he's got all this shit with her—bad break-up. What sane guy would want to get together with the cousin of the psycho he just got rid of? He probably thinks it's hereditary, Tracey.

Suddenly, the conversation between Ian and Jenny had gotten excited enough and loud enough that Tracey couldn't help but hear what they were talking about. Ian was captivating Jenny with a tale about a friend of his named Tiger (not bouncy-bouncy Tigger—growly-bite-bite Tiger—and yes, Ian had two friends named after animals) who had tried a remarkably stupid stunt that resulted in his being hospitalized. Although Tracey hadn't heard the entire story from the beginning, she was now hearing how much Jenny was trying to act totally engrossed by what Ian was saying in an effort to impress him and get him to like her even more than he clearly did already.

"Can you believe that shit? Can you believe that?" Ian asked Jenny in a boisterous tone.

Jenny laughed and said, "No way! That's an urban legend! That can't happen!"

"But I saw it with my own two eyes! I swear it! Tiger lit the lighter, farted and went BOOM! Up in flames! And I never drank vermouth again." Ian took another drink from his now fourth beer.

Jenny looked at Tracey, who appeared totally disinterested, and asked her, "Can you believe it, Trace? Can you?"

In a monotone voice, Tracey responded, "No, I can't believe it. Sounds like this Tiger guy was a real d-bag."

Ian said, "That was Tiger, man—complete d-bag! But one of the best goddamn friends I ever had. If it weren't for his antics, I don't think Charlie would have ever recovered from his brother dying."

The name Charlie—brother dying—clicked in Tracey's brain. Instantly she perked up and asked Ian, "Did you say Charlie?"

Ian answered, "Yeah, my friend Charlie—Charlie Hamor."

"You know Charlie Hamor?"

Before Ian could answer, Jenny said, "Not the Charlie you were talking about, Trace, right?"

Tracey couldn't answer; she was in absolute shock.

Then it hit Ian. Even with a buzz on, he realized who he was sitting with. "Oh shit! You're Tracey Kipper! You're Deanne-the-ho's cousin!" The vulgarity of what Ian just said clearly affected the women, which Ian picked up on immediately and apologized for profusely. "Oh man, shit, fuck, I'm sorry, ladies—I uh—I didn't—"

Jenny looked at Tracey, who smiled at Ian and said, "It's okay. She is."

Ian sighed and said, "Thank God! Wow, I can't believe we'd run into each other like—" then the realization of how late it was getting hit Ian. He looked at his watch and said, "Shit! Sorry ladies, I gotta hit it! I'm supposed to be hooking up with my friends, including Charlie! What are you two up to later? If you don't have plans, I could give you my friend's address and you two could—you know— if you don't have anything else planned! I mean, it ain't Bel Air but it ain't Koreatown either. And I know Charlie would freaking love to see you, Tracey."

Tracey didn't know what to say. She was honestly tongue-tied and overwhelmed by the odds of running into a friend of Charlie's that just asked her to go see him. What if he doesn't want to see her again? It's not like Charlie was asking her.

Jenny said, "Come on, Trace! What do you say? It'd be awesome! I bet he'd love to see you again."

"Absolutely!" affirmed Ian. "No doubt—absolutely—I know Charlie would totally dig seeing you. What do you say, huh? We can all go right now, huh?—right now?"

Tracey was still frozen, still not sure what to say or do. Finally, words came to her that she later thought might not have been wise to say. "Okay, we'll go."

"All right!" shouted Ian and Jenny at the same time.

"But," threw out Tracey, "first, I need to go back to my place— just for a second—need to get something, and then Jenny and I will hook up with you. Is it Charlie's house or the dispensary or?—"

"It's called OHM," said Ian. "And that's totally cool if you need to hit your place first—totally. Man, Charlie's gonna freak when he hears this! And I mean freak in a good way."

Tracey moved out of her seat and grabbed Jenny's hand. "Let's go, Jenny. If we're going to hook up with these guys, we should get going right now, so we can—"

"Yeah, okay," said Jenny, who was thinking to herself about the reasons why Tracey wanted to hit her place first—and all of them had to do with sex and contraception. As she moved to get out of her seat, she suddenly leaned over to Ian and gave him a quick kiss on the lips. "See you soon."

"Yeah, you too!" smiled Ian.

198

Tracey and Jenny were making a bee-line for the front door, holding tight to one another through the crowded patrons, laughing, smiling and talking to one another.

Ian got out of his seat and headed towards the back door. He knew that by now Charlie, Rita and Pony should be back with the fresh stash. He also knew that since none of them had showed up at the club like he had invited them, they must have found something out about the radio or that something not so good went down at Buddha's. Either way he knew he was going to make Charlie's whole night turn around with the news of who'd be coming over to play that night.

On the mezzanine above them Father Agosto observed the table, keeping his focus primarily on Tracey. When he watched her get up from the table and take Jenny with her, his view of Ian changed. Suddenly he got a good look at the former linebacker as he rose from the table, slapping his hands together and looking triumphant at his achievement with the women.

Suddenly there was a powerful light like a starburst that shone from behind and just above Ian's upper torso. Agosto had only seen such a supernatural corona on a few occasions in his very long career. "Halo?" muttered the priest. It was what the Revelator Glasses showed Agosto. For the first time since wearing the Glasses, the priest took them off and looked at them in doubt. He looked back down at Ian with his normal eyes and saw nothing unusual as Ian headed in the direction of the back door. Agosto slipped the Glasses back on and saw the burst again. There was no doubt in Agosto's mind. This man was somehow connected to whatever powerful forces were at play with the Augur. The fact that it was a halo suggested something even more unbelievable to the priest, but he could not deny it. He could not miss the opportunity to pursue it. The chance of the woman who knocked him to his knees meeting up with this man with a blessed mark upon him could be no coincidence. The only choice Agosto had to make was which way he should go? Should he pursue the woman who was above the Glasses being able to lock down her true form, or should he pursue this new male target?

That's when a hand grasped Agosto's shoulder from behind. It was a black-gloved hand, and the man attached to the glove wore a black trench coat, black fedora, black slacks and from between the open lapels of the trench, the purple frock and collar of a Catholic Monsignor, more precisely Monsignor Ernesto Garcia.

"Agosto?" spoke the Monsignor with a thick Spanish accent.

Agosto was neither shocked nor surprised, and didn't jump or overreact when the hand touched him.

Garcia said, "This is an interesting place for a meeting."

"Crowds are always the best form of cover, Monsignor, but we have another situation that has arisen. Individuals I must pursue have just left this establishment and I must follow them." Agosto began to walk away from the Monsignor.

Monsignor Garcia grabbed Agosto by the arm and said, "You summoned me here because you knew the Cardinals wanted an update, so give it to me! How are you progressing?"

"What is this?" Agosto asked. "I am summoned to do a job, and now for some reason I have to explain my methods. Never have I had to check in on any other—"

"The Cardinals wanted to know specifically if you have any evidence of the Opacus involved in the theft."

For the first time since his hunt began, surprise crossed Agosto's face. "The Opacus Adonai?"

"You know of another?" Garcia retorted.

Agosto looked at the bag he was holding and shook it. He said, "The Cardinals did not mention the OA when they spoke with me."

"Well, I guess that they didn't think about them until—"

Agosto interrupted his superior by saying, "Forgive my interruption, Your Eminence, but I am concerned that the Opacus isn't mentioned until I am on the road. I don't like to feel I've not been fully informed. However, I will fulfill my duty, and even if the OA is involved, or if there is any trace of their presence, I will inform the Cardinals."

"Good, good," repeated Garcia. "Now, if you haven't found any evidence of the OA, what have you found?"

Without another word, Agosto handed the duffle to the Monsignor, who had to let go of Agosto to take the duffle with both hands.

"One other thing, the young priest who found me in the Amazon, Aitor Moreno—you mentored him?"

"I did."

"He's an impressive young man and has something special. I might have need of his assistance in the future; do you have him assigned for any other long-term duty or parish?"

Without looking at Agosto, focused only on the bag, the Monsignor answered, "No, and if you want him available I will make it so. Now, can we please focus on what is important—the bag!"

When Agosto said nothing else, Garcia looked up to see the priest had apparently vanished. He knew he could not catch the Templar Priest, so he took the duffle and walked to a nearby empty table. He put it down on the top of the table and unzipped the bag. What he saw inside made the Monsignor scream and jump back. Of course, with the noise surrounding him, no one noticed the Monsignor's terror. The Monsignor moved back to the duffle and took a second look. This time his body convulsed and he turned away to vomit on the floor. Leaving the bag on the table, the Monsignor ran for the stairs and left the Troubadour.

A pair of kids saw the Monsignor vomit and then run away. They looked at each other and laughed. One pointed to the other and then motioned for him to look inside the duffle bag. The pointed-to man accepted the challenge and went to look inside. The other man followed him but kept a safe distance back.

The braver of the two opened the bag wide enough so that he could get a clear view of what was inside. What he saw made all color drain from his face. "Holy mother of shit!" He bolted from the table and collapsed, then vomited too.

The other young man ran over to the table and yes, he too looked inside, which made him scream at first. He then fell to the floor and vomited. But then he did something very odd. Out of pure anger, he stood back up grabbed the duffle bag and hurled it away from the table. "Sick son-of-a-bitch!"

However, the trajectory of the young man's throw unintentionally carried the duffle bag over the railing, soaring through the space above the heads of the unsuspecting patrons below, through the colored beams of spotlights aimed at Happy Jack's Back who were in the middle of their set. As the bag rotated towards the stage it loosened, opened and released its payload which plummeted downwards until the head of Alberich Night-dwarf landed upright on the top of the cymbals on the drum kit. His dead-eyed look aimed directly the drummer. The clang of the cymbals was loud enough but it was the drummer's terror-filled scream that assured everyone the macabre happening was not part of the act. It was a sight that no witness would ever forget—ever, which meant that the spin required to rationally explain the sudden appearance of a night-dwarf's decapitated head in a West Hollywood nightclub would be in and of itself a story worthy of telling for another time.

Chapter 26

West Hollywood, California

So while Charlie, Rita and Pony were in Calabasas at Buddha Jesus' compound, and Tracey and Jenny were getting ready for a night out at the Troubadour where they would run into both Ian and Father Agosto; outside OHM, federal agents Syde and Curb were plotting their strategy at the same time the Zealots of the Jehovah's Witnesses and the Light Warriors of the Seventh-day Adventists were plotting their strategy; all for the retrieval of the Augur. Henry Leturnoe was left alone with the Augur inside OHM once Ian had left for the Troubadour.

Being alone with the strange radio didn't frighten Henry in the least. In fact, he had worked hard to downplay his excitement at having such a bizarre item drop into his lap. Once he was alone with the radio, he could let his smile show and his glee break loose. Although he trusted his friends with his life, especially Charlie, he knew better than to give them any hint that he had suspicions as to what the radio Pony had brought them was all about.

The first thing he did once he was alone was to optically re-examine the radio. Although he and everyone else had already looked it over once, Henry did it again. He really looked for any sign, any evidence at all, that it might have once had an electrical cord that was then removed. He looked for any holes out of which a cord would come—nothing. He then looked again for any sign of a battery compartment—nothing—absolutely nothing. It was evident that no power source of any kind existed for this radio. Of course, the radio had shown no signs of working since being brought inside OHM. Henry knew what he and Pony and Rita had experienced at Pony's apartment, but now there was no sound, no evidence of operation.

Henry picked up the radio and took it to the back the dispensary to his culture room where he grew and cultivated his strains of weed. He sat at his favorite work table, clicked on the work light, while leaving the rest of the dispensary dark. He put on his magnifying glasses, placed the radio on its back and examined "the eye" in the center of the frequency dial.

At first glance, it appeared that this eye in the center of the plastic circular dial was kitschy—perhaps some kind of weird promotional idea from the mind of a madman hopped up on psychotropic drugs. Whatever its origin, Henry could not fathom the eye's purpose. Regardless, it was something that Henry's gut told him was essential to the radio. So he took a small tool from his cultivation kit which looked like nothing more than a dental pick and began to carefully touch the plastic cover on the eye.

The eye blinked.

Henry shrieked that weird kind of shriek you only hear in cartoons, but it was real. He fell back in the chair, which then flipped over and crashed to the floor. "Holy shit!"

Henry scampered up on his feet and looked down at the radio but quickly backed off, now terrified of getting too close. He picked up his pick tool and gingerly tapped on the plastic over the eye and saw nothing happen this time. The eye didn't blink.

Henry began to laugh at himself and his reaction. Clearly he thought he was seeing things, no pun intended. Clearly his anxiety made him think the radio was alive; maybe he and Pony and Rita also concocted the radio playing those songs back in Pony's apartment. Of course, that would mean some kind of collective hallucination; and as much as Henry knew about that particular phenomenon, he knew it was very, very rare.

Relieved for the moment that the radio was not somehow alive or working, Henry sat back down at the table and began to look it over as he had before, but now with the magnifying glasses. He moved the lamp light so that he could highlight different angles and looked for possible seams in the plastic—that's when something stood out which made Henry gasp and release the device.

"Oh shit—that's different."

Henry slapped his hands together and rubbed them. Whatever he caught in the light hadn't this time shocked or frightened him; it totally turned him on. He took the radio with one hand and the lamp with his other, and lined up the light with the crease of the two halves of the plastic shell of the radio so that he once again could see what he definitely knew to be runes.

Ancient markings used as both an alphabet and spiritual symbols by the ancient Nordic peoples such as Vikings and Celts, also called a futhark, these runes had become more commonly connected to the fortune-telling movement of the New Age dating back to the late 1970s.

According to those who believed in the power of paganism, wicca, New Age and similar alternative-belief systems, the runes were nothing less than symbols of power and magic, that in the right hands could either bring great fortune or conversely bring great evil in the wrong hands. In fact, it was the runes that Hitler and his Nazis used as symbols of their racist and fascist empire that even to this day are still seen as marks of evil.

Henry knew enough history of the Nordic runes to recognize their appearance on the radio's shell had nothing to do with Hitler or the Nazis, but likely had everything to do with it representing something pagan and pantheistic. In fact, Henry knew enough history to know they were once used as an alphabet by the Germanic tribes. So he began to wonder if he was looking at a message. The only problem: he couldn't remember which runes corresponded to which modern-day letters.

Henry got up from his chair and went back to the sales room. He found a laptop on the corner of the counter. He returned with it to his table, and turned it on. Once he was on the internet he searched for the word "futhark" (an ancient word for how a rune could be used to represent a current letter).

"Ah shit," was Henry's response when the choices of websites about futharks gave at least five or six different futharks from different Nordic periods and/or tribes. This meant translation could be accurate, or off by just a few letters, depending on which alphabet he used. For someone as thorough as Henry, he would have to translate the runes using each available alphabet and hope at least one made sense or said anything at all.

Henry connected the laptop to the network printer located in the lobby of the dispensary (This is where proper identification is checked on the main computer, and/or prescriptions sent from doctors' offices would be received) and printed up the different futharks. Henry walked to the front of the dispensary to get the printouts. He found them in the printer tray and picked them up. He quickly thumbed through the sheets to make sure they were good copies. Satisfied with the print job, Henry walked back to the door leading to the salesroom but stopped when he heard a scampering noise.

"What the hell?"

Henry looked around the dark lobby and could see nothing. The noise started and stopped and had come so quickly he wasn't even sure he could tell where it came from.

Henry reached into his pants pocket and took out a pack of Natural American Spirit lights. He took out a cigarette and lit it up with one of the novelty lighters located in a dispensing dish on the desk where the printer was located. Henry slipped the lighter into his pocket and waited another few minutes before walking through the door and all the way back to his work table.

Once Henry sat down at the table, he began the tedious chore of translating the runes on the radio using the different futhark printouts. From time to time, Henry had to readjust the lamp's light and the position of the radio so that the hard-to-see runes were again visible, as they kept disappearing. After spending the next thirty-five minutes transposing the runes popping up on the plastic shell to a simple piece of notebook paper ripped from a spiral, Henry began to notice a pattern with the runes that suggested, via comparison with the different futharks, missing letters (vowels) that resulted in his realizing:

"Elder! Elder futhark!" Henry shouted. Because it was the first words he had spoken in more than half an hour, it was like his vocal cords had been bursting to make noise.

It was indeed the oldest of runic alphabets appearing on the shell of the Augur. An alphabet which scholars believe began as early as 150 CE.

(These days it's necessary for scholars to use a code no longer reflective of a particular religion. That means no more BC [or even b.c.] "before Christ" or AD [or a.d.] "anno domini—year of our Lord" will be used. In short, CE [or c.e.] stands for "the common era" replacing AD, while BCE [or b.c.e.] stands for "before the common era." Sorry all of you paranoid, home-schooled, religious conservatives—we secular humanists are insidiously invading everything! Relax, just kidding—seriously, just kidding.)

A scampering noise again echoed through the large cultivation room. The sound of little feet reverberated between the rows of marijuana.

Henry muttered, "What the fuck?"

It didn't scare him, because Henry's mind immediately thought it was some kind of vermin or bug, which just pissed him off considering the delicate commodity over which he stood sentinel.

"Motherfuckers," he mumbled. "You will not take my gold. I swear to God you will not—" Henry walked the whole floor of the cultivation room, his magnifying glasses still on, to see if he could spot whatever it was. But the sound did not return, and after fifteen minutes of walking the floor he went back to his table and began to settle into the translation of what he transposed from the shell onto the spiral paper with the Elder Futhark printout.

Immediately engrossed by his translation, it took Henry another ten minutes of trying to make sense out of the runes to letter conversion before he realized, "Son-of-a-bitch! It's not right to left. These bastards wrote from top to bottom—in columns," and Henry sighed. He shook his head and cracked his knuckles. "And I thought the Vikings were only pains-in-the-ass by raping and pillaging."

With this new twist, Henry went back to translation with top to bottom replacing right to left—allowing for the fact that there were some letters in the English language that just weren't represented by runes, which then led Henry to the realization that there weren't any missing vowels like he had first thought, but although "y" didn't have an equivalent, it was all consonants that were missing. As a result there was some logical extrapolation on Henry's part to fill in any letters that might be missing in order to have certain words make sense.

Fortunately, Henry had an involved history with academia and translation of ancient languages to modern. Although he had never specifically worked with any kind of Nordic languages, he had worked with Latin and even Aramaic. Henry had spent his collegiate career in divinity and seminary studies. His friendship with Charlie and his brother Danny had led Henry away from a future in the priesthood. He had been raised by a grandmother who wanted Henry to be a learned priest or even a monk. Lucky for Henry's grandmother, she passed away before she could see how he was presently using his vast intelligence. Henry had no doubt that she would not have approved of his abandoning his pursuit of Christianity and antiquity and applied that same intelligence to pot.

No one can judge anyone's right to define either their own faith or lack of one. It's not as if Henry had woken up one day and consciously chosen not to believe in a God or, more specifically, believe in a flesh-and-blood incarnation of God named Jesus of Nazareth. He had seen cancer wither a good friend of his and the best man he ever knew, torturing his body and making his mind suffer terribly—how can that be God? And if that is God—fuck him! The creation of such a phenomenon could not be justified morally, unless it struck only those who committed equally immoral acts on others. Unfortunately, for whatever reason, that wasn't the case. Most bad people seem to make it through just fine without contracting the kind of horrible suffering as innocents or good people.

None of this meant that Henry didn't want there to be a God. In fact, if anything, his desire to see proof of God the Creator was stronger now than when he was pursuing his studies. His agnosticism had fueled Henry to investigate the power of life and death in many different cultures and languages, and all of that curiosity was about to come crashing in on him as he finally finished translating the runes he had transposed. Because what they said made Henry utter the words: "…'Wherefrom comes this that we give unto you—the gift of Augurspell.' Augurspell? Augurspell? You've got to be fucking me!"

Henry stood and banged his arms on the table in sheer frustration. The shock of the blow made the radio shake and fall over.

"That's bullshit!" shouted Henry. "What the fuck does any of that mean? What the fuck is an Augurspell?"

Henry grabbed the radio and squeezed it tightly in his large hands and screamed at it. He spoke directly to it, as if it were alive, "That is bullshit! You are not the future! There is no future! What kind of sick fucking joke are you playing?"

Having completely lost his cool now, Henry screamed at the top of his lungs and threw it across the room. It hit a wall and fell to the floor without a scratch.

"You can't be real!" Henry shouted. "Nothing like you can exist!"

Henry ran over to the radio and got ready to kick the relic when it crackled to life, causing the dial to light up and begin searching stations. Henry shouted in shock and fell to the ground with his eyes wide open.

The radio passed stations that had music, human voices and finally landed on some kind of news station, or at least that's what Henry thought it was based on how the announcer spoke.

"It was nothing the Secretary of Defense could explain. He had never in his thirty-five years of public and military service heard of United States military personnel abandoning their posts in such large numbers to disappear into the native wilderness of wherever they were posted. The commanding officers who remained at their posts said they could not explain how or why some two thousand US personnel should suddenly go AWOL.

"Meanwhile, fighting between the Palestinians and the Israeli forces intensified in Gaza overnight, with more than six thousand casualties reported from missile attacks on both sides. The president of Iran spoke before the General Assembly of the United Nations and in his address referenced the United States directly, claiming it is the US who is behind the two-week war that had broken out between Israel and Palestine; and that if the US does not admit its interference, Iran will declare war on Israel and escalate the violence which promises to engulf the whole region.

"The Secretary of State's refusal to respond to Iran's accusations is not surprising, but the rest of the Security Council is requesting the US to address Iran's accusations, or they will order a resolution to be drafted; forcing the US to account for their own recent naval movements in the Indian Ocean and Persian Gulf. It is an unprecedented move by the UN to pass any resolution ordering the US to reveal any of her national activities; however, Republican and Tea Party members of Congress have said that if this is not an indication that the US needs to pull out of the UN and declare itself the most supreme and sovereign of all free nations, with the God-given right to enforce the values of liberty and Christian freedoms guaranteed by the Founding Fathers on any and all nations seen by the US as evil and satanic, or giving aid and comfort to such a satanic nation, then the American people will take up their Second Amendment Rights and overthrow the current Democratic Administration."

Henry muttered, "This can't be real—not really happening. What the fuck is it saying? Are those Tea Party fuckers really going to kill us all?"

The radio shut itself off.

At first thought, Henry believed the station sounded like NPR or even Pacifica Radio. The timbre and educated sound of the announcer's voice made him stereotypical for NPR, and gave Henry the pit-in-the-stomach feeling that the report was legitimate.

Henry kicked the radio twice, but it didn't turn on or in any way appear physically scuffed or remotely marred by being thrown or even kicked. Henry pulled his knees to his chest and placed his hands on his head. He rocked back and forth saying, "What the fuck is going on? Charlie, get your ass back here. I don't understand what those runes mean. How did it know my name? How am I the—"

Suddenly, there was a knock at the door leading to the back of the dispensary. It was the door inside the cultivation room, and the loud banging made Henry jump. There was a second knock and Henry got up on his feet and walked over to it.

"Who is it?" shouted Henry.

No response, just a knock.

"Fuck this," said Henry. "I'm not opening the fucking door to anyone who isn't going to answer—"

Something struck the outside of the door, buckled its solid structure and knocked it off its hinges. It fell to the floor, almost hitting Henry.

Henry screamed in terror and jumped as far as he could to avoid being squashed. Shaking with abject horror, Henry saw a menacing figure standing in the now open doorway. It was a male figure, as far as Henry could see, wearing some kind of large dark cloak with hood. He had on motorcycle boots and jeans. He was the tallest fucker Henry had ever seen and nothing about him told Henry that he wasn't going to rip him in half.

So Henry gave it ten seconds with the figure standing there and Henry cowering where he was cowering, before screaming like a little girl and running towards the front of the dispensary. Unfortunately, this figure wasn't human and in the blink of an eye appeared before the running Henry and clamped his giant hand around Henry's fragile throat, lifting the weaker man off the floor.

The only sound either could hear was the sound of urine dripping from inside Henry's pants leg onto the floor.

The hooded figure looked down at the puddle on the floor.

Henry smiled meekly and shrugged his shoulders.

"Let the boy go," spoke Grim Dog from the direction of the open doorway.

Both the hooded figure and Henry looked over at the once-great deity. Grim Dog's body filled the entire doorway, and with arms crossed and the pissed look on his face it was clear to Henry this person was unlike any senior-citizen he had ever seen.

"Don't get in my way, old man," spoke the hooded figure. The voice was gravelly, almost guttural.

"Oh, really?" responded Grim Dog. "You think you got shit on me, you fucking mutt? I made you, you fucking piece-of-shit dog turd."

The hooded figure dropped Henry on the floor and turned to fully face Grim Dog.

Henry did not wait a second before he started scrambling to get out of the room. He reached the door to the salesroom, opened it but froze in his tracks as the Blessed Mother, the Virgin Mary, materialized in the doorway and blocked his way out.

"Hi," She said in as sweet a voice as Henry had ever heard.

"Hi," was all Henry could respond with.

Meanwhile, Grim Dog said to the hooded man, "I know why you're here, boy, and you will forget about it and leave."

The hooded man shook his head and said, "I will not let you leave it in the hands of mortals again."

"And you're a fucking idiot," said Grim Dog, who threw back his arm as if he were pitching a ball and opened his hand. In it appeared the most magnificent spear ever imagined. The gleaming of its iridescent silver head lit up the entire room, destroying most of the darkness in the alleyway outside.

Henry used one of his arms to hide his eyes, "Have I lost my mind? Have I lost my fucking mind?"

The Virgin Mary took Henry's free hand and said, "Far from it, Henry Leturnoe. In fact, your mind is too big now, and you can no longer stay here. You are meant for greater things."

210

As soon as the Virgin's hand touched his, Henry was no longer blinded by the light. He was no longer afraid of the hooded man or of anything his imagination or reality could muster. Henry Leturnoe was free of fear and full of unconditional love.

He looked at the Holy Mother and smiled. He said, "I know You now. I know who You are."

"Yes, you do, Henry. And I know you. I've come to take you to where you need to be next."

"But what about my friends: Charlie, Pony, Rita, and?—um— what's his name?"

The Virgin placed a finger on Henry's lips to silence him. "Theirs is a different road for now, Henry. Trust that another will look after them."

"Is Danny with You?" Henry looked behind the Virgin Mary, as if he could see Heaven there.

"You will get to talk to Danny. Will you come with Me?"

"A note—for Charlie, at least?"

The Virgin smiled and said, "You left them a note." She pointed to his translation work. "And you have not seen the last of Charlie or Pony or Rita."

"Okay," said Henry.

With that the Virgin Mary, Her hand still holding Henry's, turned around and led him through the doorway separating the growing and sales rooms—and both vanished into thin air.

Meanwhile, Grim Dog now had his brilliant spear Gunghnir in his hand. It made the old biker look more like what he must have when chief of all the Asgardian deities in his ancient palace of Valhalla.

The younger hooded man had turned both hands into fists and was bent over in a position as if he were about to launch his whole body in a hand-to-hand attack on Grim Dog. His voice was low and growling—like an angry wolf.

"Do you want to challenge this weapon, dog? Do you really want me to send your skull back to your master in a box?"

"My master will receive word of your treachery, old man."

"Go then," shouted Grim Dog. "Go and tell him! The Augur will never be his! Never!"

The hooded man threw back its head and the hood fell away. The head of a fierce wolf lie underneath and released a powerful howl that shook the whole of the dispensary. The creature lowered its head back to look at Grim Dog and said, "We will get it—one day."

"But today is not that day," said Grim Dog as he hurled Gunghnir with all his strength at the creature.

Before the spear could hit the creature it disappeared in a burst of light. The spear stuck in the floor next to the Augur radio.

Grim Dog walked over to his spear and pulled it from the floor. Instantly, it vanished. He then bent over and picked up the radio. Brushing it off, he laughed under his breath and carried it back to the table. He placed it down on the table and walked out the back door. As he passed through the doorway, the back door magically repaired itself. The cultivation room looked like something had happened in it, but any sign of deities and demigods having battled there was nowhere to be found.

Chapter 27

West Hollywood, California

It was less than fifteen minutes after the Virgin Mary had taken Henry with Her (and Grim Dog had faced off some kind of creepy-as-shit man-dog-creature) that Charlie, Rita and Pony entered through the back door of the dispensary and entered the cultivation room. It took them a little more time to unlock the magically-repaired three dead bolts, but there was no evidence that anything supernatural had taken place. Stuff had been moved around and it looked like there might have been some kind of scuffle, but it was all stuff that Henry had done when he threw the radio and kicked it around.

Immediately though, the three friends knew something was not right. Before any of them said a word they looked at each other. Rita spoke first, "Okay, so what's not right here?"

Pony shrugged his shoulders and said, "I don't know. Maybe we're just so freaked by Buddha that we're looking for stuff that's not there."

Charlie walked over to Henry's work table. He looked at the translation papers, the radio and then the lamp. "Guys, this isn't right."

Rita and Pony walked over to Charlie.

"What do you mean?" asked Rita.

"Henry wouldn't leave a mess like this. He's too anal," answered Charlie.

Pony said, "Maybe he's in front getting something to drink." Pony began heading towards the door to the salesroom. He shouted, "Henry, dude?—you out there?" as he went through the door.

Rita looked at Charlie, who had picked up the paper that had the translated runes on it. "What is it, Boss?"

Charlie shook his head. "I'm not sure. This paper has some kind of symbols, and then—'Hey Henry how's it hanging? Didn't think I'd know your name?'"

Rita asked, "That's what Henry translated?"

"I guess," answered Charlie. "I assume it's a translation of the symbols. There's more: 'I know everything. I am the Augurspell. And the secret to me is you. Wherefrom this mystery comes only you can know. Its answer comes from its power and its power is in you. So chill bro and have another'—" Charlie stopped speaking because the last word stunned him.

"What?" asked Rita, "What does it say?"

"Toke."

"I'm sorry, what?"

"Toke—the last word is 'toke.' 'So chill bro and have another toke.'"

Rita raised her eyebrows and said, "Ohh-kay! I'm thinking maybe Henry was baked when he wrote that?"

Charlie put the sheet down and said, "Yeah, maybe."

Pony came back through the door and said, "Dude's gone, man."

"What?" Charlie asked.

Pony repeated, "Dude's gone—poof!"

Charlie looked really worried. He walked around the room inspecting the plants, the grow-lamps, anything that kept him from confronting the full weight of his friend's inexplicable disappearance.

Rita said, "I'm sure he just went out with Ian."

Charlie stopped and said, "Rita, when has Henry ever gone out with Ian—ever? He hardly goes out when it's all of us together."

Rita said, "Good point."

Pony walked over to the work table and looked at the translation paper and the words Charlie had just read out loud. "What's this freaky shit?"

Rita said, "We don't know."

"We know," said a stranger's voice from the direction of the back door.

Charlie, Rita and Pony all jumped at the sound of the voice, then turned to see Brother Williams and Vice-president Eiderbrook's assistant Barker standing just inside the open back door with Williams holding a .357 magnum revolver pointed at them. Barker, looking scared as a rabbit, stood behind Williams.

Rita looked at Pony and asked, "You forgot to lock the door again, didn't you?"

Pony smacked himself in the head and shouted, "Damn it! I always forget to do that! I always forget to lock the fucking door!"

Williams shouted, "Shut up! Stop hitting yourself! Self-abuse isn't positive and doesn't help you overcome negative patterns."

Barker added, "He's right. You should forgive yourself for making the mistake and promise to improve it next time."

Pony smiled at them. "Thanks, I'll remember to do that."

Williams ordered, "Hands up! Now!"

Barker added, "But not in a negative way—are we—um—we aren't telling you to raise your hands as a negative—in fact, we're asking you to raise them to keep us from shooting—um—" Then he asked Williams, "How is that not negative?"

Williams said, "Forget it, okay? This is bigger than negatives or positives, so—hands up!"

Charlie, Rita and Pony's hands went up in the air above their heads.

Rita cleared her throat and asked, "How about you tell us what the fuck you're doing with that gun pointed at us?"

Williams said, "We're here for the Augur."

Charlie, Rita and Pony all said in unison, "The what?"

"The Augur! The Augur! The goddamned Augur!" shouted Williams.

Barker tapped his lover on the shoulder and said, "Please, honey, calm down."

"Honey?" Rita looked at Charlie and said, "Only in West Hollywood could a dispensary get knocked over by a gay couple."

"Shut up!" shouted Williams. "We aren't mugging you! We are stealing what rightfully belongs to us! We are carrying out a sanctified operation from the Lord God Himself!"

Under her breath Rita mumbled, "Okay, Jake and Elwood."

"What was that?" screamed Williams aiming his gun directly at Rita. "You said something—under your breath!"

"Nothing!" insisted Rita. "I must have coughed or something. It's all cool."

Charlie said, "Listen man, none of us has any idea what you're talking about. This is a medical marijuana dispensary, cool? We have a lot of weed, not much cash—so you're welcome to whatever you can carry. In fact, we have tote bags under the growth tables and bank bags just below the register, right? But this Augur thing—we don't know what that is."

Williams and Barker said nothing. They just looked at Charlie, Rita and Pony's surprised expressions. Finally Barker said, "Honey, I think they're telling the truth. I really don't think they know what we mean."

"Maybe you're right," said Williams.

"That means we can just take it and not hurt them," said Barker, who began to move around Williams and head for the inside of the room.

Williams grabbed Barker's arm and pulled him back behind him, "No, wait! Wait! It could be a trap!"

Barker asked, "How? How is any of this a trap?"

"I don't know—I don't—um—I say we kill them anyway."

"What?" asked Barker. "Why?"

"Yeah, why?" repeated Pony.

"We can't chance them telling Laurel or Eiderbrook they saw us or that we took the Augur."

Rita shouted, "Dudes, we don't know who you are, or who Laurel and Eiderbrook are, and we don't know about any fucking Augur, okay?"

Williams replied, "But they have ways of making you talk!"

Rita laughed a bit and asked, "Are they Nazis?"

"Worse," said Barker. "They are Seventh-day Adventists and Jehovah's Witnesses!"

Rita stopped laughing and looked at Charlie and Pony, who looked back at her. They could all see they were surprised. But the terror in Barker's and Williams' faces was legitimate, which confused the friends.

"The people who bug you by knocking on the fucking door?" asked Charlie. "You mean those kinds of Jehovah's Witnesses and Seventh-day Adventists?"

"Oh sure," said Williams, "that's how they start out—door to door—all innocent-like. But you have no idea—no real idea of how powerful, how insidious the canvassing can be…"

Barker added, "…how addictive—how evil—I mean it's a real, real high…"

Williams: "…you just crave it—gotta have it—over and over again. Gotta get into the next house…"

Barker: "…and the next…"

Williams: "… to take over every living room in the—"

They looked like they were in a trance, some kind of creepy mental Siamese Twins rote, which suddenly caused Charlie to break out laughing. Rita joined him. Pony didn't because he was just too damn scared to find the humor in anything at that moment.

Williams shouted, "Don't laugh! Stop laughing!" He fired the gun into the ceiling.

Charlie and Rita stopped laughing.

Charlie said, "Look, guys, I'm sorry, okay? I don't mean to piss you off, but I'm having a hard time accepting that, as crazy as those Apocalypse lovers are, that they're—you know…"

Pony said, "I don't know, Charlie. I've heard some weird shit about these people."

Rita looked at Pony and said, "Are you serious?"

"Yeah, I've heard the Seventh-day Adventists smuggle those portable rocket launcher things, you know, like bazookas?"

Barker shouted, "They do! They absolutely do smuggle them! They disguise it as a yearly fund-raising drive."

Williams added, "Have you ever seen fifth-graders being taught how to sell military-grade, high-powered weaponry before? It's not as cute as you might think."

Charlie said to Williams and Barker, "Then we believe you, all right? I'm sorry we laughed. You guys have the gun, and you're obviously serious. But I promise you—we don't know anything about what you call…?"

"The Augur," shouted Williams. "Um—well, we aren't sure exactly what it looks…"

Barker spotted the radio. "The radio, baby—I bet it's the radio!"

"Check it out," said Williams.

Barker walked over to the table and picked up the radio. He inspected it. "No cord, no battery compartment—there's an eye-dial-thing—this must be it! We found it, baby! We have it. We have it all to ourselves!" He jumped up and down, as gleeful as if he had just won the lottery.

"Bring it! Bring it here!" ordered Williams, a smile crossing his face.

Barker ran back to Williams, holding the Augur, and they kissed passionately.

Charlie, Rita and Pony looked at each other. None of them looked bothered in the least by two men kissing, just the fact that they appeared to be two insane men kissing.

Williams tried to keep the gun trained on them as he and Barker were overwhelmed by their personal victory of locating the most powerful relic in the world, and before their more powerful bosses did, which made it all the sweeter. But their joy didn't last long as Ian's big hands grasped the back of each of their heads and smashed them together, ala Moe, Larry and Curly, knocking them unconscious and dropping them to the floor. Ian had come through the back door and while the lovers were passionately celebrating, took them out.

Rita smiled, "Ian, I've never been so happy to see you!"

"You've never been happy to see me," said Ian.

Rita shook her head from side-to-side. "Yeah, well, I never had something good happen when I saw you before."

Charlie sighed and said, "Good timing, buddy."

Pony added, "You're the best!"

Ian said, "It's my job to guard this place, so—who are these faggots?"

Charlie, Rita and Pony all looked equally disgusted by Ian's sexual slur.

Rita said, "The whole happy-to-see-Ian-comment," followed by a loud raspberry, "forget it—right out the fucking window."

Ian reached down and picked up Williams' gun. He popped out the clip and dumped the bullets on the floor. "These assholes try to rob us, aim this," waves the gun around in his hand, "motherfucking cannon at you, and you're pissed at me for using the word faggot?"

Rita said, "Stop it, dude! Just stop it!"

Ian slipped the gun into the waistline of his pants. He scooped up the bullets and pocketed them. "So, what the hell did they want?"

Pony walked over to the radio and took it off the floor next to Barker's hand and said, "They called this the Augur. What does that mean?"

Charlie and Rita look at each other with expressions of sudden realization. Rita says, "Augur!"

Charlie exclaims, "Augurspell! Augur is a word that means to tell the future. What they meant by the Augur, I haven't a clue; but what Henry must have meant by Augurspell…"

"…was the power inside the Augur. Because spell was an ancient word for power!" interrupted Rita.

Pony looked very confused. He mouthed to himself, "Augurspell? Spell? Magic? Weed!"

Ian said, "Speaking of Henry, where the fuck is he?"

Rita said, "Don't know. But now, we have to worry about the immediate problem here."

Ian asked Charlie, "Right, okay, then what'dya want me to do with these two—uh—homos—is that a better word?"

Charlie and Rita look at each other, shrug shoulders. Charlie asks, "Can we call the cops?"

Pony shouts out, "No! We can't do that!"

Rita asked, "Why not?"

Pony thought about it for a second and said, "I don't know—I mean, I can't tell you why yet. It's just that—shit—I don't know—um—I got this weird feeling that they weren't lying about the Jehovah's Witnesses or Seventh-day Adventists."

"What the fuck are you talking about, Pony? Are you baked already?" asked Ian.

Pony held out the radio with both hands and shook it. He said, "Since this thing came into our lives, everything's gone totally weird. I mean, my dead cousin appears, Henry disappears. Now these two guys try to steal it from us—I mean, it's all kind of—"

Charlie said, "Pony, I don't think Henry not being here means—"

Rita cut off Charlie by saying, "Wait, I think Pony's onto something. I'm not sure what, but something in my gut tells me we should wait to call the cops. Whatever's going on we should try and find out before we call them in and they fuck it all up."

Charlie looked at Ian, who shrugged his shoulders. Ian said, "With Henry gone, you're kind of the only boss, Boss."

"Great," muttered Charlie, who stood for a moment rubbing his face and thinking hard about his choices. After a few more seconds he said, "Okay, okay, tie them up. Not too tight—we don't want to hurt them, just keep them from escaping."

Ian muttered, "Allll-riiight. Come on, Shaggy, help me out."

Pony put the radio down on the table and joined Ian in searching for some kind of binding. When they decided to use the plastic ties Henry kept for straightening plants to growing-posts, they bound the wrists and ankles of their captors, now captives, and sat them back-to-back on folding chairs.

Meanwhile, Charlie and Rita walked over to the work table and began looking at the notes Henry had written when studying the futhark.

Suddenly Ian shouted, "Hey, Charlie, I almost forget to tell you!"

"What?"

"I ran into your new girlfriend Tracey at the Troubadour!"

Charlie, clearly freaked out, squeaked, "You did what?—in the Troubadour?"

"Yeah, she was there with her friend Jenny, who's totally fucking hot by the way! So I invited them to come by and hang. Is that cool?"

Rita scoffed and said, "God, you're a fucking idiot, Ian! Does it look like it'd be cool? Two guys tied up, hello?"

"I didn't ask you, Rita! So fuck off!"

Charlie exploded, "Rita is right! It's not cool! How do we explain all of this to two regular girls, huh?"

"What are you getting pissed for? It's not like I could know we'd be invaded by the pink mafia when I made the date, could I? Huh? Could I? Shit, I thought you'd be happy to see her! She seemed happy at the thought of seeing you."

That made Charlie calm down instantly. "She was? How happy? I mean—could you tell how happy she was—scale of one to ten?"

Ian looked like he was giving it serious thought, then answered, "At least an eight—probably nine."

Rita rolled her eyes and muttered, "Men and their fucking dicks."

Charlie looked at Rita. "What did you say?"

"Nothing important—talking to myself." Rita turned her attention to Ian. "Sorry to party-poop on your plans, Ian, but you have to call them and, I don't know, reschedule or something? Tell them you'll meet up at Carney's later, or the fucking Ripley's museum or Zuma Beach—I don't give two shits—you can't let them come over!"

"What? I'm not cancelling pussy!"

Rita stormed over to Ian and put a finger on his forehead. She poked it repeatedly. "Hello, is there anyone in there? How stupid are you? We can't have them see this!"

Ian looked down at the considerably tinier Rita. Her poking finger wasn't hurting him in the least. He just wasn't sure how to respond.

Charlie said, "She's right, Ian. We can't have them get caught up in this. They're just innocent women. The last thing they need is to find out how fucked up our lives are."

Ian said, "Fine! I'll call them!" Ian took out his flip phone and looked at Rita who was still standing right in front of him. "Can you please move so I can a little bit of privacy?"

Rita grabbed Pony and led him over to the work table where Charlie was once again inspecting Henry's translation work.

Ian turned his back to his friends and opened his phone as if dialing a number, but in truth he gritted his teeth and cursed himself under his breath. He couldn't call Tracey or Jenny. He didn't have their number. He had only given them directions to OHM. He had no way of calling them and cancelling. But he wasn't about to say anything in front of Rita because no matter how much smaller she was or how little her finger hurt him physically, he was frightened of what else she might be able to do, like grab his balls and twist them off without a second thought. So, he put the phone to his ear and mimicked talking.

At the work table, Pony looked at the futhark printouts while Charlie and Rita read Henry's translations. While Charlie and Rita began to discuss what they could mean, Pony said, "Hey, these are runes."

"Those are the kind of symbols I saw on these translation pages," said Charlie. "You're saying they're runes?"

"Runes?" asked Rita.

Pony answered, "Sure, I've seen some of the psychics on the boardwalk use these to tell peoples' futures."

Rita said, "You're shittin' me, right?"

"No, I'm totally serious. At this psychic fair in Glendale, I had my future read using these rune-thingies. It's really pretty fucking awesome. Some people say they read better than Tarot cards. Apparently, they are like one of the oldest things in the whole world—totally been around before people could write—even used their power to help build Stonehenge, or some such hocus-pocus bullshit. At least that's what the psychic told me who read them for me."

Charlie asked, "You're saying that Henry, agnostic Henry, was messing around with runes while we were gone?"

Pony answered, "I don't know, man. I only know what these are. I don't know why Henry was fucking with them."

Rita said, "Well, we know Henry was going to try and figure out something about your damn radio, Pony. And we know that those two lunatics called it the Augur…"

Charlie continued, "…which means telling the future…"

Rita finished, "…like Pony just said! And according to what Henry wrote, this radio must be this Augur and these runes must have something to do with figuring it out!"

Charlie said, "From what Henry wrote here, there's some sort of secret to the Augur and it has to do with 'you'?"

"Me?" asked Pony.

Rita said, "No, Pony, not you specifically. Probably meant like the generic you, like whoever-the-you-is who's reading the damn things."

Pony said, "So the radio my cousin gave me has something to do with Henry and seeing the future and now Henry's gone? What's going on, guys? I'm really starting to get freaked out! I need to get high, right now!"

Pony walked off towards the side of the cultivation room with the grass that's been prepared and is ready to be put in the bottles for sale. He sat down and picked up the closest pipe he could find. He fixed himself a bowl of a nice indiga to calm him down and lit it. He took a nice long drag and let its natural medicine work.

Rita looked very worried. She asked Charlie, "Charlie, this is some real freaky-deeky shit here. Do you have any idea what any of this means?"

Charlie shook his head. "I wish I did. All I know is that we have to figure out something, because if those two guys over there are right and people are looking for this thing—we don't know if that has to do with Henry disappearing."

Ian walked over to Charlie and Rita and said, "Charlie, can I talk to you for a sec?—alone?"

Rita said, "Fine, fine, do your boy talk thing. I'm going to join Pony." Rita headed over to where Pony was and joined him in smoking the bowl.

Ian waited for Rita to get out of earshot and said, "I can't call them."

Charlie asked, "I'm sorry, what? Did you just say?—"

"I didn't get their number, man. I told them how to find us. I didn't think—"

Charlie covered his face and scoffed. "So, we might have them show up at any minute while we have two strange men tied up and—wow, this should make a great impression."

Ian said, "You want me to take these guys outside and dump them? No one ever has to—"

Charlie shouted, "Shut up! Don't even say it! We're not hurting anyone!"

"Okay, okay, chill man—just suggesting—"

Charlie took a deep breath and calmed down. "No, we have to find out what all this weird shit's about, then we start on those two. When they wake up we need to find out what they know."

Ian smiled and cracked his knuckles. "Yeah, interrogation—now that sounds like fun!"

Chapter 28

Westwood, Los Angeles, California

Tracey and Jenny reached Tracey's condo in record time. They each had their reasons, although somewhat similar, for wanting to hook up with Ian and Charlie as soon as possible; but being careful women, neither wanted to meet them without proper protection.

As Tracey unlocked the door to her place, the friends were giggling to each other about how cool they should be when they showed up at OHM. Should they be coy? Should they just jump their bones? It was mostly Jenny who verbally strategized while Tracey just made little comments about not making the men think they were all about sex. Of course for Jenny, yeah, that was pretty much all she wanted from Ian.

Keeping in mind she had neighbors, Tracey worked hard to keep both their voices at a whisper until they were inside the apartment. They walked through the door and shut it before Tracey turned on the light. It was almost pitch black in the apartment. Tracey moved her finger to the switch but suddenly stopped.

"What is it?" Jenny asked her.

"Shhh," Tracey whispered.

"What?" asked Jenny, who was still too buzzed to see that Tracey was worried.

Tracey put a hand on Jenny's mouth. She whispered in her ear. "Someone's in here. Don't make a sound."

But a sudden welling of fear made Jenny emit a tiny squeak.

That's when a light came on in the living room, courtesy of SSA Ephraim Syde. He stood up from where he was seated on the sofa and turned to face the shocked women. "Good evening, Ms. Kipper—and friend?"

Jenny screamed through Tracey's hand, which is why Tracey didn't take her hand away.

Tracey didn't act scared in the least. She was steady, confident and absolutely calm.

Jenny began digging through her purse. She pulled out a can of pepper spray and aimed in Syde's direction, of course he was well out of range.

"Don't," Tracey told Jenny. "Don't scream, okay? It won't do us any good. Just let me talk, okay?"

Jenny looked at Tracey with a quizzical expression but she nodded her head yes.

Tracey took her hand away from Jenny's mouth.

Just then, out of the hallway that led to the bedroom, walked SA Dale Curb. In his hand he carried Charlie Hamor's soiled shirt. "Sir, I heard voices?"

Before his superior officer could say a word, Curb turned to look at the women who were only a couple of feet from him. So shocked by the man's sudden appearance, Jenny instinctively screamed, "Rape!" and fired off a blast of the pepper spray straight into his eyes.

Tracey said, "No, Jenny!" and pulled Jenny's arm with the spray down to her side. Tracey's move was too late; Jenny unleashed the potent pepper spray squarely into Curb's face.

Curb made a terrible high-pitched squeal like a six-year-old girl, and fell back into the corner edge of the wall screaming, "It burns! It burns! Oh God, it burns so bad!" and slid to the floor, writhing in pain.

Syde threw his hands in the air and scoffed. "Holy shit, what did I do to deserve the nephew of the Director?"

Jenny shouted at Syde, "Watch it, asshole, or I'll spray your ass too! Trace, call the cops!"

Tracey said, "Jenny, please, let me handle this my way okay?"

Jenny looked at her friend and said, "What? These guys could be here to rape us!"

Tracey smiled at Jenny and said, "They aren't here to rape us, and even if they were I think you made it clear they aren't getting an inch closer to us."

"Damn right," said Jenny.

Tracey looked down at the squirming Curb, who had now pulled himself up to a seated position against the wall and was vigorously trying to wipe his red and swollen eyes clean. "Why don't you keep him covered, Batgirl, and I'll talk to this—person?"

Jenny shrugged her shoulders and said, "Yeah, okay, if you think so." Jenny lifted her pepper spray can, holding it with both hands, and aimed it on Curb. "One move, shitbag, one move…"

"Oh God, why?" muttered the agonizing Curb. "I'd never hurt—never touch a woman—it hurts so very, very much."

Tracey stepped past Curb in the direction of Syde but kept herself safely out of his reach. "Who the hell are you and why did you break into my place?"

Agent Syde reached into his jacket and took out his wallet. He flipped it open and showed Tracey his badge and identification card.

"FBI?" asked Tracey.

"That's right, Ms. Kipper. I am a federal agent. So's that one." Syde pointed at Curb. "I'm SSA Syde and that's SA Curb."

Jenny's eyes shot wide open. "You're a cop?" she meekly asked Curb.

Curb could only nod his head.

Jenny slipped the can back in her purse and giggled, "Sorry, agent—uh—I'm really, really sorry. Why don't we see if we can't wash that off of your face, okay?"

Curb mumbled, "Mmm, okay, okay, please—it hurts so bad."

Jenny began to make soothing sounds as she helped him to his feet and walked him to the bathroom. "I'm so sorry, mister—really. It's just, you know, it's LA and all sorts of—please, don't send me to Guantanamo."

They disappeared down the hallway and into the bathroom from where Tracey and Syde could hear the water in the sink running as Jenny began to wash Curb's face.

Tracey asked Syde, "What is the FBI doing in my place?"

Syde put his badge back inside his jacket and said, "You're awfully cool, Ms. Kipper. It's almost like, well, you're very comfortable with something so unusual for a civilian?"

Tracey crossed her arms and said, "I have an uncle who's a federal agent."

"Oh, really?"

"Not FBI, but federal, yes."

"Who?"

Tracey shrugged her shoulders and said, "It's a big government. I'm sure you wouldn't know him."

"You don't know that, Ms. Kipper. I'm very well connected."

"So am I and I am confident you don't know him, okay? So why don't we dispense with this chit-chat and get down to the fucking point."

"Do you know a Charles Hamor?"

Tracey shook her head no and said, "I'm sorry, Charles who?"

Syde snickered. "Don't be coy, Ms. Kipper. You don't play it well. I know you know Charles Hamor, owner of a medical marijuana dispensary in West Hollywood called OHM."

Tracey threw her hands in the air and let them fall back to her side. She shook her head from side to side with big wide eyes and a blank expression.

Jenny walked back from the hallway with a less-suffering Agent Curb. He had a damp t-shirt pressed to his eyes.

Syde nodded his head. "So you're going to tell me you have never heard of or had contact with one Charles Hamor?"

Before Tracey could again deny knowing Charlie, Jenny piped up with, "Charles Hamor? Do you mean Charlie Hamor, the guy who was here last night?"

Tracey gasped and shot a look at Jenny. She shouted, "Jenny, don't! Don't!"

"Ah ha!" exclaimed Agent Syde.

Jenny shouted back at Tracey, "What? What did I do? He said Charlie's name, so what?"

Tracey dropped her face and covered it with her hand.

"Well," said Agent Syde, "I think your friend just made up for attacking my partner, Ms. Kipper."

Suddenly Tracey lifted her head and clenched her fists. She stepped a few feet closer to Syde and shouted out, "Do you have a warrant, Agent Syde?"

"Excuse me?" asked Syde.

"Do you have a fucking warrant, Agent Syde? Because if you don't, you need to get the fuck out of my apartment, right now, or I will call the cops and have them kick you out for trespassing. Perhaps you would rather me not let them know you and your partner are roaming around LA busting into single women's apartments?—to rape them?—huh?"

Jenny was shocked by Tracey's sudden explosion. "Trace, what are you saying?"

Tracey continued, "Maybe I should call the Times and let them know how an Agent Syde and Agent Curb are stalking pretty girls all around LA, using their federal badges to break into apartments to violate young defenseless women like me and my friend! Huh? Would you like that, huh? Huh?"

Still being held by Jenny, Curb said to her, "I don't want to rape you, miss. Honestly, I'm not going to—"

Jenny patted Curb on the back and said, "I know, mister. My friend is just—you know—"

Syde threw up his hands and shouted, "Okay! Okay! Calm down, Ms. Kipper. We'll go. We'll go." Syde walked past Tracey, who turned with Syde to keep facing him, and then grabbed his partner from Jenny's arms. He led his partner to the front door and stopped. He looked at Tracey and said, "If you decide, Ms. Kipper, you'd like to come clean and help your government..." He reached into his outside jacket pocket and took out a business card, which he flipped across the room at Tracey. She caught it.

Agent Syde continued with his partner out the front door.

"It still burns," mumbled Curb.

"Shut up," Syde replied.

Tracey stormed up to the door, closed it behind the agents and dead-bolted the lock. She then let out a huge sigh of relief.

Jenny looked at her friend and said, "What the fuck was that about and why are feds chasing Charlie?"

Tracey looked at Jenny and was ready to respond when she suddenly realized something and asked, "The shirt? The shirt?"

"What shirt? What?"

"Charlie's shirt! That agent, the younger one, the one you..."

"Yeah, yeah, he had a shirt in his hand. So what?"

"Where is it, now?"

"I don't know! I mean, it was dirty and all, but I rinsed it off and used it to wipe the guy's eyes with, so—"

Tracey covered her eyes with her hands and shouted, "Oh shit, no! No! Don't tell me he left with it! That they have that shirt right now!"

Jenny looked totally confused and freaked out by her friend's reaction. "Yes, yes, I'm sorry, okay? I'm sorry, but yeah, he took it with him to cover his face! What did I do? What did I do wrong, Tracey? I don't understand why you're acting like this over that guy's shirt! Why?"

Tracey shook her head and began to quietly laugh. She put her back to the door and slid down to her haunches. "It's okay, Jenny. I'm sorry. I didn't mean to freak you out. Sorry."

Jenny walked over to Tracey and kneeled down in front of her so they were eye to eye. She took Tracey's hands in hers and said, "Wow, this guy Charlie's really gotten to you, hasn't he? You're really worried about him, huh? About what those guys want with him, huh? Is that it? Is it him being like a wanted man that's such a turn on? Cause I kind of like bad boys, too, you know. I mean—"

Tracey kept laughing and then lifted her face so that she was looking Jenny dead in the eye. While Jenny was still rambling, Tracey said, "I'm a federal agent too, Jenny."

Jenny kept on rambling, the words not quite sinking in yet.

"Jenny, honey, honey, did you hear me? I'm a federal agent too. Like those two guys who just left here."

That's when it sunk in and Jenny said, "What—what—what the—what did you just say? You're a…? No way—no fucking—"

"It's true. It's true, Jenny." She put her hands on Jenny's face. "I'm a federal agent like them, only I work for the NSA, the National Security Agency."

Jenny's face lost all color; her eyes rolled up in her head, her mouth dropped open, and she fainted on the floor.

Tracey looked at her unconscious friend. "Well, she took that better than I thought she would."

Parking Garage Below Tracey's Apartment

SSA Syde helped his younger partner out of the elevator and into the parking garage where they had parked their car in the reserved spot for disabled tenants. Of course, as federal agents they did not concern themselves with societal conventions like respect for the disabled or even respect for how few parking spots there was for a building the size of the one they were in. After all, putting their lives (and eyesight) on the line as such agents do each and every day should certainly allow them the privilege of parking wherever the fuck they want to, cripples be damned ("cripples" being the kind of repugnant word Syde used).

Curb kept mumbling something to Syde as they walked across the lot to reach their parking spot, but Syde could not care less about what he was saying. He was thinking about how he was going to make that girl half his age pay a heavy fucking price for standing up to him. The only acknowledgement he made of Curb, other than to keep his arm over his shoulder so that Curb wouldn't hit a wall, was to keep the wet shirt from slipping off his face and exposing the terrible irritation underneath.

Of course if Syde had listened to what Curb was saying, it might have surprised him to learn that the wet shirt was what Curb was trying to tell Syde belonged to Charles Hamor and was all the evidence they needed to get that warrant to go back and harass Tracey Kipper. But Syde didn't listen to his younger—he was too full of hate—and hating made him feel just a little bit better.

Suddenly the lights in the parking garage died.

"What the fuck?" shouted Syde.

"What?" asked Curb, who couldn't see the lights were out.

Syde let go of Curb and said, "The lights—gone out."

Curb said, "Lights? Where?"

"In the garage, stupid!"

Curb said, "Hey, don't call me stupid! I'm kind of blind here, okay?"

Syde said, "It's pitch fucking black in—"

A motorcycle engine roared to life and echoed through the whole garage like a great monster.

"Holy shit!" shouted Syde.

"A motorcycle?" asked Curb.

The light of a headlamp fell onto Syde and Curb, who had stopped in the middle of the parking lane, not far from their own car. But what caught Syde's attention was the eerie shape made by the headlamp on the floor of the garage—a kind of cross, a Templar Cross—on the floor of the garage.

"What the fuck is that?" asked Syde as he looked from the floor to the oncoming vehicle. It was a chopper motorcycle and it was accelerating very quickly towards them.

Curb started panicking. He couldn't see and was getting scared. Throwing his arms out and swinging them around, Curb shouted, "Agent Syde? Sir? What's going on? I hear it but I can't see it! Where is it?"

Syde had very little time to react. He could grab Curb and pull the younger agent and himself out of the motorcycle's path—maybe?—but maybe he wouldn't be able to pull the stronger youth or control him in his confusion? If he were to leap himself away he could definitely clear the motorcycle, even if it meant his partner being killed. Of course in the dark, in such a quick moment, who would know, right? No one would know the difference as to how or why Curb was hit by the motorcycle—not even the cyclist who was driving so recklessly—at least according to the eyewitness report of such a senior and decorated agent.

"Sir? Agent Syde, please tell me what's going on?"

The chopper was bearing down very quickly on the two agents. The driver was ready to swerve, when the older agent pushed the younger into his swerving path and leapt well out of the way. Agent Dale Curb, fortunately or not, would never consciously know how he died. Seeing the face of the priest driving the motorcycle would never be etched onto the last active seconds of his brain's life. No, Dale Curb's neck was instantly snapped when he fell forward from a combination of the push given by his superior officer and his foot getting caught on the concrete in an attempt to blindly catch himself falling. The chopper wheel struck the young man's neck at full speed, almost decapitating him.

The priest Father Agosto was too skilled to lose control of the bike, even after such a mortal collision. He used his unusually high strength and dexterity to sling the bike around so that it screeched to a stop. Through the Revelator Glasses, Agosto could see the young agent he had just killed and that it was Syde, now scrambling to where the agent thought his car was, who had pushed Curb into Agosto's deadly path. Agosto revved the bike up to full speed and opened the throttle, in the direction of the fleeing Agent Syde.

Unfortunately for Syde, his natural sense of direction wasn't very good in the dark—but then whose is? He was actually running past his car and back out into the open where the priest and bike were bearing down on him faster than he could elude them. Syde decided to turn to face the bike and draw his gun. He fired into the light of the motorcycle while screaming at the top of his lungs.

Agosto was just too—unusual. He wasn't hit by a single bullet fired from Syde's gun. In fact, he drew his own crucifix-handled guns and unloaded them into the Homeland Security agent, whose bullet-riddled body hit the floor of the garage just in time to be run over by the chopper's wheels. It was a much more gruesome and consciously painful death than Syde's younger counterpart. Agosto brought his chopper to a screeching halt and swung it around to face the two bodies. He ramped down the bike's engine and holstered his guns. He snapped the fingers on his left hand and half the lights in the parking garage flickered to life.

Clearly Father Agosto had, for his own reasons, opted to follow Tracey Kipper and Jenny Sway out of the Troubadour instead of Ian Olczwicki. Why would he do that after it was clear to him that Ian had been in the presence of something more powerful than Tracey, who had managed to drive Agosto to a knee? That decision might be learned as the priest slowly drove his bike over to the body of Dale Curb, who through all of it, still had Charlie Hamor's shirt in his hand. Agosto reached down and picked up the shirt. As he inspected it closely with the Revelator Glasses, he saw strange swirls of energy moving in and around the poly-cotton fibers of the shirt—swirls that resembled knots—Celtic and Nordic-style knots. He tightened his fist around the shirt, as if trying to break the knots of energy, and in a low voice said, "Vanaesir? Is that what all of this is about? This man-child is one of the Vanaesir?"

Agosto stuffed Charlie's t-shirt into a side pouch of the bike's seat with a sleeve unintentionally left visible. Then the priest delivered the sacrament of last rites for the soul of the young Dale Curb. As for Ephraim Syde, the priest said no such prayer. In fact, he never even glanced at the older casualty as he revved up the bike and drove out of the parking garage.

Chapter 29

Westwood, Los Angeles, California

Jenny woke up on the sofa inside Tracey's condo with Tracey holding a bottle of water to her lips.

"Just a little sip," Tracey told her. "Not too much."

But Jenny did swallow too much, and began to choke. She coughed and coughed and Tracey had to wipe the water off Jenny's chin and pat her back until Jenny caught her breath.

Finally, when Jenny was able to speak she said, "I can't believe it."

"I know," Tracey told her.

"All this time, and I never knew. You never told me."

"We're not supposed to," Tracey told her. "In fact, I'm probably going to be fired for telling you."

"Why?"

"It's a long story, Jen. Just—just know that I couldn't tell anyone I was a federal agent. Not even my family knows."

"Wow," said Jenny. "You trust me that much."

Tracey shrugged her shoulders. "Guess so."

"Does that mean then, with those agents and Charlie that—is he like an assignment for you? Is that why you're involved with him? Is he a spy or something? Is he working for the Russians or like Al

Qaeda? Hey, maybe he's like in one of those—what do they call them? Sleep-over cells?"

Tracey laughed. "No, no, Charlie isn't Russian or Al Qaeda. And he isn't part of any sleeper cell."

"Then what's it all about? Is this because he's into medical pot?"

"Well, I'm not entirely sure, but I don't think it's about that. If it was we'd have found ATF, not FBI, waiting for us. What I do know is that he's on the radar of those agents and I need to know why. So, if you feel up to it?—"

Jenny perked up. "We're still going over to see him and Ian?"

"Kind of have to now."

"Great!"

Tracey insisted, "But Jenny, you cannot tell them anything about what happened here until I say it's okay. Got it?"

"Okay."

"I'm serious, Jenny. You can't tell them a damn thing about me and those agents or anything, right? You just have to act like a girl who's gone there for a good time, right?"

"Yeah, yeah, I get it, Trace. Sheesh, you act like I'm six-years-old. I might not be a government bad-ass, but I've seen more than my fair share of 'Hawaii Five-O' and 'Criminal Minds.'"

Tracey wiggled her eyebrows and said, "I wish the job was as easy as they make it look."

"Wow, my best friend is a spy—cool. It's very, very cool. I mean, too bad you can't broadcast it—we'd get so much cock!"

Tracey broke up laughing.

"Seriously! Do you know how many guys we could bed in one weekend?"

Tracey put a finger to Jenny's forehead and said, "Enough of that now. I'm still just Tracey Kipper, independent bookstore owner, okay? And what I feel for Charlie is very real—spy or not."

Jenny mock saluted Tracey. "Aye-aye, Cap'n Sir!"

It only took the two women another ten minutes to get completely put together and head out. By the time they were walking out of the apartment, Jenny Sway was talking to her friend Tracey Kipper about Ian and Charlie as if she had never been told that Tracey was an NSA agent and she had not run into two Homeland Security Agents who were hunting down Charlie. It was an aspect of Jenny's character that Tracey very much admired—resilience.

But when they got in the elevator to ride it down to the parking garage, Jenny did ask Tracey one thing connected to what she had revealed about herself: "Can I see your badge, your NSA badge?"

Tracey smiled and reached into her purse and took it out. She handed the wallet to Jenny who opened it, looked at the shield and card and made "oooh" sounds. It wasn't something Tracey usually carried on her, but under the circumstances, she thought to put it in her purse when she was still in her bedroom changing clothes. She had a safe in her closet where she kept all such things, including her service weapon which was also now in her purse, but Jenny hadn't asked to see that.

Everything actually seemed pretty much okay between the women when they reached the parking garage and the doors opened. But when they stepped out and saw police lights and EMT vehicles along with cops and emergency medical techs swarming around the garage, they were suddenly overwhelmed with shock.

"What's all this?" Jenny asked.

Tracey said, "I don't—" but she stopped talking when she saw two bodies on gurneys. One corpse already had been zipped up in the body bag, while the second had its face still visible; the face belonged to SSA Ephraim Syde.

"Holy shit," gasped Tracey.

"What?" asked Jenny. "What?"

Tracey gulped and said, "We have to get out of here, now."

Jenny didn't see Syde like Tracey had and said, "How can we get to our car from here?"

Tracey said, "You're right. We need to call a taxi, outside—um—up on the ground level. Let's go. Let's go." Tracey pushed her friend back into the elevator and quickly punched the first floor button and repeatedly pushed the "door close" button before any cops spotted them.

As the elevator doors closed Jenny said, "What happened down there? You think?—" and from there it became Jenny's unique kind of babbling from one thought or question to the next. It was more than Tracey was able to handle at that moment.

Tracey grabbed Jenny by the shoulders and gently shook her. "Please, Jenny, honey, please stop talking for just a minute, okay? I've got to think—to think—to think—didn't see his shirt. I didn't see Charlie's shirt down there. Maybe they didn't find it. Oh God, they're cops. Of course they'll find it."

Tracey's words failed to calm Jenny. In fact she was now totally confused by Tracey's train of thought, which didn't make her stop yakking. "What are you saying? Those agents took Charlie's shirt. Why would you think Charlie's shirt was with those—what?" shouted Jenny at the top of her lungs. "That was them? Those bodies were those agents? Holy shit! Holy shit! Hooooleee shit!"

Tracey shook her friend repeatedly to calm her down. "Calm down, Jenny, please! I don't want you to faint again—"

Too late.

Tracey was ready to catch Jenny as she fell unconscious. Both sank to the floor of the elevator, which opened on the ground floor adjacent to the lobby.

"Shit," muttered Tracey, who lifted Jenny and walked her out of the elevator and over to a nearby bench. She sat her friend down and then sat next to her, leaning Jenny's body against hers. Tracey grabbed Jenny's mobile phone and punched up a number. She looked out the all-glass walls of the lobby and saw more cop cars pulling up and surrounding the building. Tracey really looked nervous, but when she saw what she knew to be an SUV from the Los Angeles offices of the FBI she made a whimpering noise. She hit the connect button to ring the number. It rang. It rang twice. It rang three times.

"God no, please—oh shit—Uncle Leo will kill me."

On the fifth ring, someone finally answered the call. It was Charlie Hamor.

"Hello?" asked Charlie.

"Hi, Charlie—um—this is Tracey—Kipper? Tracey Kipper? From the—"

"I know who you are, Tracey—of course I do—wow. Listen it's so weird you should call me, cause—"

Tracey cut off Charlie by saying, "Charlie, can you please just listen? I—um—really, really, really like you—a whole lot."

"Wow, I like you, too—really do, but—"

Tracey said, "Charlie, I know that something weird is going on for you tonight, right now even—am I correct? Weird people showing up or watching you?—"

Charlie cut off Tracey by asking, "How'd you know, huh? How did you?—" Charlie stopped talking as he lost his train of thought.

In his voice Tracey heard a kind of tone—a "high" tone which made her scoff. "You're baked right now, aren't you, Charlie?"

"Um—a little, sure, but you can't believe what's happened to me tonight! Two guys with!—"

An exasperated Tracey interrupted Charlie. "Charlie? You have to listen to me, okay? You have to do exactly what I tell you to do and nothing different, okay?"

There was only silence.

Tracey decided to start over with just, "Charlie?"

"Yes?"

"Can you hear me?"

"Yes, Tracey, I hear you."

"Then do exactly what I tell you to do, okay?"

"Okay."

"You're picking me up. This is the address—"

After Tracey gave Charlie the address, which was a good three blocks from where she and Jenny were now sitting in the lobby, she ended the call and slipped the phone back into Jenny's purse. It had been Jenny's phone, not Tracey's that she used, because her bosses at the National Security Agency (whom some people—really smart people—consider to be much more deadly than that bunch at the CIA) didn't need to know Tracey had just called Charlie. Because Tracey knew that if the NSA had not already learned about what happened in the parking garage, they were going to find out in no more than ten minutes that her address was right above the spot where two Homeland Security agents had been murdered.

What mattered most to Tracey was that the half-baked Charlie would be able to get to the pick-up spot without incident. All Tracey could do was to help her friend stand —Jenny was starting to wake up—and lead her out through the lobby doors and down the sidewalk in the direction of the intersection of Manning and Eastborne Avenues. There was a small independent convenience store there whose address Tracey gave Charlie.

By the time the two women got to the store, Jenny was awake and filled in by Tracey on what she had seen of Agent Syde. She told Jenny her biggest concern was whether or not Charlie's shirt had been recovered from Curb's body. That's when Jenny began to panic about the cops tracing the pepper spray in Curb's eyes to her particular can. Tracey quickly dismissed that fear and told her that it was unlikely anyone could actually trace the agents back to them, which was something of a lie as her bosses might if they were clued in to the incident in the garage. But Tracey was happy to lie to Jenny if it meant keeping her friend from freaking out any further.

"So, Charlie and Ian are coming to get us then?"

"Yes, well, Charlie is. I don't know if Ian will be with him."

"You said Charlie was high?"

"He sounded like he had a buzz, yes."

"And if I needed to get a buzz—would you arrest me or what?"

Tracey laughed and said, "Jenny, I'm not DEA! And yeah, I think I could do with some nice indiga myself."

"Indiga?" asked Jenny. "You know your pot, huh?"

"A bit, yeah," said Tracey. "Listen, now that you know I'm a NSA agent, can I tell you I also smoke sometimes? Right now I need a cigarette bad."

Jenny said, "Honey, me too!" Jenny dashed into the convenience store and bought a pack of cigarettes, which she opened up on the way back out to her friend. Together they smoked and tried to come down from the insanity of the weirdest Sunday night either of them had ever had.

After another few minutes of chatting and watching the road for any sign of Charlie, the women saw a tricked-out van—purple with a huge yin-yang symbol next to a giant ohm symbol—pull into the parking lot of the store and park not far from them.

Jenny shook her head and said, "Check that shit out? Who would ride in that fucking thing?"

Tracey said nothing as the side door slid open and four men with machine guns emptied out and trained their guns at her and Jenny.

"No fucking way," muttered Jenny. "They aren't doing this to us?"

Claudia stepped out next. She looked strikingly hot and sexually exotic in a sleek black skin-tight bodysuit. She said to them, "Hi, I believe you ladies were expecting Charlie Hamor?"

Jenny asked, "You're with Charlie?"

Claudia answered, "No, I'm with—"

Tracey dropped her cigarette and crushed it out with her shoe. She said, "You're Claudia. You're Charlie's ex-girlfriend and you work as a bodyguard for the drug lord Buddha Jesus."

Claudia looked at Tracey with a big cat grin. "My, my, my, you are impressive for a Midwestern twat."

Jenny shouted, "You'd better not fuck with us, bitch, 'cause my friend here is a—"

238

Tracey punched Jenny unconscious before she let out the critical information that would be their ace-in-the-hole as long as it remained unknown.

Everyone watched Jenny drop to the ground.

Claudia nodded and said to Tracey, "Well, you are a strange little bird, aren't you?"

"You want me," offered Tracey, "you can take me. But you leave my friend here, all right? You obviously want me because of Charlie, right?"

"Well, yes, to get his attention about something."

Tracey walked towards Claudia with her hands and purse up in the air and said, "He's going to be here to pick us up any minute. Leave her and she can give him the message."

Claudia grabbed Tracey's purse and tossed it to one of the gunmen, who held onto it without looking through it. Claudia walked around Tracey and pulled her arms down behind her back and bound her wrists with a plastic tie. "You are smart, and definitely more than you appear to be."

Tracey said, "All you need to know is, that whatever game you and your scum of a boss think you're playing at, is way beyond your intelligence to grasp. Trust me when I say that you've taken a very big step into a very large pile of shit by kidnapping me."

Claudia whispered in Tracey's ear, "You don't scare me, Bitch-any Spears. Whatever you think you know about me and my boss, you don't know about me and my boss. Now, get—" and Claudia shoved Tracey at two of the gunmen, who grabbed Tracey by the arms, picked her up and physically carried her to the van. They threw her inside.

Claudia walked over to Jenny and kneeled down. She grabbed Jenny's chin and lifted her head. She slapped her face a few times until Jenny began to wake up. Claudia said, "Tell Charles to come to Buddha's compound if he wants to see his girlfriend again—and tell him to bring the radio."

Jenny, barely conscious, mumbled, "Big mistake—stupid bitch—she's—agent with—"

Claudia may have heard the words Jenny said, but her mind wasn't connecting them. She was already walking back to the van by the time "agent" came out of Jenny's trembling mouth. Claudia climbed inside the shotgun seat of the van and shifted the rearview mirror to see her prisoner sitting against the wall of the van, looking very pissed. As the van started up, a gunman closed the sliding door.

Suddenly one of the gunmen shouted, "Federalé! Federalé!"

Claudia shouted back in Spanish, "What the fuck, Gomez?"

Gomez scrambled up behind Claudia with Tracey's purse and handed it to her. Gomez kept shouting, "She's a fed! She's a fed!"

Claudia looked inside the purse and found the gun and the wallet that said Tracey Kipper was a National Security Agent. "Oh you have got to be shitting me! This is too fucking good. This is too fucking good." Claudia broke out laughing.

Tracey turned to look at Claudia laughing in the rearview mirror.

Back in the parking lot of the convenience store, Jenny began to regain consciousness just in time to see the ugly purple van disappear down the street. She fought to rise to her feet and just as she made it up to her full height, she saw Charlie and Ian pull into the parking lot and stop just a few feet from her.

Ian popped his head out at Jenny and said, "Hey, babe! Whoa, you okay? You look kind of—wrecked."

Jenny began to speak, to try and describe what happened when Charlie climbed out of the passenger's side of the car and walked up to her. He said, "Hey, you okay? Where's Tracey?"

Jenny leaned against Charlie and was still fighting to find the words.

Charlie looked back at Ian and said, "Ian, I think something's wrong with her. She's acting—I don't know—fucked up."

Leaving the engine running, Ian climbed out of the car and helped Charlie by supporting Jenny with his bigger strength. "Hey, sweetheart, what's wrong?"

"Kidnapped," muttered Jenny.

"What?" shouted both men.

"Kidnapped by some cat-eyed bitch named Claudia. In Buddha Jesus—compound."

"Oh shit," said Ian. "What the fuck is she saying?"

Charlie said, "I don't know, but it sounds bad. It sounds real bad. Hey, Jenny? Jenny?"

Jenny looked at Charlie and asked, "Are you Charlie?"

"Yes, I'm Charlie."

Jenny slapped Charlie, but good.

Ian broke out laughing, while Charlie rubbed his stinging cheek with his hand. Ian grabbed his friend's shoulder and said, "I think I'm love with this girl."

Jenny said, "This is your fault—you fuck! I don't know why, but Tracey—cares for you—nightmare people want to kill you—kidnapped my friend because of you and a radio?"

Ian and Charlie looked at each other and simultaneously said, "Radio?"

Jenny said, "Yes, cat-woman-bitch said bring—radio to—compound?"

Charlie looked at Ian and said, "We've got to help Tracey. Can you?—" as he nodded towards Jenny and ran back to the car.

Ian asked, "What the fuck is up with this radio?" Ian lifted up Jenny into his arms and went back to the car. He opened the back door and gently laid Jenny down across the back seat. Ian climbed in after her and lifted Jenny just enough so that he could rest her head on his lap.

Charlie sat behind the wheel of the car, shifted into drive and tore out of the parking lot with his brain going a hundred miles faster than the car.

Chapter 30

West Hollywood, California

"Right—okay—yeah—we'll be right here." Rita closed her mobile phone and stared off into space with a completely stunned expression.

Pony was captivated by Rita's look and glanced into the same space, as if he could see whatever it was she was seeing inside her head. But Pony was stoned—not too much for him, but enough—and when he realized there wasn't actually anything in the air for him to see, he looked back at Rita and asked, "What? What did Charlie have to say?"

Rita shook her head and came back to the present. She had taken another toke or two before Charlie called her from the car, just after leaving the convenience store parking lot in pursuit of Claudia and the kidnapped Tracey, but two tokes wasn't enough to even get her decently buzzed. Still, the shock of what Charlie had reported to her was stunted a bit by the indiga. So as she recited back to Pony, it seemed as if she were describing a strange dream. "Apparently, Buddha Jesus wants the radio—the one you got from your cousin—and is holding Charlie's not-quite-yet-girlfriend Tracey hostage until he gets it."

"Holy shit, how did he find out about the radio?" Pony pondered.
"You don't remember?"

Pony genuinely looked like he didn't recollect the incident.

Rita rolled her eyes and said, "Pony, maybe—just maybe—could you not be so fucking stoned for six seconds? We told him about it when we had to get a new supply of his blend after you traded it for that fucking radio!"

"Oh yeah, now I remember."

"Good! Now that you remember that little detail, maybe you'll realize that same psycho has kidnapped a real-life person to fucking get it?" Rita asked in response.

Pony walked over to the Augur and picked it up. He looked it over so closely his nose was almost touching it. "What has my dead cousin given to us? And what?—" Pony spun around and looked at Rita with an excited look on his face. "Hey, did Charlie say what we're supposed to do? Like, do we take it to him or is he coming here or?—"

"Nothing!" shouted Rita, who was now feeling some jealousy creep through her calm façade over Charlie's involvement or would-be involvement with Tracey.

"Huh?" Pony was confused by Rita's apparent anger.

Rita caught her reveal and shook it off. In a much calmer voice she said, "No, no, sorry, I just don't understand what's going on! No, uh, Charlie said for us to just keep an eye on it and wait for his next call."

"Right," said Pony, who now sat down in the chair at Henry's work table and began to run his fingers over the radio, trying to switch it on.

Rita on the other hand took her mobile, slid open the text table and began to text Henry's number. It was a standard message: "Yo Henry, where in the hell are you?" But instead of a reply she got back the service provider message that his phone was no longer in service. Frustrated, Rita closed up her phone and shouted, "I don't get it—where the fuck is Henry?"

Pony said, "Still can't get ahold of him?"

Rita walked over to Pony and said, "That's the thing, man. I get the provider-bullshit that his number's not in service, but I know it is. It was this morning. And if anyone pays their bill on time it's Captain Anal Henry!"

Suddenly the voice of Brother Williams caught both Rita and Pony by surprise when he asked, "You really don't have any idea what you have there, do you? You are both so lost and so damned."

Rita and Pony looked at Williams and the still-unconscious Barker.

"Oh, and you fucking know something about it?" shouted Rita.

"More than you faithless douchebags!" shouted Williams.

"Fuck you, you lunatic! I might not have gone to church in a decade but don't you fucking tell me my fucking soul is fucking damned, you fucking fuckhead!" Rita balled her hand into a fist and went running at Williams, ready to knock out every tooth in his head.

Pony leaped up from the chair with such speed and strength, he knocked not only the chair but the entire work table over, which sent the radio flying through the air. But Pony caught Rita's arm before she reached William's face. "No, Rita! Don't!"

Rita stopped and looked at Pony, who was holding back her arm.

"Shit!" screamed Williams as the radio hit the floor. "Don't break it, fuck-face!"

Rita shot a burn-in-hell look at Williams and actually growled. "I hate you, motherfucker, and I don't even know—"

The radio crackled to life.

Rita stopped in mid-sentence.

Everyone else in the room, including Barker who was coming back to consciousness with all the yelling, gasped as they all looked at the radio, except Barker who wasn't able to see the radio because of how he was tied to his chair.

The radio dial began to turn itself as the plate lit up and electricity from no visible source began to surge through the relic in search of a station.

Barker screamed, "What is it, honey? Is it?—is it—?"

"Yes!" screamed Williams, "It's come to life! The Augur's alive!"

Rita and Pony had no words as they looked at the radio do whatever it was doing.

Within seconds, the radio had found a working station and they all heard a broadcaster's voice come through crisp and clear.

"As those of you who have been listening to our coverage of the war since it began less than two weeks ago, you are aware of how difficult it has been for any of the news services to get reporters into the war zone to verify some of the more fantastic reports coming out of the battlefield, especially regarding the kind of air-based phenomena rumored to be involved in combat."

Another broadcaster, a woman, broke in at that point to say, "No one, least of all us, wants to suggest for even a moment that any of the service members, especially our own brave young Americans who have reported the strange happenings, are in anyway false or not telling exactly what they believe to be the truth. However, there have been rumors now for at least a week that perhaps some kind of other biological warfare is involved, which may be affecting the sensory perception of those troops locked into combat."

The male broadcaster returned to say, "That's correct, Dianne. That's correct. These rumors of some kind of affectation of our troops, which may have led to the strange reports, have been supported by our own government; perhaps in an effort not to dispute the legitimacy of what our troops report, but to somehow persuade news organizations from pursuing validation of our own. Fortunately, many organizations have learned, especially since the recent debacle of embedded journalism during the Iraq and Afghanistan wars, that we simply cannot trust any government not to manipulate and lie to journalists and use the media to further their own propaganda.

"As a result of NPR's renewed mission to stay free of censorship, propaganda and any commercial or governmental influence—including any and all corporate interests who use their money to try and alter our independent voice—we have worked harder than ever to get our veteran foreign correspondent Kyle Huntley into the region to send us a report."

The woman broadcaster's voice returned to say, "And to Kyle's credit and courage, he has sent us the following report—the first of its kind since the beginning of this new war—directly from the battlefield."

Rita and Pony looked at each other, wondering what was coming next.

Williams struggled with his ties, while Barker began to cry.

Kyle Huntley's voice came over the radio and said, "Ron and Dianne, I am presently located somewhere just outside the most recent city under siege. Although I cannot give any information specific to my location for obvious reasons, I can tell you unequivocally that the reports of strange aerial phenomena are not exaggerated. What I can tell you is that with my own eyes I am seeing seven—yes, seven—well, the best way I can describe them are creatures possessing multiple wings with their human-like bodies covered with multiple—eyes? They are all blinking at different intervals. Each of these creatures must be at least seventy feet—maybe one hundred feet high. They began their slow descent above this city some three hours ago, and the weather has been stormy ever since. They ended their descent a short time ago and have been hovering. I kid you not when I tell you that the sound of thunder and yes, even trumpets—or something like trumpets as if made out of Boeing Jet engines—have been heard intermittently since these creatures first appeared. At first their wings were not flapping in unison; however, just a few short minutes ago the wings began to flap in unison. And it appears that giant bowls have materialized in the hands of these creatures.

"Allied troops gathered in this city and surrounding its perimeters have attempted to fire on the creatures, but no apparent damage was taken by any level of ordinance. As for the creatures, they seem to have no recognition of the assaults. And now—yes, now—I can report that the creatures have taken the large bowls and are turning them upside down to pour out—I cannot believe what I'm seeing! It is—blood! I repeat—blood is being poured from the bowls onto the city and the troops—and on—it's burning! The whole city! Everyone hit by the blood! Fire! Exploding into fire—"

Suddenly the radio shut off as it had before, as if it never had broadcasted at all.

Rita and Pony looked at each other.

Williams was whispering to his partner Barker in an effort to comfort and calm the distraught Adventist.

Rita said, "Wow. That was the most fucked up thing…"

Pony finished, "…I've ever heard in my life."

Rita asked, "Did it sound like war coverage to you?"

Pony nodded. "Totally—absolutely totally—I mean, do you think it's about the Iraq war or Afghanistan?"

Rita shook her head, "No, they made it pretty clear that they weren't talking about either of those—that they were talking about something that happened…"

Pony finished with, "…afterwards?"

Rita said, "But what sense does that make? I mean, Iraq is technically over, but we still have troops there. They've also said we're drawing-down in Afghanistan—over by 2014—but I mean—"

Pony shouted, "What the fuck was that Huntley describing? Is this some sort of Orson Welles' 'War of the Worlds'-type-hoax-thing?"

Then a light shone in Rita's eyes, something that Pony could not remember ever seeing before. A feeling, a weird intuition, gripped Pony's gut; something was happening in Rita that was deeper than the sexy, intelligent, temperamental, and often angry woman to whom he was powerfully attracted. He asked her, "Rita, what're you thinking?"

"Angels," she muttered.

"Angels?"

Brother Williams and Barker tried to look at Rita, because what she said registered with them.

"Yes, angels," repeated Rita.

Pony asked, "What about them?"

Rita said, "Seraphim, to be exact. Oh man, shit man, I haven't thought about that stuff in a long time. But I remember now—"

Pony said, "Angels? What do they have to do with anything?"

Rita grabbed Pony and said, "Honey, I'm telling you that what that reporter guy was describing were angels! Or a type of angel called Seraphim."

"Sera-who?"

Brother Williams and Barker began to sing quietly—well, as quietly as fundamentalist Christians can sing hymns about their favorite subjects: the Rapture, the Tribulation and oh-Jesus Christ's-a-come-again!

Rita put her hands on Pony's face and said, "Don't worry about it, honey. It's weird, deep Christian stuff that I'm just now remembering from my days at the convent." Rita caught the sound of the singing captives and turned towards them.

Pony was still on Rita's comment about her "days at the convent." He said, "Oh right, yeah, didn't you used to be a nun?"

As Rita was walking over to Williams and Barker she said, "No, I never got that far, Pony. I was a novitiate for two years, but never took my final vows."

Pony laughed and clapped his hands together, "Oh shit, that's right! You left after they found out you'd been boinking that priest!"

Rita grabbed Williams by the shoulders and shook him with her full strength. Although Rita was physically petite, she was far from weak, and had strength belied by her size. "Hey you, stop the singing, asshole! Stop it! Jesus ain't gonna save you or your sorry asses!"

Barker stopped singing but Williams kept going. He smiled at Rita and said, "None of us is getting out of here alive, wetback!"

Pony shouted, "What?" and ran over to Williams and started slugging him in the face three times before the shocked Rita could push him off the JW.

Barker shouted, "Leave him alone! I love him!"

Williams was groaning as blood ran down his chin from his split lips and nostrils.

Rita said, "Pony, it's okay, honey! It's okay. I don't care what that shitbag calls me."

Pony said, "I do! I care!" He ordered Williams to, "Apologize! Apologize for calling her that hateful word!"

Williams laughed and spat at Pony. "I condemn your hell-bound soul!"

Rita held back Pony from attacking Williams again. "Please, I can handle this, okay? Just go over and keep checking out the radio."

Pony reluctantly walked back to the table and the Augur.

Rita rested her hands on her knees and leaned into Williams' damaged face. "Okay, now I know you really do believe your apocalyptic bullshit—rapture—tribulation—all that second coming horseshit. Fine—but what would make fanatics like you come after us with a gun for the radio? What are we, all doomed here?"

Williams just laughed.

Barker answered with, "They are coming for it—the radio."

Rita walked around to the side Barker was facing and leaned over to get into his face. She asked him point-blank, "Who's coming for it and what's so damn special about it?"

Barker said, "They are Watchtower and the Light Warriors of the Seventh-day Adventists."

Rita stood up and laughed, "You've got to be kidding me! A bunch of door-knocking loonies are going to try and get that from us?"

Barker said, "You have no idea who these people are! They are not what you think! They are frightening! They will kill you because they think you guys stole it from the Vatican, and they will kill us for betraying them!"

Rita said, "Stole?—from the Vatican?"

Williams finally piped up with, "Yes, you stupid bitch! The radio isn't a radio! It's the Augur—the most powerful object in the entire world! And now that it's started broadcasting, Watchtower and the

SDA will know it! They have satellites that can detect its power! Those satellites will lead them here, and they will kill each and every one of us!"

Rita shouted, "Are you out of your fucking mind? There's no such thing as the Augur! That's just a fairy tale from Sunday school or for naïve believers in all that Christian mumbo-jumbo!"

Williams said, "How can you say that? You heard what it broadcasted! It's describing the End-times—Apocalypse—fucking Armageddon! It's the fucking Rap—"

Rita walked back to Williams and slugged him so hard he slumped over unconscious.

Barker began to scream, "Are you all right, baby? What have you done to him, you crazy bitch? What?"

Rita sighed and walked back to Barker and slugged him unconscious, too. Afterwards, she shook her fist and showed how much pain it was in. "Damn, those were two of the whiniest bitches ever—"

Pony asked, "Rita? What they said? The radio?—"

Rita walked over to Pony and touched the radio. "The Augur—yeah, I've heard of it. It's like the Ark of the Covenant, Holy Grail or the Spear of Destiny—"

Pony said, "Like the Holy Grail?"

Rita nodded. "It's supposed to be the most powerful of all relics because it can predict the future."

"Well, look at it. I mean, it is kind of weird, you know? It powers itself, tunes itself and—"

Rita shook her head. "No, it's not possible. I don't know what this thing is, but I can't believe—one—it's that powerful, and—two—they didn't have radios two thousand years ago. Damn, I just wish I knew where Henry was. He's like—a hundred times better at remembering the biblical shit from seminary."

Pony asked, "So we don't have to worry about anyone else coming after it or us?"

Rita said, "Nope. I don't buy that whole Watchtower, Light Warriors bullshit. Look, I'll agree there's something weird about that radio, but ancient power? Those guys are freaks and just trying to scare us. We just need to wait for Charlie to call—or hear from fucking Henry!"

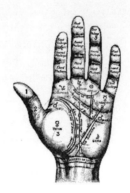

Chapter 31

Calabasas, California

Tracey knew that Claudia's laughter at discovering her NSA identification was not a sign that Claudia was comfortable about the situation. Having been an agent with plenty of undercover experience, she knew she had the upper hand and wasn't going to give anything away until she was at least in front of Claudia's boss. It wasn't that Tracey couldn't see that Claudia's demeanor and apparent skills showed her to be a worthy adversary—someone with specialized or even governmental training. The question was the source of that training.

What made Tracey the most curious was how Claudia kept looking at her through the rearview mirror with eyes that spoke not of enemy to enemy but something else—something very, very competitive but in a much more personal way. Tracey wasn't psychic, but she had been in her job long enough to know the difference between the gleam of an impersonal enemy and a personal one. This was personal—there was something deeply personal in how Claudia was looking at Tracey.

Why that was is what Tracey wanted to know most of all. But how she was going to find that out without in some way tipping her hand, or giving Claudia any sense that she had something on her, was the mystery.

Both her years of training and instinct told Tracey to just stay quiet—no matter what.

For Claudia's part, the personal glaring was all about Charlie—or Charles, as Claudia always preferred to call him—because Claudia believed she was the only woman who had ever seen the full blossom of potential trapped below a slacker's façade. At the height of his success as an author, Claudia and Charlie were a dazzling couple who appeared at many high-class events and were never shy about the media attention. Claudia was never happier or more in love with anyone than she was with Charlie in those days. However, Danny's cancer and untimely death tore down whatever structure Claudia demanded for Charlie and for them. According to Ian and Pony, crash and burn described what happened. Claudia's apparent lack of support of Charlie during his brother's illness and death was what turned everyone the couple knew against her. Not that Claudia would have ever said so, but that hurt Claudia. She had not made the mistake of being in a couple since then.

Now, Claudia had at her mercy perhaps the first woman who had the skills and power to rival her. Women like Deanne were of no threat to Claudia, because she believed she could take Charles back anytime she wanted, but this Tracey Kipper was an altogether different kettle of—kippers? And Claudia didn't like thinking she had any competition for what she could or couldn't have (but really wanted although she wouldn't ever admit she wanted it—or him—or whatever). But Claudia knew she couldn't do anything about it either way, until after Buddha Jesus had done with Tracey whatever he was thinking about doing in order to get that radio from Charlie. So Claudia would just sit back and observe—to see if Charlie had the balls to come after her. Now, the thought of that kind of Charles made Claudia tingle—in a way she had not tingled in a very long time. Maybe if nothing else, she could get her Charles back by forcing him to challenge her over this blonde-haired Kewpie doll; which Claudia could then eliminate and have Charlie take all his anger out on her in one glorious and brutal fuck session. That thought made Claudia grin from ear to ear.

Regardless of what was running through Claudia's mind or privates, Tracey's mind was focused on how this person, this Buddha Jesus, had the balls to take a federal agent and, more importantly, what his real target was in connection with Charlie. She had studied just about everything there was to know about Charlie, first as an objective agent of the United States government, then as someone who broke every rule of her profession because her feelings for Charlie grew stronger the closer she got to him. Through all her work, she could not find anything other than the obvious edginess of his general lifestyle—marijuana dispensary owner and radical-thinking author—which made him what the government felt was a threat. Claudia had mentioned to Jenny a radio of some kind. Tracey wondered if that was code, because the kidnapping seemed a bit extreme for just a radio.

Then Tracey began to remember something she had not thought about in quite some time. It was something she felt embarrassed to have forgotten as it was the last face-to-face conversation she had had with her handler Uncle Leo, before she left to begin her assignment in Los Angeles.

Uncle Leo had come to Tracey's apartment in Washington DC and found her packing it up for the move. He was as kind a man as one could imagine any agent's handler being towards his charge. Without an overt appearance of paternal affection for Tracey, Uncle Leo was always asking Tracey her feelings or her thoughts on an assignment and the particulars regarding that assignment. It was the kind of interaction that made Tracey feel truly appreciated as well as protected, especially when she was isolated in the field and unable to rely on immediate back-up. While Tracey was sealing up a box of bric-a-brac, Uncle Leo placed his hands in his trench pockets and said, "I checked into the coincidence of your cousin Deanne Ripper dating this target which you've been assigned to monitor."

"And?" asked Tracey.

"Just that—a coincidence."

Tracey didn't respond. She moved the just-sealed box over to a stack of other boxes and put it on top. She then walked into the bedroom without looking at Uncle Leo.

Uncle Leo followed her into the bedroom and found Tracey putting the last of her clothes and necessities into a duffle for carry-on during her flight from DC to Los Angeles

Tracey asked, "And the movers will be here tomorrow to get my stuff out there? I don't like being stuck in hotels for more than a day or so when I'm supposed to be relocating for a long assignment."

"They'll be here, Kipper. I have it all covered. But I don't think you believe the answer—just a coincidence."

Tracey shrugged her shoulders. "What's to believe? It's not a matter of what I believe. It's a matter of what I do and don't do. Need to know, right?"

Uncle Leo looked at the bed and saw that only one corner wasn't covered with something. He sat down on the corner and slapped his hands on his knees in a concerted effort to catch Tracey's full attention. Tracey sighed and stopped packing. Although her face was stony, she gave Uncle Leo her full attention.

"Cut the 'agent speak,' Kipper. You and I don't talk like that, okay? Not unless you're really pissed off. Hell, I was the one who recruited you, so I think I've gotten pretty good at reading you. On this, though, I need you to tell me."

"It's nothing you or the agency's done, Sir. I feel like—like the problem may just be in me. It makes me nervous to have someone in my family so closely connected to an assignment—not that Deanne and I are exactly close. Maybe I think I won't be able to…"

"Stay objective?"

Tracey shrugged.

Uncle Leo stood up and walked over to Tracey. He rested his hands on her shoulders and shook her very gently. "I know you, Tracey. I know you'll be fine. I understand you're a fan of this guy's work. Hell, even I liked his first book—the others were so-so—"

Tracey's stony look broke and she smiled. For everything else this job did to make a genuine connection between handler and field agent impossible, beneath all the protocol Tracey knew Uncle Leo genuinely cared for her.

Leo continued, "The point is that sometimes it's to an agent's advantage to have some kind of vesture in a target."

Tracey looked surprised to hear that come from of a veteran like Uncle Leo. "You really believe that?"

Uncle Leo stepped away from Tracey and paced the floor of the bedroom concentrating hard on how he said his next words: "I know that every handbook, every instruction given to an agent says to stay objective, to detach, be cold, etc., etc.—but that denies our most basic, most advantageous instinct—humanity. The more human we are, the better we actually become."

Never in her life had Tracey ever thought she would hear anyone inside the agency tell her exactly the opposite of what every bureaucrat from the highest office in intelligence to the lowest page in Congress would tell the outside world.

Uncle Leo went further, "The very thing that makes an agent a good agent is their love of country or service or hopefully both. So I don't think it does any good to deny that very thread throughout any operation. You clearly have an understanding, if nothing else, of what this target—um—forget that term, right now—um—this person thinks. You've got a better understanding of the material he's produced, and whereas I know that it's not material that the higher-ups are exactly happy with, you get it. That means you can get close to him—better than any other agent in the entire intelligence network.

"But it isn't just as simple as saying it's okay to have feelings. The point of my telling you this is to let you know you must trust your gut. What I need to know from you is that you know when not to cross the line—and that no matter what your feelings are, you won't go there."

That was the million-dollar question, wasn't it? At that time, before Tracey had spent some six months orbiting Charlie's world, she could tell Uncle Leo that no line would be crossed—but she had crossed that line the night she took Charlie out of Deanne's apartment, drove him home and saved him from his own over-imbibing. She had spent the next two hours checking out his apartment while he slept, not for anything that would help her assignment, but to give her more insight into the depths of this complicated person. The searching was for herself, to satisfy herself that she could be whatever he needed, whatever he wanted.

What Tracey couldn't find in Charlie's house and still had no idea about as she bounced around the back of Buddha Jesus' van, was what it was about Charlie that got him marked by the NSA. As she replayed the last face-to-face with Uncle Leo in DC, she plumbed the depths of her memory for anything he might have said to indicate what it was, so she could ascertain if this drug lord had figured out what that something was. Tracey wanted to know why the drug lord was willing to kidnap her and talk about some radio or whatever else to get at Charlie.

Even when Tracey had asked Uncle Leo, "What doesn't make sense to me, Sir, is that other authors who've written more openly radical and even threatening material about the government haven't been marked for personal tracking like Charles Hamor? So, why him? What's the real reason, Sir?"

Uncle Leo smiled and said, "Not good enough to just tell you to do it? That no matter how thinly veiled his writings are, they've really got the bosses pissed and they…"

Tracey shook her head and said, "Pardon my interrupting, Sir, but—please, I do have enough experience to know that what I'm told the reasons are for an assignment is pretty much never the reason."

"And this time you really need to know the reason?"

"I think I deserve it, yes. I mean, from what you've said the bosses know that I'm basically their only option to get close to this guy."

Uncle Leo laughed and rubbed his chin. "Ah, so that's what I gave away, huh?"

Tracey shrugged her shoulders and sat down on the bed.

"Okay, here's the deal, Kipper. If you repeat what I'm going to tell you to anyone else, ever, I'm going to disavow you and throw your corpse under the nearest bus, got it?"

"Absolutely, Sir."

"It's genetic," was all Uncle Leo said.

Tracey waited for more words to follow but they didn't. Uncle Leo just looked at Tracey with a blank expression. "It's genetic?" she repeated, but in the form of a question.

Uncle Leo said, "And that's all you get. The rest is need-to-know and you don't need to know." And before Tracey could follow up with a million questions to drag out a clarification, Uncle Leo was out of the bedroom and out of the apartment with these final words, "I'll call you when you land in LA. And we never had this conversation, ever!"

Which had left Tracey in the same spot six months ago that she was in now as she bounced up and down in the van—obsessed with the word "genetic," but unclear as to how Charlie's genes were of any interest to the US intelligence network. Her search that night of Charlie's house had yielded nothing to indicate anything out of the ordinary—and no medical records of any kind. And in the first days of her investigation, she had even looked for any doctors that Charlie had seen in Los Angeles, but it's as if the man had never been sick a day in his life, or even gotten a physical. Now she was on the verge of meeting someone who might have a deeper knowledge of this enigma, and she was willing to go as far as necessary to find that answer.

But Tracey's mind was shaken from both its memories and preparation for meeting the Buddha when the van made a turn and stopped. Although she could not see outside the van, Tracey could hear the noises made by the front gates of the compound as they opened.

As the van drove through, Claudia climbed out of her seat and walked back to Tracey. She kneeled in front of the smaller woman, took out a knife, reached around her and cut the binding.

Instinctively, Tracey rubbed her wrists because the tightness of the plastic bindings caused an almost unbearable pain. She shook her arms and rolled her shoulders several times to relieve them of tension and pain. "Thank you."

Claudia never looked Tracey in the eye. She said, "Don't thank me, bitch. You'll need help from God himself to escape whether you're bound or not."

The van stopped and Claudia moved to open the side door, but Tracey grabbed her arm first, which made Claudia lash out with her other arm to punch Tracey as if under attack. Tracey wasn't attacking Claudia, but she knew how to defend herself. She blocked Claudia's arm with hers, something that anyone without Tracey's training wouldn't have been able to do.

"You're good," said Claudia.

"So are you," returned Tracey. "Now tell me, please, you have a thing for Charlie?"

"Have? Honey, I did. He and I are ancient history."

"I see."

"You have a thing for Charlie?" Claudia asked in return.

"He's dating my cousin."

Claudia laughed. "You're cousins with that plastic-enhanced bitch?"

Tracey nodded.

Without another word, Claudia opened the sliding door and pushed Tracey out into the waiting grasp of the two gunmen. Tracey didn't resist. She was smarter than that. She was also skilled enough to know how to land outside the van when Claudia tossed her.

Claudia watched with unrevealing interest Tracey's reactions to her situation and being shoved by Claudia, her defense of Claudia's attack, all signs that this woman could be a formidable opponent and was absolutely more than she appeared to be, even as a NSA agent. Claudia jumped out of the van and led the gunmen, each holding one of Tracey's arms, up the steps and through the front doors of Buddha Jesus' home. They made their way through the foyer and then up a huge stairwell that curved around to the second floor and then further on to a third floor.

Once they reached the third floor, Claudia led them down a long hallway to a set of double doors. Depictions of Hindu and Buddhist deities, spirits and heroes locked in legendary struggles decorated the double doors. It might have impressed someone other than Tracey, but she had seen too much in her life to be impressed by the clear pretentions and insecurities of this would-be Buddhist drug dealer.

Claudia looked at Tracey and said, "Your shoes."

"What about them?"

"Drop them. Here."

Tracey kicked off her shoes and then motioned to Claudia to open the doors.

Claudia opened the doors.

Without any prompting, Tracey entered the large chamber to find Buddha Jesus seated in lotus position on a liter (the cot-looking thing Liz Taylor laid upon, carried by huge slave-extras in "Cleopatra") at the far end of the room upon a dais between two pyres with lit fires inside the bowls. A reflecting pool in the center of the room between Tracey and the Buddha was the first of features to catch Tracey's attention, followed by the statues of Hindu spirits lining the walls, with a single statue of the Great Buddha at the end of the reflecting pool just before the dais. The two gunmen followed Tracey inside the chamber while Claudia remained outside and closed the doors.

"Welcome to my private meditation chamber, Agent Kipper," greeted Buddha Jesus.

"I see you practice the humility side of Buddhism," responded Tracey.

Buddha stood from his lotus position and laughed. "You are well acquainted with the path?"

"I know a middle path from an extreme."

"Very good."

Out from seemingly nowhere, although it was really from the recessed corners of the dais which are well out of sight, appear two beautiful women who wrapped Buddha in his traditional Tibetan red and gold robes.

Buddha said, "I imagine you're wondering why a man such as me would dare challenge the government by kidnapping one of its intelligence officers, especially during the War on Terror?"

Tracey said, "Look, you obviously think you're—uh—whatever this is, and you think you need something from Charlie Hamor and that taking me is the way to get it and…"

Buddha motioned with his hand for the gunmen to bring Tracey closer to him. The gunmen grabbed Tracey by the arms and walked her around the pool, stopping her at the bottom of the dais. Buddha walked down the steps and stopped one step above Tracey. He placed his fingers under her chin, but she pulled her face away from his hand with a burning glare in her eyes.

"I see," said Buddha.

"You see what?"

"You and him—connected."

"Fuck you."

Buddha clicked his tongue and waved a finger in her face. "Now that is beneath someone of your skills and capabilities, Agent Kipper."

"What do you think it is that Charlie has?"

Buddha said, "He has a radio—the radio, of course."

"Radio?"

"Don't act like you don't know what I'm talking about."

"I don't. I don't know anything about a radio."

Buddha slapped Tracey across the face. She took the blow without so much as a mild bother in her eyes and brought them back to meet his. She said, "I hate to tell you, but I don't know anything about any fucking radio. And if you hit me again, you will pay a price no amount of karma can settle. Do you know what it's like when the NSA comes down on your ass for kidnapping one of their agents?"

Buddha nodded. "Well, clearly you are excellent at lying. And you are clearly lying because there is no other reason why the NSA would be interested in Charlie or his pathetic stoner crew. The fact that Homeland Security has also taken an interest just proves that you are a liar. Now you can go on and try to scare me further about your awesome NSA, or you can confirm for me that the radio in Charlie's

258

possession is the Augur and that you will give it to me before I kill you and kill Charlie—once he gets here, of course."

"The Augur?" Tracey asked. "What's an Augur?"

Buddha slapped her again. "Fine. I shall wait for him, and I shall see that he is more motivated."

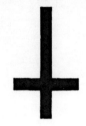

Chapter 32

(Still In) Calabasas, California

Charlie, Ian and Jenny were only a few minutes from the gates to Buddha Jesus' compound. Charlie was driving and holding Ian's mobile phone to his ear. He looked scared, very scared. In the backseat, Jenny still had her head in Ian's lap and was looking up at him with a growing attraction for this giant man who was so gently stroking her hair. Ian wasn't noticing Jenny as he was focused on Charlie.

"Fuck!" screamed Charlie as he handed Ian's phone back to him.

"Still nothing?" asked Ian.

"It's fucked up, man! Henry's number keeps coming back as not in service—no direct to voicemail, no memory full and not temporarily disconnected. It's like it doesn't exist, man! What the fuck has happened to him?"

Ian said, "I don't know, man. Look, I'll try Rita's phone again." He began to dial Rita's number.

Charlie spotted the gates at the edge of the headlights and said, "Finally, we're here. We're here."

Jenny finally sat up, her interest now fully focused on her friend Tracey. She grabbed Charlie by the shoulder and said, "Don't fuck this up, okay?"

Charlie looked back at Jenny. "Excuse me?"

"My friend's life is in danger in there, okay? Because of you!"

Charlie shrugged off Jenny's hand and shouted at her, "Listen, you, I'm sorry you got beat up, okay? And I'm sorry that Tracey's in this situation, but don't fucking blame me for that fucking psycho Buddha, okay? I'm not a bad person! And I'll do whatever it takes to get Tracey out of there, so just sit back and stop blaming me!"

Jenny was stunned by Charlie's tone and outburst. It wasn't that she thought it unfair, but she suddenly realized that taking out all her anxiety on Charlie for what was happening was too much. She thought about apologizing, but Charlie had already pulled into the driveway, rolled down the window and pushed the intercom button.

Charlie shouted, "Hey, motherfuckers! Motherfuckers, wake up!"

There was no response.

Ian hung up his mobile and said, "I couldn't reach either Rita or Pony, so I left a voice mail telling them to call us, ASAP. I'll try the store phone." Ian began dialing the phone number of OHM but suddenly stopped when…

The gates to the compound opened. But it wasn't like it had ever seemed before—watching and listening to the entrance beckoning to come inside. Maybe because lives were on the line it seemed that for a moment—just a moment—the gates of Hell itself were opening. But it wasn't a three-headed hound that greeted them from inside. Claudia stepped out into the light of the headlamps.

Charlie slammed the gearshift into park and jumped out of the car. Without even closing the door, he walked around to the front of the car and stopped just a few feet from his ex-girlfriend. He shouted, "Where the fuck is she, Claudia? Where's Tracey?"

"Take it easy, big guy. She's inside with Buddha."

"She's inside with Buddha?" Charlie started laughing and looked back at the car. He saw Ian and Jenny climbing out of the back doors. "Hey guys, she's inside with Buddha. No worries, huh? Nothing to worry about."

Suddenly, Charlie jumped at Claudia and tried to punch her, but Claudia being Claudia easily side-stepped the blow. She caught Charlie's fist in her hand, twisted his arm and spun him around so that his whole body was facing the car and his arm was twisted against his back.

Ian hissed. "Ow, that fucking bitch."

Charlie's eyes were watering from the pain, but he wasn't going to cry.

Claudia whispered into Charlie's ear. "Calm down there, tiger. No need for you to lose your cool or your arm." She pressed his arm a few times, straining the rotator cuff between his shoulder and arm.

Charlie hissed and spat a few times before Claudia released his arm and pushed him towards the car. Charlie fell against the front of the car, planting his hands on the hood to break his fall.

Jenny came around to help Charlie stand up. "I'm sorry—for yelling at you—before."

Charlie looked at Jenny and smiled.

Ian came around and stopped between Charlie and Jenny and Claudia. He said, "Hey, Claudia."

"Ian."

"You want to tell that sick motherfucking boss of yours we're here? Or would you rather try those moves on an ex-linebacker?"

Claudia smiled and walked to the driver's side of the car. She got inside and shifted it into drive. "Get in, guys."

Jenny and Ian looked at each other and then at Charlie. Charlie motioned for them to get back into the car. They returned to the backseat, while Charlie climbed into the passenger's side next to Claudia.

Claudia looked at Charlie and said, "You have the radio?"

Charlie said, "Fuck you."

Claudia nodded and said, "Right." She drove the car through the open gates and up the driveway to the front of the house.

As the gates began to close, a chopper with its headlamp off pulled into the driveway and slipped between the gates before they closed completely. Father Agosto stopped his chopper just as the gates closed and looked back at it. In his hand he held Charlie's shirt lifted from the dead body of Agent Curb. He looked up the driveway and saw the lit house in the distance.

As Claudia reached the front of the house, she parked the car behind the van in which she had transported Tracey. She climbed out at the same time as Charlie, followed by Ian and Jenny. The three waited for Claudia to take the lead up the steps then followed her up to the front door. Charlie stayed just ahead of Ian and Jenny.

Claudia opened the front door and led them through the foyer; taking the exact same path she had led Tracey until they were up on the third floor and by the doors to Buddha Jesus' meditation chamber. She opened the doors and stepped aside.

As the doors opened, all three saw Tracey standing on the far side of the pool at the dais below Buddha Jesus who was now seated again in lotus position on the liter.

Jenny's eyes widened and she shouted, "Tracey!" She broke into a run past Ian and Charlie and across the room to greet Tracey with a huge hug.

Tracey returned the hug but said, "Honey, honey, it's good to see you, too, but you've got to calm down, okay—not a good situation—not a good one."

Jenny pulled back and said, "Yeah, right, sorry. I'm just so happy you're not hurt!"

"Are you okay? Did they hurt you when they—"

Jenny shook her head, "No, no, Ian—Charlie too, but especially Ian, really took good care of me. They found me. They're over—"

Tracey looked at the doors and saw Charlie and Ian step inside followed by Claudia, who closed the door behind herself. She locked eyes with Charlie and gave him a small but sweet smile. He returned it along with a mouthed, "Sorry." But Tracey shook her head, closing her eyes and smiling. She clearly didn't blame him.

Ian shouted, "Hey, Buddha, how the fuck?—what the fuck is this place supposed to be, huh? Is it like that freaky-ass dome building in New Delhi with those giant creepy-as-shit-eyes on it?—like the eyes of God or some such shit?—stare right through to your?—hey, where are those giant-ass spinning posts, you know?"

"Prayer wheels," answered Charlie. "You make a prayer to the gods and spin them to put the force of the spirit in motion."

"Right!" shouted Ian. "And how about some of those?—what do they call them, Charlie?—those monkeys that jump around free as birds?"

"Hanuman monkeys," answered Charlie.

"Hanuman monkeys, right! You know, they are allowed by law to run around and shit!—literally shit!—in the streets and steal food and all that kind of!—"

"Shut up, Olczwicki!" shouted Buddha Jesus. "Your mocking is not helping your situation!"

Ian shrugged his shoulders and said, "Maybe not, but it does make being in this shitbox a lot more bearable."

Charlie patted Ian on the shoulder signaling him to chill. Ian nodded and crossed his arms. Charlie walked around the pool and made his way to where Jenny and Tracey were standing. Ian followed directly behind Charlie. When Charlie reached the women, he moved past them, and put a foot up on the first step of the dais, leaning slightly to rest an elbow on his knee.

Ian took Jenny's hand and stepped her back about ten feet so that Tracey could move in just behind Charlie. Jenny didn't fight Ian; in fact, she smiled up at him.

Charlie said, "All right, Buddha, no bullshit—straight up—what the fuck are you doing kidnapping people and threatening us for some antique radio?"

Buddha Jesus did not speak right away. He looked into Charlie's eyes and saw in them the truth of his not knowing what the fuck was going on. "You really don't know about the radio, do you?"

"I know that Pony has some crazy story about his dead cousin visiting him and giving it to him, and that it somehow operates without batteries or power cords, and that my best friend Henry has vanished into thin air—do you have Henry? Are you holding him hostage, too?"

Buddha walked down to the step just above Charlie and looked him straight in the eye. "I don't have Leturnoe, but I do want that radio. Bring it here and I will let you all leave unharmed."

"Fine."

Everyone looked at Charlie with a surprised look, including Buddha Jesus—the only person Charlie was watching for a response.

Buddha Jesus asked, "That's it? Just like that?"

"What you don't get, Buddha, is that what I care about most is the safety of the people I love. Unlike you, I'm not a fucking hypocrite."

Buddha Jesus narrowed his eyes and through gritted teeth said, "What did you call me?"

"I called you a fucking hypocrite! You call yourself Buddhist, but you threaten people's lives, kidnap people, deal drugs!—you're a fucking cartoon character!"

The gunmen in the room raised their weapons, chambered rounds and took aim at Charlie.

Ian and Jenny gasped and held onto each other.

Instinctively, Tracey placed her body against Charlie's back as if to protect him.

Buddha Jesus raised his hand to stay the gunmen. "No. Charles, I daresay you have very little basis upon which to formulate any kind of opinion on my spiritual ethics. Unlike you, I understand the nature of karma, dharma and I know what my nature in this life is, and I am that—purely. Are you?"

Charlie laughed and said, "Damn, you're so full of shit, but whatever." Charlie turned around to look for Ian and suddenly saw Tracey was right up against him. It took him back for a moment. It also took Tracey back, so she stepped away, suddenly very nervous and unsure of what to do or say.

Charlie smiled at her. He then spotted Ian with Jenny and said, "Ian, go back to OHM and get the radio. Bring it back here, okay?"

Ian said, "You sure? I mean—"

Charlie insisted, "Please, dude, let's just get this shit over with."

Jenny to Ian said, "I'll go with you."

Buddha Jesus then said, "Claudia, go with them. I want to make sure they don't try anything stupid."

Claudia nodded and walked over to Ian and Jenny. "Well," Claudia said to Ian, "let's go!"

Ian gave a last look at his friend and walked with Jenny out of the chamber, followed by Claudia.

Buddha Jesus motioned for two of his gunmen to approach the dais. The men walked up and the Buddha ordered them, "Take them to one of the bedrooms down the hall and hold them there until I give word, understand?"

The men nodded and turned their weapons on Charlie and Tracey, who began walking in the direction which the men motioned for them to go with the barrels of their guns.

The Buddha Jesus shouted, "Oh, by the way, Hamor?"

Charlie, Tracey and the gunmen stopped and gave Buddha their attention.

"Your girlfriend there—she's a spook."

"What?"

Tracey dropped her head and scoffed. She covered her face.

Buddha said, "She works for the government, stupid—a fucking spy. That should give you plenty to discuss while we're waiting for your friends to return."

Charlie looked at Tracey with a shocked expression.

Tracey couldn't return the look. All she could do was to turn her face away and cross her arms. The gunmen shouted for them to get walking and prodded them on with the barrels of their guns. Reluctantly, the couple began to walk. As they made their way out of the meditation room, Charlie kept looking at Tracey, while Tracey kept staring ahead with her arms crossed.

The door to a huge bedroom that was lavishly, if impersonally, decorated opened and Tracey entered, followed by Charlie. They were more or less forced in through the doors by one of the gunmen. The other stayed outside the door and closed it. The other gunman, his weapon still trained on the couple, made his way across the room to the French doors and opened them to reveal a balcony. He went out onto the balcony and took his position after closing the door.

Charlie and Tracey were now alone in the room, although still in clear view of the gunman on the balcony. Neither spoke at first.

Tracey walked over to the California king-sized bed and sat on the edge. She looked at the four garish posts with no canopy overhead.

Charlie immediately looked for a bathroom and spotted it. He walked into it, switched on the light and went to the sink. He turned on the cold faucet and splashed his face with water. The blast of much-needed energy set his body tingling and made him shiver. Splashing his face twice more, he then grabbed a nearby hand towel and wiped his face, hair and neck dry.

Tracey watched Charlie walk back into the bedroom, still wiping his face and hair with the towel. "I suppose you have a million questions?"

Charlie didn't answer at first. Instead, he looked around the room, really studied it, trying to catch any and all distinctive characteristics. As he scanned, he reached into his pants pocket and took out a crushed box of cigarettes with lighter crammed inside the half-empty box. He took out a cigarette and the lighter. Without looking at his companion, he offered, "Cigarette?"

"Thanks." Tracey stood from the bed and walked over to Charlie; she took the cigarette and lit it. Once she had put it between her lips, Charlie lit his own.

Charlie put the box back into his pocket, while Tracey turned to walk away. But Charlie grabbed her arm, forcing her to stop and look him in the eye. Charlie asked, "I only have one question."

Tracey said, "Anything."

"Is he lying?"

Tracey looked down before speaking, but Charlie took her chin gently in his hand and forced her to look him in the eye. "No," he insisted, "to my face—my eyes."

Tracey was shaking now. Whether it was Charlie's touching her skin or his forceful will, Tracey had never felt more exposed, more frightened in the whole of her personal or professional life. There was something powerful in Charlie's hazel eyes. She knew it was there before now, but never before had she seen it set against her. This seemingly ordinary guy was tearing down every emotional defense Tracey had put up.

"He's right," Tracey said. "I am a spook—a spy—NSA, National Security—"

Charlie took his fingers from her chin and spun away with his whole body tensing from the anger seething inside. Before she could finish the agency's full name he said, "Yes, I know what NSA stands for. I'm not—or didn't think I was—a total idiot." Charlie walked to the credenza across from the baseboard of the bed and slammed his palms down on the top.

The sound made Tracey jump, which made her really feel uneasy. To be so easily shaken by Charlie's emotional state, nothing about this situation made her feel anything like an agent and everything like a woman being caught in a lie by the man with whom she had fallen in love. There was nothing left that Tracey could think to say or do, except reveal the truth. So she shouted, "You're not an idiot! I am! I'm the idiot! And I'm so sorry." She went back to the bed and sat on the edge, resting her arms on her knees and bending over so that all she could see was the floor.

Charlie turned around to see Tracey hunched over and vulnerable. He sighed and walked over to her. He sat down next to her, but she tried to scoot away. Instead, Charlie wrapped his arm around her and pulled her body back to his. He asked, "It's the books, isn't it?"

Tracey didn't respond.

"Henry told me they were gonna piss off powerful people."

Tracey said, "They did."

"How many people?"

"A lot."

"Him?"

"Him who?"

"You know—"

Tracey looked up at Charlie with a quizzical expression.

Charlie gave her a smirk and said, "You know—the wannabe cowboy and his shoot-'em-in-the-face master?"

Tracey turned back to the floor and shrugged her shoulders. She let out a tiny smile and said, "Maybe?—yeah."

Charlie clapped and said, "Ha! I hoped it would! I told Henry I wanted to create a presidential character who was so fucking clueless and emasculated, that when he discovered there was this whole generational caste system built into the government that determined who would be elected and who would be sacrificed, the real people in power would be terrified the public would believe what we had written was real and rise up against them!"

Tracey asked, "You want people to overthrow the government?—because of your book?"

"Well, yeah, sure—I mean, no, of course I don't really think—well, actually, I mean—that's what Jefferson did, right? John Locke? Mills? Machiavelli? It's what all those guys hoped would happen when people read what they wrote. The unwashed masses would rise up against their tyrannical oppressors and change the whole government—from the ground up!"

Tracey smiled and said, "Holy shit—you are a revolutionary."

Charlie nudged her and said, "Of course I am—and you're an advocate—a defender of the status quo. We're archenemies, you and I."

"Are we?"

"Sure we are. I co-wrote a series of books about an underground group of revolutionaries who discover that they are reincarnated over and over as a group of rebels hell-bent on overthrowing a race of megalomaniacs, who reincarnate over and over as an Illuminati-type caste that dominate the human race in an effort to keep them from evolving and reaching their full potential as a spiritual force with the power of transforming all evil into good.

"Meanwhile, you are an incredibly beautiful and intelligent patriot who has sworn to defend the ideals for which our country stands, but really carries out the instructions of a bureaucracy who uses your love and patriotic devotion to those ideals to enforce their hypocritical agenda and crush the likes of true patriots and free-thinkers like me and Henry."

Tracey laughed and said, "Wow, you really do have it all figured out, don't ya? And now I suppose you are going to pull the blinders off my eyes and reveal to me the true duplicity of the evil bureaucracy, thereby turning my skills against the very forces that created them in an effort to create a champion for the people?"

"A super-sexy, super-secret, super-powered champion for the people then? I guess those skills of yours makes you like Wonder Woman or better yet—Black Widow from 'The Avengers' who wears one of those hot-as-hell skin-tight leather body-suits!"

"Oh okay, so now I'm like some super-bad-ass-bitch-champion-and-a-half -Scarlett Johannson?"

"Bingo!" shouted Charlie. "Now you got it! No wait!—wait! Not Scarlett!—hotter even!—Kate Beckinsale from the 'Underworld' movies! That's it!"

"Oh, well, what can I say? You've just got it all figured out."

"Actually, no I don't. You aren't like either of those make-believe women. You're a thousand times better. You're real, completely and totally real—the most real, the most beautiful—the most brilliant person I've ever met." Charlie put his face very, very close to Tracey's and added, "And for all that's happened since you've come into my life—you make it all not only worth it but give me a reason to face all of it."

Tracey did not answer because she could not. Blood was pounding in her ears. Her cheeks were blushing and her limbs trembling. Only her eyes were steady and they studied every inch of Charlie's face and eyes. Her whole career was about lying to people and making them believe what she wanted them to believe whether any of it was true or not. So she had to make sure he was telling her the truth—that he was as sincere as her heart was hoping he was. "You're saying I make you believe you can beat someone like Buddha Jesus and all of these gunmen?"

"You make me want to fight someone like Buddha Jesus—take on the kind of bastards who would try to hurt you," whispered Charlie.

Tracey had been holding back her passion and attraction for Charlie long enough, and when those words came from his mouth her desire broke through her better reason and drove her lips into his. Charlie eagerly welcomed them and, fueled by his rising body temperature, decided that regardless of their imperiled situation—he wanted Tracey more than anyone or anything else ever. How far they were willing to go given their imperiled situation was about to be tested.

Chapter 33

(Still In) Calabasas, California (Just Outside Buddha Jesus' Compound)

From a distance of two hundred yards, seated atop his chopper, Father Agosto watched Ian, Jenny and Claudia get into the same car that he saw Charlie, Ian and Jenny arrive in. This told him that Charlie was still inside that compound, and Charlie was still his key to finding the Augur. Of course, for all his formidable capabilities, the Templar Priest had no way of knowing that following the three who just left in the car would take him directly to the radio—he wasn't telepathic. All he knew was that the Revelator Glasses showed him the power and energy on this shirt was the same power and energy he saw on Charlie and Charlie only, and that meant getting inside that well-guarded house.

He waited until he saw the car drive down to the opening gates and head out onto the street before he started up his chopper. He kept it dark and drove down towards the gates and then rolled it onto the driveway. He knew he couldn't stay hidden from the gunmen and whatever other security was set up on the grounds for much longer. But the priest had one more trick up his sleeve. (Pardon me.

I shouldn't say it's a trick up his sleeve. It's not this book's intention to insult anyone who genuinely believes in the instruments of faith; it's just an expression. Perhaps it would be more apt to describe it in the same way St. Paul the Apostle described it to the Ephesians:

> "Wherefore take unto you the whole armour of God, that ye may be able to withstand in the evil day, and having done all to stand…Above all, taking the shield of faith, wherewith ye shall be able to quench all the fiery darts of the wicked. And take the helmet of salvation and the sword of the Spirit, which is the word of God…"

These were the words the Templar Priest Agosto spake [Oops, sorry. After reading the King James Version or anything by Shakespeare, I have a strange habit of slipping into that "middle-English" kind of thing—again, sorry]—spoke as he revved up the engine of his bike.) The recitation of such verses flipped a switch inside the priest's head and set off a kind of transformation of his conscious mind. The barrier between his conscious and subconscious dropped, allowing for the full capacity of his vast knowledge in combat and warfare to take over. Agosto opened the throttle of his bike and roared down the driveway reaching higher and higher speeds. His target: the front doors of the mansion.

Inside, Buddha Jesus had seated himself back on the liter at the top of the dais, and was for all intents and purposes meditating. Of course, it was more likely that Buddha Jesus' mind was thinking about the power he imagined he would possess once he had the legendary Augur in his possession.

The perimeter alarm went off—blaring and squealing and making the kind of inhumanly horrific sound those kind of electronic devices make.

Buddha Jesus' eyes popped open, and he saw one of his gunmen burst into the meditation chamber shouting, "Buddha! Buddha! Intruder! Intruder!"

Buddha Jesus stepped off the liter and shouted, "Who?"

"A motorcycle! Someone on a motorcycle!"

Outside the main house the priest on the chopper was getting closer, about to reach the front steps.

About a dozen gunmen came running from all directions, three from around one side of the house, three from the other side, four from out of the front doors and two from positions on top of the roof, all aiming their automatic weapons on the Templar Priest.

Inside their prison-bedroom, Charlie and Tracey were lip-locked, tongue-locked and in the early stages of removing each other's top when they heard the perimeter alarm go off.

It so caught Charlie by surprise, he slipped off the edge of the bed and crashed to the floor. He shouted, "Son-of-a-bitch!"

Tracey on the other hand, as a trained agent, wasn't shocked or surprised. Instead she simply stood up, returned her top and manner to normal and began to watch the man positioned on the balcony outside. She saw him touch the wireless headset in his ear and begin talking to someone.

"What the fuck is going on?" asked Charlie in a rhetorical fashion. His mind was more focused on getting his own shirt and the tent in his pants back to normal positions.

But Tracey, who stepped over Charlie on her way to the balcony door, said, "Shh, something's happening outside—I think it's our ticket out of this asylum."

Charlie got up on his knees and rested his arms on the bed. He watched this beautiful woman who had mere moments earlier been on the way to unveiling for him at least 45 out of the 50 shades of a particular color work a different, if not just as mysterious, kind of magic to help them escape.

Tracey positioned herself against the wall, next to the French doors onto the balcony so that—

The gunman on the balcony opened the door to enter the bedroom and was surprised to see Tracey's fist for about a quarter of a second as it smashed his nose into his skull and sent him flopping to the floor for another second before the blow ruptured his brain and he died.

"Holy shit!" shouted Charlie. He shot up to his feet and watched Tracey bend down and pick up the gunman's automatic weapon and his earpiece.

"Did you?—did you fucking kill him?"

Tracey was walking over to Charlie and said, "Yeah, you knew him? Would you like to send his mama a card or something?"

"No, but he was a human being, right?"

Tracey put her free hand on the back of Charlie's head and pulled him into a powerful kiss—an open-mouthed, passionate-as-hell, knee-buckling and instant-erection kind of a kiss. In fact, Charlie made a squeaky noise like a teen-age girl. Finally, after what seemed an explosive half-hour of kissing, but was really only a minute or so, Tracey pulled away from Charlie and said, "You ready to stop talking bullshit and get the fuck out of this place?"

Charlie's mind was totally blown and his face showed how blown his mind was, but he managed to nod his head and said, "Um—uh-huh."

While outside the front of the main house, but only for a few more seconds, the gunfire leveled at the Templar Priest atop his chopper never hit their mark. As impossible as it seemed, the bullets either veered away at the last moment or some kind of invisible shield (perhaps what St. Paul dubbed "the armour of God"?) deflected them. But it was a moot point as the chopper rode up the steps and headed for the open front doors.

The gunmen who originally came out through the front doors continued to fire on the chopper until the last possible second, when they had to abandon their duty and either leap out of the way or be run down. They flew to the porch as the bike entered the house at a speed of eighty-nine miles an hour.

Just inside the foyer, seven more gunmen entered from adjoining rooms and hallways with weapons trained on the barreling chopper. High above them at the third floor banister appeared Buddha Jesus, who had run the distance of the floor from his meditation room, accompanied by the two gunmen who had first alerted him to the motorcycle.

What he beheld two stories below made him shout, "What the holy fuck is that?"

"A padre, Buddha!—a padre on a motorcycle!" shouted a gunman.

Buddha grabbed the hapless employee by the collar of his t-shirt, pulled him to his face and said, "I can see who it is, you dumbfuck! I want to know what he is! Got it?"

The poor man nodded.

Buddha Jesus took a .357 Magnum revolver from out of the gunman's shoulder holster and shoved him aside. Now properly armed, the drug lord ran back in the direction he came from, to the closest staircase.

As Agosto rode through the foyer, he circled around on his bike more than a few times, freaking out several of Buddha's men who were trying to hit him with their onslaught of gunfire, but nothing—nothing seemed to hit the man.

Finally, Agosto brought the bike to a halt and stared at the gunmen, who also stopped firing. They saw clearly now that this was a man of God—a Catholic priest (albeit one wearing a leather jacket, biker boots, jeans, sunglasses and riding a bad-ass motorcycle). These men were, with the exception of a few, Latino, and regardless of their employer and specific form of employment, instilled with a reverence and fear of the Cloth in a way that no one not raised with or by Roman Catholic grandmothers could understand.

Of the ten who had come together in the foyer to attack the Templar Priest, eight of them were just that kind of Latino, and they lowered their weapons and crossed themselves. Six of those eight began to silently recite prayers.

The other two looked at their fellows and saw them lower their weapons. The fact that these two freckle-faced ex-Marines were Anglo-Americans raised in the Midwest meant they saw the priest with the same disdain they felt towards stupid ghost stories. So they took aim and were about to fire on the priest when Agosto drew out his automatic pistols and fired two bullets into each freckle-face: one in the chest, one in the skull. They dropped like bags of wet cement.

Despite their fears, four of the other gunmen raised their weapons to fire but were equally shot at and equally killed. That left four others who lowered their weapons and bolted out the front door. Agosto let them. He stepped off his bike and viewed all the ways out of the foyer through the Revelator Glasses. He saw a flash of light when he looked at the hallway above that led towards the meditation chamber, the same hallway down which Charlie and Tracey and been led. With guns in hand, he walked down the hallway.

As he entered the hallway, he saw all the lights inside the house go dark. Agosto cracked a smile.

Suddenly, a voice spoke over an intercom system through every corner of the house. It was Buddha Jesus' and it said, "Whoever you are, you would be wise to lower your weapons and surrender to us. I have an army and you have nothing."

"You are wrong," spoke the priest. "I have the Word of God."

Just then an array of machine gun fire unloaded on the priest from down the hallway and out of rooms adjacent to the hallway. Like the gunfire aimed at him before, nothing appeared to hit Agosto. Although the darkness was broken from the flares of gunfire, Agosto was able to return gunfire and hit each of the gunmen with absolute precision, dropping body after body as he walked towards the staircase leading up to the meditation chamber.

While the firefight below had stolen the attention of Buddha Jesus and every one of his employees, Tracey and Charlie exited the bedroom to find an empty hallway. This was when Buddha Jesus and two of his men ran to the front of the house so they could see Agosto in the foyer. This gave Charlie and Tracey an opportunity to break for the staircase close to the meditation chamber and run down to the second floor. By the time the couple had reached the second floor and disappeared from sight, Buddha Jesus and his gunmen had run back to the meditation chamber. As they passed by the bedroom/prison cell, none of them noticed that the door was left open and whoever was posted outside had gone down to fight Agosto.

When they reached the second floor, Tracey stopped herself and Charlie with a firm arm to his chest because of the roaring sound of the motorcycle and gunfire.

Charlie whispered to Tracey, "Is that a motorcycle?"

Tracey nodded.

"Inside the house?"

Tracey whispered back, "I have no idea what any of this about."

"So, it isn't like your gang sending reinforcements?"

"My gang?"

Charlie shrugged his shoulders.

Tracey narrowed her eyes and said, "You're so lucky I've fallen for you, because if I hadn't, I'd dump you right—"

Charlie interrupted Tracey with, "You've fallen for me?"

Tracey heard what she said coming back from Charlie and audibly swallowed—hard! "Look, we are in a life and death situation and we don't have time to talk about this, okay?"

"You brought it up!" said Charlie, as if the volume of his voice was no longer a concern. "You're the one who said it!"

Tracey poked Charlie in the stomach with the butt of the gun to calm him down. In a strong whisper she said, "Shut up, okay! We don't want them to hear!—"

That's when the lights went out, and any further discussion of who had fallen for whom and who had said it first had flown out the proverbial window.

As quickly as she could, Tracey brought the gun up so she could look through the infra-red laser-scope and scanned the staircase up and down, as well as the areas directly adjacent to them. That's when Buddha Jesus' voice crackled over the intercom and spooked Charlie.

"Shit, I hate his voice! I fucking hate him! I hate that we're fucking trapped here!"

Tracey grabbed Charlie's arm and decided that getting him out of the house was the fastest way to save them both from his complete ignorance of subterfuge and firefights. With no words, she guided him downstairs where they both heard and saw the flashes of the firefight between Agosto and Buddha's men.

Charlie whispered, "Who the fuck is attacking the house?"

Tracey used the laser-scope to hone in on—"Holy shit," she whispered, "I think I've seen this guy before." She had seen him. It was Agosto, the man she had bumped into at the Troubadour.

Still whispering, Charlie said, "Are you shitting me? And this guy isn't one of yours?"

"No, he definitely doesn't work for our government." Tracey took Charlie by the hand and led him down the hallway until she saw Agosto coming from the opposite direction. "What the fuck is he doing?"

The priest was firing both his pistols, laying waste to anyone who tried to attack him.

Tracey was dumbfounded. She could make out a priest's collar around his neck. "What the fuck is a priest doing with two guns?— firing two guns?"

"I'm sorry," said Charlie, "did you just say a priest is firing two guns?"

Before the Templar Priest could make out Charlie and Tracey, the NSA agent pulled them into the nearest room: a huge music room which ran the length of the hallway and had a doorway that opened out next to the foyer.

Agosto's senses were so focused on the gunfight and following what he thought was Charlie's energy trail, which by this point was actually a crossing of both the first trail that went up the stairs and the recent one made by Tracey and Charlie coming back down. As a result, the Glasses missed what was Charlie's escaping into the music room. Agosto was not practiced enough in reading the nuances of the Revelator Glasses' detection of the spiritual energies to catch the difference himself. By the time Agosto reached the staircase, the onslaught of gunfire had vanished. All but a few men still with Buddha Jesus physically were dead. However, the priest took no chances and kept his guns out and ready.

Suddenly, the lights came on and Agosto saw himself in the crosshairs of three gunmen at the second floor landing of the stairs. Standing with these three was Buddha Jesus holding the .357 Magnum against the priest.

Buddha Jesus asked, "Who the fuck are you?"

Agosto answered, "I am a messenger of The Lord Thy God and He demands your fear!"

"Not my god, priest. Now what the fuck do you want?"

"I want the Vanaesir and his Valkyrie."

Buddha Jesus laughed and asked, "What the fuck? Valkyrie? Van-what? You talk some crazy shit, padre!"

Agosto fired on all three men, dropping them dead at Buddha Jesus' feet. "Bring me the Vanaesir and the woman guarding him."

Before Buddha Jesus could say another word, the sound of Agosto's motorcycle revving up stole both the Christian's and the Buddhist's attention.

Buddha Jesus said, "Something tells me they're stealing your ride."

Which was exactly what was happening: after Tracey and Charlie exited the doorway next to the foyer, they spotted the bike. Tracey signaled for Charlie to stay quiet and follow her. They ran across the hallway and into the foyer, the voices of Agosto and Buddha Jesus echoing down the hallway.

When they reached the bike, Tracey climbed on to drive and motioned for Charlie to get on behind her. He followed orders very well, wrapping his arms around Tracey's waist while she revved up the engine. While Tracey got the chopper rolling towards the door, Charlie turned his head to see Agosto running after them at full speed.

Charlie said, "Uh, he's coming."

Tracey said, "And we're going." She cranked the accelerator with her right hand, going almost full throttle, pulling a wheelie as she tore across the floor and out the front doors.

Charlie gave a victory howl, followed by a throaty laugh.

Agosto slid on his heels and came to stop just seconds after his ride left the building. He had his guns trained on the rear-lamp as it hit the porch steps, but knew he couldn't chance harming the riders and lowered them.

Outside, down the steps and hauling ass towards the gate, Charlie shouted, "Goddamn, you're sexy and fucking awesome!"

Tracey laughed. "Thanks!"

Then Charlie spotted the gates, the fast-approaching gates and shouted, "Oh sweet Mother of God!"

Tracey reached for the automatic gun hanging from her side and lifted it—taking aim at what she hoped was the control panel. It was attached to a fencepost connected to the gates. She fired three rounds into the metal box. The shells pierced the covering, which blew the box apart, forcing the gates to open—but not at a speed fast enough for the chopper to…

Charlie screamed at the top of his lungs and dropped his head so that he wouldn't see what he feared would be them spread like peanut butter on the driveway. Fortunately, all Charlie missed was Tracey turning the chopper in time to avoid a collision. She made a full doughnut and came back onto the driveway when the gates were opened enough for them to go through safely.

As they reached the road and headed in the direction of Los Angeles, Charlie shouted, "Will you marry me?"

Tracey laughed and accelerated the bike to a speed of eighty-five miles an hour.

Charlie felt the pressure hit his face and screamed, "Yippie-Ki-Yay, motherfuckers!" followed by more laughing. He then yelled, "Tracey Kipper, I am your bitch for life!"

"Damn right you are! I own your flat butt!"

"You've noticed my butt?"

Tracey laughed. "It's not all I've noticed!"

Then without thinking Charlie spat out, "Please just marry me!"

Tracey said, "I'll have to think about the marriage thing. I'm not sure we can find a dress in your size." Then something caught Tracey's eye. She noticed—yes, the sleeve of Charlie's t-shirt which Agosto had stuffed into the side pouch of the chopper's seat. It was flapping furiously but from Charlie's continued laughing and yapping, Tracey assumed he couldn't see it himself.

How the hell this t-shirt got into the hands of the biker priest turned Tracey's stomach. It confirmed that whatever this question of the radio was and how it was connected to Charlie was getting bigger and bigger; and this one single NSA agent was quickly discovering she had a score of enemies closing in on her assignment. So far, Tracey could count the two dead Homeland Security agents, the crazed Buddhist drug dealer, and his hit woman Claudia. Third, she was now seeing a gun-wielding, chopper-riding Catholic priest who had survived a barrage of gunfire closing in on Charlie and in the possession of a shirt that suggested the priest might have been the killer of the Homeland Security agents.

All of this meant Tracey had only one person she could call to help figure out what the hell all this mess meant: Uncle Leo. Since she didn't have her mobile phone and Charlie didn't carry one, she would have to wait until they were back at OHM, which she knew posed a whole other set of problems with Claudia on her way there, presumably holding a gun on Ian and Jenny. That's when Tracey said out loud, "Shit!"

Charlie had been rambling about how awesome Tracey was in getting them out of the compound alive and how lucky he was to have her attracted to someone like him, but stopped when he heard Tracey's pronounced swearing. "What is it?"

"We're not out of the fire yet."

"What specific fire are you referring to?"

"Your bitch of an ex."

"Oh shit," scoffed Charlie. "Claudia has Ian and Jenny! Do you really think Buddha Jesus is going to tell her to kill them and everyone else at OHM?"

Tracey shook her head and said, "I honestly don't know. I don't know if Buddha Jesus is even alive, given what that dude who broke into the compound was doing. My dad told me some pretty hairy stories about the Jesuits who taught him back in the day, but wherever that priest comes from has got to be one hell of a parish. Let's hope he does kill Buddha and that Claudia won't find out about it before we can get the jump on her."

Charlie said, "Hey wait, if you can get us to a pay phone—"

"In LA? Are there any left?"

"A few?—I think?—I hope?—I can call Rita or Pony on their mobiles and let them know what's about to go down."

"That's what we'll have to do."

Chapter 34

West Hollywood, California

Barker and Williams were still unconscious from Rita's earlier "sleep therapy," while Rita sat at Henry's work table, the radio in front of her, on her mobile phone cursing under her breath.

Pony was seated next to one of the growing tables, smoking a joint and singing a catchy tune. He looked over at Rita who was in a totally different space than he was and said, "Rita? Hey, Rita? You want some?" He held the joint out in her direction.

Rita just looked at him and said, "I love you, Pony, but the fact you're sitting there smoking weed while I'm over here trying to get a hold of someone—anyone—unsuccessfully, while trying to figure out what the fuck the thing is with this fucking radio of yours, isn't really endearing you to me and is actually—maybe—making me think about picking up this radio and planting it squarely in your fucking skull."

Pony stood up and walked over to Rita saying, "Yeah, you definitely sound like you need some mellow." When he reached Rita he handed her the joint. Without a question or remark, Rita took the joint and took a nice, long drag.

"Still can't get anyone?" Pony asked while he picked up the radio.

"Nope. It's like we can't get reception of any kind in here, you know? Like?—"

"Like interference?" offered Pony.

"What did you say?" asked Rita.

Pony said, "It's like something is keeping our devices from connecting outside this building," while looking the radio up and down very, very carefully.

Rita nodded and said, "Yeah, yeah, it is kind of like that. How did you think of that?"

Pony shook the radio, hard. "I don't know, baby. It's just like—it's just like—this fucking thing is fucking with us, you know? It's like, alive and it's—" Pony lifted the radio above his head and with all his strength hurled it to the floor, "—fucking with us!" His voice was as loud and as full of anger as Rita had ever heard.

"Holy shit!" shouted Rita, as she jumped up to see the radio crash into the floor but not a scratch or mark was left on it.

Pony said, "See? The fucking thing is like—it's cursed—like the Holy Grail in that 'Last Crusade' movie."

Rita was amazed. She hadn't had the balls herself to do what Pony just did—or wasn't high enough to do it. Either way, she was glad because it gave her the chance to pick it up off the floor and really shake it hard to confirm that Pony's assault left no outside marks and from inside she could hear absolutely no damage to the unit.

Pony took the joint from Rita and walked back to his seat by the growing table.

Suddenly, Rita felt her tummy muscles constrict, followed by a groaning, popping noise that always for her meant one thing and one thing only: "Oh shit, I think I have to—" as the fart came quickly and not too quietly.

"Oh shit," said Pony, laughing lightly. "You okay there, Rita?"

"I don't know. I don't—" again, a fart—a loud fart and a painful fart, the kind of fart that vibrates your anus and makes your hips roll because you're trying to shift your whole body so the acid burn that follows this kind of fart won't hurt quite as much as it hurt Rita at that moment.

Then the smell—the smell hit Pony and he went, "Whoa! Whoa, shit, baby, shit!" but he didn't want to say that. He didn't want to make

Rita feel worse, but he couldn't help but say something because the smell was the kind of sick, sweet, cheesy smell that only comes from gas trapped inside the body for a really long, long time.

Barker and Williams didn't move, didn't react, because they were still unconscious.

Rita put down the radio and held her stomach, whose muscles were still cramping. "Oh shit, I guess I need to hit the bathroom and—"

Just then through the back door entered Ian, Jenny and Claudia, who was holding a gun on Ian and Jenny. But before any of those three could speak a word, before Rita or Pony could greet them or comment on the gun in Claudia's hand, the smell of Rita's flatulence hit all three of them like slaps across the face.

"Damn!" shouted Ian. "What the fuck?"

Jenny gagged—no words—just gagged.

Claudia coughed and felt water fill up her eyes. She was almost disorientated from the shock of the smell, which could have meant her losing her hold on the gun, but everyone else who was conscious in the room was as overwhelmed as Claudia, and missed their chance to grab it.

Rita had tears in her eyes and shouted, "I'm sorry! I'm so fucking sorry! I can't help it!"

Ian shouted, "Bathroom, Rita, motherfucking bathroom!"

Jenny shouted, "Incense? Don't headshops have incense by the fucking ton?"

Claudia joined in, "Yes, yes, must be something in this place! Potpourri, any-fucking-thing, light a whole goddamn plant, Pony! Just do it!"

Rita ran as fast as her cramping body would let her into the employee bathroom that was located between the doors that went into the salesroom and the room that went into the special hydroponic growth room. She slammed the door, locked it, and they could hear the sound of the seat being dropped on the porcelain followed by more of Rita's very audible flatulence, succeeded by her groans of pain and discomfort.

Pony ran into the salesroom and grabbed several ounces of sandalwood incense sticks and brought them back into the larger growing room. He took the lighter on Henry's worktable and lit the handful of sticks that he grabbed. After blowing the flames dead, he handed a few sticks to each of the conscious people, until he reached Claudia. That's when Pony actually registered she had a gun out and pointed.

Pony screamed, "Holy shit, Claudia!" and dropped the incense sticks he had been carrying to hold up his hands. "What's up with you?"

Claudia said, "Just don't do anything stupid, Pony, and no one will get killed."

Ian and Jenny managed to collect themselves after the olfactory onslaught to realize that Claudia still had her gun, still had it pointed at them and was still: "A crazy bitch, Pony," Ian said. "She's always been a crazy bitch. I mean, I know you have a slammin' fuck-me-all-over body, Claude, but what the fuck Charlie was ever thinking sinking his dick in your well is so fucking beyond me I can't—"

Claudia fired the gun in Ian's direction, purposefully missing his head. But the shock, sound and potential near-death experience was enough to make Pony, Ian and Jenny hold their positions, if not pee—just a little.

"Care to say anything else really fucking stupid, Ian?" asked Claudia.

"Nope," answered Ian. "Nope, I'm good."

Claudia motioned with the gun for Pony to join Ian and Jenny opposite her.

Pony nodded vigorously and walked over to Ian and Jenny. Without looking at Ian, Pony said, "Hey, big guy, Charlie still with Buddha Jesus?"

"Yeah, we tried to call you and Rita but—"

"Yeah, seems our phones, the store phone—pretty much everything's all fucked up right now. Don't know why."

Ian scoffed, "Great, now we have no way of getting out of this fucking mess."

Jenny said, "Sure! Just give her the radio!" Turning to Claudia, she said, "Hey you, don't you want that radio for your boss, right—right?"

Claudia didn't respond. Instead she walked over to Henry's work table and saw the radio there. "Is this it?"

Pony nodded. "Yeah, that's it, but I'm warning you, Claude, it's kind of fucked-up and weird and—"

Rita groaned loudly from inside the bathroom.

Pony said, "Oh, poor baby. That must really be hurting bad."

Jenny said to Claudia, "Well, that's the radio, right? So take it! Take it and call your boss and let our friends go, okay? Okay?"

Claudia aimed the gun at Jenny and shouted, "Shut the fuck up, you stupid bitch! Goddamn, your voice is annoying! Blah! Blah! Blah! You sound like my chatty cousin Margarette! God, I hated that girl! She was always rambling on and on about something useless like mascara or 'what shade of red is this lipstick'? Yeeech! So just shut the fuck up, okay? Shut up!"

"Okay, okay, okay," begged Jenny. "I heard you the first time."

Claudia sat down at Henry's work table, grabbed the radio with her free hand and pulled it over to her while keeping her gun trained on the three captives. "Now we sit and wait, give it about fifteen minutes or so, maybe just ten, and see if we hear anything from Buddha. If not, I'll call, get word and we can settle this whole ugly affair."

Ian asked, "Can we sit? Can we get?—"

"No!" shouted Claudia.

Pony begged, "Please, Claude? I mean, weren't we all friends once?"

"No, Pony, we weren't all friends once. I had Charles and I tried to get him away from you losers. I hated all of you because you turned him from the brilliant literary future he had, to all of—" she waved her gun around in the air, "—this! You took advantage of his depression after Daniel's death and turned him into the same kind of pathetic losers you are. No, I saw you all for the rotten parasites you are. I couldn't convince him to leave you, so—I had to dump him."

"Wow," said Ian, "Really? Is that how you see it?"

Jenny prodded Ian in the side and said, "Please be quiet, okay? Please?"

"No, no, Jenny, I'm not going to be quiet about this! You don't know about this because you didn't know this monster when she was sucking Charlie dry!"

"Excuse me?" shouted Claudia. "I was draining him?"

"Yes! You were a fucking vampire—um—a—um—succubus!"

Jenny started to cry, "Please, Ian, please, I don't want to die. I really, really don't!"

Ian walked towards Claudia screaming, "You were the one who tried to turn him into something he wasn't! And how dare you call us losers, when you're the one who fucking kills for a goddamn scum-of-the-earth drug lord?"

Claudia got up from the chair, walked up to Ian and forced him to stop walking when she pressed the barrel of the gun into his forehead. "I swear to God, Ian, I will pull this trigger and I will blow your fucking brains out all over this fucking rat trap!"

Through gritted teeth, Ian said, "I dare you, bitch! I dare you!—do it!"

Jenny started crying. "No!—no!—no!—"

Pony put his arms around Jenny, no longer worried about what Claudia would do when he dropped his arms.

Claudia cocked the hammer back on her gun and said, "Pray to whatever druggie god you have, stoner—"

The radio crackled to life.

Claudia slowly returned the hammer to its safe position and lowered the gun. She turned to look at the radio, as did everyone else including Ian, who also sighed with relief.

Pony said, "See! See, the fucking thing works!" Pony released Jenny and walked over to it. He was about to pick it up when Claudia intercepted him and hit his hand away with her gun. "Ow!" cried Pony.

Ian went back to Jenny and hugged her. She pleaded with him, "Don't do that again, okay? Please, don't ever do that again!"

Ian couldn't help but smile as she hugged him back. "It's okay, babe. I won't. It's all good."

Claudia was captivated to see the dial move itself and the indicator dance back and forth looking for a live station. "Is this thing?—running itself?"

Pony sucked on his aching hand as he said, "Yes, that's what I've been telling everyone. The thing—it's like—it's fucking alive—on its own—ow! You really fucking hurt my hand!"

Without looking at Pony, while also trying to figure out what the weird eye-looking-thing in the center of the dial was (one of those fake plastic-ridged-3D-things that moves from side-to-side, depending on the direction at which you look, maybe?) she said, "Please, Pony, don't be such a baby, okay? It wasn't personal. I'm here doing a job. Now what the fuck do you know about this?"

Pony chuckled and pointed at Claudia saying, "Ha, see, I knew you couldn't really hate us! I know you think of us as friends no matter what you say."

Claudia looked at Pony and patted him on the cheek. She said, "If it makes you feel better for me to say you're my friend, okay, you're my friend, Pony."

"Yes!" cried Pony, pitching his arms straight up into the air.

Claudia grabbed one of his arms and forced it back down. Pointing the gun at his face she said, "Now, friend, why don't you tell me what you know about this radio?"

But before Pony could speak, everyone conscious heard the first noises out of the bathroom in which Rita was sequestered for several minutes: a loud scream, followed by another loud fart, followed by the sound of big diarrhea.

Ian and Jenny both cringed.

Even Claudia hissed and showed concern. "Man, what the hell is wrong with her?"

Then the radio found a live station and a song came through loud and clear. It was the progressive-rock group Rush playing their 1984 classic "Red Sector A" from their album "Grace Under Pressure." As the music blared forth, immediately Claudia realized that the sound was digital 5.1 quality, which wasn't possible for such an old radio.

"The sound," Claudia said. "The quality of that sound—not possible—stereo quality sound coming out of an old mono radio—but how the hell can it do that?"

"Who is that?" Jenny asked Ian.

"Rush."

"Rush?" asked Jenny. "Blech!—I can't stand that heavy metal shit!"

"It's not really heavy metal," replied Ian. "It's hard but not, you know, really like metal." Although Jenny's ignorance and reaction to Rush bugged the shit out of him, he wasn't about to blow his chances with so fine a woman by arguing the point.

Pony on the other hand, he wasn't happy with what Jenny said either, and shouted out, "First, Rush is not heavy metal—they are progressive rock! Second, they are one of the most seminal bands ever assembled! A trio of musicians whose talent on their instruments and classical understanding of music allows them to create music unlike anyone ever—"

Ian was signaling Pony to shut his mouth, but it wasn't working.

Claudia, on the other hand, ended Pony's rant by hitting him on the shoulder blade with the barrel of her gun.

"Ow!" shouted Pony. "Why are you always trying to hurt me?"

Claudia said, "Fuck your music lesson, professor! The point is not who it is or why they're good! The point is, how the fuck is it playing that song?"

Unexpectedly, the voice of Brother Williams could be heard from the almost-forgotten corner of the large growing room where he was tied to his also now-conscious partner Barker, and the JW said, "None of that is the point, you idiots! Listen to the words! Listen to the words of the song! That's the key to why the relic is playing it!"

Claudia walked over to the two lovers and said, "Oh my fucking God. Who are you two fucks?"

Pony said, "Those guys showed up earlier trying to steal the radio before you did."

Claudia put her foot on the chair between Williams' legs and bent over so that her face was in Williams' and her gun was pointed at the JW's crotch. "Oh, so you two are also interested in this radio? My boss sent me here to retrieve it for him. I'm wondering if your interest is the same as his."

There was no response from the defiant Williams, who, because of his sexual proclivities, was in absolutely no way influenced by the incredible beauty and tight-fitting outfit covering Claudia's body. The fact that his eyes never left hers gave her the idea that he probably was gay, and she hoped she could use that to her advantage.

"Well," Claudia continued, "what about it? What do you know about that radio?"

Brother Williams said, "I know this: all of you are going to die in a fiery blaze of Jehovah's Glory when—"

Claudia broke out laughing and cut Williams off by waving her hands back and forth and shouting, "No way! No way! You've got to be kidding me! You guys are motherfucking Jehovah's Witnesses?"

Williams said nothing.

Barker on the other hand finally spoke up and said, "Actually, he is. I'm Seventh-day Adventist."

Claudia continued laughing.

Meanwhile, Pony actually did what Williams suggested. He listened to the lyrics of the Rush song; they describe a dystopian future where the world is at war: concentration camps, families destroyed—absolute horror—but ends on the hope of revolution and change for the better.

Then Pony's mind began to spin, as he remembered two of the other songs played by the radio: the Phil Collins' classic "Something In the Air" and Credence Clearwater Revival's "Bad Moon Rising," which lyrics, combined with those that Pony had just heard, all spoke to terrible evils, unspeakable horrors, and apocalyptic disasters coming in the near future for everyone.

When he put those kinds of songs together with the horrible news report he had heard about a battle with angels, and the broadcast sounded as if it was happening in the present, Pony's mind reeled and all he could do was start to groan and cry out, "Oh my God, they're right! It's the end of the fucking world, man! That radio is talking about the end of the world!" Everyone gave their attention to Pony when they heard his pronouncement.

Barker said, "See—at least one of you believes us now."

Claudia said, "No, no, no! You might be the biggest stoner I've ever known, Pony, but I can't believe you're actually buying into this bullshit!"

Pony looked genuinely terrified as his head filled with the dynamism of everything that he had seen, heard and viscerally experienced since Claire, or what Pony now absolutely accepted was Claire's ghost, had shown up at his door with that infamous bowling bag. Moreover, the part of Pony's mind which most everyone who knew him accepted was operational—the logical and analytical part of his brain—was seeking some kind of reference point from which to operate in light of his sudden epiphany. All that Pony's brain could match up with what was happening to him now was the story of Moses and the burning bush. Pony's brain said to itself, "Is this how Moses felt, must have, had to have felt when he realized there is a piece of shrubbery in front of me that spontaneously ignited and started speaking with the Charlton-Heston-like voice of God?"

"Son-of-a-bitch," mumbled Pony. "This thing is really real and it's really telling us how the fucking world is going to end!"

Another terrible groan came from the bathroom, followed by Rita's crying out, "Please, God, I beg of you! I'll do whatever you ask! I'll go back to the convent and become a nun this time! Just please, let this shitting stop! Please!"

Ian shouted, "Rita, it's Ian—you've got to stop it there, girl! You keep that up and you'll blow out your sphincter! At best, you'll have a hemorrhoid for life!"

"Tell it to my ass, dude! Tell it to my ass! I swear to God, Pony, if that damn radio has anything to do with what I'm going through, I'm going to take the bowling bag it came in, fill it with cement, and smash your balls with it!"

At that moment Ian noticed Jenny staring, staring directly at Pony, who was walking back to the radio with his hands outstretched, a look of reverence on his face. The look on Jenny's face, though, truly bothered Ian. He didn't know exactly how to read it, but there was definitely something happening inside Jenny's head towards Pony, that much he knew for sure, and he didn't like it one bit.

Claudia put the barrel of her gun against Williams forehead and said, "Okay, I don't know what kind of weird shit is going down here, but seeing as you and your butt-buddy there are the only ones who seem to have any real understanding of what that radio-Augur thing is, you better start explaining it in detail to me so I can tell my boss."

Ian asked Jenny, "Jenny, you okay? What's going on?"

But Jenny didn't answer. Instead she just walked over to Pony who was staring at the radio, which was now broadcasting some kind of news report that no one could really clearly understand—not so much from a volume problem, but because it wasn't broadcast in English, or any other language any of them understood. He took it in his hands and lifted it up above his head. Pony said, "Behold! It is the Augur! The Word of God made of plastic and transistor wire!"

"Yes," muttered Jenny. "Yes, you are right." Then her voice got loud, really loud as she put her hands together as if to pray and screamed, "Behold all mortals, this is The Word of God made plastic! His Revelation made by—"

"Philips, I think," said Pony, "or maybe by Sony—either way, it is the Revelation of God and we must heed it!"

Jenny went down on her knees next to Pony and said, "I will heed it! I will heed its word!"

"Oh shit," muttered Ian. "Great, the first chick I've really been interested in—in like months—and she's turned into some kind of Jesus freak right in front of my fucking eyes."

"Rise, rise, Little Sister," said Pony to Jenny, as he reached down with one hand, while holding the radio aloft in the other.

Jenny placed her hand in Pony's and cried out, "Yes, yes, I rise up, Brother." Her pupils dilated as if she had just taken a hit or two of acid.

Pony put the radio between his and Jenny's ears and said, "Do you hear? Do you hear the words spoken?"

Jenny's eyes began to water as if she were crying from ecstatic joy, and she said, "Oh yes, it is the sacred—the sacred language of Christ himself—Aramaic."

Claudia was met with silence by Williams. He and Barker were both looking at Pony and Jenny. Claudia said to Williams, "Hey, don't ignore the bitch with the gun—not smart!"

Williams shouted at her, "Go ahead! Kill me! Do it! I'd rather go to the Kingdom Hall of the Great Father then witness all of you burning by His Fiery Hand."

"Shit!" shouted Claudia as she lowered her gun and kicked Williams in the face, knocking him unconscious. "I hate religious fanatics!"

"You demonic bitch!" shouted Barker. "Don't you dare hurt him! God will have his wrath on you! You will burn in Hell!"

"Fuck this," said Claudia. She walked around to face Barker and aimed the gun at him. Without a word, she shot him in the forehead. Barker was dead before he could speak another word.

Ian shouted, "Holy shit, Claudia! Did you have to do that? Did you have to fucking kill him?"

"Yes," Claudia said. "He was too fanatical. I wasn't going to get anything out of him—utterly useless. Plus he was pissing me off."

Meanwhile, Pony and Jenny seemed to take no notice of the gunshot. They were listening intently to the broadcast in Aramaic.

From inside the bathroom Rita shouted, "What happened? Ian? Pony?"

Claudia shouted, "Shut it, Rita! I killed the Seventh-day Adventist butt pirate! Everyone else is fine! Now can you please finish up in there? I don't like you being where I can't see you!"

"Then come in, Claude! I'd love to share this with you!"

Pony said to Jenny, "Listen, Sister, do you hear? The Sons of Light have arrived to battle the Sons of Darkness. They have arrived at Armageddon and are ready to do battle."

Jenny smiled and said, "Yes, yes, Brother, I hear it! I hear the Glory of God!"

Ian sighed and shook his head, "You know, Claudia, between you killing that guy, Pony and Jenny turning into Holy Rollers, Rita being stuck in the toilet shitting out her insides, and that fucking radio doing whatever the fuck it's doing—I'm getting the odd feeling things are really starting to get out of hand here."

290

Claudia took out her mobile phone and dialed Buddha Jesus' number. While she waited for an answer she said, "Thanks for pointing that out. I hadn't noticed."

A sudden piercing whine came through Claudia's phone, hitting her eardrums with an unholy pain.

"Holy shit!" shouted Claudia. She dropped the phone and covered both ears with her hands.

Ian took the chance and punched Claudia square in the face with his huge fist. She dropped to the floor completely disoriented. Ian kicked her in the jaw, knocking her backwards. While she groaned and struggled to maintain consciousness, and fought to get back on her feet, Ian grabbed the gun and pulled it from her hand.

"Well," Ian said, aiming the gun at Claudia, "how about that?" He cocked the hammer of the gun and took aim at the back of Claudia's head.

Chapter 35

(Still In) West Hollywood, California
(Inside OHM)

Holding Claudia's nine millimeter automatic to the back of her head gave Ian a conflicted sense of both bravado and pity. Claudia was not by any stretch of the imagination Ian's favorite person or even a person Ian liked. Even if he saw her save a schoolbus full of orphans and their nun guardians who were careening towards the edge of a cliff, he'd still dislike Claudia. Several years ago, he watched Charlie suffer an emotional hell after Claudia dumped him because she dubbed him a failure after he chose a route in life inspired by his brother Danny. It was Ian's primary reason for hating Claudia. However, with all that aside, Ian was not a totally cold person without any moral compass. To kill a bitch like Claudia in cold blood made his testicles pull up in his body—a sure sign that it wasn't the manly thing to do.

"Aw, shit!" shouted Ian, who lowered the gun and stepped away from Claudia. Her nose was bleeding and her jaw was almost broken from Ian's kick. "I can't do it," he said. "I can't kill you!"

"Smart—" mumbled Claudia. "Buddha Jesus would make you pay big—"

"Shut up, bitch! Fuck I hate you!"

Someone knocked on the back door.

"What the hell?" Ian turned his head to look at the door.

Again someone knocked on the back door.

Ian looked at Pony and Jenny, but they were rambling on to each other about whatever unintelligible religious bullshit was spewing from the radio.

Rita could be heard cursing from the bathroom.

Claudia was now seated on her butt, still too out of it to be of any assistance.

A third knock on the back door told Ian that it was unlikely he could just ignore it and have whoever it was go away. He knew it couldn't be Charlie or even Henry; they had keys and would have just come right in. The only people left for Ian to look at was the dead Adventist and the Jehovah's Witness who started to regain consciousness. Williams was shifting and raising his head and Ian nudged Claudia with his foot.

"What?" Claudia asked, still pissed from being beaten to give a shit about anything.

"You have to tell that fruit you killed his lover."

Claudia looked back at Williams and scoffed, "Great. Of course I do. Now are you going to answer that fucking door or should I switch jobs with you?"

"Fuck you," and Ian walked to the back door, raising the gun to shoulder-level. With his other hand he took a hold of the knob and began to turn it. Slowly he opened it and put his face and the gun close enough to the opening so that both an eye and the barrel had a clear shot of whoever was outside. But what he saw—who he saw made him sigh and lower the gun. Ian mumbled, "Son-of-a-bitch," and opened the door.

Two women, one in her early forties, the second in her late teens, and a man in his late twenties stood at the door, each holding their own Bible and dressed in typical "Sunday wear" as if on their way to church. The women were made up plainly with long hair woven into a single braid, while the man looked like he just walked out of a 1950s Montgomery Ward's catalog.

Yes, they were Jehovah's Witnesses. Not the kind seen through the eyes of Brother Williams or Brother Laurel. No, these folks looked like the kind of stereotypical Jehovah's Witnesses who come to ordinary American suburban doors just about every day of the week.

The middle-aged woman said, "Good evening, Sir. My name is Abigail. May I ask yours?"

Ian scoffed and shook his head, laughing at the absurdity. "Oh God, you've got to be shitting me!—Jehovah's Witnesses?—tonight of all nights?"

Abigail smiled at Ian and asked, "I'm sorry, Sir? Yes, we are Jehovah's Witnesses. How observant you are," and Abigail looked back at her smiling companions. Then she looked back at Ian and asked again, "May I ask your name?"

Ian swung the gun in the air above his head and shouted, "Sure! Why the hell not? My name is Ian!"

Abigail began her spiel with, "Hi, Ian. Have you wondered why such a loving God would allow so much suffering the world?"

Ian responded, "Lady, I wonder why a loving God would create fucking lunatics like you and that fucking radio over there?—it's the middle of the fucking night, Abigail! Don't you people ever sleep?"

Abigail tried to look past Ian as subtly as she could to see if she could spot the radio and answered, "Oh, the radio? Yes, I'm sure you must wonder, Ian. Well then, let's get to the point, shall we?" Abigail stepped back and looked to her younger companion who stepped up and took Abigail's place.

The younger woman said, "Hi, Ian, my name is Sarah."

Ian checked out Sarah because even in her plain dress and with little make-up, she was definitely attractive. "Hi, Sarah—now you just might be able to get me to listen to the Word."

As if Ian had not said anything, as if she was reading from a memorized script, Sarah said, "Ian, I'm Sarah and we know the terrible weight of what Jehovah has placed in your hands. We have been sent here to relieve you of it." Sarah opened her Bible to the exact page from which she intended to read. "Zachariah, Chapter 11, Verse 15, 'And the Lord said unto me, 'Take unto thee yet the instruments of a foolish shepherd.'"

Ian might not have been what anyone would call a studied Christian (or unstudied Christian for that matter), but he was raised by a Pentecostal grandmother who took him to church, followed by Bible study every Sunday from the earliest age he could remember until he was seventeen. As a result, he knew what was being said to him and how.

Ian said, "Did you say I was a foolish shepherd? Did you just call me a motherfucking—" Ian snorted and blew out air, trying to keep himself from really freaking out. "Look, I'm gonna be nice with you people because I have a gun and even though I don't think he cares, I'm not gonna cross the Big Man by blowing away three of his worshippers no matter how fucked up you people are. So—"

Ian moved to close the door on the Jehovah's Witnesses, but Sarah jumped aside so that her other companion Michael could jump forward and put his foot between the door and the jam to keep it open.

Ian looked at Michael's foot, then at Michael's face and said, "What the fuck?"

Abigail said, "We were sent by Watchtower's Zealots, Ian, and if you don't give us the Augur of Jehovah, we will do whatever is required to take it from you—even by force."

Ian aimed the gun at Michael and said to Abigail, "Are you guys the fucking lunatics that asshole over there said you are? Because right now, what I see is me with a fucking gun in this fucking pretty boy's face, and the three of you have Bibles—not fair is it? Now, how about you fuck off and leave the radio with us?"

Abigail and Sarah each pulled a pair of combat knives out of their Bibles and tossed the books to the ground. Within seconds, they had assumed battle postures with a knife in each hand.

Michael released the kind of bone-shaking, diaphragm-deep-martial-arts howl, "Ki-yah!" made famous by Bruce Lee and comically warped by Jackie Chan, followed by a series of high kicks and punches to the air close to Ian's face.

Ian was too overwhelmed by what he was seeing to react by firing his gun. Instead, he took advantage of Michael's having pulled his foot from between the door and jam in order to display his respectable martial talents and closed the back door, locking in succession the knob lock, first dead bolt, second dead bolt and safety bar. After which the former Niner linebacker shook his head and mumbled, "Those are some funky-ass fundamentalists."

Suddenly, the sound of banging on the back door made Ian jump away from it and shout, "Knives?—martial arts?—now a battering ram? What the fuck is with these Jesus-freaks?"

Almost as shocking was the immediate proximity of Pony to Ian, causing him to jump when Pony said, "Let's be glad they weren't Seventh-day Adventists. Word on the street is those fuckers use rocket launchers."

Ian could only stare at his friend who now appeared to be normal, out of the control of whatever phenomenon had drawn him into a "Jesus-freak" dialogue with Jenny over the broadcasts on the radio and acting as if nothing had ever happened to him at all.

Pony added, "You know, rocket launchers? I heard they have those Javelins—like Al Qaeda or the Mujahedeen?—"

Ian grabbed Pony by the shoulders and shook him. "What the fuck happened to you, man? You were like, totally freaking out and talking to the radio, and then to Jenny about the radio, and about Sons of Light, Sons of Darkness—"

Pony looked very distressed by Ian's grasping him and yelling into his face. He interrupted Ian with, "What are you talking about? I don't know what you mean? I don't remember—"

Ian continued rambling, "—city of Armageddon? Does that mean Armageddon is an actual city?" Then Pony's words and state of normalcy sunk into Ian's head and the thought of Jenny returning to normal overtook him. He let Pony go and headed over to Jenny, who was still standing by the work table listening to the radio. Ian grabbed Jenny's shoulders and spun her around. He looked into her eyes and said, "Are you okay, Jenny? Are you back?—"

But Jenny's face and eyes were as blank and void of recognition as they were when she and Pony went off into the La-La Land they previously occupied. She looked at Ian as if he were any stranger and said, "They have it all wrong about God, Brother. They think their mega-churches and their televangelist TV stations and Eight-hundred-and-Fifty Clubs can hold God, be any place God would visit, but they lie! They lie about God! They violate little boys—some do little girls, but mostly boys—boys! They take the innocence away from boys! And they claim to know God? They know nothing of God! They are the Sons of Darkness! I know the truth of God! The Augur tells me the truth of God! The truth of God is revealed before my eyes—my ears—and you hear it too, Brother!"

Ian tried to follow Jenny's diatribe about ministers raping children and the Augur telling the truth. But the fact that Jenny was gesticulating wildly made it difficult for Ian not to focus on her flailing arms and crazy eyes instead of hearing anything substantive she was preaching. He realized that she was gone—maybe for good—and that he was going to have to accept it. So Ian sighed and said, "That's nice, Jenny—real nice."

As Ian guided Jenny down on the table chair to listen to more of the radio, he felt a tapping on his shoulder. He turned to look at who it was and met four incredibly fast, incredibly painful and incredibly effective punches from Claudia's fists. They knocked Ian unconscious and laid him flat out on the floor.

Claudia took back her gun and said, "Thanks for giving it back—shithead."

Pony said, "Why did you do that, Claude? Why?"

Claudia looked at Pony and said, "Because I'm a bad guy, Pony. He punched me and took my gun, so I returned the favor. Suck it up, stoner-boy, and have another joint."

"But how did you get over there, hit him—I mean, I didn't even see you move over there and—"

"I'm good at what I do, Pony. Now shut the fuck up."

Then Pony realized he was missing some time—not much—a few minutes maybe, but it really started freaking him out. "Wait, did I forget something? How is it?—why don't I remember Ian getting the gun and you being punched and?—" Pony noticed the dead Barker in the chair and screamed. He pointed at the body and gasped, "What the fuck happened to him?"

Claudia aimed her gun at Pony and said, "I happened to him, Pony! I shot him!"

"Killed him? You killed him dead?"

"Yes, yes, you idiot! Now shut the fuck up or I will kill you too."

Pony's freak-out over not remembering several things that had clearly just happened and having no memory of his actions with the radio was creating more anxiety than the reality of Claudia's gun. He kept on shouting, "Why don't I remember any of this? Is it the weed? Weed's never fucked with my memory before! I don't get it! Who took a chunk out of my brain?"

Claudia couldn't believe how out of control Pony's anxiety attack was getting. She knew her threats meant nothing to him, so she lowered her gun and said, "I've got to get another job. No money is worth this shit."

The banging on the back door suddenly stopped, which was refreshing enough to make Claudia look at the door and say, "Thank God for that at least."

That's when the sound of all Hell breaking loose outside the dispensary, not just outside the back door but now from the front of the store, loud enough to be heard by everyone who was alive or conscious or not in the grip of some weird religious fugue-state in the growing room. And now they could also hear the sounds of feet and equipment on the roof of the building. More specifically, the sounds were gunfire, heavy footsteps (as in marching troops), heavy equipment of some kind, and loud voices chanting in something resembling Latin.

"What the fuck is that?" Claudia asked rhetorically.

Jenny began to shout, "They've come! They've come to steal the Voice of God!" She grabbed the radio in her arms and held it against her breasts. The look on her face showed desperation and attempted defiance. She began to slowly make her way towards the bathroom. "I have to hide it! I must defend it with my life!" But when she reached the bathroom door she couldn't open it because Rita was still locked inside.

"Fuck off!" shouted Rita. "I'll come out when my ass stops exploding! But I can't come out! The smell! It will kill you all! Fissures! Fissures! I'm going to have them for the rest of my fucking life! Kill me now! Please, kill me now!"

Claudia rolled her eyes, then looked at Jenny and said, "Ian, she needs to stop with that crazy Jesus-shit! If she doesn't, I'm going to shoot her like I did that loser. Since you and her have a thing, shut her up now!"

Ian sighed and said, "Like I can do anything about it? It's that fucking radio, man! It's taken her over."

"Fine, then she dies." Claudia began walking towards Jenny, who was still fighting to open the bathroom door and babbling about defending the Augur.

"No!" Ian ran to block Claudia from Jenny, putting his much larger body in between the killer and her target.

"Stop it!" shouted Pony.

Then a sound came from outside the back door that made everyone who could react to it forget everything else and turn their attention to it—gunshots! Loud, intense, repetitive automatic gunfire right at the back door coupled with a savage banging and shouting, "Open up! Let us in! For God's sake! There's a fucking army out here!"

"Charlie!" shouted Pony, who was the first to get to the back door.

"An army?" questioned Claudia, as she moved to the door, putting both hands on her gun, ready to fire.

"That's Charlie, all right!" joined Ian, who helped Pony once he got to the door to unlock it as quickly as both he and Pony could manage.

It took less than a minute, but felt like an eternity as Charlie screamed and begged for them to open the door and let them in. Only the continued firing of the automatic weapon that Tracey was using kept her and Charlie alive from whatever forces were outside attacking them; however, no one inside OHM knew that just yet.

"There!" shouted Pony, as he and Ian popped the last of the locks and threw open the door.

Immediately, Charlie fell through the door panting, gasping and swearing at the top of his lungs. Tracey tried to come in after him, firing her gun, but almost tripped over him before Ian and Pony could grab both of Charlie's arms and pull him into the room.

Claudia, no questions asked or answers given, joined Tracey and fired out of the door into the alley that appeared crowded with gunmen—at least a dozen—garbed in black bodysuits, balaclavas and night-goggles; all armed with submachine guns similar to the one used by Tracey. Although at least seven or eight gunmen were already lying on the alley floor dead, more gunmen seemed to leap off the roof of the building and join their brethren in barraging the women who were quickly running out of ammo.

Claudia's clip went empty and she shouted, "Shit! I'm empty! She ejected the clip and searched the belt of her catsuit for one of three pouches.

Tracey shouted, "I've got it covered if you have more?"

"I do!" answered Claudia as she hit one of the pouches, opened the flap, took out another clip, and slammed it into the grip of her gun. "Hey, Ian, can you get your fat ass over here and close this fucking door for us?"

"Fat-ass?" shouted Ian, who left Pony to help Charlie get up into a chair, and ran back to the women. He grabbed the door and said, "Ok, you have to stop shooting at some point for me to close this fucking thing!"

That's when the two women jumped back away from the door and hit the floor as gunfire flew in through the doorway, almost hitting them, and slicing up the many marijuana plants and warming lamps in their pathway.

"Son-of-a-bitch!" shouted Pony. "They're killing our weed, man! They're killing our beautiful weed!" As if his life was suddenly of no value whatsoever, Pony left Charlie at Henry's work table and ran serpentine through the growing room, fiercely picking up whatever clones he could that were in the path of the incoming bullets. "No! Weed is it, man! Weed is it!"

As quickly as he could, Ian used his superior strength to slam the door shut against the onslaught of gunfire, which took both considerable power and full-throated grunting and howling until the door was shut and he had the locks secured.

Claudia and Tracey sat up and sighed, looking at each other.

Tracey was the first to say, "You are a hell of a shot! I think I saw you take down at least four."

Claudia returned the compliment with, "And you clearly took out more than half-a-dozen from what I counted on the ground."

Pony stopped his serpentine run and collapsed to the floor, holding at least eight plants in his arms. "I tried, my babies! I tried to save you all!"

Charlie stood up and in one incredible burst of savage anger picked up the chair and smashed it on Henry's work table—over and over until both chair and table were in pieces. Everyone in the room now looked at Charlie; all except Jenny, who was slumped down by the bathroom and stroking the radio, mumbling something to it, and the now-conscious Brother Williams, who was quietly crying.

"I've had it!" Charlie shouted. "Tracey, cover that crazy bitch with your gun!"

Tracey stood up and said, "Charlie, she just helped save your life and everyone else's."

Charlie screamed, "Fuck her! Fuck her boss! I don't care! I want that gun away from her!"

Ian added, "Seriously, Tracey, that bitch not only shot that dead dude over there, but has been threatening to shoot the rest of us for like the last half an hour!"

Tracey looked at Claudia, who shrugged her shoulders and said, "Clearly you and Charles got out of that compound alive, so you must have done something with my boss?—with that gun of yours?—" as she presented her gun to Tracey.

Tracey took the pistol and said, "Actually, your boss was alive, if not so well, when we left. There was some kind of killer priest there who took out every guard on the compound."

"A priest?" Claudia asked.

Charlie walked over to look at the dead Barker, and then at the weeping Brother Williams, whose head was covered in Barker's gore. "Hey, dude?—dude?"

Williams lifted his head and looked at Charlie.

"Why are you here?"

Williams answered, "We—he was my lover—we came here to get the Augur. Our bosses are leading those forces outside trying to get in here to get the radio. Barker and I thought if we got it first and used it against our bosses we could escape our pathetic lives and live together in open peace and love."

Charlie shook his head and said, "You came for the radio too? Who are you, though? Who are your bosses?"

Ian joined Charlie and said, "This living dude is a Jehovah's Witness and the dead dude is—was a Seventh-day Adventist."

Charlie looked at Ian with a totally mystified look. "So, those guys?—those fucking soldiers outside?—are Jehovah's Witnesses and Seventh-day Adventists?"

Pony threw in, "Did you see any rocket launchers or Javelins? That's what those Seventh-day Adventists use."

Charlie looked at Pony with a shut-the-hell-up look.

Pony threw up his hands and said, "Okay, I'll just check on the rest of the weed."

Charlie looked back at Ian. "Let me get this straight—the door-knocking/pamphlet-loving?—"

Claudia shouted, "Charles, shut it! I can make this real simple for you!"

Charlie walked over to Claudia shutting her up with the most incredulous stare anyone there (including Claudia) had ever seen him muster. He replied, "Me?—shut it? You can explain this all so easily?"

Claudia started to answer but Charlie's palm in her face told her he was far from finishing. The only fact that kept Claudia from overreacting or even speaking was what still smoldered in her for him.

Charlie continued, "No Claude—sorry—your delusional boss is like any of these Christian freaks. He's just as obsessed with getting that fucking radio—am I wrong?—am I?"

An expression—a shadow—passed over Claudia's face that told everyone watching that she was hurting—pained by Charlie's clear distrust and disdain of her. It was the first time the paid enforcer had actually looked like just a woman to any of them, and Tracey could sense Claudia's heart breaking.

Before Claudia could speak, Charlie piled on: "Actually, Claude, I'll tell you what—fuck giving me an answer—fuck what happened to my friend Henry and to my store being assaulted and this woman I love being kidnapped—"

The words "woman I love" got a shocked look from Pony, Ian and Tracey, but they said nothing.

Charlie continued, "How about this?" He walked over to Jenny and grabbed the radio.

But Jenny wasn't going to give it up that easily. She resisted Charlie, who used all his strength to get the artifact away from the crazed woman. It became a tug-of-war with Jenny screaming curses at Charlie and Charlie begging Tracey to help him with her friend.

Tracey couldn't believe how Jenny was acting. She came to Charlie's assistance and wrapped her arms around Jenny's torso to hold down her arms. This allowed Charlie to pull the radio out of Jenny's grasp. She screamed, kicked and wailed. More than a little freaked, Charlie backed away while Tracey applied a technique (thanks to her NSA training) of hitting a pressure point in Jenny's neck that knocked her unconscious. Gently, Tracey set her friend down on the floor.

Charlie took the radio over to Claudia and said, "Here! Take the fucking thing! Get the fuck out! Take it and go fight those insane bastards outside, okay? Do me a favor and draw all of them the fuck away from us!"

Claudia looked at the radio and then at Charlie. After a few seconds, she walked away from Charlie and the radio, taking a position near the back door and leaning against the wall.

Charlie said, "Pony, get over here, please?"

Pony walked over to Charlie. "Yeah?"

"Hold this." Charlie handed Pony the radio.

Pony took it and held it away from his body like it was covered with filth. He began walking it over to Ian, who put his hands up, showing Pony he wanted nothing to do with the damned thing either.

Charlie walked over to Tracey kneeling on the floor, holding her unconscious friend in her lap. The tears in Tracey's eyes showed Charlie how scared she was for her fallen friend. "Is she?—"

Tracey looked up at Charlie, tears rolling down both cheeks, and said, "God, I don't know, Charlie. There's something wrong with her. She feels like she's on fire—feverish—but I don't see anything wrong physically. I just don't get it."

Charlie put a hand on Tracey's face and kissed her wet cheek. He kept his lips there for several seconds, and Tracey shut her eyes, placing her hand on his face too. She liked the touch of his lips and wanted to hold it there. But Charlie had to let her go and stand up.

Ian and Pony walked up to Charlie. Ian said, "Dude, we haven't even told you about Rita."

"Rita?"

Pony said, "She's in the crapper, dude. She's having a Titanic-sized shit in there—iceberg and all."

"What?"

Ian said, "True, man. We don't know what it is, but she's been screaming in pain for awhile now."

Charlie headed over to the bathroom door and grabbed the doorknob.

Simultaneously, Ian, Pony and Claudia all reached out towards Charlie and screamed, "No! Don't open that door!"

Charlie stopped and said, "Rita, you in there, babe?"

Rita moaned.

"I hear you're having a bad?—"

That's when the sound of a ripping fart and the terrible dropping of feces into soiled water echoed from inside the bathroom accompanied by Rita's cries of pain.

Charlie hissed and stepped back from the door. With hands raised he said, "Okay, yeah—um—if you?—um—need any Pepto Bismol? I think we have some in the fridge with the edibles, okay?"

Charlie walked back to Ian and Pony and said, "Uh, yeah, that sounds bad—real bad."

Pony said, "Honestly, Charlie, I think it has something to do with this radio, you know? I think everything that's happening is because of this radio, man."

Both Ian and Charlie said, "Ya think?"

Ian popped Pony in the back of the head and said, "Don't say stupid shit like that!"

Charlie lifted a hand to Ian and said, "No, wait. I know Pony's stating the obvious—but he's the first person to actually say out loud what we are all thinking and what it is that's bound us all together."

Everyone who could looked at each other, maybe for the first time in the light of the realization that they were all in the same boat with the same goal—getting out of the situation alive.

Claudia asked, "Then what are you thinking, Charles? None of us can use our mobiles and the landline is dead."

Charlie nodded and said, "I'm thinking what you just said, Claude. We have no help coming. All we have is ourselves. And we all need to just chill so we can figure out what our next step is going to be—and whatever it is, it is not going to be to kill each other, got it?"

No one spoke, just looked at each other.

"Have you all got it?" shouted Charlie.

Slowly, some nodded and some mumbled, "Yes," but for the first time everyone (well, everyone who was alive and conscious and not trapped in the bathroom experiencing hellish bowel problems or tied up to their dead lover, that is) was in absolute agreement. And it was from this position that Charlie Hamor hoped, for the first time since he made the mistake of trying to believe he could reason with Buddha Jesus about anything, that he could unite everyone in that room full of weed against their common foe—apocalyptic Christians.

Chapter 36

(Still In) West Hollywood, California
(Still Inside OHM)

During the next thirty minutes, the captives in the growing room had moved out into the lobby where there was a sofa, a love seat and two very big, very cushy chairs.

The love seat was occupied by Tracey, who had the unconscious Jenny's head in her lap. She held a damp cloth to her friend's forehead and looked very worried. Of course, she also had her submachine gun standing against the loveseat and her leg, well within her reach if needed.

Charlie was pacing, deep in thought about what options, if any, the group had.

Ian and Pony were sitting on the sofa smoking a bowl. They had done well in the last half hour to rid themselves of as much stress as they could, even allowing themselves a few moments of laughing at the Adult Swim cartoons playing on Cartoon Network, which they were watching on the high-definition TV.

Claudia was seated in one of the comfy chairs, checking her gun and counting the number of rounds and magazines she still had in the three pouches on her belt. Of course, most of the time she had her eyes on Charles and then she'd look at Tracey, who seemed to be more interested in the state of her friend than him. Neither Charlie nor Tracey had said a word to each other, not even looked at each other. This pleased Claude, as her once-friends had slipped into calling her.

Over the course of thirty minutes they had continued to hear gunshots, battling and struggling of some kind on the roof and out front of the dispensary. The windows were covered by horizontal blinds as well as safety bars outside. The front door was also heavily protected, not to mention the security cage. No one had dared to look out the blinds and the windows seemed not to have been touched, let alone attacked during that time.

To the shock of everyone, Rita entered the lobby. She looked none-the-worse for having had what anyone might consider the worst possible bathroom experience.

Pony was the first to spot her and shouted, "Rita!" He jumped up from his seat, leapt over the coffee table on which all the gear and weed was set up and caught his foot on the edge of the table. Ian broke up laughing as Pony crashed face first into the shag carpeting at Rita's feet.

Rita looked down at Pony and said, "Hi, Pony, nice to see you too."

Charlie walked up to Rita and gave her a great big hug. She gladly welcomed his comforting grip. He said to her, "I'm glad you survived being in there. Pony and Ian kind of explained to me what happened. Do you think?—"

Rita didn't even let Charlie finish his sentence before she said, "Yeah, I think it was that piece-of-shit radio. I mean, I'm not sure I want to buy into all the Augur talk that's been going down, or that every broadcast coming out of it is legit, but what I can't deny is that something—" Rita stopped to take a deep breath and look around at everyone.

Charlie said, "Rita, come on, we're willing to believe just about anything right now. And since Henry's still nowhere to be found, you are the smartest person in this dispensary."

Rita smiled and nudged Charlie in the stomach with her fist. "Enough with the flattery, Boss. But you're right. I am the smartest person here. Anyway, I do think something supernatural is at work here. And the grossest part—that eye in the middle of the dial—dudes, I don't think it's fake."

Everyone, including Claudia, looked at Rita with genuinely shocked expressions.

Ian was the first to say, "Oh shit, no way! You're saying that's a real fucking human eye?"

Rita looked at Ian and shrugged a shoulder. "I don't know whose, but yeah, I think it's fucking real."

Pony lifted his head up from the shag carpet and said, "Dudes, that is one fucked-up radio!"

Claudia was now finished cleaning her gun and checking her ammo. She put it all back in its pouch and the gun in her belt. She stood up and said, "We have to decide on what move we make next. If we assume that it's Jehovah's Witnesses and Seventh-day Adventists who have been duking it out, whoever wins that rumble will do whatever they can to break through into here next. We need to figure out our next move before they really unload on us."

Tracey gently lifted Jenny's head and, as she moved to stand up from the love seat, placed it gingerly on the sofa so as not to disturb her friend. Once she was standing, Tracey said, "Claudia's right. We need to get ourselves ready for what will clearly be an all-out siege. When Charlie and I approached OHM on the chopper, we drove with our lights off and circled the block to assess how big the situation is."

Claudia looked at Charlie and then at Tracey with a seriously pissed expression. "And you're telling us this just now? What the fuck? You could have answered a dozen questions by now! What the fuck, Charles?"

Charlie said, "Claude, you're one to talk about secrets and holding back information! It wasn't anything we were keeping just to ourselves! It's more like—we had a ton of other bigger, more immediate shit to deal with, huh? Like you killing people? Like Rita? Like still not knowing what happened to Henry?"

Claudia waved her hand and said, "Fine! All right! Just tell us what you saw!"

Tracey said, "You're right, Claudia; there are definitely two distinct paramilitary units. We now know who they are. I assume from what Ian said about the Witnesses who pulled out weapons on you, the group who uses the most ammunition is the Seventh-day Adventists, while the Witnesses are more hand-to-hand. In any case, what concerned me most was the appearance of deputy sheriffs and even SWAT."

Claudia said, "Holy shit! You're saying the cops are working with both groups?"

"How?" asked Ian, his buzz quickly fading. "Why the fuck are the cops helping those lunatics?"

Rita said, "Ian, if you think cops aren't some of the most religious people in the world you'd be even stupider than I thought. Most cops—"

"—and Feds," threw in Tracey.

Rita continued, "—are very religious. If it turns out that we are dealing with Christian apocalyptic sects with paramilitary and/or death-squad-like units, then it's not a stretch to think—"

"—that cops, maybe even a majority of them, are part of those sects," finished Claudia.

Pony sat lotus-style on the carpet, resting his chin on a fist and said, "Man, there really isn't a way for us to win. If the cops are involved, backing them up, we haven't a hope in Hell."

Ian said, "Skinny-fuck is right. There is no hope." Ian plopped down on the sofa. "Maybe we should just surrender to them now and pray for their mercy, which includes death by lethal injection."

Tracey said, "The thought is terrifying, Ian. I know that. I'm not saying we shouldn't be scared—but we can't just give them the radio."

Ian argued, "Of course we can, 'Mizz' NSA! That's one I'm still getting used to. Hey, Charlie, what is it with you and chicks with guns?"

Charlie spat out, "Fuck you, Ian."

"No, we can't give them the radio, Ian," countered Tracey. "Two reasons—first, it's our only bargaining chip, the only thing we have that they want and that means they can't kill us—and two, from what we've heard coming out of that radio—there is no doubt that whoever has the radio and used it could become very powerful, very rich and very, very destructive."

Ian said, "Fine! Let them take over the fucking world! I don't give a shit about the world! I only care about us—me and my friends. If we set up a negotiation with them, we can set up the exchange—safe passage for all of us to go wherever the fuck we want. Charlie, Rita, I know you two can see the sense in what I'm saying."

Charlie said, "Sure."

Rita said, "Absolutely."

Ian said, "Great! Stoners outnumber girls-with-guns!"

Charlie added, "But we can't."

Ian was shocked by Charlie's reply. "I'm sorry, we can't what?"

"We can't give in to them. This thing is too big. I will not be responsible for putting something into those bastards' hands that could cause untold damage and harm."

Ian started laughing and pounding the coffee table, knocking all the contents onto the floor. "Son-of-a-bitch—son-of-a-bitch!"

Then something popped into Rita's mind, an idea that made her smile and clap her hands. "But maybe we can make them think we're giving them the radio."

Claudia said, "Make them think?"

Tracey walked over to join Charlie and Rita, and for the first time did something in front of everyone that displayed something more between Charlie and her. Tracey took Charlie's hand into hers. Tracey asked Rita, "What are you thinking, Rita, some kind of charade?"

Rita nodded. "Something like that, Tracey. See, they are still counting on us knowing either exactly what they know about this radio or not knowing as much as they do. What if we convinced them that not only do we know about the radio, but we have actually tapped into its mystical power source and can manipulate it for ourselves— create whatever dreadful thing they are afraid we'll do with it?"

Ian said, "I need to take a shit. So I leave you Einsteins and Oppenheimers to figure this shit out." Ian disappeared into the back of the store, presumably to the same bathroom that Rita had just left.

Once Ian was out of the lobby, Claudia walked up to Tracey and extended her hand. Rita, Tracey and Charlie all looked at her hand and then at Claudia's eyes. Claudia said, "I know, I know, no reason to trust me. I get it. I killed that loser in the back and I threatened to kill you guys. Look, I'm not stupid. I can't get out of here without you and you can't get out of here without me. You," to Tracey, "are the only one here I can really expect to have the same skills I have to get us out of here. I'm offering a truce—a partnership."

Tracey smiled and shook Claudia's hand. "Agreed—fact is I can't call in reinforcements because we can't call out—nothing works. It's likely my handler will think something's gone wrong when he realizes I didn't report in at my regular time, but that doesn't mean we can expect the cavalry."

Rita and Charlie looked at each other. Rita said, "It's like Batman and Superman teaming up against the League of Evil-doers."

Charlie said, "More like Catwoman and Black Widow."

Rita nudged him and smiled. "You wish."

Tracey and Claudia broke their shake and turned to begin discussing the plan further with Charlie and Rita when Jenny woke from her unconscious state screaming, "The Augur! He is trying to steal the Augur!"

By the time the four had looked at Jenny, she was off the love seat and running towards the door to the salesroom. Pony was closest to her, literally on the floor near the door, and Tracey was the first to scream, "Pony! Grab her leg, now!"

Perhaps Tracey didn't know that study after study has proven weed does not impair physical functions of the smoker. But because Pony's mind was in a weed-induced relaxed state, the best Pony could muster in response to Tracey's order was, "Um—what?"

Jenny was through the door and into the salesroom before Tracey, followed by Claudia, followed by Charlie, followed by Rita, who was then followed by Pony, who was actually walking behind them after putting the pipe and lighter down on the table.

Jenny charged through the door from the salesroom to the growing room screaming, "You will not take the Augur! You will not give it to them!"

Ian did indeed have the radio in his hands and he was at the back door, unlocking the dead bolts. It looked like he was leaving with the Augur. Although he was almost twice the size of Jenny, she was all over him like a wild cat—clawing, biting, and kicking to get the radio out of his hands. Ian was so shocked, so overwhelmed by the assault there was little his brain could manage to do other than fall to the floor, after dropping the radio.

By the time the others had entered the growing room, they found Ian rolling on the floor, Jenny on top of him, screaming and clawing at him, with Ian begging, "Get her off me! What the fuck is going on?"

Tracey and Claudia ran up to Jenny and used their training to catch her arms while in mid-swing and yank her off Ian, dragging her to the chair occupied by the dead Barker. Without a word between them, while Jenny was spitting and shouting curses in Aramaic, Tracey and Claudia grabbed Barker's corpse with one hand each and pulled him from the chair to the floor. Now empty, they forced Jenny down onto the chair and combined their strength, speed and skill to tie her arms behind her, using her own belt to secure them to the chair.

While they fastened Jenny to Barker's chair, Williams whipped his head side-to-side, shouting, "No! No! Do not put that crazy-ass banshee woman behind me!"

Claudia moved her head around Williams' shoulder so that he could see her fiery eyes. "Listen end-timer, you will shut the fuck up right now. If you do not, you will be joining your butt-buddy in the land of Rapture, got it?"

Williams fell quiet. He dropped his head but caught a glance of his dead lover on the floor—a tear fell from his eye.

Tracey said, "Claudia, I'll finish with Jenny. Please, see that the radio is secure."

Claudia ran to scoop the radio off the floor and held onto it.

Meanwhile, Charlie, Rita and Pony all helped Ian off the floor. But Rita was not happy with Ian and let him know with a series of hits and punches to his arms and gut, followed by, "What the fuck were you thinking? What the fuck were you going to do?"

Ian said, "Do? What none of you will! I was going to end this! I was going to give them the fucking radio and let them fight over it so we could get the fuck out of here!"

Charlie said, "No, Ian! We are not giving up on this! Something too weird, too strange and too damn apocalyptic is happening here to just!—"

Then came the sound that for everyone in the dispensary was the one sound that terrified them the most, the sound that told them all Hell had broken loose and the fat woman was singing at the top of her lungs—an explosion. An almost deafening explosion from the lobby of the dispensary which could only mean—

"The rocket launchers!" shouted Pony. "Those motherfuckers have unleashed the Javelins!"

"Holy shit," muttered Charlie. "Claude, Trace, you have to come with me, now! Rita, I need you and Ian to stay back here with Pony, the radio and Jenny. Whatever happens to us, whatever, do not give up that radio, okay?"

"Okay," said Rita, tears forming in her eyes.

Charlie said, "If you have to, make a run for it out the back. Just don't—"

"I know! I know!" said Rita.

Claudia and Tracey, each with their weapons, said, "Come on, Charlie! Come on!"

Charlie ran for the door to the salesroom with Claudia and Tracey just ahead of him. As they entered the salesroom, they heard the terrible sounds of machinery and human voices, all gnashing together. They got to the door of the lobby, and Charlie grabbed the knob. He looked at the two beautiful women and nodded. They nodded back. Charlie opened the door and saw the weirdest sight he had ever seen. He stepped through followed by Claudia and Tracey, each with their weapons trained to fire on whoever was opposite them.

What the three of them saw was a lobby littered with glass and plaster, mortar and smoke. Something like the rocket Pony shouted about must have hit the front door of the dispensary, blown it apart and then contacted with the security cage inside. Fortunately, the construction of the cage was such that the rocket didn't hit it with full force, and only buckled from the explosion. With the security cage having contained the main force of the blow, the windows that made up the greater part of the dispensary's front wall were completely blown out, but the bars were still intact.

Claudia, Tracey and Charlie saw at least thirty armed men and women and two Hummers armored with rams standing just on the other side of what feeble barriers still stood. The floodlights mounted to the top and sides of the Hummers shone through and lit up the whole lobby. It made it impossible for the three to see individual details of the attackers.

Charlie said, "You're the ones after the radio?"

Every man and woman raised their submachine guns and readied to unload them.

Claudia and Tracey did the same—as futile as it seemed considering how outnumbered they were.

Finally, a single man made his way to the front of the attackers and said, "I am called Eiderbrook. I am the Vice-President of Reliquaries and Acquisitions from the Seventh-day Adventists Church of America. I apologize for the damage to your personal property, because as a registered Republican I am a firm believer in small business, but the Lord Father has commanded us with the duty of retrieving the Augur. If you do not do so, we will unleash more ordinances and destroy your business completely."

Charlie asked, "Are you just Seventh-day Adventists or are there Jehovah's Witnesses out there too?"

Eiderbrook responded, "Well, I'm sure you've been hearing some calamity out here?"

"Yes, a bit," answered Charlie.

"That was us fighting Watchtower's Jehovah's Witnesses. After some conflict, we proved to have greater numbers and greater power and, well, they are gone. It is just us now. We alone will take the Augur. Are you ready to?—"

The ceiling above the lobby buckled and the front half, closest to the part hit by the explosion, collapsed completely. It was sudden, shocking and loud as it forced the SDA forces outside to fall back so as not to be hit by rubble. Claudia and Tracey both grabbed Charlie and pulled him out of harm's way and back through the door separating the lobby from the salesroom.

Once the ceiling had finished collapsing, a horde of different men dressed in black combat suits and body gear leapt through the hole, shouting "Watchtower eternal!" and "Jehovah's Swords attack!"

It would appear the SDA had spoken prematurely. The JWs were far from defeated and far from giving up on taking the Augur.

Charlie, Claudia and Tracey hunkered down behind the sales counter to catch their breaths. What they heard was the maddening sound of the two forces screaming at each other, gunfire and hand-to-hand melee. Bottom line, protestant Christians who essentially share the same beliefs, give or take the Holy Trinity or transubstantiation versus transmutation during the Eucharist, were slaughtering each other wholesale.

Charlie was about to say something to Claudia and Tracey when Rita, holding the radio, and Pony and Ian, carrying a screaming Jenny still tied to the chair, burst through the door into the salesroom. Once they were all inside, Pony slammed the door shut and locked it.

Charlie asked Rita, "What's wrong? What's happened?"

Rita shouted, "They did it! They broke down the back door! Some kind of battering ram—poured into the room! They were like!—they were like!—"

"Zombies!" shouted Pony. "They were like the mouth-frothing, army-garbed, rabid religious undead!"

"It was fucked up," added Ian. "They were shouting 'The Augur! The Augur!' It was totally fucked up, man! I swear they aren't human!"

"Used their hands Romero-style!" continued Pony, "Clawing! Growling! It was fucked up!"

Ian put the seemingly ever-screaming Jenny down near Tracey. Tracey stood up and walked over to Jenny. She said, "Jenny, honey, I'm sorry but—" Tracey punched Jenny unconscious.

"Finally," mumbled Claudia.

"What do we do?" asked Rita. "It's 'Night of the-fucking-Dead' out there—but worse! It's 'Night of the Fundamenta-pocalypse'! And we have absolutely no help coming! We don't have enough ammo or weapons! Madre de Dios, minorities always die first in those films!"

Both doors to the salesroom began to rattle. They were locked with solid dead-bolts, but no one thought that would keep the paramilitary end-timers out for very long.

Chapter 37

Three Guesses? Yep, Still OHM

Seated beside one another in a Hummer were Father Agosto in the front passenger seat and Buddha Jesus behind the wheel. As unlikely as it seemed, both men agreed—after reaching a stalemate and watching Charlie and Tracey escape the compound on Agosto's chopper—that the only way to get what each of them wanted was to unite and follow where Charlie and Tracey had gone. Good thing they did too, because when they pulled into the Sunvalley Organic Market's parking lot and saw what amounted to a full-on siege of the dispensary OHM, they knew the time was short for them to intervene.

Buddha Jesus looked at Agosto and asked, "You realize what we're looking at, right?"

Agosto didn't look at Jesus; instead he lifted a pair of binoculars to his eyes and scanned the specifics of what lay before them: the two factions of Seventh-day Adventists and Jehovah's Witnesses were to the Templar Priest clearly discernible. Amongst the two factions, however, he saw what were both city and county cops which, while to any normal person seemed distressing at best, was to him not at all surprising. Of course, these two sects were battling with each other both in the street and on the roof, and were doing as much to destroy each other as destroy the building wherein the radio was being held.

Agosto said, "Your knowledge of the Augur, although impressive for a lay person, is severely limited. It is neither a force of good nor evil; it is an altogether self-revealed power that has its own agenda. Once activated and brought into the sphere of conflict, it will use its own kind of will to affect the minds of all those believers in higher powers to fight against one another until the last surviving forces prove themselves worthy enough to use it."

Buddha Jesus asked, "You mean it plays both sides against its middle and may the worthiest man win?"

Agosto said, "That's one way of putting it. The question for you now, is do you have enough of your own men to make a dent in those numbers?" He held out the binoculars for Buddha Jesus to take.

Buddha Jesus took the binoculars and looked out at the melee. He said, "Yeah, that's a shitload, but I've got a shitload myself. It would have been nicer if you hadn't killed every one of my employees at the compound. They were my best men."

"It's of no importance now. I need you to draw enough fire away so that I can get inside."

Buddha Jesus lowered the binoculars and motioned with his fingers for Agosto to hand him something.

Agosto took off the Revelator Glasses and looked at them one last time before he placed them in Buddha Jesus' hand.

Buddha Jesus put them on and smiled at Agosto. "Don't worry, padre, I know it's a high price to pay, but I also know that the Augur is worth a million times more than these glasses—no matter what their power is."

With the Revelator Glasses on, Buddha Jesus saw the leather-clad, gun-wielding Templar Priest no longer; but saw what he could only describe as someone out of a mediaeval film epic. His leather jacket was a white surcoat with the huge red cross emblazoned across the front with a huge red cloak. It was an all-together surreal effect. Buddha mumbled, "Shit, this reminds me of doing peyote at Joshua Tree."

Agosto moved to open the door and step out of the truck, but before he stepped all the way out, Buddha Jesus asked, "You aren't human, are you?"

"Excuse me?" asked Agosto looking over his shoulder and into the reflective-rainbow glasses he had just used as payment.

"These things are showing me—"

"Look," said Agosto interrupting Buddha Jesus, "I am as human as you are. Everything else is more than you can handle. Don't let what you see through those glasses unravel what you know to be true inside your own heart.

"Now, if you wouldn't mind calling in your soldiers? I don't know how much longer the thieves inside will be able to stay alive, and that means the Augur will not get in my hands. And you want me to get it so you can keep those glasses."

"Right," said Buddha Jesus, so he took out his mobile phone and dialed an associate who picked up the call on the other side. "Yeah," opened Buddha Jesus when he heard his associate's voice. "Are you and the other five leaders in position and ready?"

Agosto watched Buddha Jesus' face for the answer.

Then Buddha Jesus said, "Good. Do it." He hung up the phone.

Agosto looked at the drug lord for some kind of signal.

The drug lord looked at the priest and said, "Go on. You'll know when you see them."

Agosto climbed out of the Hummer and took out both his guns. He checked each magazine to see they were fully loaded. They were. He slid them back into the guns and began to walk out of the parking lot, onto the sidewalk and across Santa Monica Boulevard, in the direction of OHM's front door—well, where OHM used to have a front door.

Fascinated by what he was seeing as the "true form" of this Templar Priest, Buddha Jesus continued to watch Agosto as he stepped onto the crowded street called Santa Monica Boulevard, which was completely occupied by the paramilitary vehicles and forces of the SDA and JWs. Suddenly, Agosto stopped and crossed his arms across his body. Although Buddha Jesus could not see Agosto's face, he saw the priest bow his head.

The drug lord wondered if the priest was in prayer.

Suddenly, Buddha Jesus witnessed a phenomenon that only the greatest of lamas had ever described seeing before: a light like a waterfall fell out of the sky and bathed Agosto entirely in its brilliance. Flashes like wings—or perhaps what Buddha Jesus would later recall was a bird of some kind—came through that shaft of light and into the head of the priest. Immediately the priest lifted his head and crossed himself with guns in hand and looked skywards as the light faded. Whatever it was, Buddha Jesus would later say he witnessed a moment of true enlightenment for the priest—a moment in which Agosto achieved the perfect union of mind, body and spirit. For the priest Agosto, it was nothing less than the Holy Spirit entering his body for battle.

It was at that moment both Santa Monica Boulevard and Fairfax Avenue were invaded by at least thirty different street vehicles. From motorbikes and SUVs to low-riders and full-sized trucks, out of which emerged street thugs, the likes of which none of the religious paramilitary soldiers had ever seen in person. These thugs were armed to the teeth with weaponry at least as advanced (and maybe in some cases better) military-grade than what the SDAs and JWs were sporting. They didn't have rocket launchers, but they had submachine guns and automatic pistols which were as impressive as anything the fundamentalists had ever seen. This was Buddha Jesus' street army, and they were there to wage war as adjunct soldiers for the Templar Priest sent by the Vatican.

Without a single word spoken by the priest, the street thugs fearlessly moved against the paramilitary forces and opened fire on them. Without orders to actually invade the dispensary and retrieve anything at all, they could hold their positions and simply unload on the fanatics until they were no longer moving.

This gave Agosto the cover he needed to break into a run across Santa Monica Boulevard, weaving his way through the vehicles and bodies of SDAs and JWs, firing his guns on anyone who tried to stop him. As it was in the compound, it appeared that whatever force had entered Agosto's body was acting as a deflective shield that prevented him from being hit by either bullets or stray fire of any kind.

Agosto found the SDA and JW forces beginning to scatter. Even under the power of the Augur, both the fear of being slaughtered by incoming fire and the instinct for survival overrode their fanaticism, which drove them back to those vehicles they had that were still operational. When Agosto reached what used to be the security cage, he kicked down the weakened structure and entered the ruined lobby. He stepped over bodies of JWs and SDAs until he reached the door to the salesroom. When he found it locked and still strong enough not to fall from his efforts to kick it open, he fired several times at the weakened lock until it popped out of the door.

Agosto kicked opened the door and stepped inside to find Claudia and Tracey aiming their weapons at him. Behind Claudia and Tracey, the four stoners were on the ground trying to keep the radio and Jenny, still unconscious, covered from view. For a few tense seconds no one knew what anyone's next move would be, until the door to the growing room (still rattling from the attacks on the other side) collapsed into the salesroom, unleashing at least five screaming Jehovah's Witnesses, faces were contorted in horrific screams, swinging bladed weapons from swords to fighting knives.

Agosto shouted, "Behind you!" to Tracey and Claudia.

The women spun around, dropped to a knee, trained their guns on the same targets as Agosto and unleashed holy hell on them.

The four stoners screamed and covered each other and Jenny as the hail of gunfire from their friends and the frocked stranger cut down the first-wave of protestant killers. But no sooner had that first wave been taken down, another wave poured through, and this time it was ten Witnesses instead of five. They were also met with a hail of gunfire but two got through and reached the defenseless Jenny, whom they tried to pull off the chair.

"Jenny!" screamed Ian, who jumped up and tackled one of the attackers.

Charlie and Rita leaped at the other attacker and each grabbed a leg, sending the attacker face-first into the floor.

This left Pony alone to hold the Augur tightly against his chest. He was screaming in fear and scooting across the floor in an effort to reach the farthest wall.

Another wave of ten zombie-like fundamentalists broke through from the growing room and used their fellows ahead of them as body shields against Claudia, Tracey and Father Agosto's gunfire to sneak through the attack line to hone in on Pony and the radio.

By the time Charlie spotted Pony isolated and four Jehovah's Witnesses closing in on him, he was too tied up in the leg of the person he and Rita had brought down to help Pony. Instead he shouted, "Claude! Tracey! It's Pony! They're after him and the radio! You have to save him! Forget about us! Save Pony!"

That was what the Templar Priest needed to hear—the radio was in danger. To his spontaneous allies, Agosto said, "Keep shooting them! I'll save Pony and the radio!"

Something in Agosto's voice made Claudia and Tracey trust him, and they kept their gunfire unleashed on the invading zombie-fundamentalists.

Agosto swung around to face the backs of the four JWs who were clawing and cutting up poor Pony, who was screaming at the top of his lungs, using his own body to protect the ancient relic. Agosto realized he could not use his guns, or he might kill this brave soul giving his own life to defend the Augur. Holstering his guns, Agosto drew out of each boot daggers so thin they were almost poniards. Like a dervish, the Templar Priest launched himself across the room and swung at the backs of Pony's attackers, slicing them open and hacking their limbs off (and in two cases, their heads) before they could turn to see who was killing them.

Suddenly, Pony felt all attacks on him stop. He opened his eyes and looked up into the face of Father Agosto, who gave him a tiny smile. "You are very brave, young man."

"Thank you—for saving my life."

Crazed Jehovah's Witnesses seemed to continue pressing through the doorway from the growing room until finally there was the sound of additional gunfire behind those invading the room, as Buddha Jesus' men entered through the back door and cut down the enemy, ending the salesroom invasion.

With all the attackers down, Claudia and Tracey dropped their guns and dropped to their knees, exhausted.

Charlie and Rita let go of their Jehovah's Witness, who was cowering and begging for them to spare his life. Rita stood over the man and said, "Fuck you!" She punched him unconscious.

Charlie walked over to Tracey and fell to the floor beside her. Smiling at each other, they hugged and kissed each other passionately.

Claudia looked at the new lovers only a foot or two away and scoffed. She picked up her gun and walked out towards the lobby, done with everything that was left of the building.

Ian kneeled down in front of Jenny and reached behind her to break the bonds holding her onto the chair. She was still unconscious but alive. Ian lifted her chin with his hand and said, "You in there, pretty girl? Can you wake up now?"

Jenny's eyes opened but it wasn't Jenny's voice that said, "You truly have a loving heart, Ian Olczwicki."

Ian fell back onto his butt out of shock. What he heard was distinctively not Jenny Sway's voice, but whatever it was, it definitely used Jenny's vocal chords.

Ian asked, "Who are you?"

Jenny reached out and placed a hand on Ian's face and said, "Be good, pure of heart, and this will not be the last time we meet."

"Huh?"

As Jenny rose from the chair, it was as if time itself froze in the dispensary and maybe beyond its walls, but no one would know or even remember this happening, except—

Jenny turned to see Agosto and Pony with the radio in his hands.

Agosto and Pony realized that something weird was happening. No one was moving and there was no sound of any kind around them. The two men began to look for an answer when they both saw Jenny Sway standing in front of them. A beatific smile and shining eyes with a light that shone behind her head gave the Templar Priest all the information he needed.

Agosto bowed to his knees and lowered his head before Jenny and said, "Holy Mother, I am Your humble servant."

Pony looked at Agosto, and then at Jenny, and said, "Huh, what? That's just—" Then Pony stopped speaking. It wasn't that he consciously realized he was facing the Virgin Mary channeling through Jenny Sway, but he felt great emotion and comfort from being in the presence of a Great Unconditionally Loving Feminine Force, which was enough to make him mute.

The newly merged Virgin Jenny looked at Agosto and said, "You are one of only a handful of true warriors left who has the Glory of My Son in your heart. Those men whose orders you follow are not, do you understand?"

"I do," answered Agosto without lifting his head to look upon the Virgin Jenny.

"Then you must know it was Me who hired the dwarf Alberich Night-dwarf to steal the Augur from the Vatican."

Agosto still did not lift his head. He said, "Yours is the Will of Our Lord and Savior. I am Your instrument. I do as You will."

"Good," spoke the Virgin Jenny. "Then know also that the Augur was taken from the Rock upon which My Son first chose to build His Movement because they no longer follow the Movement of My Son. They are wholly corrupt and willfully ignorant of what they've allowed to enter Our world. They would use the Augurspell to take the power of that darkness and threaten the world. So I have chosen those who they would not recognize, because of their ignorance, to face that darkness. They are of a people older than even you."

"What is Thy Will for me, Holy Mother? How may I serve Your Will?"

Pony was amazed to see this exchange, but still he said nothing. He could only watch.

"Look upon the one who now holds the Augur."

Agosto, still on one knee, turned his head and saw the pie-eyed stoner, mute with awe, gripping the Augur to his chest.

Pony returned the Templar Priest's gaze. His voice suddenly returned to him and he felt Someone had given him permission to say, "Hey dude, the name's Pony—what's up? Thanks for like, saving my life, you know? You were—um—like—"

The Virgin Jenny interrupted Pony. "This child is beloved of Me—one-half of a whole, whose destiny is to unlock the mystery of the Augurspell. I will place him high in the order of the corrupt and ignorant, because such visibility will protect him from the Enemy who chooses to dwell in the shadows. It is My Will you protect him with all your might and power because the Enemy has soldiers, too."

Agosto turned back to the Blessed Jenny. "And where in the order will You place him?"

The Virgin Jenny smiled. "You'll see."

Suddenly, Pony's conscious mind connected that these two people were discussing him and they were going to be taking him somewhere else. "Um—hey?—uh—where are you taking me?"

Back of OHM, Growing Room

Not far from the glory of the Blessed Jenny, in the ruins brought on by the invading hordes that had battered down the back wall, shifted rubble and mortar. Still alive, Williams pulled himself out from underneath the mess, ripped bonds and pieces of the chair falling from his cut-up clothes and bleeding scalp. He groaned and spat out blood.

A shadow fell across Williams as he stopped crawling, and looked up to see what his eyes could only believe was a tall, powerfully built man wearing some kind of wolf-like mask under a leather hood. It was the same creature, or one just like it, that had come to claim Henry but had failed.

"What the fuck are you?" asked Williams, whose voice cracked as he unleashed a coughing fit. His lungs were full of dust and smoke.

Without speaking, the creature reached down and grabbed Williams. Unable to resist, the JW could feel claw-like fingers grab what was left of his tattered jacket and lift him from the floor. There would be no Grim Dog or other force to come and save Williams from the creature and whatever fate lay ahead for this once-faithful servant of Jehovah.

Chapter 38

I Think We All Know
Where We Are By Now—

Pony, Father Agosto and Jenny were all gone—physically gone from the ruins of what was once the dispensary OHM.

Rita was the first to notice. She shouted, "Pony's missing!"

Ian snapped out of his trance, remembering only that for a second he was seeing Jenny wake from unconsciousness, touch his face and say, "If you are pure of heart, this will not be the last time we meet." After that, he remembered nothing. He stood up and said, "Jenny was just here too, and now she's gone! What the fuck?"

Tracey and Charlie turned to face their friends.

Tracey said, "Jenny's gone?"

Ian said, "Yeah, she was sitting right here in the chair and I remember her waking up and then—well, I don't know where she went."

324

Charlie said, "Pony's gone? What about the radio?"

Rita walked over to where Pony and Agosto had last been standing and saw what looked like the weird radio on the ground. She bent over and picked it up. "Well, it's still here."

Tracey asked Charlie, "What about that weird priest? Wasn't he just here, too?"

Charlie said, "Yeah, what the hell? First Henry, now Pony and Jenny, we get attacked by total lunatics—what is with this radio? Hey, has anyone seen Claude? I don't see her either."

Suddenly, the thunderous sound of helicopter blades and the blinding power of flood lights attached to the sides of military gunships filled the air above the collapsed roof of the dispensary.

Everyone in the salesroom looked up and saw real military soldiers and governmental agents descend rappelling lines into the salesroom, lobby and the growing room. In total, twenty-two masked NSA and FBI agents appeared everywhere in the building within two minutes.

Charlie looked at Tracey and said, "Your people?"

Tracey shrugged her shoulders and nodded.

Rita and Ian looked totally freaked out as the agents began to try and round up the street thugs sent in by Buddha Jesus, as well as the still living JWs and SDAs, but none of these groups wanted to stay and discuss their actions to the United States government. So without firing on them, they ran from the scene as quickly as they could. It was quite a chaotic reversal from invading OHM, to escaping it as quickly as possible.

One of the masked government agents made his way up to Tracey and Charlie. He took off his mask and revealed himself to be Tracey's handler Uncle Leo. "Agent Kipper!"

"Yes, Sir." Tracey stepped away from Charlie and assumed a more professional stance in face of her superior.

"Well, I can see that this is a supreme cock-up!"

"Well, Sir—none of this could have been foreseen. It wasn't exactly part of my assignment."

Uncle Leo nodded and said, "And could you tell me why you would get involved in something that wasn't part of your assignment?"

Tracey shifted only her eyes to Charlie, who then made a quick look over to Rita, who instinctively hid the radio behind her back.

Uncle Leo could see that something weird was going on between all three of them and said, "I think a debriefing is in order, Agent Kipper."

Tracey said, "Yes, Sir."

Without another word, Uncle Leo took Tracey by the arm and began walking her away from Charlie and the others, towards the street. Tracey took a look over her shoulder at Charlie, whose face suddenly turned kind of pouty.

Ian walked up behind Charlie and put a hand on his right shoulder. He said, "Dude, is that it?"

Charlie said, "Maybe?"

Rita walked up behind Charlie, the Augur in hand, and put a hand on his left side. She said, "Well, at least we still have the radio."

Charlie and Ian both looked at Rita with burn-in-hell looks.

Rita threw her hands up and said, "Hey, we almost got killed over it, maybe it's worth something after all?"

A few of the helicopters that had landed amidst the outside wreckage began to take off—one held Tracey Kipper. Other governmental vehicles and agents remained behind and were soon joined by county and city emergency crews that showed up to clean up the bodies and begin taping off the site for investigation.

Seeing the flood of personnel getting bigger, Charlie said, "We need to get the fuck out of here before someone corners us for interviews."

Ian asked Charlie, "Your place?"

"Yeah, we need to figure out what we have to do next. This place is totally destroyed."

Rita added, "And we still have two friends missing."

Charlie held out his hands to Rita and said, "May I?"

Rita shrugged her shoulders and handed the Augur to Charlie. "Sure."

Charlie took it and looked it over. "Let's figure this thing out."

As quickly and stealthily as possible, the three remaining stoners escaped without anyone appearing to notice them. When they reached the alley, they tried to very casually step over the many dead bodies until they found where Charlie's car was parked and all climbed inside. They drove to Charlie's house because it was the closest.

Along the way, none of them spoke a word or listened to the radio. All they did was stare out the windows and listen for the sounds of any sirens. Once they reached the house, Charlie pulled into the driveway and onto the front lawn. He slammed it into park, and all three ran from the car into the house. Charlie was the last to leave the car as he made sure he had the radio in his hands when he went inside.

Once inside the house, Rita and Ian plopped down on the sofa and fell against each other, exhausted. Charlie entered after them and locked the door. With the radio still in hand, he walked to a recliner and dropped into it. Within seconds the fatigue of their ordeal knocked them out.

What seemed only a few seconds later to Charlie, he was woken by a familiar voice. "Hey, Charlie—wake up, dude. Wake up."

Charlie opened his eyes and saw Henry kneeling in front of the chair. "Henry! Dude! Where the hell have you been?"

But Henry didn't answer right away. Instead, he looked over at the sleeping Ian and Rita. He said, "They can't see me, Charlie, only you."

Charlie sat up and covered his face with his hands. He shook his head and scoffed. "Shit, don't tell me this is some kind of dream?"

"It's kind of a dream, yeah."

Charlie sighed and asked, "Then you're not physically here? Are you dead, man? Just please tell me you're not dead."

Henry stood up and smiled. He said, "No, I'm not dead—per se. It's kind of hard to explain, but just suffice it to say, I'm where no one can reach me or hurt me. Not so with you."

"What the hell does that mean?"

"It means your life is always going to be in danger because of that radio."

"Fine, I'll get rid of it!"

Henry shook his head. "You can't, man. It's your destiny to have that radio."

"What the fuck does that mean?"

"It means it's in your blood—your genes, man, and Tracey knows it."

"Tracey? What's she got to do with this?"

Henry said, "Dude, I gotta split, before I'm seen here. Just believe me when I say, you got to trust the girl. Tracey is more than you know."

Charlie woke with a start and shook his head. It was drenched with sweat, and he wiped his hands across his damp hair. He shook the excess on the floor and looked around to see not a trace of Henry, but instead saw Tracey standing right in front of him. A big happy grin crossed his face, "Hi, are you a dream too?"

Tracey shook her head. "No, I let myself in though. Hope you don't mind?"

Charlie stood with a smile and hugged Tracey with all his strength. "Oh God, no, I don't mind. I just—I wasn't sure I'd see you again. Your boss seemed pretty pissed, you know?"

"Uncle Leo has a way—listen, Charlie, we have to talk. There's something I have to tell you and—um—well, I don't want it to change how you think of me."

Charlie said, "Baby, I found out you were a government spook; I've had my livelihood decimated; two of my best friends in the world have vanished; and I've survived a zombie-apocalypse waged by registered Republican fundamentalists. What could you possibly say that would make me change how I feel about you?"

Tracey smiled and said, "Well, you've got a point there, but—" Tracey sighed and said, "—you were my assignment."

Charlie shook his head and said, "I'm sorry?"

Tracey looked at the sleeping pair on the sofa and took Charlie by the hand. She led him into the back of the house where Charlie's bedroom stood dark and quiet. Again Tracey said, "You were my assignment, and I'm sorry I didn't tell you before."

Charlie sat down on the bed and asked, "But I don't get it—how am I an assignment? What does that mean?"

Tracey said, "Well, you were right about the government not liking what you wrote in your books—but it's more than that. I don't know how else to say it—um—it's your genetic makeup they want—and how it's tied to the radio."

Charlie shot up from the bed and said, "Are you saying there's something in my genes that connects me to the radio— the Armageddon 420 fucking radio?"

Tracey shrugged her shoulders and gave him the tiniest smile. Her eyes were getting wet as the fear of losing Charlie to this truth made her want to cry.

"And your government bosses want to—what? Study me—study me and the radio?"

Tracey released a broken sigh and sniffled. She wiped away the tears from her eyes and took his hands in hers. She squeezed them tightly, gave him a solid kiss and said, "I don't know, Charlie. I don't know what about your genes interests them. All I know is that my bosses wanted me to come and talk to you to see—"

"What—if I'd come along with you? Just throw my whole life away to let the motherfucking US government poke and prod me and that fucking radio to find out what makes us tick?"

Tears rolled down Tracey's cheeks as she could now see the anger as clearly in his eyes as hers showed absolute heartbreak. This was what she feared was going to make him hate her forever. "I don't know Charlie, I don't. I just—I want you to trust me—just know that if you come with me I'll be with you every step of the way. I'll never leave you alone with them. I'll be—" Tracey's voice broke completely and she had to take in a deep breath to keep from losing it altogether. She wiped her eyes, her dripping nose and decided not to say another word.

"You'll be my own private guardian angel?" Charlie asked in a softer voice, followed by a smile.

"In a heartbeat."

"Well—" Charlie sat back down on the bed and lay down on his back, looking up at the ceiling. "How about this for a deal?" He patted the bed next to him.

Tracey wiped the last tears from her eyes and smiled. She slowly sat down where Charlie patted and asked, "Well, I've been given latitude to make a deal, if necessary."

Charlie took her arm and pulled her down so that she was lying face up next to him. Tracey giggled. He said, "Okay, how about this: I'll go with you, let your bosses find out what they can; but they have to give my friends, all my friends, protection from whatever other lunatics try to come after them because of that radio. Also, none of them get prosecuted whatsoever for anything we had to do to keep ourselves safe. Does that sound doable?"

"I'm sure I can get them to agree to that."

"Oh, and something else," Charlie added. "I want them to help me find my friends Henry and Pony. It's because of this whole fucking mess they've gone missing."

Tracey sat up and looked down at Charlie. She said, "I will personally head-up whatever operation is necessary to find Henry and Pony—I promise."

Charlie shook his head and said, "Not good enough. I need more than just a promise."

"Oh really?" asked Tracey with a wry grin. "What else can I do to make you believe?—"

Charlie reached up and pulled Tracey down on top of him and kissed her deeply, passionately. She laughed and willingly exchanged the kiss, which led to something a lot bigger, better and more convincing than just a promise.

Several hours later, Rita woke from her impromptu nap and found herself leaning against Ian's shoulder on the couch. Ian was still asleep. Rita sat up and looked around for signs of anyone else. All she saw was the radio in the loveseat but no sign of Charlie.

Not wanting to wake up Ian, Rita kept quiet as she stood up and looked around the house. When she arrived at the door to Charlie's bedroom, she slowly opened it and stuck her head inside. She saw Charlie and Tracey asleep under the sheets. A twinge of jealousy stung her stomach, but Rita realized it would be a lost cause to say anything to Charlie about how she felt, let alone try to fight for him. After watching Claudia and now Tracey through the whole experience, Rita knew what it was Charlie liked, and she was not it.

Rita shut the door and walked back into the living room. She stopped off at the kitchen first, to dig into the fridge and get out a beer, and returned to the living room. She sat back down on the sofa, this time with distance between her and the still sleeping Ian, and reached for the remote control, clicking on the cable and TV at once.

As always, Charlie's cable opened on MSNBC. With it being Monday morning, the early show hosted by the only recognized Republican on the news network was in its last half-hour. On that morning, however, coverage was targeted on the Vatican. Rita had forgotten in the wake of the last couple of days that the Pope had died. The College of Cardinals had begun Conclave just after sending Agosto out on his hunt for the Augur to choose the next Pope.

Rita took a drink of beer as she watched the reporter interview some faithful Catholics about who they hoped would be named the next Pope. Of course, only really faithful Catholics would give a shit about who would carry on two thousand years of poorly-updated dogma which in no way reflects the actual needs of their congregations or the needs of the world in general. Regardless, it seemed that that's the way it was, until the bells of St. Peter's Basilica rang loud just as the white smoke was released into the air.

On the TV screen appeared a wide shot of the balcony of the Basilica overlooking St. Peter's Square. The crowd below was applauding and screaming and calling out in celebration of the new election. Finally, as Rita took the last drink of beer in the can, she saw two men walk out onto the balcony. Rita didn't recognize the first, the Camerlengo Cardinal Tindiglia, but the second was the Templar Priest Agosto, whose name Rita didn't know but remembered well from the Battle of OHM. Then she saw a third person, the newly-elected Pope walk out onto the balcony, and as the camera closed in on this person—Rita shot up to her feet and screamed at the top of her lungs.

Ian woke up shouting, "What?—what?—not more of those fucking Jehovah's?—"

Rita shouted, "On the TV!—he's on the fucking TV!"

Ian sat up and began wiping the sleep from his eyes and the goopy build-up in the corner of the lids. "Who?—what?"

"Pony! Pony's on the TV!" shouted Rita.

Just then Charlie and Tracey, who was wearing Charlie's robe while Charlie was pulling on a pair of boxers, entered the living room. They asked in unison, "What is it?"

Rita pointed furiously at the TV screen, "You have to look! You have to see this!"

Ian saw it—saw the sight that made Rita totally lose it and his jaw dropped wide open. "Holy shit, I've got to be dreaming!—or dead!"

Charlie moved closer to the TV and saw Pony Macreedy, stoner extraordinaire, robed in the raiment of the Pontiff, the Holy Father, and the Pope of the Catholic Church. "Holy shit," muttered Charlie, "The Pope? Pony's become the fucking Pope?"

Tracey crossed her arms and said, "Well, at least we don't have to find out where he was taken."

Charlie responded, "But if Pony's the new Pope, does that mean Henry's going to show up on CNN as the new Dalai Lama?"

The End.

Our stoners and Father Agosto will return in:

Toke of the Templar – Book 2 of the Augurspell Mystery
Explore the world of the Augurspell Mystery at
www.tradingohm.com.

Acknowledgments

With whom else can I start but my incomparable wife Laura Tooley, who has not only put up with me for longer than anyone not genetically attached to me, but has given me her unwavering and unconditional love and support in the creation of this book and the ongoing series. In addition to being my hero, she is the gifted editor of this work.

My sons Dominic and Jakob, my always little girl Dylan, and nieces Lexi and Jillian, who have never let me forget the power of imagination and the magic of play.

My mother Nancy, who was my first teacher, first champion, first friend and has never second-guessed my choices even when she knew they weren't in my best interest. My father Charles, who has always been my biggest critic and taught me from day one to always go with first ideas, and, whether he likes it or not, gave me the gift of music. My brother Christopher, who through our ups and downs, estrangement and flat-out arguments, was the first to make me believe I could be a hero.

My cousin Gavin who is more than just family, he is the most loyal of friends and a spiritual brother. My cousin Stephanie, who promises to push me around in the wheelchair I'll inevitably be stuck in, no questions asked. Also my most recently-discovered cousin Debbie, who reached out to me because of this book, adds to the totality of love necessary to undertake this kind of project.

My sister-in-law Teri for being Laura's best friend and supporting both Laura and I through all the medical battles we fight each and every day, and for helping to remind me that my love of British comedy is not a disease but the key to my insane sense of humor. And, lastly, but by no means last, my wife's baby brother and the one person who knew best the horror with which I live, Brian. Too young to be gone from the Earth, his love and friendship, too big for the cancer that took him from us, continues to guide us, love us and makes us all see what is best in our selves.

I cannot separate easily my friends from family, because when I first arrived in Los Angeles fresh from the wasteland of Texas, it was David Gold who took me in and not only got me my first job but made me a brother. Together we became "The Vault Monkeys" and with his support I was able to literally physically transform myself and embark on the creative life that has led directly to the creation of this book. Laura and I both love you, Monkey—never ever forget that.

My manager and friend David Rosenblatt, who grabs the lapel of every creative exec and actor who comes into his office and demands they read my manuscripts. His is the only number I see on my caller ID after 10:30 p.m. that I will bother to answer, because whether he has good or bad news to share, he always makes me laugh.

Another friend and my production partner, whom Laura and I have unofficially adopted as our little sister, Haylee Homs. It took me decades to find a mind, a sense of humor and a heart that could not only understand what my ambitious goals were, but had the genius to bring my insane writings into reality—that is who Haylee is—a genius, and I could not love her more if we had the same blood in our veins.

My ex-boss and eternal friend Patricia Laucella—if Haylee is my little sister, Patricia is my big sister. The only boss I ever had that didn't ever ask me to think, act or do my work differently from who I am. She gave me the opportunity to see how the big bad Hollywood machine operates from the inside, and never, ever for a moment made me feel like anything other than fully appreciated, fully trusted, and fully loved. Your faith and unwavering support, Patricia, is vital to this book coming into the light.

A very special thank you has to go to my friend Juliana Dever—a beautiful soul and one helluva an actor. Although I had already written the first screenplay of "Trading Ohm" when I first sat down and talked to Juliana, it was her sharing with me about her own amazing life journey that helped me to fully actualize a vital aspect of this story. She was my choice to be "Tracey Kipper" in my early efforts to produce this book as a film, but became more than just a player in the drama—she became a teacher, my teacher.

Although no longer on the Earth, Reverend Al Donsbach and Dr. Bill Painter were my great mentors. Each of them taught me what God, Christianity and human history are from the spiritual and intellectual viewpoints. Nothing I have read, seen or written since Al first sat with me in my hospital room at age 10, or Bill Painter instructed me about in my freshman year at university has not been affected by the genius they both made me believe I possessed and gave to me as a gift. If it weren't for them being in my life, such a book as this one could never have even been conceived.

To the music of the following artists whose poetry, power and innovation created the energies I used to push me through the physical pain I sometimes found blocking my creativity or the doubt and fear in my mind: Hawkwind, Rush, Yes, Led Zeppelin, Cream, The Band, Deep Purple, Wishbone Ash, Big Brother & the Holding Company, Black Sabbath, Crosby Stills Nash & Young, Warren Zevon, The Alan Parsons Project, The Beatles (of course) and Steely Dan, whose music cannot be described simply as rock or jazz or even fusion. Like the book, Steely Dan cannot be fit into any existing mold. Also like this book and Steely Dan, the incomparable musical artist Glen Hansard has played a vital part, for Laura in particular, in helping to create an atmosphere of creativity, love and emotion which has guided the editing of "Trading Ohm."

I am a child born in the waning of the counter-culture 1960s, who some argue came of age in Regan's 1980s—not so. Whatever historians say of my generation, we came of age in the 1970s—about whatever else is said—a true decade of the counter-culture. Is that counter-culture dead some forty years later? I sure as hell hope not. What I do wish is that something of the musical artists' geniuses listed above could be found in more than just a few musicians and bands of today.

And to those visual artists whose films, writing, and performances have in all ways that matter to how an artist crafts his skill have left an indelible mark on my own creative process and, therefore on the structure, humor and story told in this book. I suppose to list all of them might not be possible, but I would like to give special admiration to the following: David Lynch & Mark Frost, Paul Haggis, Gary Shandling & Peter Tolkan, Stephen Fry & Hugh Laurie (as a duo and as individual artists), David Mitchell & Robert Webb, Danny Boyle, Terry Gilliam, Alfred Hitchcock, the whole of Monty Python's Flying Circus as a unit and separate entities (especially Gilliam, as noted above), the great one himself Mr. Stan Lee, Craig Ferguson &

Jeff Pederson and a little known and truly unappreciated artist but someone who I must fully acknowledge as a genuine influence in all I do, William Shakespeare, whose spirit has been a muse for me since I first read "A Midsummer Night's Dream" at 10 years old.

Finally, there is one person who throughout the course of my life has been a true compass for what I have done creatively and who I have sought to be as a person—my grandfather, Gilbert Van Vlack. When I was ten and trapped in my body cast, he sent me postcards from Poughkeepsie, N.Y., telling me a story of how the legendary Bigfoot was making a special trek down from the Catskills to the flatlands of North Texas just to visit me in the hospital. He even drew little "big feet" across each postcard to help me believe that kind of magic was real. Well, Granddad, that magic you taught me at ten is the same magic I give back to you and to anyone else who picks up this book, or indeed any book.

I thank each one of you, and the many others I did not have the time or space to include in this section, for helping to bring this dream, my first dream, to life. I love you, brothers and sisters, mothers and fathers, children, living and immortal, factual or fictitious. Peace to you all.

List of Artwork Above Chapter Headings

Chapter 1 – Our Lady of Guadalupe (aka The Blessed Virgin Mary)
Chapter 2 – Cover of wallet-sized State of California Health and Safety Code 11362.5 Physician's Statement (medical marijuana card)
Chapter 3 – Odin's Rune Shield
Chapter 4 – Buddhist Wheel of Law
Chapter 5 – Pope's Mitre
Chapter 6 – The Augur (in radio form)
Chapter 7 – Caduceus (Greek God Hermes' magic wand for alchemy and/or healing)
Chapter 8 – Knights Templar Cross
Chapter 9 – Buddhist Prayer Wheel (hand-held)
Chapter 10 – Yin-Yang Symbol
Chapter 11 – The Revelator Glasses
Chapter 12 – Roman Soldiers (bas-relief)
Chapter 13 – Qiblah (Islamic compass)
Chapter 14 – Nodic Gods Odin, Thor and Frey (from 12th century tapestry)
Chapter 15 – Trefoil of the Trinity (symbolizing Christian Father, Son and Holy Ghost)
Chapter 16 – Constantine's Cross
Chapter 17 – Cretan Ax (often associated with Greek God Zeus)
Chapter 18 – United States Department of Homeland Security Logo
Chapter 19 – Osiris (Egyptian god of the dead and underworld)
Chapter 20 – Cannabis Leaf
Chapter 21 – Baphomet (aka "The Beast" – Hermetic deity of hedonism)
Chapter 22 – Russian Orthodox Cross
Chapter 23 – Zeus (King of the Greek Gods and god of the skies)
Chapter 24 – National Security Agency Logo

About the Author

Matthew Van Vlack has had a unique life experience which has definitely given him both a skewed view and style in his writing. His unusual circumstances began at age 10 when he was diagnosed with a crippling form of arthritis called Perthes Disease. Able to overcome this childhood trauma, Matthew was living in Los Angeles and working for Warner Bros. Studios when he underwent a total hip replacement at age 33. He had to overcome a lifetime of obesity and lose more than 100 pounds in order to undergo the procedure. Over the next several years Matthew endured further deteriorating conditions including spinal disease, neuropathy and fibromyalgia. This has left Matthew battling chronic pain on a daily basis, as well as using a cane or walker to move about. None of that matters to Matthew in comparison to how it has driven him to focus on his mind, imagination and goals to create novels and other artistic work that illuminate the world and the people in it from a humorous and nakedly honest viewpoint. Other than the nine medications Matthew takes each day, his wife Laura and his two step-sons are the best treatment possible for what nature has thrown at Matthew. Currently, Matthew and his family reside in Albuquerque, New Mexico. If you would like to find out more about Matthew's artistic work, please visit his Traumatic Artists website: www.traumaticartists.com.